WENDY CORSI STAUB

P9-CEK-345

THE
GOODSISTER

HARPER

An Imprint of HarperCollinsPublishers

This is a work of fiction. Names, characters, places, and incidents are products of the author's imagination or are used fictitiously and are not to be construed as real. Any resemblance to actual events, locales, organizations, or persons, living or dead, is entirely coincidental.

HARPER

An Imprint of HarperCollins*Publishers*
10 East 53rd Street
New York, New York 10022-5299

Copyright © 2013 by Wendy Corsi Staub
Excerpt from *The Perfect Stranger* copyright © 2014 by Wendy Corsi Staub
ISBN 978-0-06-222237-4

All rights reserved. No part of this book may be used or reproduced in any manner whatsoever without written permission, except in the case of brief quotations embodied in critical articles and reviews. For information address Harper paperbacks, an Imprint of HarperCollins Publishers.

First Harper mass market printing: October 2013
First Harper mass market special printing: May 2013

HarperCollins ® and Harper ® are registered trademarks of Harper-Collins Publishers.

Printed in the United States of America

Visit Harper paperbacks on the World Wide Web at
www.harpercollins.com

10 9 8 7 6 5 4 3 2 1

If you purchased this book without a cover, you should be aware that this book is stolen property. It was reported as "unsold and destroyed" to the publisher, and neither the author nor the publisher has received any payment for this "stripped book."

*For Laura Blake Peterson: after two decades together,
you aren't just my agent or
even merely a friend—you're family.
Thank you for everything, always—
but especially for conjuring
the concept that started the creative wheels turning
for* The Good Sister.

*And for my guys: Mark, Brody,
and—with great maternal pride—
my college man, Morgan.*

Acknowledgments

Thank you to my editor, Lucia Macro, and the gang at Harper-Collins (too many of you to safely name names without missing someone—please know that your daily efforts on my behalf are most appreciated); to my indispensible agent, Laura Blake Peterson, and the gang at Curtis Brown, Ltd.; to Carol Fitzgerald and staff at Bookreporter.com; to Peter Meluso; to John Valeri; to my ever-widening circle of family and friends; to the many supportive fellow authors whom I would include in the aforementioned circles; to librarians and booksellers everywhere, particularly the Donovans at my hometown Book Nook; to my loyal readers, whose endless enthusiasm helps me keep writer's block at bay; and to my Facebook Gang for helping me with research and brainstorming—particularly Sherrie Saint, Michelle Mathews Gullo, and haberdashers everywhere. Finally . . .

thx to my son brody staub 4 hlpng me get the txt mssgs righttttt

THE
GOODSISTER

Chapter 1

That it had all been a lie shouldn't come as any surprise, really.

And yet, the truth—a terrible, indisputable truth that unfolds line by blue ballpoint line, filling the pages of the black marble notebook—is somehow astonishing.

How did you never suspect it back then?

Or, at least, in the years since?

Looking back at the childhood decade spent in this house—an ornate, faded Second Empire Victorian mansion in one of the oldest neighborhoods in the city—it's so easy to see how it might have happened this way.

How it *did* happen this way.

There is no mistaking the evidence. No mistaking the distinct handwriting: a cramped, backhand scrawl so drastically different from the loopy, oversized penmanship so typical of other girls that age.

Different . . .

Of course it was different.

She was different from the other girls; tragically, dangerously different.

I remember so well.

I remember her, remember so many things about her: both how she lived and how she—

Footsteps approach, tapping up the wooden stairway to this cupola perched high above the third-story mansard roofline, topped by wrought-iron cresting that prongs the sky like a king's squared-off crown.

"*Hellooo-oo.* Are you still up there?" calls Sandra Lutz, the Realtor.

"Yes."

Where else would I be? Did you think I jumped out the window while you were gone?

Sandra had excused herself ten minutes ago after finally answering her cell phone. It had buzzed incessantly with incoming calls and texts as their footsteps echoed in one empty room after another on this final walk-through before the listing goes up this week.

The entire contents of the house are now in storage—with the exception of the rocker where Mother went undiscovered for weeks.

"I don't think that chair is something you'd want to keep," Sandra said in one of their many long-distance telephone conversations when the storage arrangements were being made.

Of course not. The corpse would have been crawling with maggots and oozing bodily fluids, staining the brocade upholstery and permeating it with the terrible stench of death.

Presumably, someone—surely not the lovely Sandra—tossed the desecrated rocking chair into a Dumpster.

Everything else was transported to the storage facility somewhere in the suburbs.

As for Mother herself . . .

I'd just as soon someone tossed her into a Dumpster, too.

But of course, the proper thing to do was arrange, also long distance, for a cremation.

"We have a number of packages," Glenn Cicero, the undertaker, said over the phone, after remarking that he remembered Mother from all the years she worked part-time at Russo's Drugstore as a pharmacy clerk.

"Packages? She's not just in one . . . urn? How many are there?"

"No, that's not what I meant. I was talking about funeral packages. It just depends on how you want to set up visitation hours and—"

"No visitation. I live almost five hundred miles away, and I can't get up there just yet, and . . . there's no one else."

Pause. "There are no other family and friends here in the Buffalo area who might want to—"

"*No one else.*"

"All right, then." He went over the details, mentioning that there would be an additional seventy-five-dollar charge for shipment of the ashes.

"Can you just hold on to—" *It? Her?* What was the proper terminology, aside from the profane terms so often used to refer to Mother—though never to her face—back when she was alive?

"The remains?" Cicero supplied delicately.

"Yes . . . can you hold on to the remains until I can come in person?"

"When would that be?"

"Sometime this summer. I'm selling the house, so I'll be there to make the final arrangements for that."

The undertaker dutifully provided instructions on how to go about retrieving what was left of the Dearly Departed when the time came.

The time is now here, but of course there will be no trip to Cicero and Son Funeral Home. Mother's ashes can sit on a dusty shelf there for all eternity.

As for the contents of this old house . . .

"I'm sure you won't want to go through it all just yet," Sandra Lutz said earlier, handing over the rental agreement, with the monthly payments automatically deducted from Mother's checking account, and a set of keys to the storage unit. "Not when the loss is so fresh. But empty houses are much more appealing to buyers, and this way, at least, we can get the home on the market."

Yes. The sooner this old place is sold, the better. As for the padlocked compartment filled with a lifetime of family furniture and mementos . . .

Good riddance to all of it.

Well . . . not quite *all*.

Right before she answered her phone, Sandra took a Ziploc bag from her pebbled black leather Dooney & Bourke satchel.

"These are some odds and ends I came across after the moving company and cleaning service had finished in here. I didn't want to just throw anything away, so . . . here you go."

The bag contained just a few small items. A stray key that had been hanging on a high nail just inside the cellar stairway door, most likely fitting the lock on a long-gone trunk or tool chest. A dusty Mass card from a forgotten cousin's funeral, found tucked behind a cast-iron radiator in the front parlor. A tarnished, bent silver fork that had been wedged in the space behind the silverware drawer.

And then there was . . .

This.

The notebook, with a string of pink glass rosary beads wrapped around it twice, as if to seal it closed.

According to Sandra Lutz, the notebook, unlike the other relics, hadn't been accidentally overlooked. Someone had deliberately hidden it in one of the old home's many concealed nooks.

"I stumbled across it last night when I stopped by to double-check the square footage of the master bedroom," she reported. "I noticed that there was a discrepancy between the measurements I took a few weeks ago and the old listing from the last time the house sold, back in the late seventies."

"What kind of discrepancy?"

"The room was two feet longer back then. Sure enough, that's exactly the depth of the secret compartment I found behind a false wall by the bay window. I was wondering whether you even knew it was there, because—"

"The house is full of secret compartments. My father always said that they were used to hide slaves on the Underground Railroad."

"That's the rumor about a lot of houses in this neighborhood. Probably because we're just a stone's throw from the Canadian border, and there was considerable Underground Railroad activity in western New York. But I don't think this would have been an actual safe house."

"Why not?"

"Because historical documentation shows that there just weren't very many of them in Buffalo. Slavery was abolished in New York State years before the Civil War started, so escaped slaves who made it this far either stayed and lived openly, or they were taken from rural safe houses into the city and directly across the border crossing at Squaw Island."

Sandra added quickly, as if to soothe any hard feelings from her announcement that the home hadn't served some noble historic cause, "I've always admired this house though, and wondered what it looked like inside. Did I mention that this is my old stomping grounds? I grew up a few blocks away, and I just moved back to the neighborhood."

Yes, Sandra mentioned that over the phone several times, and in e-mail, too. She also had no qualms about sharing that she's a recent divorcee living alone for the first time in her life.

"I bought a fabulous Arts and Crafts home on Wayside Avenue, just down the street from Sacred Sisters High School," she prattled on, as if she were revealing the information for the first time. "Not that I went to Sisters, even though it was right in the neighborhood; I went to Griffin instead."

Ah, Griffin Academy: the upscale, all-girls Catholic boarding school. No surprise there.

"Anyway, when I saw the house on Wayside come on the market, I snatched it up. It might not be as big or as old as this one, and it doesn't have any secret compartments, but it does have all the original—"

"The notebook—what were you saying about finding the notebook?"

"Oh. Sorry. I guess I tend to ramble."

No kidding.

If there's anything I can't stand, it's a motor mouth.

Sandra shrugged. "I was just going to point out that the secret compartment where I found it was different."

"Different how?"

That was when Sandra's phone rang. She checked the caller ID, said, "Excuse me, but I have to take this one," and disappeared down the steps.

Now she's back.

And now that I've seen what's in that notebook, I really need to know what she meant about "different."

"Sorry about that. I thought that call was only going to take a minute." Slightly winded from the climb, Sandra adds, "Those stairs and my asthma are not getting along today! Oh, it's warm up here, isn't it?"

The windows are open, but there's not a breath of cross breeze to diminish the greenhouse effect created by four walls of glass on a ninety-degree July afternoon.

Looking not the least bit overheated, Sandra fans herself with a manila folder—gently, though, so as not to send a hair out of place. A perfumed, expertly made-up fortysomething blonde wearing a trim black suit, hose, and high-heeled pumps, she's probably never broken a sweat outside the gym or had a bad hair day in her life.

When she introduced herself, she pronounced her first name "Sondra." Most locals would say it *Say-and-ra*, the

western New York accent stretching it out to three syllables
with a couple of distinct flat A's. Not her.

"I'm *Sahndra*," she said as she stepped out of her silver
Mercedes on the driveway to shake hands. Heat shimmered
off the blacktop, yet her bony fingers were icy, with a firm,
businesslike grip. "It's so nice to finally meet you in person.
How was the drive in last night?"

"The drive?" *Oh, so we're doing the small-talk thing.
Let's get it over with.* "It was fine."

"Did you come alone, or bring your family?"

*Is she fishing for information, or did I tell her I have a
family?*

There had been so many questions through their two
months of long-distance phone calls and e-mails, it was difficult to keep track of what Sandra had been told—truth,
and lies.

"I came alone."

"It's about nine hours, isn't it, from Huntington Station?"

Huntington Station. Not Long Island, not Nassau County,
not even just Huntington, but Huntington Station. So
damned specific.

"I went to college in the Bronx, at Fordham," Sandra mentioned, "and my boyfriend back then was from Long Island.
Levittown. A nice Irish boy—Patrick Donnelly . . . ?"

She paused, as if to ask, *Do you know him?*

Question met with a cursory head shake, she went on,
"Well, anyway, I know exactly where you live."

She has the address, of course, to which she's been Fed-
Exing paperwork for a couple of months now.

Sandra went on to inquire about the suburban Marriott
she had recommended for this weekend stay. After being
assured that the room was satisfactory, she said, "Be sure
and tell the front desk manager, if you see her, that I referred
you. Her name is Lena."

"Friend of yours?" *I'll be sure to steer clear.*

"Oh, I've never met her, but she's a dear friend of a client's sister."

And so it became clear early on that Sandra Lutz is the kind of woman who not only tends to ramble on and make dreary small talk, but who also remembers the most mundane details about people she meets in passing.

That characteristic probably serves her very well when it comes to her line of work, but otherwise . . .

Someone really should warn her that sometimes it's not a good idea to pay so much attention to other people's lives.

Sometimes, people like—people *need*—to maintain more of a sense of privacy.

"I try not to take calls when I'm with a client," Sandra says breezily now, pocketing her cell phone, "but that was an accepted offer for a house that's only been on the market for a week. I thought it would be a hard sell, but it looks like this is my client's lucky day. And mine, too. Let's hope all this good fortune rubs off on you. Now that we're finished looking the place over, we can—"

"Wait. When you said the compartment was different, what, exactly, did you mean?"

Sandra's bright blue eyes seem startled at, then confused by, the abrupt question. "Pardon?"

"When you found the *notebook* behind the *wall*"—*Careful, now. Calm down. Don't let her see how important this is to you*—"you said the compartment was different."

"Oh, that's right. I meant that it wasn't original to the house. Here, let's go downstairs and I'll show you what I mean."

She leads the way down the steep flight to a noticeably cooler, narrow corridor lined with plain whitewashed walls and closed doors. Behind them are a bathroom with ancient fixtures, a couple of small bedrooms that once housed nineteenth-century servants, and some large storage closets that are nearly the same size as the bedrooms, all tucked above the eaves with pairs of tall, arched dormers poking through the slate mansard roof.

The third floor hasn't been used in decades, perhaps not even when the second-to-last owners, a childless couple, lived here.

When Mother and Father bought the house, they found that the first two floors were plenty large enough for two; large enough, even, for four.

And then there were three . . .

No. Don't think about that.

Just find out where the notebook was hidden, and how much Sandra Lutz knows about what's written in it.

Down they go, descending another steep flight to the second floor.

Here, the hallway is much wider than the one above, with high ceilings, crown moldings, and broad windowed nooks on either end. A dark green floral runner stretches along the oak floor and the wallpapered walls are studded with elaborate sconces that were, like most light fixtures throughout the house, converted from gas to electricity after the turn of the last century.

"The same thing was probably done in my house," Sandra comments as they walk along the hall, "but I'd love to go back to gaslights. Of course, the inspector who checked it out before I got the mortgage approval nearly had a heart attack when I mentioned that. He said the place is a firetrap as it is. Old wiring, you know—the whole thing needs to be upgraded. It's the same in this house, I'm sure."

"I'm sure."

The mid-segment of the hall opens up with an elaborately carved wooden railing along one side. This is the balcony of the grand staircase—that's what Sandra likes to call it, anyway—that leads down to the entrance hall. Or foyer. (Pronounced *foy-yay* by *Sandra-sounds-like-Sondra*.)

The master bedroom at the far end of the hallway isn't

large by today's standards. And it isn't a *suite* by any stretch of the imagination, lacking a private bath, dressing room, walk-in closet . . .

But that, of course, is what Sandra Lutz calls it as she opens the door for the second time today: *the master suite*.

The room does look bigger and brighter than it did years ago, when it was filled with dark, heavy furniture and long draperies shielding the windows. Now bright summer sunlight floods the room, dappled by the leafy branches of a towering maple in the front yard.

A faint hint of Mother's cloying talcum powder and Father's forbidden pipe tobacco seems to waft in the air, but it might very well be imagined.

The lone floor lamp, plugged into an electronic timer that will turn it on for a few hours every evening, was Sandra's idea. There's one downstairs in the living room, too.

"You don't want to advertise that the house is empty," she said.

"Why not? There's nothing here to steal."

"Yes, but you don't want to tempt kids or vandals to break in."

I really don't care.

"Here." Sandra walks over to the far end of the room, indicating the decorative paneling on the lower wall adjacent to the bay window. "This is what I was talking about. See how this wainscot doesn't match the rest of the house? Everywhere else, it's more formal, with raised panels, curved moldings, beaded scrolls. But this is a recessed panel— Mission style, not Victorian. Much more modern. The wood is thinner."

She's right. It is.

"And this"—she knocks on the maroon brocade wallpaper above it, exactly the same pattern but noticeably less faded than it is elsewhere in the room—"isn't plaster like the other walls in the house. It's drywall. Did you know that?"

"No."

There wasn't even wainscoting on that end of the room years ago. Obviously, someone—Father?—rebuilt the wall and added the wainscoting, then repapered it using one of the matching rolls stored years ago on a shelf in the dirt-floored cellar.

"There's a spot along here . . ." Sandra reaches toward the panels, running her fingertips along the molding of the one in the middle. She presses down, and it swings open. "There. There it is. See?"

Dust particles from the gaping dark hole behind the panel dance like glitter into sunbeams falling through the bay windows.

"Like I said, it's about two feet deep. I wish I had a flashlight so that I could show you, but . . . see the floor in there? It's refinished, exactly like this."

She points to the hardwoods beneath their feet. "In the rest of the house, the hidden compartments have rough, unfinished wood. So obviously, this cubby space was added in recent years—it must have been while your family owned the house, because as I said, the room was two feet longer when it was listed by the previous owner."

"When you opened the panel, was there . . . was this all that was inside?"

"The notebook?" Sandra nods. "That was it. It was just sitting on the floor in there, wrapped in the rosary. I gave it to you just the way I found it. I figured it might be some kind of diary or maybe a prayer journal . . . ?"

The question hangs like the dust particles in the air between them and then falls away, answered only by the distant whistle of a passing freight train.

Predictably, Sandra waits only a few seconds before filling the awkward pause. "I just love old houses. So much character. So many secrets."

Sandra, you have no idea. Absolutely no idea.

"Is there anything else you wanted to ask about this or
. . . anything?"

"No. Thank you for showing me."

"You're welcome. Should I . . . ?" She gestures at the
wainscot panel.

"Please."

Sandra pushes the panel back into place, and the hidden
compartment is obscured—but not forgotten, by any means.

Does the fact that the Realtor speculated whether the
notebook is a diary or prayer journal mean she really didn't
remove the rosary beads and read it when she found it?

Or is she trying to cover up the fact that she did?

Either way . . .

*I can't take any chances. Sorry, Sandra. You know "ex-
actly" where I live . . . now it's my turn to find out the same
about you.*

That shouldn't be hard.

An online search of recent real estate transactions on
Wayside Avenue should be sufficient.

How ironic that Sandra Lutz had brought up Sacred Sisters' proximity to her new house before the contents of the
notebook had been revealed. In that moment, the mention of
Sacred Sisters had elicited nothing more than a vaguely unpleasant memory of an imposing neighborhood landmark.

Now, however . . .

Now that I know what happened there . . .

The mere thought of the old school brings a shudder,
clenched fists, and a resolve for vengeance. That Sandra
Lutz lives nearby seems to make her, by some twisted logic,
an accessory to a crime that must not go unpunished any
longer.

They descend the so-called grand staircase to the first
floor. Here, a faint mildewed smell permeates the musty air,
courtesy of the damp cellar below. It's always been prone
to flooding thanks to a frequently clogged drain. Earlier,

Sandra needlessly pointed out that a vapor barrier, French drain system, and even new roof gutters would help.

I'm sure it would. But that's somebody else's problem.

"Shall we go out the front door or the back?" Sandra asks.

"Front."

It's closer to the rental car. The need to get out of this old house with its unsettling secrets and lies is growing more urgent by the second.

"I thought you might like to take a last look around before—"

"No, thank you."

"All right, front door it is. I never really use it at my own house," Sandra confides as she turns a key sticking out of the double-cylinder dead bolt and opens one of the glass-windowed double doors. "I have a detached garage and the back door is closer to it, so that's how I come and go."

Oh, for heaven's sake, who cares?

"You know, your mother had these locks installed after your dad passed away. She was so afraid to be alone at night."

Mother? Upset that Father passed away?

Mother, afraid to be alone?

Mother, afraid of anything at all—other than the wrath of God or Satan?

I don't think so.

"What makes you assume that?"

"It's not an assumption," Sandra says defensively, stepping out onto the stoop and holding the door open. "Bob Witkowski told me that's what she said."

"*Who?*"

"Bob Witkowski. You know Al Witkowski, the mover? He lives right around the corner now, on Redbud Street, in an apartment above the dry cleaner. His wife divorced him a while back and took him for everything he had."

Oh, for the love of . . .

"Anyway, Bob is Al's younger brother. He's a locksmith. I had him install these same double-cylinder dead bolts in my house when I first moved in, because I have windows in my front door, too. You can't be too careful when you're a woman living alone—I'm sure your mother knew that."

"Yes."

The wheels are turning, turning, turning . . .

Stomach churning, churning, churning at the memory of Mother.

Mother, who constantly quoted the Ten Commandments, then broke the Eighth with a lie so mighty that surely she'd lived out the rest of her days terrified by the prospect of burning in hell for all eternity.

"A lock like this is ideal for an old house with original glass-paned doors, because the only way to open it, even from the inside, is with a key," Sandra is saying as she closes the door behind them and inserts the same key into the outside lock. "No one can just break the window on the door and reach inside to open it. Some people leave the key right in the lock so they can get out quickly in an emergency, but that defeats the purpose, don't you think? I keep my own keys right up above my doors, sitting on the little ledges of molding. It would only take me an extra second to grab the key and get out if there was a fire."

"Mmm hmm."

The place is a firetrap . . .

"Of course, now that it's summer, I keep my windows open anyway, so I guess that fancy lock doesn't do much for me, does it? I really should at least fix the broken screen in the mudroom. Anyone could push through it and hop in."

It's practically an invitation.

Stupid, stupid woman.

Sandra gives a little chuckle. "Good thing this is still such a safe neighborhood, right?"

"Absolutely."

Yes, and thanks to Sandra's incessant babble, a plan has taken shape.

A plan that, if one were inclined to fret about breaking the Ten Commandments—*which I most certainly am not*—blatantly violates the Fifth.

Thou shalt not kill.

Oh, but I shall.

It won't be the first time.

And surely, it won't be the last.

Entry from the marble notebook

Tuesday, August 20, 1985

   Another bad day.
   Father visited my room again last night. I've de-cided to start writing it down whenever it happens, because I can't keep it all inside anymore. I have no one to talk to other than Adrian, and he's only five years old and I can't burden him with it.
   So this is going to be my Bad Day Notebook from now on. And if I ever get brave enough to tell someone what goes on around here, this will be my evidence.

Chapter 2

On steamy nights like this, there's something to be said for living in a solid old house.

Sandra Lutz is certain that her ex-husband wouldn't agree, but to hell with him and his newly built waterfront condo and his newly built—thanks to an expensive boob job the SOB denies having paid for—live-in girlfriend.

The old box fan humming on the windowsill above the kitchen sink creates a pleasant, if warm, breeze as Sandra takes a carton of mango Häagen-Dazs sorbet from the freezer.

Really, with all the windows open and the fans spinning, who needs air-conditioning?

Heat waves like this occur maybe once a year in western New York, and even then, this property's ancient maples shade the home's gabled roof by day, and the thick plaster walls keep the warm air and humidity at bay.

Plaster walls . . .

That reminds Sandra of the conversation she had with her new client this afternoon in the Addams House.

That's what all the neighborhood kids used to call the magnificent Victorian over on Lilac Street.

Addams, as in *The Addams Family*, an old sitcom that was popular in syndicated reruns back when Sandra was growing up. On the television show, the family lived in a Second Empire Victorian mansion that was strikingly similar to the one on Lilac Street, with its paired dormers and iron-crested cupola tower poking high above the mansard roof.

The neighborhood streets were lined with old houses, but most of them had been built in the 1900s, not the 1850s. Conspicuous as a tiered butter-cream wedding cake perched on a platter of supermarket corn muffins, the Addams House was a magnet for kids with lively imaginations—especially during the two- or three-year period when the place stood empty after elderly Mr. and Mrs. Normand died without heirs.

Sandra and her friends used to dare each other to sneak inside. As far as she can recall, no one ever went through with it, and eventually, they all became more interested in spin the bottle than in truth or dare—probably right around the time the new family moved in.

Sandra vaguely remembers the parents, having occasionally crossed paths with them: the father worked at the local bank branch where she used to deposit her babysitting money in a savings account, the mother at Russo's Drugstore where she picked up her asthma inhalers.

The father is long dead and now the mother is, too; their son is an adult, and the Addams House stands empty once again.

Empty, scrubbed clean, aired out, and ready to receive new owners.

There are plenty of similar homes listed—homes that need a lot less work and don't have the pall of tragedy hanging over them—but Sandra is guessing that the Addams House probably won't be unoccupied for long this time. Regardless of the sagging market and rust belt location, property tends to move when you have an owner who's open to lowball offers, eager to sell and move on.

Sometimes that's the case with an estate property, but just as often, Sandra encounters sellers who are reluctant to close the door on the past—particularly when there are several inheritors in the will. Typically, you have sentimental, nostalgic children or grandchildren, nieces or nephews, locking horns with their calculating, greedy cousins or siblings—or worse, siblings-in-law. Divvying up the contents of any house is always a potential issue, as is setting an asking price, and deciding whether to hold out for it.

None of that here, though. The sole inheritor to the Addams House has been all business, if noticeably skittish—even before the stilted conversation about the rosary-wrapped notebook and the secret panel Sandra had found.

That, clearly, was a touchy subject for him. Why?

The old house certainly has its share of secrets. Most old houses do. In this case, so, apparently, did its final residents.

What the heck was in that notebook and why was it wrapped in a rosary, as if to . . . to . . .

To keep the devil at bay, maybe?

Sandra wishes she'd taken the time to at least glance inside before she'd handed it over to him. She was naturally curious—who wouldn't be?—and she'd fully intended to take a peek, but she hadn't gotten around to it before he showed up for the walk-through.

Oh well. For all she knows, the pages are full of prayers from a long ago CCD class, or they're completely blank.

Why would anyone have hidden it, then?

And why bother to build a new secret compartment? The house is already full of them.

Clearly, the elderly owners were pretty desperate to hide something. Most likely money or jewelry, and the notebook simply wound up there.

Still, it doesn't make sense. Why not just use one of the existing hidden cubbies?

Because they wanted to keep whatever it was from someone who would already be familiar with the home's existing nooks and crannies.

Someone—like their own son?

It had to be. The Normands and all other previous occupants of the house are long dead, and the most recent owners were hardly social butterflies who welcomed in flocks of friends or neighbors. Even Bob Witkowski, when he installed the new locks, said he never got past the front foyer.

"The old lady watched me like a hawk through the doorway from the parlor the whole time," he told Sandra, "just like she used to watch us from behind the counter at Russo's when we were kids, like she thought we were trying to shoplift condoms or cigarettes."

"You probably were."

"Not always! Anyway, I'm not a kid anymore, but she had that same way of watching—it gave me the creeps. She just sat there in her rocking chair with her rosary beads, rocking and muttering her prayers and staring at me."

Rumor has it that the reclusive family was overtly religious—not unusual in this old Roman Catholic neighborhood, where small front yard grottos housing statues of the Virgin Mary are nearly as prevalent as lofty maples. But according to Bob's brother Al, who owns the moving company that hauled away the contents of the house, the owners were ultra-conservative fanatics who kept to themselves even before the terrible tragedy years ago—a tragedy Sandra doesn't even recall.

"It was definitely in the paper," Al said, "because I remember my mother reading the article out loud to my father, saying what a shame it was, and that we would all have to go to the wake. I was dreading that. Not that I was sad about it—I barely knew them, but I hated wearing a suit coat and tie and my mother would have made me. But then it turned out there wasn't one, so I didn't have to worry."

"No wake?"

"No wake, no funeral. My mother thought that was strange."

Al's mother, Sandra remembered now, had been the neighborhood busybody. One of many, actually. But Al always liked to talk as much as his mother did, which meant Sandra was privy to all the gossip he gleaned from his mother.

"Mom thought it was even more strange," he went on, "when the parishioners wanted to organize a volunteer circle to bring over meals for a while afterward, but the family didn't want even that."

"Maybe they heard about those heinous liver and onion casseroles Mrs. Schneider used to make," suggested Sandra, who had been treated to the volunteer circle's offerings one summer when her own mother had bunion surgery and was laid up for two weeks.

Al chuckled. "That's probably it. Anyway, my mother always said, 'If people want to help you, you should let them do it, because sometimes they need to for themselves, as much as for your own sake.' But I guess some people would just rather grieve in private."

Yes. And some people—like the skittish man she met today—leave home and never look back, all but estranging themselves from elderly parents.

Perhaps with good reason. Sometimes a parent doesn't agree with an adult child's choices or lifestyle—an ugly divorce, a child born out of wedlock, a same-sex lover . . .

Sandra prides herself on being open-minded; she would never condemn her own children for any of those so-called sins. But she's met plenty of people who would. So when her client deflected her questions about whether he had a wife or children back home on Long Island, Sandra sensed that he had something to hide, and that his God-fearing mother probably didn't approve of whatever it is.

She mentioned that to Al Witkowski, whose bushy eyebrows nearly disappeared beneath his graying comb-over. "Yeah, I'll bet. The mother homeschooled him, so no one ever really knew him, but from what we could tell, he was a real weirdo. Remember the rumors that went around about him?"

"Which rumors?" She wondered whether Mrs. Witkowski had a hand in spreading them.

What Al told her fueled her suspicion and sparked sympathy for the misfit kid her client had once been, and for his widowed mother living out her years in gloomy solitude. No one even discovered the body in the rocking chair until the power was shut off after the electric bill went unpaid. Finally, a neighbor noticed that the windows had been dark—behind the perpetually drawn curtains and shades—for weeks.

Such a shame.

Ugly rumors and past differences aside, you'd think a person's own flesh and blood would show a bit of remorse about that harsh, lonely death. But no. Talk about a cold fish.

However, a client is a client; a commission is—

Suddenly, the house goes dark.

What in the . . . ?

Oh. The power grid must be overloaded by all the air conditioners running tonight.

The window fan slowly winds down and falls still, its whir giving way to the steady chirp of crickets beyond the screen.

Sandra puts the carton of sorbet back into the freezer, then tugs open a stuck drawer and fumbles around looking for a pack of matches. Wrong drawer. She tries another, and then, growing more anxious by the second, a third—bingo! Matchbook in hand, she feels her way into the living room to light the fat three-wick lavender spa candle on the coffee table.

What are you afraid of? Ghosts? She can almost hear her ex-husband's voice mocking her jitteriness. *There's no such thing.*

Most of the time, Sandra would be in complete agreement. But once in a while, when she shows an old house—or now that she lives in one—she gets that creepy feeling that she isn't quite alone.

She's probably just imagining things, not yet used to living solo for the first time in her life.

Again, her thoughts drift to the old woman who died alone in her rocking chair in the Addams House.

This time, along with pity, she feels a shiver of trepidation.

That's just because you're alone in the dark. Hurry up and light the candle.

She does; it takes her a moment to realize that a faint glow is falling through the sheer curtains.

Moonlight?

No, it can't be. There was just a slender white sliver in the sky when she stepped out of her Mercedes on the driveway a little while ago.

Walking over to look out the window, she's startled to find it closed and locked. So, she realizes, is the one across the room.

That's strange. She hasn't been in the living room since she fell asleep in front of the television last evening, but she could have sworn that she left the windows open overnight to ventilate the house.

Who knows? Maybe she groggily closed them all when she woke up and dragged herself to bed in the wee hours.

Maybe? She must have. There's no other logical explanation.

Peering through the glass, she sees that the light spilling into the room is coming from the streetlights out front. They're still ablaze up and down Wayside Avenue, as are her neighbors' porch lights, their windows bright with lamplight.

So this isn't a blackout. It's some kind of power failure affecting only Sandra's house.

Okay. Old homes *do* have their drawbacks—like old wiring.

And the inspector *did* warn her that the electrical system is not in good shape. A fire hazard, he called it.

She sniffs the lavender-scented air. No hint of smoke. That's a good sign.

It's probably just a blown circuit breaker. Too many fans plugged in or something.

Realizing she's going to have to inspect the ancient fuse panel in the basement, Sandra misses her ex-husband for the first time in months. It would be nice to have a man around the house, even if he is a complete SOB.

There's always Al Witkowski. He personally oversaw her move a few months ago and said to call him if she ever needs anything.

"Remember, I'm just a few blocks away," he reminded her, lingering long after the job was done. "Even if you just get sick of being alone and want some company some night . . . I know how that is."

A teddy bear of a man with a beer gut, the recently divorced Al is definitely not Sandra's type, and she isn't in the mood for company tonight. But when she thinks about the damp, still-unfamiliar basement and the spiderweb-draped electrical panel—and the fact that she isn't sure whether she even has a flashlight in the house, let alone one with working batteries . . .

Yes. She's calling Al.

Sandra reaches for the cordless phone on the end table before remembering: It's useless without electricity.

As usual, her cell phone was down to one battery bar

at the end of the workday; she plugged it in upstairs when she got home. Opting to conserve what little charge it might have picked up since, she makes her way back to the old wall telephone in the kitchen. A landline comes in handy when the power goes out.

She lifts the clunky-by-today's-standards receiver to her ear, feeling as though she should be dialing the number of one of her childhood girlfriends. The same phone, but in a burnt orange shade that matched the flower-power wallpaper, hung in her own childhood kitchen. She spent many an hour stomach-down on the speckle-patterned beige linoleum beneath the curly cord, chatting and swinging her legs around in the air.

Sandra's happy burst of nostalgia vanishes when she realizes that there's no dial tone on this phone.

Frowning, she presses the metal cradle and lifts it again. Still nothing. She jiggles it up and down. Nope.

That's strange, because it was in perfect working order when she first moved in. She used it to order takeout Chinese before she dug the cordless phones out of the moving boxes, and she marveled at how long it took the dial to circle back to its original position after each digit. People must have had a lot more patience back in the old days, before the whole world evolved into an instant gratification electronic extravaganza.

Now the old phone is offering zero gratification.

Which doesn't make sense, because a landline should work even with the power out. A blown fuse wouldn't have impacted the telephone line inside the house, and it's not as if there's a storm raging outside, toppling trees and taking down wires.

Perplexed, Sandra stands holding the receiver, wondering how it stopped functioning.

Then she sees it, out of the corner of her eye: the slightest movement in the shadowy corner of the kitchen, where two steps lead down to a small, windowed mudroom and back door.

Her instinct is to cry out, to turn and stare at the spot, or to bolt from the room.

She doesn't do any of those things.

Instead, just in case someone really is there, watching her, she pushes back the panic rushing up from her gut, forcing herself to stand absolutely still.

Her mind races through possibilities.

One, she's imagining things . . .

Two, it's a ghost . . .

Three, it's a human prowler.

Seeing another flicker of movement, she rules out the first option and decides that the second is much more appealing than the third.

More appealing, but perhaps less likely, especially when she considers the abrupt power outage.

Someone could have cut the telephone and electric lines, instantly isolating her in the dark.

The house is locked, of course, with the fancy new dead bolts Bob Witkowski installed for her after she moved in. A hell of a lot of good they do now, with all the windows open.

Sandra's own words about the broken screen, spoken so glibly just this morning, come back to haunt her now.

Anyone could push through it and hop in.

But it's such a safe neighborhood . . .

That doesn't matter. Someone—some, some *night predator*—could have easily found his way here.

Someone could have been watching from the shrub border as she walked from her car to the back door a little while ago. He could have climbed in the window while she was upstairs changing her clothes, lying in wait down here the whole time . . .

Oh dear God.

What do I do?

He's positioned between Sandra and the back door. If she goes in the opposite direction and makes a run for the front door, he'll surely catch her before she reaches it.

There's a drawer full of knives a few feet away, but she can't remember which one it is.

All right. All right. Neither flight nor fight is a reliable option.

She can scream for help, but chances are no one will hear her above the hum of air-conditioning or window fans.

What do I do?

What do I do?

In the still, dark room, she can feel the predator poised, getting ready to pounce.

She has to take a chance.

With a silent prayer—*Please, God, please, God*—Sandra bursts into motion, running with all her might toward the front of the house, certain she's going to hear footsteps chasing her, and yet . . .

Yet there's nothing, not a hint of movement behind her.

But he's there; I know he's there, and he's coming.

I have to get out.

Cursing the fact that she doesn't keep the dead bolt key inside the lock, she frantically reaches for the strip of molding above the door, knowing now that the extra second it takes to grab it could very well cost her her life.

Her straining fingertips settle at the center of the door frame, where she always places the key after locking herself in.

It isn't there.

She fumbles along the shallow ledge a couple of inches to the right, and then to the left.

No key.

Biting her trembling lip to keep from crying out in frustration, she swipes her hand across the ledge again, trying to control her movement so that she doesn't knock the key off and have to dive for it. The ledge is empty.

How can that be?

Her mind races. She rarely uses the front door. But whenever she opens it, she puts the key back where it belongs.

So what happened? Where is it?

It doesn't matter. She's trapped.

Any second now, he's going to grab her from behind . . .

She spins around.

He isn't there.

Was her mind playing tricks on her after all?

Of course. It makes sense.

Who doesn't start imagining scary things when the lights go out?

Relieved, Sandra presses a hand against her pounding heart.

Okay. Okay. I'm okay. It was a false alarm.

But . . .

What about the missing key?

And why *did* the lights go out?

And how did the living room windows wind up closed and locked?

Even as the questions flit into her mind, even as her pulse slows to a slightly less frantic rhythm, she hears it . . .

The unmistakable sound of a floorboard creaking in the kitchen.

Someone is there.

Someone is coming.

Steady footfalls approach.

Sandra looks around wildly for something to throw through the window.

Before she can make a move, a voice—eerily calm, jarringly familiar—says from the shadows, "Don't, Sandra."

It's *him*.

What is *he* doing here?

"I have a gun, and I'll use it."

A whimper escapes her as she shrinks back against the locked door like a cowering doe helplessly waiting for the hunter's kill.

Entry from the marble notebook

Wednesday, September 4, 1985

He came to my room again last night.

I wasn't feeling good so I had gone to bed early, but he woke me up. As usual, after he left I was so upset that I got no sleep, and I was exhausted today for the first day of school.

I'm a sophomore now. At Mass on Sunday, I prayed that this year will be better than last, and that I might find a friend. But so far, it's the same as last year. The other girls either look right through me like I'm not even there, or they stare at me like they feel sorry for me, or worse, like they hate me.

I don't know how I'm going to get through another whole year of this, let alone two more after that. If I complain, Mother will threaten to homeschool me again—that's what she's going to do with Adrian, poor baby.

I would never survive that. Never. School might be miserable, but it's my only escape. But I don't think she'd really go through with it for me. She doesn't want me at home all day, every day, where he could get to me while she's out working. It's not that she's trying to protect me from him, because God knows she doesn't do that. When I was little and it first started happening, I used to go crying to her, begging her to make him stop. I would get beaten and locked in my room, and I learned to keep my mouth shut. So she doesn't try to keep me from him for my own sake. It's for hers. I think that in some weird, warped way, she's jealous. She'd be thrilled if I walked out the door one day and never came back. I would, too, if it weren't for Adrian. I would never leave him here alone with them, ever.

If I stay in school I can get a good job someday and then I'll take him to live with me. We'll move away and make a fresh start someplace—in a big city where no one will know us, or on a peaceful ocean beach—someplace where we can be safe and sound and far away from the two of them, and we'll never look back. That's the only thing that keeps me going.

Chapter 3

February might be the shortest month of the year, but it feels exactly the opposite, Carley Archer decides as she strips off her wet parka on a dark winter Monday morning.

February seems to drag on endlessly here in Buffalo, where regardless of what the calendar and the groundhog say, there are still at least two more months of depressing weather ahead—usually more.

Carley drapes the hood over a hook in her locker, crams the rest of the puffy nylon coat into the narrow space, and slams the door, knowing that when she opens it later, it's going to smell like mildew again. That's what happens, she's discovered this winter, when you hang a wet coat in a closed-in, dark place all day, every day. There are no open cloakroom hooks here at Sacred Sisters High School like there were at the parochial school where Carley spent the first nine years of her education.

She takes a deep breath, air that smells of pencil sharpener shavings, old books, and, still lingering faintly, the fish casserole the cafeteria served for lunch on Friday. Time to get through another week.

Backpack over her shoulder, she heads down the hall toward homeroom, keeping an eye out for Johnny, the part-time janitor.

The first time she saw him, not long after she started school here last fall, he was outside at the edge of the parking lot, leaning on the rusty bike rack no one ever uses, simultaneously reading a book and peeling an apple. He was using a pocket knife and peeling carefully so that the skin dangled in a continuous red coil.

He wasn't great-looking—tall and wiry with black hair cut stubbly short—but there was something appealing about him. Carley assumed he must be someone's boyfriend from Cardinal Ruffini, the neighboring all-boys Catholic school.

He saw her looking at him and instead of glancing away, said hello.

"Hi," she said, expecting him to go back to his book, but he was still looking at her, as though he expected her to say something else.

So she gestured at the apple. "How do you do that without even looking at it?"

"Practice."

"Really? Aren't you afraid you're going to cut your fingers?"

He shrugged. "Nah. I've peeled a million apples and I've never cut my fingers once."

"Still . . . that must be a really good book," she said. "What is it?"

He held up the cover, and she recognized the Ray Bradbury novel she'd been assigned to read for freshman English.

"Do you like it?" she asked.

"I love it."

"Really?" Carley, who loves so many books, didn't like that one at all. Too shy to tell him that, much less find out what he thought made the book so great, she hurried away.

She occasionally spotted him out there after that, always with a book and an apple and a perfectly unfurled peel. As the weather grew more frequently inclement, she started to notice him inside the school, too. She can't quite remember how she found out his name, or that he's not someone's boyfriend after all—rather, part of the custodial staff—but she does recall feeling an odd little spark of pleasure at the news.

Not that she has a particular affinity for janitors, but . . . well, at least he's not dating one of the other girls. Not that *she* wants to date him, because he's too old for her and they have nothing in common but Ray Bradbury and finding themselves in the same little corner of the world at the same time, and he's probably not interested anyway, but . . .

She just happens to like the fact that he was obviously reading the Bradbury book because he wanted to. Not because he had to for an assignment.

She began not just to notice him, but to look for him. She figured out, for example, that on the first Monday of every month, he can always be found outside by the big signboard in front of the school. It's his job to change the listing of events using the big black letters he carries with him in a plastic case. She liked how in December, he wrote "MERRY CHRISTMAS!!!!" using plenty of exclamation marks.

When she worked up the courage to compliment him on that one day, he told her that he would have used more, "But that was all they had in the box."

On the last day before Christmas break, he saw her in the hall and called, "Merry Christmas! I hope you can tell I said that with lots of exclamation!"

She laughed longer and harder than she should have.

Today, there's no sign of Johnny in the hallway. Just the usual crowd of uniformed girls making their way to class-rooms, and the occasional habited nun hustling them along or waiting in doorways to greet them.

"Hi, Carley!"

She turns, surprised to have been greeted—by name!—by a pair of passing girls from her social studies class.

"Oh . . . hi."

She rounds a corner and another girl spots her and waves. "Carley, what's up?"

"Not much." Carley waves back and walks on, feeling a smile playing at her lips. Maybe, at long last, she's starting to fit in here. Mom promised that it would take some time but would eventually happen. "You'll see, Carley, before you know it, you'll feel as much at home at Sacred Sisters as you did at Saint Paul's."

She doubted that. After all, Saint Paul's was within walking distance of her house in Woodsbridge, not way up here in the city. And she was enrolled there from kindergarten through eighth grade, year after year, in the same building with the same kids and the same teachers who weren't all nuns like they are at Sisters—well, *almost* all of them, anyway. And at Saint Paul's, the nuns didn't wear habits as they do here, where they're part of a more conservative religious order.

Plus . . .

Nicki was at Saint Paul's.

Carley's smile fades. She doesn't want to think about Nicki right now. Not on a day that's started out so well, despite the stormy weather outside.

In homeroom, she greets Sister Thomas Katherine, who's standing at the chalkboard writing something.

"Good morning, Carley!" Sister Thomas Katherine is cheerful, as always, and Carley's mood lifts another notch as she heads down the row to her seat.

"Hi, Carley." The girl in front of her, a pretty blonde named Renee, turns around. "How was your weekend?"

"Oh—it was pretty good, thanks."

"That's good." Renee faces forward again before Carley remembers that she should have asked, in turn, how Renee's weekend was.

"The best way to make new friends," Mom coached her at the beginning of the year, "is to ask people about themselves."

So far, that's been easier said than done. You can't just walk up to someone who doesn't know you exist and ask if she has any hobbies.

Mom can't relate to that particular problem, though. She's the kind of person people notice—and like—right away. Dad calls her a social butterfly. Carley's younger sister, Emma, is the same way: never at a loss for words and completely at ease wherever she goes, even surrounded by strangers.

It must be nice to have that kind of confidence. Carley would trade places with Emma or Mom any day.

But now, for the first time since she started high school, she wonders if her loneliness might be temporary after all, like her mother said. Weird the way it seems to have happened overnight, though. Or maybe friendliness is contagious: several other classmates say hello to her before it's time to stand for the Pledge and morning prayer, read over the loudspeaker by a pair of seniors.

Listening absently to the morning announcements, Carley decides February isn't so bad after all.

It's definitely looking better than the fall months, when she was so new here she couldn't find her way from her locker to homeroom without consulting her photocopied map.

And it's better than December and January, too, by far. Nicki's absence in her life made the holidays—always Carley's favorite time of year—seem oddly depressing this year. The lake-effect snow hurtled across the frigid waters of Erie and Ontario seemed even crueler than usual without her best friend around to coax her into sledding or brownie baking when blizzards canceled school.

"And last but not least," the girl on the PA system is

saying, and her voice makes Carley picture her as petite, ponytailed, and bubbly, "this morning, the Spring Fling elections will be held in homeroom. Winners will be announced on Friday."

The other senior joins her to deliver the usual signoff in unison: "Have a blessed day!"

The intercom clicks off, and an excited buzz goes up in the room.

Carley first heard about Spring Fling from her mother, who also attended Sacred Sisters, along with Carley's four aunts. The dance, a longtime tradition, is a collaborative affair between Sisters and Cardinal Ruffini, held annually on a March weekend in the gym of one school or the other. There's a royal court, consisting of one princess and one prince chosen from each grade, along with a senior queen and king.

Naturally, Mom was voted princess her sophomore year.

"Why not freshman year?" Emma wanted to know, the night Mom shared that memory at the dinner table.

"I was a late bloomer. Freshman year, the prettiest girl in the class got elected."

"You mean she wasn't you?" Dad shook his head. "I don't buy that for a second."

Mom laughed. "I know it's hard to believe, but not everyone fell in love with me at first sight. Just you."

At that, Emma rolled her eyes at Carley, who—the older she gets—finds it more sweet than disgusting when her parents get flirty. Maybe someday, she'll be grown up and sitting at the dinner table with her own kids and a husband who fell in love with her at first sight. Maybe she's a late bloomer, too.

"Listen up, ladies," Sister Thomas Katherine calls from the front of the room, brushing chalk dust from her black habit. "Before we each write down the name of the girl we'd like to represent the class at Spring Fling, we're going to go over some of these points I've written on the board. This is *not* a beauty contest or a popularity contest."

Sure it is, Carley thinks. It's a beauty contest *and* a popularity contest, because (a) those two things go hand in hand, and (b) who wants an ugly nobody as Spring Fling princess?

For weeks now, her fellow freshmen have been talking about the obvious choice: Melissa Kovacs, the prettiest girl in the class.

Also the meanest.

Carley figured that out on the first day of school, when she heard Melissa mocking an elderly cafeteria lady's speech impediment within earshot of the poor woman.

"Let's go over the qualities we want to see in our princess," Sister Thomas Katherine is saying.

Chin in hand, Carley scans the list on the board: *good citizenship, solid morals, impeccable manners, intelligence, a charitable heart* . . .

Melissa Kovacs possesses none of the above. She might win, but it won't be a unanimous vote, Carley decides, as Sister Thomas Katherine walks up and down the aisle, handing out ballots.

The sky beyond the windowpane is dismal as ever this morning, pulsing blue-black clouds pushed by a gusting west wind that tosses icy pellets against the glass like slingshot gravel. But nothing, not even western New York weather, can put a damper on this glorious day.

Yet another phase of the plan has been set into motion. At last, it's all coming together.

Nineteen months.

It's been nineteen months since the black marble notebook, with its papery brown shards of pressed flower petals, surfaced in the old house on Lilac Street.

Nineteen months since the terrible truth was revealed.

Nineteen months since Sandra Lutz became the first to pay for the sins of the past—though not her own sins. No, she merely got in the way. Said too much, knew too much . . .

But the others—the original trio of sinners—are about to discover what it means to truly suffer.

The bell rings, signifying the end of homeroom period. In exactly four minutes, another bell will announce the start of first period. A minute after that, a distant whistle will blow, bells will clang, and a freight train will burst onto the grade-level track a few blocks from the school, rattling along its route to Cleveland and on to Detroit, maybe, or Chicago. Ten, fifteen minutes later, a brown UPS truck will pull into the big parking lot alongside the yellow brick building and the driver will climb out with the day's packages. In the big industrial kitchen adjacent to the cafeteria, plain-faced women in hairnets chop tomatoes and shred lettuce. Monday is always taco day.

You get to know the rhythm of a place after a while. Week after week, month after month, the same routine, marred only by winter storms that warrant school closings or the occasional fire drill, though not in a while, and not today for sure. No one wants to stand around the parking lot, coatless, on a morning like this.

Today will be unremarkable, with one exception.

But I'm the only one who knows about that.

With a scraping of chairs and excited female chatter, the girls of Sacred Sisters leave their homerooms to fill the drably tiled hallways of the old school, oblivious to the tragedy that started to unfold here almost three decades ago this very day—or to their own unwitting roles in the new one about to begin.

Entry from the marble notebook

Monday, October 7, 1985

Today is my birthday. Sweet sixteen—what a joke. There is nothing sweet about it. Nothing sweet about my life.

Father came to my room after midnight saying he had a special present for me. He was laughing. I hate him. If I could figure out a way to get away with killing him, I would. But I don't want to spend the rest of my life in jail, and I don't want to go to hell for committing a mortal sin.

Before he left my room, he said I have to go down to Motor Vehicles to get my driving permit tomorrow, because he and Mother need me to start doing my share around here. As if I'm not already their slave. They want me to take over the grocery shopping and running errands. Usually I'm glad to get out of the house for any reason but I don't want to drive if he's the one who's going to teach me. I begged him to wait until spring, at least, when the other sophomores will start turning sixteen and I can take driver's ed through school, but he won't let me.

I hate being older than the rest of my class—it's because they held me back a year in school when we moved here from California. It's just one more thing to set me apart from everyone else.

We don't do birthday cakes in our house, but on Adrian's fifth birthday last winter, I got him a Hostess cupcake, put a candle in it, sang to him, and told him to make a wish when he blew out the candle. That night when I tucked him in, he told me he had wished that I was his mom instead of her. I reminded him that you're not supposed to tell what your wish is, or it won't come true.

Today, Adrian was crying because he couldn't figure out how to get me a cupcake and a candle so that he could sing to me and give me a wish. I told him we would make believe. When I blew out the pretend candle, he told me I had to make a wish.

I wished that my father were dead. That's not the same thing as killing him. It's not a sin. You can wish anything you want.

Adrian warned me not to tell him what I wished because it wouldn't come true. I didn't tell him, of course. But it doesn't matter. It was a fake cupcake and a fake candle and anyway, none of my wishes have ever come true.

Chapter 4

"How was school?" Jen Archer asks Carley as she blows in the door on a damp March gust.

Seeing the look on her daughter's face, she immediately regrets the question that had impulsively escaped her mouth, as words so often seem to do.

Way to go there, Mom.

How was school?

How do you *think* it was?

Sometimes, it seems that Jen has spent the better part of her life reminding herself to think before she speaks—or trying to undo the inevitable fallout when she forgets.

Growing up the youngest of the five Bonafacio sisters, each more outgoing than the next, she was known by the childhood nickname "the Yapster." She never quite outgrew her loquaciousness; in fact, it served her well in her postcollege career as a sales rep for a packaged goods corporation.

Not so well, though, as a stay-at-home mom to two daughters whose moods go awry based on the slightest inflection—real, or imagined—in Jen's tone.

"Carley, I—"

"Mom, school was *fine*." The last word lands as heavily as the backpack she drops on the polished hardwood floor, fiercely walloping Jen with maternal protective instinct.

For Carley, school wasn't *fine* today. It hasn't been fine for weeks now, as far as Jen knows. Probably a lot longer.

But it's been two weeks, exactly, since the Friday morning when she got the phone call from Sister Linda, the school's part-time social worker. Two weeks since Jen and her husband, Thad, found out that their fifteen-year-old freshman has become the target of vicious bullying.

Jen bends to pick up the backpack and move it to a cushioned bench. "This weighs a ton, sweetie. Doesn't it make your back hurt?"

"Yes, but what am I supposed to do? Not worry about homework at all, like Emma?"

Conscientious Carley dutifully hauls around a stack of thick textbooks every day, unlike her slapdash eighteen-months-younger sister, Emma, whose eighth-grade assignments—if she remembers them at all—are usually crumpled in her school uniform pocket with a litter of Juicy Fruit wrappers.

Not that Emma's even allowed to chew gum with her braces on.

Not that she cares.

That her daughters are extreme opposites used to give Jen pleasure. "They balance each other out," she'd say when they were younger, "and opposites attract, right?"

Right. That was back in the good old days when Carley and Emma were so close that they walked around holding hands, completely of their own accord. Strangers would smile and say, "Awww . . ."

Now that the girls are both teenagers, opposites most certainly don't attract; they repel. When they're actually speaking to each other, they're arguing.

Jen can't help but think this isn't how it's supposed to be. She and her four older sisters didn't always get along perfectly, but at least they all had similar personalities and temperaments and grew up to be good friends. Whenever they actually see each other—which isn't as often as anyone would like since Jen is the only one still living in western New York—conversations are laced with laughs and the camaraderie of women who view the world from similar perspectives.

She can't imagine that ever happening with Carley and Emma, given their extreme personalities. If they could just find a happy medium once in a while, life would be so much . . . well, happier.

Happy. When was the last time Carley was happy?

Yesterday, Jen reminds herself. *Yesterday she almost smiled, for a moment there . . .*

Yes, because when Carley came home yesterday, Jen greeted her not with questions about school, but with a funny account of the fat, persistent squirrel who'd invaded the backyard birdfeeder, only to be repeatedly chased off by a tiny, bossy bird. Jen embellished the story into a Disney-esque romp—anything to see her daughter's face light up the way it used to.

Carley's always been passionate about anything having to do with nature, particularly animals. Jen will never forget the pure pleasure—or resulting heartache—of surprising her on a long-ago birthday with a tiny white kitten. When she and Thad decided on the gift, they had no idea yet that Emma was asthmatic with a fierce allergy to cat fur. All fur, actually, and feathers, too.

The kitten—whom Carley had named Cutie Pie—had to go.

"Why can't *she* go?" Carley had sobbed, cradling the purring ball of fluff and glaring at Emma, whose eyes were equally swollen and teary, courtesy of said fluff.

In the end, Cutie Pie went to live a few miles away with Jen's sister Bennie and her family. Carley took solace in being able to visit any time she wanted—until Bennie's husband was transferred to California. She didn't return the cat—Emma was still allergic—but she did give the Archers her piano.

"Consolation prize?" Jen asked wryly.

"Maybe your girls can learn to play it. My kids were never interested and I didn't want to force lessons on them the way Mom did on us."

"But we actually liked piano lessons, remember?"

"Not really. We just liked Marie Bush," Bennie pointed out, and Jen smiled, recalling the vivacious teacher who would come to the Bonafacio house on Wednesdays and teach one sister after another to play scales and eventually Beethoven.

Jen accepted the cast-off upright from her sister, and Cutie Pie moved to the West Coast. Following an extended mourning period, Carley survived the loss and started piano lessons. She hasn't mentioned the cat in a long time now, though she remains affectionate toward furry creatures.

Predictably, Jen's rogue squirrel story yesterday was rewarded with—well, not a smile, exactly. But at least there was a fleeting spark of interest in her daughter's big brown eyes.

Bent on seeing an actual grin today, or maybe even getting a laugh, Jen was hoping to find a new anecdote to share. But woodland creatures were nowhere to be found in the backyard, thanks to the monsoonlike weather so typical of early springtime in western New York.

As the uneventful day wore on without yielding a shred of amusing material—nature-related, or otherwise—Jen resorted to scouring the Web for a good joke or a comedic video clip suitable for her fifteen-year-old.

She's never spent much time on the Internet. Not compared to the rest of the world, anyway. Maybe she'd be more tech-savvy if she were still in the workforce, or a teenager, but she prefers to do most of her communicating and shopping and reading the old-fashioned way.

Aghast at what popped up via the search engine today, she's more worried than ever about what her girls are being exposed to online.

"Whatever happened to good old-fashioned *clean* comedy?" she asked Thad during his regular lunchtime phone call, after she'd explained Mission: Cheer Up Carley.

"You mean like Charlie Chaplin?"

"Not *that* old-fashioned."

"The Three Stooges? Abbott and Costello?"

"You know what I mean. Everything is so raunchy, and I—I don't know. I just want her to laugh again."

"She will, eventually. But it's going to take a lot more than a laugh to get her past this thing. You can't just fix everything."

Sure I can, Jen thought. *I'm her mom. That's what moms do. We fix things for our kids and we worry about them and we ask about their day when they walk in the door . . .*

Dammit. Why, just when Jen felt like she was starting to get the hang of this motherhood thing, sisterly squabbles and all, did the rules have to go and change?

To make matters worse, the local bus Carley takes to and from school, so often running late, had to go and show up five minutes early today, catching her off guard. And so, rather than greeting Carley with an amusing anecdote or even a raunchy YouTube clip to take her mind off her troubles, Jen simply blurted the first thing that came to mind.

How was your day?

Carley was never forthcoming with details about her life even *before* the whole school nightmare started.

But Jen wouldn't hesitate to ask Emma that same question on any given afternoon. She's not necessarily less prickly than her older sister—if anything, she's far pricklier—but she's not nearly as private.

Never in a million years would Emma merely tell Jen that school was "fine." She'd pronounce it "horrifying" or "amazing," then launch into a superlative-heavy account of something that had happened during recess or lunch. The spectacular incident typically would feature at least half a dozen of the gaggle of girls Emma refers to as her BFFs—a term that used to amuse, but now only aggravates, her big sister.

"You can't have twenty people you call best friends forever," she often tells Emma. "If there are twenty of them, then they aren't BFFs. They're just friends. A person can only have *one* BFF."

"Maybe *you* only have one," Emma shoots back, "but I have twenty. Actually, twenty-three."

Yes, and poor Carley no longer has even one. Not since Nicki Olivera switched to public school after their eighth-grade graduation from Saint Paul's Parochial.

Inseparable from Nicki since preschool, Carley had asked if she, too, could go to Woodsbridge High, rather than commute to Sacred Sisters, the all-girls Catholic high school in the working-class Buffalo neighborhood where Jen had grown up.

"Try Sisters first," Jen told her. "If you don't like it, you can change to Woodsbridge sophomore year."

Once Carley got to Sisters, she wouldn't want to leave, Jen was certain. After all, she herself had gone there, along with all four of her siblings, and her mother and aunts a generation before them.

So had Debbie Quattrone Olivera, Nicki's mother and one of Jen's closest friends back at Sisters. They drifted apart when they went off to college, but rekindled the friendship about a decade ago as married young moms living in adjacent developments here in Buffalo's South Towns suburbs.

"If I ever have a daughter," Debbie used to say back when they were teenagers, "I'll *never* send her to Sisters."

"Why not?"

"Because I want her to have freedom to choose where

she goes, not be forced into it like we were just because our moms went here."

Yes, Sacred Sisters was a tradition among Catholic families in the old neighborhood, but Jen didn't consider herself forced into attending. On the contrary, having wistfully watched her older sisters enroll one by one, she couldn't wait to go.

The Bonafacio girls thrived there, academically and socially. Firstborn Maddie was class president all four years. Brainy Jessie graduated a year later as valedictorian. Bennie and Frankie were standouts—and eventually captains—on almost every athletic team.

Night after night, year after year, they sat at the supper table brimming with tales of high school life.

When at last it was Jen's turn to walk into that three-story yellow brick building as a student, she found her niche on the yearbook and newspaper staffs. She loved every minute of those four fleeting years, with the exception of her on-again, off-again high romance with Mike Morino.

Genuinely taken aback when the ever-irreverent teenage Debbie declared that she'd sell her future daughter into slavery before she'd send her to their alma mater, Jen had asked, "But what if she *wants* to come here?"

"Why would she?"

"Why *wouldn't* she?"

Famous last words.

Last spring, when Carley started asking about public high school, Thad wasn't opposed to the idea of forgoing high school tuition payments for the next four years. He's always worried about money, thanks to the dismal economy, bills piling up, taxes and college costs on the rise, and regular rounds of layoffs at the accounting firm where he's a principal CPA.

"Just think—we could save more in the girls' college accounts if we send them to public high school, Jen, and they'd still get a great education."

"You and I both went to private high schools, though . . . so how would we know?"

"I don't know . . . but I'm guessing my experience wasn't as warm and fuzzy as yours."

Having grown up in a wealthy suburb of Rochester, Thad had gone to a four-year prep school. He isn't Catholic—or religious, for that matter. While his parents had been Presbyterian, they weren't practicing, and the first time he set foot in any church was when he married Jen. He never considered converting, but he occasionally attends Sunday Mass at Saint Paul's with her and the girls. He likes to refer to himself as a lapsed agnostic.

"Look, I know Sacred Sisters is a tradition in your family, Jen," he said. "But if Carley feels that strongly about it—"

"She doesn't," Jen cut in. "She's always planned on going there. She's just worried about being separated from Nicki after all these years. I told her they can still be friends."

"You and I both know it won't be the same."

"Well, it's not really good for the two of them to be joined at the hip anymore. Nicki's the type who might be tempted to walk on the wild side when she gets a little older." Lord knew her mother certainly had. "Carley's not like that. She's a good girl, and anyway, it's time for her to branch out and make new friends, don't you think?"

"Sure, but you've said yourself that Sisters is too small—"

"I never said *too*. I just said small."

"Okay, you've said that it's small, and insular—"

"*Insulated*. That's not a negative quality. Crazy, terrible things are going on out there in the world, Thad."

"Crazy, terrible things can happen anywhere. Isn't high school a time for Carley to broaden horizons instead of narrow them?"

"That's what I just said. I want her to branch out and—"

"And you want her to be insulated. I feel like you're talking in circles, Jen."

To be honest, so did she—and it wasn't an unfamiliar sensation. But whenever she feels passionately about something, she fights for it.

Not about to let her daughter miss out on a wonderful high school experience, she told Thad firmly, "I have a feeling she'll love Sisters if she just gives it a chance."

So.

Thanks to Jen, Carley gave it a chance.

And thanks to me, she's absolutely miserable. Look at her.

There are dark circles under Carley's bespectacled eyes. Her skin is broken out thanks to stress and hormones—also the culprits behind a noticeable recent weight gain. She's never been a thin, wiry kid like Emma, but she wasn't necessarily plump, either. Lately, however, sedentary habits, an insatiable sweet tooth, and a tendency to turn to food for comfort have caught up with her. She's getting a double chin, and the buttons on her white blouse strain as she leans to drape her windbreaker over the coat tree by the door.

She sees Jen staring at her and scowls suspiciously. "What?"

About to remark that it's much too chilly on this raw day for just a thin jacket like that, Jen thinks better of it. No need for criticism right now.

"Nothing." She lifts her gaze away from the gaping buttons, away from the round, pimply face, and notices that Carley's brown ponytail is damp.

Resisting the urge to pat her head or—God forbid—pull her into a big hug, Jen weighs her words carefully before asking the most innocuous question she can think of: "Is it sleeting out there again?"

"I don't know. Maybe a little bit."

"I was thinking the sun might peek out this afternoon, but it doesn't look like it's going to, does it?" Jen glances up at the gray, misty world beyond the glass pane in the door.

Carley mutely stares at her sneakers as she backward-skates the rubber soles over the mat, leaving thick streaks of March mud.

"It was snowing out this morning, did you see?"

Still no response.

"I'm glad it didn't stick," Jen goes on. "I was planning to put those pansies I bought yesterday into the window boxes, but it was too wet out there, you know?"

"Mmm hmm."

Following her daughter's gaze to her once-white Nikes, Jen finds herself wondering if things would be different, maybe, if Carley didn't wear them, along with opaque navy stockings, to school.

While uniforms are still required at Sacred Sisters—although the plaid skirts are shorter and the navy blazers less boxy than they were in Jen's day—they no longer have to be paired with low-heeled brown loafers.

Jen can't imagine stiletto heels being tolerated, but she's seen girls wear cute sandals and boots that almost border on sexy when paired with above-the-knee-hemlines. That particular style might not do pudgy Carley any favors, but there must be a look that would be more flattering than those clunky old—

No. Stop thinking that way. It's not Carley's fault. It's not about what she wears, or doesn't wear, and it's not about her face being broken out or the weight she's gained. Other girls at the school are in the same boat, or worse off; girls who are tremendously obese, or physically disabled, or utterly impoverished charity cases, or brazenly nonconformist with shorn hair and hidden tattoos . . .

Why Carley? Why did the bullies have to set their sights on her, of all people? Why a sweet girl who'd never hurt a fly?

Carley isn't talking, except to insist that she doesn't want to leave Sacred Sisters.

Jen's first instinct had been to pull her out—and she still might have done it, despite Carley's determination to stay put, if both Thad and the school's social worker hadn't urged her not to react so drastically.

"If she's willing to give it another chance," Thad said, "then I think we should back her up. Situations like this can build character."

He had a point, but . . .

"You should be proud of her for wanting to stick it out," Sister Linda told her over the phone. "Your daughter isn't a quitter. That's something we admire here."

She had a point, too, but . . .

Jen couldn't stand—still can't stand—the idea of her little girl facing down cruel bullies day after day.

Sister Linda repeatedly assured her that she would be meeting regularly with Carley and her team of teachers to make sure the situation had been nipped in the bud.

"I'd like to come in and meet with them, too," Jen said, "and my husband could probably—"

"Mrs. Archer, I know you're concerned, but let's not blow this situation out of proportion."

Jen bristled at that, but when she repeated later the comment to Thad, he shrugged. "I can see her point."

"*What?*"

"You do have a tendency to get a little—"

"Don't you dare say melodramatic!"

"I wasn't going to say that."

"Or even just dramatic."

"I wasn't going to say that, either."

"What were you going to say, then?"

"Just that you can get a little worked up sometimes when—"

"I do not get worked up!"

"When it comes to the kids? Really?"

All right, maybe she does. But this is serious, not something to be brushed off like an overdue library book.

To be fair, the social worker has touched base by e-mail several times since the initial phone call. Still, she's made it abundantly clear that Carley is in high school now, and parents are encouraged to foster independence in their daughters.

You don't have to cut the apron strings, Mrs. Archer, Sister Linda wrote, *but it's not a bad idea to loosen them a bit. We aren't doing our young women any favors if we fight their battles for them, are we?*

In that moment, Jen hated her with all her heart. Almost as much as she hated the bullies who chose Carley as their target.

She's since conceded that Sister Linda wasn't saying anything that wasn't previously drilled into the parents of incoming freshmen. At Sacred Sisters orientation last spring and again at Back to School night in September, the message came with different phrasing, depending on who was delivering it: the principal, the guidance counselors, various teachers and coaches, even the school nurse.

But the basic theme was this: *It's time to let go, Mama Bear.*

In other words, the school dress code and the staff aren't the only things that have changed in the twenty-five years since Jen graduated.

Back then, no one was encouraging the girls of Sacred Sisters to think for themselves or solve their own problems. They weren't exactly coddled, but it wasn't sink or swim, either. The prevailing message, when you had a problem, was "Give it up to God."

Nearly all the teachers in the old days were nuns with a few priests thrown in, and unlike at many local Catholic schools, that hasn't changed at Sisters.

Still, in some ways, the credo was somehow less conservative back then than it is now. Most of the staff when Jen was here had started teaching in the wake of Vatican II, and the nuns wore street clothes.

The pendulum has since swung back. Weekly Latin Mass has made a comeback. The current crop of teachers includes many nuns who belong to a conservative order and still wear traditional habits.

The only one who remains from Jen's day is Sister Margaret, the elderly home economics teacher. Back then, her job—ironic in many ways—was to teach the girls to be competent housewives. She still conducts cooking and sewing classes, according to Carley, but her title is now home and career instructor, and computer courses have been added to her curriculum.

"Sister Margaret uses a computer?" Jen was incredulous. "She was half blind when I knew her."

"She's pretty much all blind now," Carley said. "But that's why she likes the computer. She has voice recognition software."

That conversation took place early in the school year when Carley seemed tentatively optimistic about her future at Sisters. At that point, Jen was a lot more comfortable with the idea of letting go.

It's not so easy to do now, when she feels like her daughter is dangling by a fraying thread—or, all right, by an apron string—high above a pit filled with rabid cats. Her maternal instinct is to yank Carley back to safety and hang on tight.

Jen looks at her, again noticing the weight gain and problem skin—and again hating her own critical eye.

She herself wasn't a perfect teenager. She didn't have acne and she wasn't overweight or nearsighted, and she was considered pretty and popular, but there were other things . . .

She remembers her long dark hair being far too straight and flat at a time when curly, frizzy big hair was in style.

And she remembers thinking that her nose was gigantic, even begging her parents to let her have surgery on it.

"Are you crazy?" her mother shouted—shouted, because the Bonafacios weren't exactly a soft-spoken bunch. "People would kill for that nose! That's a good, strong Roman nose!"

"It's *my* nose!" her father put in.

"That's the problem!" Jen wailed. "It's a gigantic *man* nose on *my* face!"

But her parents assured her that she'd grow into it, and they were right. Either that, or she eventually stopped caring so much, learning to be comfortable in her own skin . . . which was much easier to do once she was away from her high school boyfriend, who always made her feel as though she didn't measure up.

Now that she's in her early forties, she's noticing tiny wrinkles around the big brown eyes she always thought were her best asset. There's a faint network of wrinkles, too, at the corners of her wide mouth.

As for her figure—nothing is as taut as it used to be. The pounds have crept on over the years, settling around her hips and thighs. She's not obese by any stretch, but she's hardly the super-fit middle-aged woman she'd always assumed she'd become. Losing five, ten, fifteen pounds is no longer the no-brainer it was back when she was getting rid of postpregnancy flab. Somehow, it takes a hell of a lot more diet and exercise to get rid of far less weight. And somehow, she's not very motivated these days. As long as she's healthy, do her looks truly matter?

Not most days. And on days when she finds that her appearance actually does matter to her, she's careful never to vocalize self-criticism when she looks in a mirror—not if her impressionable girls are in earshot.

Does Carley even care about her own looks, though? She doesn't ever talk about it, and Jen doesn't dare bring it up.

I'm her mom. I'm supposed to think she's beautiful, no matter what.

And I do, she reminds herself hastily. *I just don't want others hurting her because they don't agree.*

But again—she doesn't know if what happened has anything to do with the fact that Carley doesn't conform to the other girls' standards of physical beauty; she's only using her own past experience as a frame of reference.

When she was at Sacred Sisters, the only girls she remembers being teased and taunted were—to put it kindly—rather unconventional in appearance. And certainly what happened to them was nowhere near as disturbing as what happened to Carley.

Although there was one—

No. Jen doesn't like to think about that.

Sensing that her daughter is about to bolt for the stairs and disappear behind closed doors for the remainder of the afternoon, she returns her focus to the conversation, determined to keep it going, even if it is mainly one-sided.

"Oh, before I forget to tell you—guess what?"

"What?" Carley asks in a monotone.

"Guess who's coming to visit next weekend?"

"Who?"

"Your godmother."

"Aunt Frankie? Really?" Carley's brown eyes, behind her glasses, connect with Jen's at last.

Encouraged by the spark of interaction, Jen nods vigorously. "She called me today"—actually, it was the other way around—"and she said she's been thinking it's been too long since she's visited."

In truth, Jen reached out to her closest sister—in age, friendship, and proximity, as Frankie lives in Albany—and updated her on the situation with Carley. Not only is Frankie a social worker, but as both godmother and childless aunt, she adores Jen's daughters.

"What can I do?" she asked immediately.

"Is there any way you can come this weekend? Maybe Carley will open up to you more than she has to me."

"I have to go to Long Island for a conference. But I'll be there next weekend—Ma's doing Saint Joseph's table on Sunday, remember?"

Somehow, Jen had forgotten. Saint Joseph's Feast Day is right up there with Thanksgiving and Christmas in their family. They used to celebrate on the actual day, March 19, but now that everyone is scattered, her parents gather everyone on a weekend before or after. That means Jen will be spending the days leading up to it in her mother's kitchen as usual, helping to prepare the labor-intensive feast.

"When is Aunt Frankie coming?" Carley asks now.

"Friday, as soon as she gets out of work. She wants to take you out to the Cheesecake Factory"—that's Carley's favorite restaurant—"and maybe to a movie."

"Me and Emma?"

"Just you."

Carley digests that. "How come?"

"Because you're charming and adorable," she quips, hoping her daughter will crack a smile.

Nope.

"Is Aunt Patty coming, too?"

Patty is Frankie's longtime significant other. A rotund woman with a magnetic personality and an easy laugh, she might be just what the doctor ordered for Carley right now. But alas—

"She's working next weekend, Aunt Frankie said."

Carley looks disappointed. "She's always working."

"It seems that way, doesn't it?"

Patty, a paramedic, seldom has enough time off to make the four-hour drive to Buffalo with Jen's sister.

"Aunt Frankie is always working, too. I bet they wish

they could trade places with you and do nothing all day every day."

Carley's comment is intended to be innocent enough, Jen knows, but it stings nonetheless. She's tempted to point out to Carley that she's hardly a lady of leisure.

It's all she can do to keep up with the housework around here, making sure everyone has everything they need on a daily basis, like prescription refills and permission slips and today, a last-minute egg carton for Emma's overdue science project . . .

Jen hastily emptied the eggs right onto the refrigerator shelf and sent Emma on her way. But when she opened the door again to grab the coffee creamer, several loose eggs rolled into each other, then onto the floor.

No surprise there. She's always dropping things, a life-long klutz. Clumsiness goes hand in hand with impetuous-ness. But so, for Jen, does resourcefulness.

Rather than let the eggs—which cracked, but didn't actu-ally break—go to waste, she started baking. First, she made a sponge cake to bring to the people who just moved in two houses down the street.

Well, not *just*. It's been a few weeks since she spotted the moving van in the driveway, but she wanted to give the new residents—a single dad and his teenage son, according to Carley, who babysits for the Janicek family next door to them—some time to settle in before showing up to welcome them to the neighborhood. She's been hoping to catch them coming or going so that she can introduce herself, but so far, that hasn't happened. Not that she's noticed, anyway. She's been distracted by what happened to Carley at school.

While the sponge cake was in the oven, she mixed a batch of peanut butter cookies, Carley's favorite.

It seemed like a good idea at the time. Probably because that's how her own mother always shows her love or handles a crisis: by feeding people. It's a wonder Jen and her sisters weren't overweight, growing up—especially Frankie, a notorious junk food fanatic.

But kids were so much more active back then. These days it's all about technology and screens—television, smart phones, e-readers, laptops . . . they don't even call each other on the phone anymore so that they can hear each other's voices; they just send text messages back and forth . . .

"I have to go do homework." Carley is on the move, brushing past Jen, heading for the stairs.

"On a Friday afternoon?"

"Math test Monday."

"Wait, Car, guess what? I made some peanut butter cook—"

"No, thanks."

"But—"

"I'm not hungry." Carley bounds up the steps. Seconds later, her bedroom door closes—not gently, but not hard, either.

Jen finds herself wishing her daughter would just slam the damned door. Good old-fashioned healthy adolescent anger—she'd welcome that any day over this . . . this preternatural calm.

Door slamming isn't Carley's style, though. She isn't the household hothead by any stretch. That honor belongs to Emma—or perhaps to Jen herself.

Aside from her looks, Carley takes after Thad's side of the family.

"In other words, she's quiet and reasonable and sane," Thad used to tease Jen whenever she mentioned the similarities between him and their firstborn.

"Hey! Are you accusing me of being loud and unreasonable and insane?"

"Absolutely," he'd say, or he'd raise an eyebrow at her—just one—and the conversation would invariably end in a few more traded quips and grins.

Around here lately, though, lighthearted moments have become as scarce as . . . as . . .

As songs played on that piano, Jen thinks as she passes it on her way back to the kitchen. Back before the girls' lessons got lost in the busy household shuffle, Emma complained constantly and could barely bang out a scale. But Carley seemed to have some actual talent.

Maybe she should get back into music, Jen muses, moving on down the hall. Maybe that will help somehow.

Back in the kitchen, she eyes the trays of cookies cooling on the breakfast bar.

Maybe those will help somehow.

Maybe something, somehow, will help.

You can't just fix everything, Thad's voice reminds her.

No? Watch me.

She grabs a rubber spatula, slides the edge under a cookie, and starts to move it from the still-hot baking sheet to a waiting plate. She'll take a couple up to Carley's room with a glass of milk and see if she wants to talk.

She won't. But at least she'll know I'm there for her if she needs me. At least she'll know she's not alone. And sooner or later, she'll—

As she tilts the spatula, the cookie, still too hot, lands on the plate in an accordion heap of crumbly goo.

"Crap!"

Shaking her head, Jen tosses the spatula aside in frustration.

Once again, she was too impulsive. Once again, she forgot to think things through before she acted.

When, Jen asks herself, *will you ever learn?*

A quick visual inspection assures Carley that her lavender and white bedroom is just as she left it this morning before school: bed neatly made; books, binders, folders, and note cards stacked just so on her desk; closet door and dresser drawers slightly ajar—just slightly, so that it'll be easier for her to tell whether anything is amiss.

Nothing is.

Good.

Now that Carley has moved on to high school, she has to catch a metro bus that departs half an hour before Emma leaves for Saint Paul's. That's a problem in a house without any locks on the interior doors. Sometimes her sister sneaks in after she's gone and snoops around or borrows something. Usually not clothes, of course—Emma is one of those petite girls who will never be more than a size two, while Carley, already a twelve, is the same size as Mom.

Too bad that doesn't keep Emma from rifling through her things, helping herself to accessories or school supplies or, more often, to Carley's secret chocolate stash. No matter where she hides it, Emma usually manages to sniff it out.

Not today, though. It's a pretty good bet Emma's not going to go browsing on Carley's bookshelves. She's always making fun of her for keeping dog-eared copies of *Charlotte's Web*, *Amelia Bedelia,* and the Little House series.

After removing two fat hardcover volumes of the Hunger Games trilogy from her bookshelf, Carley takes the bag of miniature Twix out from behind them.

When, she wonders as she reaches into the bag, was the last time she devoured a book as fervently as she did these? Back when she was in parochial school, she read the entire trilogy one title right after another, lost in a futuristic world where terrible things happened to kids just like her.

If only it were so simple to escape the real world now. If only terrible things happened just to fictional kids. If only . . .

If only I didn't have to spend so much time thinking if only this or if only that.

She counts out three candy bars, starts to return the bag to the shelf, then grabs one more Twix. No, two more.

It's been a rough day. She deserves it.

She crams the bag back into its spot, replaces the books, unwraps a candy bar, and pops it into her mouth.

Another if only: If only chocolate could make it all better.

If only something, someone, could make it all better.

Someone . . . like who?

Nicki, her ex-best friend?

Aunt Frankie, who won't be here for another whole week?

Mom, down there in the kitchen baking Carley's favorite peanut butter cookies?

The house smelled so good that her mouth started watering the moment she opened the door. But she didn't dare make a detour to the kitchen. She couldn't bear the thought of sitting there eating cookies with her mother's eyes on her, pitying her.

"How was school?" Mom asked, like Carley is just some regular kid. How would her mother react if she told her the truth?

I sat alone at lunch, alone at Mass, alone at the assembly. Oh, and I also sat on a thumbtack someone put on my chair in earth science, and it really hurt, but I pretended I didn't notice anything and I left it there, sticking out of the back of my skirt, until I could get to the girls' room after class. Even though I could hear them all laughing about it behind my back when I walked down the hall. Oh, and I was the last one picked for volleyball in gym.

Actually, it was worse than that.

So much worse.

Ever since she started freshman year, Carley has always been the last one chosen in gym—that's bad enough. She's never exactly been a star athlete. Who can blame the competitive team captains for picking the best players?

But only recently—since the Spring Fling debacle—has she been tripped by her own teammates, or pegged so hard with the ball that her back is bruised. The other girls actually aim it right at her. If Mr. Klerman—hardly the warm and fuzzy type—catches them, he blows the whistle and glares at everyone, including Carley.

"This is volleyball, ladies," he shouts, "not dodgeball!"

A couple of times, he benched the offender. But no one ever minds that, not even the jocks. There are worse things than having to sit out a volleyball game on a bench behind the teacher's back, where you can text and check your Peopleportal page from the cell phone smuggled in your shorts pocket, even though phones are supposed to be left in the locker room during gym.

Yes. There are far worse things than any of that.

What happened to Carley at school was unbearable. She still isn't over it. She'll never get over it.

But I have to stick it out. I have to, because . . .

"What are you going to do, Carley? Leave school? Let them win? Wouldn't you rather hold your head high and show them that they can't get the better of you?"

"But . . . I can't. I just . . . I can't . . ."

"You can't hold your head high? Sure you can, if you grow a spine . . ."

She just didn't understand. No one understands.

But maybe she was right. Maybe it's time to grow a spine. Carley's been trying to do just that—when she isn't dwelling on what happened, replaying scenes over and over in her head like a horror movie that keeps you tossing and turning long after the final credits.

Why, oh why, wasn't Carley suspicious when she found out that she'd been elected Spring Fling princess?

Because it was the biggest thrill—the best surprise—of your life, that's why.

Because you thought things were finally starting to turn around after what happened with Nicki.

You thought you were going to be popular after all, and maybe have a group of friends, like a normal high school girl, like Mom promised.

You thought they must have voted for you because you embody all the qualities Sister Thomas Katherine said a Spring Fling princess should have: good citizenship, solid morals, impeccable manners, intelligence, a charitable heart . . .

To think Carley actually got tears in her eyes—happy tears—when she heard her name over the loudspeaker during the morning announcements. "And now, we have the election results for the royal court at the Spring Fling dance. Representing the freshman class will be Carley Archer . . ."

Sitting there in homeroom, she gasped aloud.

That can't be right! she thought wildly, surrounded, as she was, by over a dozen girls whose names she wouldn't have been surprised to hear—except maybe Kendra Hyde's.

Kendra is what Mom would call "a little rough around the edges." She wears eyeliner and big earrings and sometimes she smells faintly of cigarette smoke, and she seems much older than she is. Carley heard that her mother died when she was little, and she lives alone with her dad, who isn't exactly hands-on.

She isn't Spring Fling princess material by any stretch, but Carley had written her name on the ballot anyway, the prior Monday morning. At least she's kind of friendly, unlike snotty front runner Melissa Kovacs.

But then Carley's name was announced, and she knew that it had to be real because everyone was congratulating her, and they seemed so sincere . . .

Stupid. It's your own fault for being so stupid, so gullible.

Everywhere she went, people were smiling at her. That's what she thought, anyway.

Smiling at you? They were laughing at you. Laughing

*right in your face, and you made a fool of yourself, telling
them how happy and excited you were . . .*

She floated through school that day, even working up the
courage to give Johnny, the janitor, a flirtatious grin and
hello when she saw him in the basement hallway on her way
to the computer tech lab. He had his book and apple and
was just about to open the door to the custodian's storage
closet, skirting around several cans of red and black paint
that blocked his way, along with a trio of gigantic papier-
mâché ladybugs the decorating committee had been working on for Spring Fling.

Spring Fling! I'm Spring Fling princess!

"Ready any good books lately?" a newly emboldened
Carley asked Johnny.

He looked surprised—pleasantly so—and nodded. "A
bunch. How about you?"

"Not really. Maybe you could recommend something to me."

"I just finished *A Farewell to Arms* for a lit class," he
said as he flicked on the storage closet light. "Do you like
Hemingway?"

"You're taking a lit class? Are you . . . I thought . . ."

"I'm getting my GED at night," he said, reaching into
the closet toward a shelf right beside the door. It was lined
with cleaning supplies, but he plucked a pocket knife from
among them.

"What's your GED?" Carley asked.

"High school diploma," Johnny explained, setting to
work peeling his apple. "I had to drop out. I work two jobs."

"Oh!"

She stayed there talking to him for another minute as
he impressively peeled the apple and tucked the knife back
onto the shelf, but then told him she had to hurry to class.

She wasn't sure how she felt about Johnny being in school.
It meant he wasn't the kind of guy who reads Hemingway

for fun. And maybe it meant he wasn't quite as old as she'd assumed, that a lot of things about him weren't as she'd assumed.

"You know what they say," Nicki used to tell her, with a big grin. "Whenever you assume, you make an 'ass' out of 'u' and 'me'!"

Carley loved that clever saying, but she never repeated it because she tried to avoid using words like "ass"—unlike Nicki, who delighted in it.

On that day, the day she found out she'd been voted Spring Fling princess, everything Carley had ever assumed about anything seemed to have been proven all wrong.

She ran home from the bus stop to share her big news with Mom, who was so thrilled that of course she started crying, because that's how Mom is.

"Oh, Carley! Oh, I'm so proud of you! See? I told you! I told you!"

Her joyful tears were contagious and Carley found herself crying, too. Crying and trembling and laughing in her mother's embrace as they stood there in the front hall on a glorious winter afternoon when the sky was a deep, perfect blue and the sun was shining . . .

Or maybe it wasn't.

Maybe Carley just remembers it that way.

In any case, that day was drastically different from today.

Drastically different, too, from the day not long after when Carley found out the truth: that it had all been a cruel prank.

The social worker, Sister Linda, called Mom and told her.

"Sweetie . . . are you okay?" Mom asked when Carley came home from school that afternoon.

That time, Carley didn't say she was fine.

She said, simply, "No."

There were tears in Mom's eyes, and this time, too, they threatened to be contagious.

"You don't have to go back there," Mom said. "Not ever again. I'll arrange for you to switch to Woodsbridge right away."

Woodsbridge—with Nicki.

Carley longed to say yes; longed to leave Sacred Sisters behind without a backward glance.

But . . .

At Woodsbridge, she'd have to see Nicki every day. Plus . . .

What are you going to do, Carley? Leave school? Let them win?

She forced herself to tell Mom that she wanted to stay at Sisters. Then she went straight upstairs and shut herself into her room, where no one could see her as she wept toxic tears laced not just with grief, but with shame.

Ever since that day, Mom has behaved differently toward Carley. Either she's bending over backward to be nice, trying to engage her in awkward conversations, or she's looking at her sadly, maybe critically, as if she wishes she could make Carley over into the perfect daughter.

As if she'd been hoping I'd turned out differently, more like her. As if I let her down.

Dad gives off pretty much the same vibe, when he's around—which isn't very often now that it's tax season. He's always busy at work, worried about losing his job like a lot of other people at his company.

Only Emma treats her the same as always—which is, basically, like crap. But she almost welcomes her kid sister's bad attitude these days, because it makes her feel like her old self.

Carley tears the gold foil wrapper from another candy bar and crams the whole thing into her mouth. Chewing hard, she feels a twinge in one of her molars as the chocolatey caramel coats what is probably the beginning of another cavity.

Great. She had perfect teeth until she turned thirteen.

"You're the lucky one," Mom used to tell her. "You won't even need braces like Emma."

No, but she needed two fillings and a root canal.

There are worse things, even, than needles in your gums and drills in your teeth and braces.

Worse things . . . like having everyone you know turn against you—including your ex-best friend.

That, more than anything else, is what hurts. She could probably have handled everything the girls at school have dished out—the taunting, the snickering behind her back, even the Spring Fling nightmare.

But what Nicki did? She can't bear to even think about it.

So don't. It's over. It happened months ago. Who cares about her?

Carley moves her stuffed animals off her bed, carefully rearranging the collection on the built-in window seat, where they seem to watch her like an audience of supportive friends. Some of these guys, like a fluffy flamingo named Bubblegum, have been sleeping with her since she was a little girl and afraid of the dark.

Maybe she'd still be afraid of the dark if it weren't for them.

Imagine how the girls at school would react if they knew she still sleeps with stuffed animals and sometimes even talks to them in her head.

Nicki knew that—well, not about the talking-to-them-in-her-head part. But she's slept over in Carley's room a million times and she knows Carley sleeps with the stuffed animals carefully arranged around her pillows. She's the one who gave Carley many of her fake-furry friends, including Bubblegum, as gifts over the years.

Nicki knows, too, that Carley sometimes still reads *Charlotte's Web* and the other books from her childhood, and that she even takes out her Barbies once in a while to change their clothes and brush their hair.

Nicki knows all her deepest, darkest secrets.

That never bothered Carley until now.

Lying on her stomach on her bed, she opens her laptop and pops a third Twix into her mouth before typing in the first few letters of the Web site she visited late last night.

B . . . U . . . L . . .

The rest of the link pops up. She clicks it and is transported to a virtual world populated by people who are exactly like her.

Well, not exactly: Many are female but a few are male; most are kids, though some are adults. They all have one thing in common with Carley, though: They are—or were— victims of bullies.

They post their stories here in a public forum; stories that tend to begin with lines like: *It all started in sixth grade*, or *I don't know what I did to deserve this, but . . .*

More often than not, the entries end with variations of: *I wish I were dead.*

Yeah. Carley knows the feeling.

Not that she's brave enough to actually do anything about it.

There's a lot of talk of suicide on the forum, but that, Carley knows, is a sin. If you kill yourself, you don't go to heaven.

But sometimes, when she climbs into bed after a cruel day, knowing that tomorrow will bring more of the same, she wishes that she could just go to sleep and never wake up.

Who cares about heaven when your life is pure hell?

QT-Pi is online.

The message flashes in a corner of the screen like a beacon.

"Ah, there you are. I've been waiting for you."

QT-Pi—whose real name, of course, is Carley Archer— will have just gotten home from school.

The dismissal time at Sacred Sisters is 3:12, and the metro bus ride home to the South Towns should take anywhere from thirty to forty minutes, with stops. Carley—concealed, or so she believes, behind the QT-Pi screen name and the little portrait of a kitten—usually pops up on the Internet after four o'clock.

But here she is, and it's only 3:55 right now. Either the bus was early, or she was in a particular hurry to get online today.

Probably the latter. Misery loves company.

"Aw, what's the matter, Carley, did you have another bad day at school? Is that why you're here?"

Here, as in an online forum populated by fellow victims of bullies.

Safely concealed behind the screen name Angel 770—a meaningful screen name created just for this Web site—it's tempting to engage QT-Pi in a private chat or at least bait her for comments on the message board.

But maybe that's not a good idea.

No, given Angel's plan for tonight, it's probably wise to keep a low profile right now. And in the days ahead, for that matter.

No one would ever in a million years think Angel might be responsible for what's going to happen tonight—or, for that matter, to the others, including Carley Archer, when it's her turn.

Still . . . you never can be too careful.

Angel was careful when it came to Sandra Lutz.

The Realtor's death, widely covered in the local papers and on *Eyewitness News*, was ruled accidental. Her body was found just inside the front door of the fire-gutted house, which was locked from the inside. The key to the double-cylinder dead bolt turned up nearby in the rubble.

The fire investigators reported that the fire had started in the living room, where a burning candle had ignited draperies.

Sandra must have been frantically trying to get out, couldn't locate the key, and was too overcome by panic and smoke to escape through a window. Those closest to the door, facing the street, were all closed and locked. And the smoke detectors on both floors were useless without batteries.

The fire chief used Sandra's sad demise to teach the viewing public a fire safety lesson.

"This woman's death could have been prevented," he grimly told a television news reporter, "if she had taken a few simple steps. Smoke detectors should be in working order. Lit candles should not be left unattended. Keys should be left in locks that open from the inside, in case an emergency makes it necessary to get out quickly."

Sandra, he made it clear, had done everything wrong.

Ah, but she hadn't—other than talking too much, asking too many questions, snooping and finding that notebook . . .

It was Angel who removed the batteries from the smoke detectors. Angel who closed and locked the front windows. Angel who hid the key to the front door lock before Sandra even came home.

It was Angel who held the lavender candle to the curtain panel until it caught fire, then set it on a table beneath the window as flames hungrily licked the wall.

And it was Angel who hastily climbed back out the mudroom window, replaced the old-fashioned screen, and scurried away as flames engulfed the house.

Sandra Lutz's body was burned beyond recognition, according to ghoulishly graphic reporters. That meant the investigators wouldn't have realized—or suspected—that the woman had been lying unconscious by the locked door long before the fire started.

Smiling faintly, Angel remembers the satisfaction of knocking her out by shocking her carotid artery and jugular vein with a well-practiced, well-placed sharp blow to the side of her neck.

It had been so easy.

All of it.

No problem finding the house, the broken window screen, even the key above the door . . .

Angel has Sandra herself to thank for that.

You just didn't know when to shut up, did you?

You got what you deserved.

And now, so will the others.

Angel leans away from the keyboard with arms folded and hands clenched around fingers that are twitching, eager to type, eager to reach out to QT-Pi . . .

No. Not yet.

For the moment, all Angel can do is watch her.

And wait.

But it won't be long now.

Entry from the marble notebook

Saturday, November 30, 1985

When I heard someone unlocking my bedroom door late last night I thought it might be Mother, having a change of heart about locking me in here as punishment or at least bringing me water. But it wasn't.

It was him.

"I thought you might be lonely," he said. Bastard. I'd rather be locked in here alone for a year—for the rest of my life, even—than spend one minute with him.

Before he left, I begged him to sneak me some food or even just water and let me out to go to the bathroom, but he wouldn't.

"You heard what your mother said," he told me. "You have to stay in here until it's time for church Sunday morning. You have to make atonement."

My sin this time: sneaking up to the third-floor bathroom to wash my hair while she was at work at the drugstore. She found hair and shampoo residue in the drain. She must inspect it every day like she inspects everything else around here.

She won't let me take a bath more than once a week because she says it's sinful to be vain and wasteful of hot water. I think she wants to make me ugly because of him. As if he cares what I look like.

I wish no one else did. I'm the only girl at school with dirty, greasy hair and it makes everyone hate me even more. But not as much as I hate myself, or as much as Mother hates me. She knows what he does to me and she doesn't stop him. And worse yet, she blames me for it, I know it.

At church tomorrow morning, I'm going to pray that something terrible happens to him. That's not a sin, is it? It's the same thing as just wishing someone dead when you blow out your birthday candles. You can't go to hell for that.

Chapter 5

After wiping her eyes again on the soggy cuff of her flannel pajama top, Jen fumbles in her pocket for the wad of damp Kleenex she's been carrying around the house with her for the past hour, ever since the first wave of grief washed over her with the grim news that arrived when the phone rang at six, much too early for a Saturday morning.

"I just don't understand," she tells Thad, pressing the useless clump of tissue against her streaming nose, "how a sweet, beautiful girl who had everything to live for could . . . take her own life."

Take her own life . . .

They might mean the same thing, but the words sound less jarring than the phrase that was on the tip of her tongue: *kill herself.*

For once, she'd caught herself. Or maybe it wasn't so much that as having been unable to say the ugly word.

Kill . . .
Kill . . .
Kill . . .

Dear God, it's so violent, so utterly out of place in this safe suburban world.

Crazy, terrible things can happen anywhere.

That's what Thad told her last spring, when she said she wanted to keep Carley insulated at Sacred Sisters.

"I feel sick." Trembling, she sinks down beside him on the couch. "This is so . . . it's so . . ."

"It's tragic." He shakes his head, putting an arm around her. "That's what it is. Tragic. What a waste."

They fall silent, sitting side by side in the formal living room they so rarely use.

Hearing footsteps and creaking floorboards overhead, Jen looks at Thad. "That's Carley."

He nods, well aware that Carley has the steadier, heavier footfall, while Emma tends to bounce and prance, even at this hour.

"What are we supposed to tell her, Thad? Kids aren't supposed to die. Not this way. Not at all."

"No. But they do."

She nods mutely and they listen as the footsteps go down the hall, away from the stairs. After a brief lull, the toilet in the hall bathroom flushes, the footsteps retreat, and Carley's bedroom door closes again.

She's gone back to sleep—for now, anyway.

Relieved by the momentary reprieve, Jen tells Thad, "She's going to be devastated. How is she possibly going to deal with something like this?"

"She'll have to."

"But how?"

"She'll face it and eventually she'll get past it. It's a part of life. It happens to everyone, growing up. You lose people."

She nods bleakly, remembering how her beloved Pop-Pop, who lived two houses away, had a heart attack and dropped dead in his backyard one morning while he was pruning his fig tree.

"My grandfather died when I was in high school," she tells Thad. "But that was different. He was old. When you lose someone your own age . . ."

"Kids die suddenly, too. When I was a junior, a friend of mine, Chase Rivington— Did I ever tell you about him?"

"No. Yes. I think so."

Her brain is shrouded in a fog of grief right now. Still, she remembers, long ago, commenting about the name: Chase Rivington.

"He sounds like such a prep school kid," she told Thad at the time. "Even more than Thaddeus Leland Archer the third."

"What's wrong with prep school?" he asked.

"Nothing. I just forget sometimes that we grew up worlds apart. If we'd met back then, we wouldn't have given each other the time of day."

"If we'd met back then, you would have told me you were going to marry Mike what's-his-name."

Morino was his name. Mike Morino.

They grew up in the same neighborhood but attended different Catholic schools and never met until the summer after her freshman year, when their paths converged at a church lawn fete. She wore his class ring on and off through high school and beyond, enduring quite a few breakups and an unfounded pregnancy scare before he finally drifted out of her life for good—just as Thad walked into it.

Thank God for that. Thank God for Thad.

They were both twenty-two and recent college graduates when they met at a bar on the Elmwood Strip, though Jen assumed he was younger. He had a baby face, and a sweet, kind disposition that grabbed her attention immediately.

"He's the type of guy," she confided in her sister Frankie the morning after she met Thad, "who would never hurt someone."

"Everyone in the world is capable of hurting someone, Jen."

"But not on purpose. Not like . . . you know."

"The jerk."

Mike. Right.

Frankie didn't even know the extent of what Mike had pulled. Jen had never confided the whole truth about him: how he'd pressured her to go farther than she wanted to, dumping her several times when she wouldn't. And then, when she finally did sleep with him senior year, then thought she was pregnant, he told her she'd just have to have an abortion, and broke up with her again when she told him she wouldn't.

Of course he came back. He always did. And she took him back every single time for years, until finally she grew up, came to her senses, and realized that Mike Morino was sorely lacking a heart.

It wasn't just about how he treated her. It was how he treated other people, as well.

"This guy," she told Frankie, after meeting Thad, "just wouldn't deliberately hurt me or anyone else."

"And you know this how?"

"I just know," she said with a shrug.

Some deep-seated instinct told her that Thad, a virtual stranger, was obviously kindhearted. So different from Mike, whom she knew well enough to realize that he was capable of hurting others—not just Jen—for the perverse pleasure, it seemed, of inflicting pain.

The night they met, she and Thad danced to U2's "The Sweetest Thing." It became their song, the one they first danced to at their wedding a few years later. The lyrics seemed to have been written for them.

Blue-eyed boy meets a brown-eyed girl . . .

Those blue eyes, at the moment, are focused on the window opposite the couch. Jen knows that Thad isn't gazing out at the sun-splashed morning beyond the panes. He's remembering his lost friend.

"Chase was a year older," he tells her, "but we were on the lacrosse team together . . ."

"What happened to him?"

"Car accident."

"Isn't it always?" she says, remembering names from tragedies in her own past.

Jimmy Fazzoleri . . .

She hadn't known him; he was in her sister Maddie's class.

Ruthie Bell.

Jen had known her, of course. They were sophomores together at Sacred Sisters when Ruthie was killed. Not friends, not by any means, because . . .

Because she was *Ruthie Bell*. Even the name itself is light years away from *Chase Rivington*. But it comes readily to Jen's mind, ushered in by the memory of Mike Morino's cruel streak.

Ruthie was the gawky, ginger-haired girl everyone made fun of; the girl Jen was thinking about just yesterday afternoon when she was wondering whether Carley's appearance has anything to do with her being bullied.

But of course Carley is nothing like Ruthie.

Anyway, what happened to her daughter at school seems much more insignificant now. At least it wasn't life and death. At least Carley is alive.

But somehow, they have to break the news to her that last night, Nicki Olivera took a chef's knife from a kitchen drawer and slit her wrists.

Morning sunlight streams across Carley's bed, falling across the carefully arranged menagerie of stuffed animals at her side and the laptop propped against her pillow.

She tilts the screen to cut the glare, but it doesn't help much.

Why does the sun have to shine today? It hardly ever does at this time of year.

It hardly ever shines around here, period.

Nicki is always complaining about the western New York weather. *Was* always complaining. Past tense. Nicki isn't in Carley's life anymore, because she apparently decided she no longer wanted to be best friends.

But when she was around—always around, *always*, for as long as Carley can remember—she'd sometimes say, "When I grow up, I'm getting out of here. I'm going to live someplace where it's always warm and sunny, like Florida or Arizona or L.A."

And then Carley, who never wants to move that far from home, would remind her of their plans to be college roommates and then get an apartment together and then, after they were married, live next door to each other. And their kids would play together and their husbands would play golf and they would be best friends, closer than sisters, forever.

Yeah. Not happening.

Stupid sun.

Carley can always go pull the shade down or move the laptop over to her desk, but she's in the middle of instant messaging with a new friend and she doesn't want to interrupt it even for a few seconds.

Finally, somebody gets it.

Gets *her*.

Finally, she has someone to talk to about what's been going on at school.

Who would have thought she'd find more comfort in a total stranger she met on the Internet than in anyone she knows in real life?

QT-Pi: do u think i can evr trust her again?

Angel 770: y wd u want 2?

QT-Pi: cuz shes been my BFF 4ever its not like i nvr want 2 see her again

Angel 770: tru friends dont do what she did 2 u last fall who needs thatttt?

Carley finds herself nodding. Angel is right. Who needs Nicki?

QT-Pi: i dont need it not anymore

Angel 770: good then stay away from her

QT-Pi: believe me i will

That isn't very hard to do now that she and Nicki are in different schools. She just hopes the Olivera family doesn't show up at ten-thirty Mass tomorrow. Some Sundays they don't make it to church at all, because Nicki's mom isn't as much a stickler about it as Jen's mom is. Unfortunately, though, they usually do go during Lent.

They were there last Sunday morning. Ordinarily, Carley and Nicki would have been rolling their eyes at each other in silent agreement that Father Peter's long-winded sermon was ridiculous. But this time, Carley avoided making eye contact.

When it was time to go up to receive Communion, she whispered to her mother that she wasn't feeling well and slipped out to wait for her parents and Emma in the car. Otherwise, she'd have had to come face to face with Nicki as their mothers chatted in the vestibule after Mass.

If the Oliveras are there tomorrow, she'll have to do the same thing.

Or maybe she should just look Nicki right in the eye; stare her down. Make her feel super uncomfortable about how she treated Carley.

That would be good . . .

Except I could never pull that off.

Staring people down isn't her style. Her style is . . . pretty pathetic. A typical Carley move would be to take one look at Nicki and burst into tears.

She needs to work on getting a thicker skin—or at least try acting like nothing bothers her.

Angel 770: u still there qp?

QP. Short for QT-Pi. It's Angel's little nickname for her.

Nicki has one, too. She's always called Carley "Carls," and Carley calls her "Nicks."

Well, they did when they were speaking, anyway.

Okay, enough. Forget Nicki.

QT-Pi: sry im here just spacing

Angel 770: yeah its early rite?

QT-Pi: not as early as where u r!

Angel lives in California. That means it must be, like, four A.M. there.

QT-Pi: do u always get up so early?

Angel 770: u mean do i always stay up so late?

Carley smiles.

QT-Pi: night owl?

Angel 770: yepppppppp

Beyond her bedroom door, Carley can hear the phone ringing.

She glances at the computer clock. It's pretty early for a phone call on a Saturday morning.

It's probably Grandma Bonafacio. She and Grandpa are always up early, out and about before the sun comes up, even on weekends. They go to seven-thirty Mass at Our Lady every single day without fail, and then over to Tim Horton's for coffee with a bunch of old people from church. When Carley was younger, they would often pick up a box of doughnuts and bring it over here afterward. They always remembered to get extra chocolate-frosted ones with sprinkles, Carley's favorite, and extra powdered sugar with jelly, Emma's favorite.

But then one Saturday morning a few years ago, they knocked on the sliding glass door in the kitchen and scared the heck out of Dad, who was standing there in just his boxer shorts pouring coffee. He splashed it and burned himself— plus, his in-laws saw him in his underwear. After that, he told Mom to tell her parents to please call first from now on.

Grandma and Grandpa weren't thrilled about that, but they said they'd try. Most of the time, they remember.

Carley wonders if they're on their way over with dough-nuts. Ordinarily, she'd welcome that. But lately, she doesn't feel like seeing anyone, not even her grandparents.

Glancing back at the computer screen, she thinks that might be different if Angel lived close by instead of on the opposite side of the country.

If she were around, I'd be into seeing her.

No one else.

Just Angel, because she understands. She's been through this, too.

Angel 770: i wasnt always a night owl but when things started getting bad at school i had a hard time sleeping how about u?

QT-Pi: same here

Angel 770: do u take stuff to help u sleep?

QT-Pi: warm milk and honey doesnt help

Angel 770: not what i meant

What did she mean? Drugs? Like sleeping pills?

Before Carley can reply, another question pops up.

Angel 770: do u have nightmares 2?

QT-Pi: major nightmaressssss the other night i—

She breaks off typing, hearing the phone ring again.

Unsettled, she wonders who keeps calling at this hour, and why.

Maybe she should go downstairs and see what's up.

She will—just as soon as she finishes this chat with Angel. She looks back at the screen.

Angel 770: u there?

QT-Pi: yeah sorry i—

Again, she pauses, hearing footsteps creaking up the stairs. Two sets of footsteps; her parents are coming up together, which is as unusual as the fact that the phone keeps ringing.

So, come to think of it, is the fact that Mom and Dad's bedroom door was already open when Carley got up and went down the hall to the bathroom earlier. They usually sleep much later than seven on Saturday mornings, and whoever gets up last always makes the bed and opens the shades before leaving the room.

Today, Carley could see that the bed was unmade and the shades were still drawn, but it didn't faze her—until now.

The footsteps approach, and there's a knock on her door.

"Sweetie?" Mom calls. "Can we come in?"

We?

It's never a good sign when both parents want to talk to her. In fact, that's the kind of thing that usually happens only to Emma, who lately manages to get herself into trouble at home or at school every other day. But Carley follows the rules, does her homework, and gets good grades—except in math, but she's working on it.

What can this possibly be about?

Maybe they just want to rehash the whole bullying situation again, try to talk her into switching schools. If that's the case . . .

The only person I want to talk about it with is Angel.

Carley quickly types *brb* in the instant message window, shorthand for *be right back*.

Angel 770: kk wuzup?

QT-Pi: prnts

Parents.

"Carley?" Dad calls through the door. "Are you awake?"

She hurriedly takes off her glasses, then closes the laptop and stashes it beneath the bed, knocking Bubblegum the stuffed flamingo off in the process.

The door opens just as she's settling back against her pillows, still clutching Bubblegum.

Pretending to stir as if she's just waking up, she rubs her eyes and looks up at her parents.

Mom is in her pajamas and bare feet, Dad in boxer shorts and a T-shirt, as though they just rolled out of bed. Mom's obviously been crying.

Maybe Dad, too, Carley realizes, looking from one to the other.

Her heart starts pounding and she sits up quickly. "What? What is it?"

Her parents look at each other.

Mom opens her mouth as if she's going to say something, but only a strange, choking sound comes out.

"Mom? You're scaring me. What's wrong?"

Dad takes over. "Carley," he says gently, and sits down on her bed, reaching for her hand, "we have some bad news."

It's been half an hour, at least, since QT-Pi informed Angel that her parents had interrupted their instant messaging.

I bet I know why.

Now that this cold, sunny Saturday morning has dawned, the shocking news is undoubtedly spreading from house to suburban house in Woodsbridge.

All night, Angel had been wondering how long it would take before Nicki's parents found their only child's body.

They were both out last evening when it happened.

Angel had watched them leave, all dressed up, probably headed out to dinner or something—but not together. No, never together. Not those two.

Debbie Olivera left in her Lexus and her husband in his BMW, an hour apart, headed in opposite directions.

Having watched them for months now—and well aware of their secret lives—Angel wasn't surprised that the two so obviously had separate plans on a Friday night.

Which of them came home first?

It would be nice to think that it was Debbie herself. How

satisfying it is, just picturing how Nicki's mother might have reacted to the horrific scene . . .

Imagine if I could have been there to witness that moment in person?

That would have been tricky to pull off, but well worth shooting for.

Maybe next time.

Or the time after that . . .

Angel checks the computer screen again to see if QT-Pi has returned. No, not yet.

At this very moment, she's probably distraught over her best friend's violent suicide.

Ex-best friend.

Angel found it almost as delightful to hear Carley's version of Nicki's betrayal as it had been last summer to plan—and then instigate—the rift in their friendship.

Just think—that was only the beginning.

With a happy shiver, Angel reaches for the keyboard.

Angel 770: hope evrything is ok qp gtg cya l8r

Before hitting enter, Angel thinks better of that last phrase, deletes it, and replaces it with *ttyl*.

There. Much more authentic. *L8r* seems to have fallen out of favor recently.

Angel has spent months lurking on the Internet, studying the way kids communicate with each other online, learning the ridiculous text message shorthand and paying close attention to the nuances in their interaction. Now it's almost second nature to type run-on sentences heavy with abbreviation and slang and nearly devoid of punctuation or capitalization—unless, of course, one wishes to express excitement, in which case one must type in all caps and sometimes hold down a key to repeat the final letter in a word many times.

None of it makes much sense, and yet it's paid off.

You sound just like one of them.

Carley honestly believes she's chatting with a teenage girl who lives in California.

She has no idea that Angel is right under her nose.

But she will. Soon enough, she'll find out exactly who Angel really is.

Just like Nicki did.

Entry from the marble notebook

Friday, December 13, 1985

I didn't realize until I wrote down the date that today is Friday the thirteenth. I just got a chill when I noticed. I wonder if it's a sign?

Do you remember how I prayed in church for something terrible to happen to Father?

This afternoon, he made me go out with him to practice driving after school. I was nervous, because it was snowing and the roads were slippery. Whenever I had to brake for a stop sign or light, the car would slide into the intersection. He kept yelling at me to be careful, and I was crying so hard I could hardly see. Then he got really quiet and I looked over and he had passed out. For a minute I thought he was dead.

The funny thing is, that is exactly what I had been hoping for, but in that instant, I forgot all about it. I was in the middle of practicing parallel parking in front of Cardinal Ruffini High School and a couple of guys were just coming out. I started yelling, "Help, help!" to them and they came running. They checked Father. He had a pulse. One of them ran back inside to call an ambulance while the other two stayed with us.

I don't remember if anyone said anything while we waited for the ambulance to show up—it didn't take very long. All I could think was that God had heard my prayer and Father was going to die, and if that happened, would it be my fault? Would I burn in hell for eternity?

The paramedics put Father on a stretcher and told me to go get my mother and meet them at the hospital. They rushed away with the sirens going and they didn't even hear me telling them that I don't have a driver's license.

The Cardinal Ruffini guys heard me, though. They said they would drive me home.

They were all wearing basketball jackets, so I know they're on the team. One of them was really good-looking. I see him sometimes at church but I don't know his name. He sat in the backseat with me and I couldn't stop staring at him.

Eric, the one who got behind the wheel, was a terrible driver. Twice, he drove up over the curb. The first time, he scraped the side of the car in some bushes and the next time, we were inches away from slamming into a tree. That's how I found out his name— the cute one yelled, "Eric, you almost just got us all killed!"

I didn't find out until we were almost back to my house that Eric didn't even have his permit. None of them do. By that time it was too late so I just thanked them and they walked off down the street. I hope I see him again soon. The cute one, I mean. Maybe I'll dream about him when I close my eyes. I hope so.

For the first time I can ever remember, I don't dread climbing into bed tonight. Father is staying in *the hospital at least through the weekend. He had a heart attack.*

Do you think God answered my prayers and punished Father because he's evil? Do you think He'll listen if I ask Him to make it so that Father never comes home again?

Chapter 6

On a monochromatic Monday afternoon, Jen turns the car onto a wide boulevard near Delaware Park, where large houses are set against a sky the same shade as the dirty slush in the gutters. Absently noticing that the wet March snow is already starting to stick, she turns the windshield wipers a notch faster. According to AccuWeather, the temperature will have plummeted into the twenties by dusk, with well over a foot of new snow in the forecast before the thermometer boomerangs up into the sixties by midweek.

The storm started earlier than predicted, though. The meteorologists had said it would begin snowing late this afternoon, but already a coating of white dusts the rooftops, bare branches, and grass on meticulously landscaped properties.

If it weren't for the unobtrusive wooden signpost and awnings that shade the tall windows and stretch along the front walk, the three-story white house in the middle of the block would look like any other. But it isn't like them at all.

People live in those other homes. Some of the aging residents have been there since Jen was growing up on a nearby block lined with equally old, albeit far smaller and less dignified houses set much closer together than they are here.

But in her lifetime, no one has ever actually lived in the stately black-shuttered mansion with the signpost and the awnings. It's been used for one purpose only, as evidenced by the signpost:

"CICERO AND SON FUNERAL HOME."

Back in the old days, the sign read just "CICERO FUNERAL HOME." But then Glenn Cicero grew up and followed in his father's footsteps, and old Mr. Cicero proudly changed the name. He passed away a few years ago, but Glenn has left the sign the way it is.

When Jen last saw him, about a year ago at her great-uncle Frank's funeral, he said, "No reason to change it. My son Connor tells me he might want to go into the family business, too."

"How old is he now?"

"Seven."

Jen nodded, smiling politely, wondering whether any seven-year-old truly wants to think about growing up to become a mortician, even if it is the family business.

The Ciceros have presided over many a Bonafacio family funeral, and quite a few others Jen has attended over the years. Just the sight of the stately old structure is enough to send a pall over her on an ordinary day, when she barely gives it a second glance.

Today, however, she drives past the funeral home with slow deliberation, noting that the large gravel parking lot alongside it is already full, and the street is lined with parked cars.

The wake for Nicki Olivera doesn't even start for another fifteen minutes, but dark-clothed mourners are lined up out the door. Groups of teenagers cluster on the walkway; crying girls shivering bare-legged in dresses console each other alongside uncomfortable-looking boys in dress pants, down coats, and sneakers.

Jen takes a deep breath; exhales shakily.

Oh Lord. Suddenly, Nicki's death has gone from surreal to shockingly real.

This is going to be brutal enough for the adults who are attending. But for those poor kids . . .

For Carley . . .

Jen fleetingly considers sparing her daughter the ordeal.

No. She has to go. She *needs* to go, in order to fully grasp the shocking reality that Nicki is gone.

On Saturday morning, Jen had faltered right before they told Carley the news, when she saw her lying there in bed. She was clutching her stuffed flamingo, Bubblegum: a long-ago birthday gift from Nicki. Childhood innocence personified.

She knew that Carley was about to lose something that she'd never get back. Not just in the literal sense—not just the monumental loss of her friend, which in itself would leave a void that would never be filled.

But Carley's world was about to be shaken because of the way Nicki had died. An accident, or an illness . . . that's one thing. But when someone deliberately chooses death, without explanation or warning . . .

But you don't know that, Jen keeps reminding herself. *You haven't seen Nicki in a while; you don't know, and Carley probably didn't know, what was going on with her.*

When they told their daughter the news, she went from disbelief—asking "*What?*" over and over—to hysterical tears.

They had to reveal that it was suicide. There was no point in lying.

"But . . . but that means she's not going to go to heaven!"

Jen tried to console her, telling her that the church had changed its views on suicide, but she could tell Carley wasn't buying it. She'd spent too many years in an old-fashioned parochial school to completely disregard what she'd been taught about the mortal sin of taking your own life.

It wasn't until hours later, when the initial shock and grief had subsided, that Carley wanted to know exactly how Nicki had done it.

"With a knife," Jen said reluctantly and then, seeing the look of horror on her daughter's face, she hugged her close and consoled her as a fresh wave of tears broke.

The violence of Nicki's death, more than anything else, is what's been troubling Jen.

You always read that it's the male victims who use knives or guns to kill themselves. Not women. Certainly not young girls who cower behind the couch pillows just trying to watch one of the old Scream movies at a sleepover.

"No! I can't look!" Nicki shrieked as Carley giggled. "Are there blood and guts, Carls? You know I can't deal with blood and guts!"

Remembering the many overnights Carley and Nicki spent together, Jen wonders, yet again, how Nicki could have changed so drastically in six or seven months.

What was going on in her life that made her decide to end it?

If Carley has any idea, she's not talking about it.

Now Jen is grateful that the girls have drifted apart, for her own daughter's sake. This would have been even more torturous had it happened when they were inseparable.

But then, maybe it wouldn't have happened at all. When Jen thinks about Nicki, about how alone and desperate she must have been feeling, her heart aches for the girl.

Could a friend have saved her?

Could her mother have saved her?

Jen remembers what she was thinking just the other day when she and Thad were discussing Carley's trouble at school.

That's what moms do. We fix things for our kids and we worry about them and we ask about their day when they walk in the door . . .

Was it only a few days ago that it seemed like the worst thing in the world was to have your daughter victimized by the mean girls at school?

Jen thinks about her friend Debbie, wondering how she's coping, wondering how you can possibly go on when you've lost a child.

Whatever you do, she warns herself, *don't go and ask her that when you see her. Don't blurt out anything stupid.*

She's had two days now to figure out exactly what she can say to Debbie at a time like this, and she's come up with only one acceptable thing.

I'm so sorry.

It's what she said when she called Debbie's house on Saturday morning and got voice mail. "It's Jen. I just heard, and I'm so sorry . . ."

Too choked up to go on, she hung up mid-message.

When she finally pulled herself together and called back, the voice mailbox was full and no longer accepting messages. She sent a carefully composed e-mail. When that went unanswered, she texted Debbie's cell phone a few times—no reply.

Yesterday, she made a tray of ziti and took it over there, along with a dozen of the untouched peanut butter cookies and the sponge cake she'd intended for the new neighbors.

Debbie's sister-in-law from Ohio, whom Jen had heard about but never met, answered the door. She said Debbie and Andrew were at the funeral home, "making arrangements."

"Tell them that Jen was here, and that I'm so sorry, and—"

Again, she choked on a lump in her throat and couldn't finish the sentence.

"What's wrong with me?" she asked Thad later in frustration. "Why can't I be one of those people who always says the right thing and has perfect composure, grace under pressure . . ."

"Because you're a Bonafacio," he reminded her, and he was right.

How many times has Jen—or one of her sisters, or her mother—said just that, in an effort to explain why when they talk, they talk too much; when they laugh, they laugh uncontrollably; when they cry . . .

Same thing.

"It's because we're Bonafacios." Her family—the women in her family, anyway—tend to be overly emotional, and they lack filters. That's just how it is.

At this point, Jen feels as though she's drained every last teardrop in her body. But she knows that when she sees Debbie, she's going to start sobbing again.

She drives on past the funeral home, flipping her turn signal and braking carefully on the slick pavement at the stop sign. She makes a right and brakes at the railroad tracks, looking both ways before bumping across them.

Once, years ago, the signal failed at a crossing in the neighborhood. That was the official story. But an eyewitness claimed that the teenage driver, Jimmy Fazzoleri, was trying to beat it.

He didn't make it.

Jen was just in elementary school then, but she remembers the horror of that accident, the tragic, violently morbid tale told and retold by her sisters and their friends until Jimmy had taken on folk hero status.

Still—it was an accident. No one ever speculated that Jimmy had taken his own life. Either he'd been the victim of malfunctioning electronics or he'd done something foolish and reckless, and he was killed. Tragic, but hardly inexplicable.

Not like this. Not like Nicki.

Jen drives on, heading toward Sacred Sisters to pick up Carley for the wake.

She had expected her daughter to jump at the chance to stay home from school today, but Carley insisted on going.

"I have an algebra test sixth period, Mom."

"You can make it up."

"He only gives you one chance to make up a test."

He is Carley's dreaded math teacher, Mr. Sterne, one of the few laypeople on the staff. She's convinced he doesn't like her.

What a shame that gentle Sister Louisa, who taught algebra back in Jen's day, has long since retired. Life would surely be more pleasant for Carley if she'd been greeted at her new school with smiles of recognition and "Isn't one of the Bonafacio girls your mother?"

When Jen was there, it was "You must be the Bonafacio girls' baby sister!"

Debbie once asked her if it ever bothered her, but it never did. Rather, she felt welcomed into the fold.

But today's teachers—other than half-blind Sister Margaret—don't know Carley from any other student, and Mr. Sterne, in particular, seems to be making things difficult for her.

"If I don't take the test today, I'll have to do it tomorrow," Carley told Jen this morning, "and I can't because I have the funeral."

"Carley, no teacher would penalize you for missing a test for something like this. Woodsbridge High is excusing anyone who wants to go to the wake or funeral."

"But that's because Nicki went to Woodsbridge, and anyway, Mr. Sterne's really strict! Those are the rules." Carley, with her fierce sense of right and wrong, was on the verge of fresh tears.

"It's not so black and white. Trust me, sweetie, you can—"

"He only bends the rules if you have a doctor's note!"

"I'll write him a note."

"You're not a doctor!"

"Then I'll come in and talk to him. Just don't worry about school rules at a time like this."

"Mom, I'm only getting an 87 in algebra so far this quarter and it's going to drag my average down. This test can bring my grade up if I do well, but I'll forget everything I studied if I don't take it now."

To her credit, Emma, having eavesdropped on the exchange, waited until Carley left the room before announcing, "She's crazy."

"Emma—"

"She acts like she's failing with an 87! I *wish* I had an 87 in math! Or in anything!"

"You *can* have an 87. You can have 100."

"No one gets 100."

"Sure they do."

"I mean besides Carley. And I almost got a 90 one time last year. I got an 88, but I almost—"

"Almost doesn't count, Emma. Almost isn't good enough."

"I hate when you say that."

"Well, it's true. You should be getting nineties. Or hundreds. You just need to work harder at it like your sister does." As soon as she'd said that, Jen wanted to take it back.

She does try not to compare the girls, knowing it only contributes further to their resentment of each other. But she was overtired and overemotional and overprotective, in that moment, of Carley.

"Why can't I stay home for the wake?" Emma wanted to know. "Carley's not the only one who's sad about Nicki around here."

"I told you, Daddy and I think you should just go to the funeral on Tuesday."

"Can you please stop calling him Daddy? Can't you just say Dad?" Emma rolled her eyes.

Jaw clenched, Jen amended, "*Dad* and I think you should just go to the funeral."

"But why?"

"Because the wake will be too upsetting for you."

"I went to Uncle Frank's wake."

"That was different. He was old and sick for a long time. When it's someone your own age, it's much harder."

Plus, Emma can be such a drama queen that there's no telling how she might react at the funeral home. It would be just like her to fall apart and create an emotional scene, robbing a quietly grieving Carley of her parents' attention at a time when she needs it most.

Reaching the next stop sign, Jen makes a left onto Dogwood Street, feeling as though she's driving on autopilot. Good thing she knows this neighborhood as well as she does the one where she now lives with Thad and the girls. Better, really, in some ways.

There's still constant new construction in their suburban development, and businesses on the highways surrounding it are mostly chain stores and restaurants that seem to come and go or change hands with startling regularity.

But some of the houses in this neighborhood have stood for well over a century, many with a single last name on the mailbox for decades. Countless small factories that thrived here in her childhood have long since closed, but Jen drives past a number of flourishing locally owned businesses that, like the funeral home, have been run by the same family for generations. Sgaglio's Market, Mackowiak's Polish Deli, Louie's Bar on the corner of Redbud, where generations of neighborhood kids learned to hold their liquor . . .

Rounding the corner onto Wayside Avenue, Jen spots one of the few brand-new houses in the neighborhood, one that would be far more at home on a suburban cul-de-sac. The white center-hall Colonial, an architectural anomaly on a block lined with close-set homes dating to the early 1900s, spills over the small lot like a fat man in a middle airplane seat.

The house was built to replace the Arts and Crafts bungalow that burned to the ground a year or two ago, tragically killing the female owner.

"That was Joe and Betty Bardin's daughter Sandy," Jen's mother, Theresa, said when it happened. "She was your sister Madonna's age, but she went to Griffin. She boarded there even though it's only fifteen miles from her house. They were always trying to be fancy, the Bardins. Remember?"

Jen did, but only vaguely.

Now she pitied the poor woman Maddie and her friends used to call Snobby Sandy. What a horrible way to die, trapped inside a burning house.

"She's going to be laid out at Cicero's," Theresa Bonafacio reported, and asked Jen if she wanted to accompany them to the viewing.

She declined. It seems her aging parents are always telling her about wakes and funerals these days, or talking about their own.

"When my time comes . . ." her mother will say.

Her father is less delicate. "When I croak," he'll begin, and proceed to give explicit directions—usually involving his belongings. He's convinced that his daughters are going to fight over his wheat penny collection or autographed Connie Francis albums.

Jen's parents will be at the wake today.

"You know, if this had happened years ago," her mother said, "there wouldn't have even been a wake or funeral. But the church has softened its views on suicide, thank goodness."

That was exactly what Jen had told Carley. The difference is, Carley wouldn't accept it.

Jen does. There's no way that a merciful God would keep a troubled child from going to heaven. Absolutely no way.

Her mother agreed, and added, shaking her salt and pepper head, "It would have killed Ro if her granddaughter couldn't have a Catholic burial. It might kill her as it is."

Mom and Debbie's mother, Rosemary Quattrone, go all the way back to when they attended Sacred Sisters together many years ago. That schoolgirl connection was the first in three generations of female friendships between the two families.

Carley and Nicki used to push their dolls around in baby carriages talking about how their "babies" would grow up to be best friends, too.

And now . . .

Jen swallows hard as the familiar yellow brick facade looms up ahead. The building rises two full stories atop an elevated foundation with low basement windows where the science labs, locker rooms, and custodial quarters are located. On the two main floors are symmetrical rows of tall, paired windows framed and paned in peeling, white-painted wood.

The sight of her alma mater has always filled her with fond nostalgia. But seeing the school for the first time since she learned what's been happening to Carley there, she feels sick to her stomach.

Especially today, seeing the brick-pillared signboard that lists events for the month of March. Prominently featured in big black block letters alongside next Saturday's date on the glass-fronted panel: "42ND ANNUAL SPRING FLING."

Carley has to look at that every day. Why, oh why didn't she agree to switch schools? Why didn't Jen insist?

It's still not too late to pull her out of Sisters; not too late for her to make a fresh start far from the girls who tormented her. But now that Nicki is gone, Jen can't bear the thought of transferring Carley to Woodsbridge. There are plenty of other private schools around, though . . .

The last time she brought that up to Thad, he said they can't afford to pay additional tuition this school year. He said that if Carley is willing to stick it out at Sisters, they should support her decision.

With a sigh, Jen turns into the parking lot and pulls up alongside the walkway to the main entrance, putting the car into park. Glancing at the dashboard clock, she sees that she has at least another five or ten minutes before Carley gets out of math class.

Seized by an impulsive idea, she shifts the car back into drive and pulls back around, into an empty parking spot marked "Visitors."

Before she can change her mind, she steps out and hurries toward the door through the falling snow, her somber black pumps tapping hollowly along the slush-slicked concrete.

$$13 + (b \times 12) - 18 = 271$$

Staring blankly at the algebraic equation, pencil in hand, lump in throat, Carley can't stop thinking about Nicki.

About what she did.

It's impossible to imagine Nicki even holding a big, sharp knife, much less . . .

The Nicki that Carley knew was always squeamish about—well, everything. When they were little, she cried when she lost a tooth or scraped her knee because she couldn't bear the sight of blood. Even as a teenager, she shied away from the vampire books and dark movies the other girls loved.

Had she changed so much in these past few months that she had been able to take a sharp blade and press it against her own skin, pressing, cutting, slicing . . .

That's what Carley heard: that she slit her wrists.

Mom and Dad didn't tell her that part. She saw it on Peopleportal, the social networking Web site more commonly known as Peeps. Not on Nicki's own page, because Nicki removed Carley from her connections list and blocked her when they had their falling out.

But all Carley had to do was search the social networking site for Woodsbridge High School students, scanning through the wall posts on the pages of Nicki's classmates who didn't have their settings set to private.

Carley's own page is private, of course. She's not one of those girls she and Nicki used to call "connection collectors" because they gauge their own and others' popularity by the number of Peeps connections they have. Collectors write public, provocative posts solely to attract attention and accept Peeps requests from total strangers just to send their number of connections into the desired thousand-plus range.

Carley, who has less than fifty, knows better than to post provocative thoughts or personal business on the Internet for anyone to see—not unless she's guaranteed some kind of anonymity.

That's why her user name on the bullying forum is QT-Pi—a tribute to Cutie Pie, the beloved kitten she had to give up thanks to stupid Emma and her stupid allergies.

On Peopleportal, she's just Carley Theresa. No last name.

"How are people supposed to find you that way?" asked her sister, who recently created a Peeps page—without private settings—under her full name, Emma Sue Archer.

"That's the point. I don't want anyone to find me—including Mom and Dad."

Her parents had never specifically forbidden her from online networking, but something tells her they wouldn't approve.

"You shouldn't use your name, either," she warned Emma. "They would kill you if they found out."

"Why?"

"Because it's dangerous. Everyone knows that. You have to be really careful what you put out there."

"You're so paranoid, Carley. And anyway, I *am* careful."

"Really? You posted the other night that you were psyched to have the house to yourself while I was babysitting and Mom and Dad were out. That's like an open invita-

tion to any creep: *Here I am, all alone—come and get me!*
If Mom and Dad found out you did that . . ."

Emma shrugged. "They're not going to find out because
they're not on Peopleportal, and you'd better not tell them I
am."

"Don't worry. I won't."

That day, Emma changed her Peeps settings so that her
sister could no longer see her page. Whatever. Carley had
other things to worry about.

She still does—now more than ever.

Nicki . . . oh God, Nicki . . .

How could she have done it? Especially knowing she
wasn't going to go to heaven . . .

Mom had tried to convince Carley that wasn't true, but
she's not a nun or a priest or God Himself.

Mom's just doing what she always does, trying to make
things easier by saying things she doesn't know for a fact.
Like when she tells Carley that the trouble at school will
blow over, that things will work themselves out, that she'll
eventually have plenty of friends and be able to put all this
behind her . . .

Yeah. Right.

Tears flood Carley's eyes and she wipes them on her
sleeve, hoping no one noticed.

"Ladies, please keep an eye on the time." Strolling up and
down the aisles, Mr. Sterne cuts into Carley's reverie.

Never was a person's name more suitable than his. Tall,
dark, and gaunt, Mr. Sterne has thick black eyebrows that
always make him look as though he's scowling, even when
he's smiling. Which Carley has seen him do maybe a couple
of times all year—most memorably, when he announced
that there would be a major test on the first day back after
Christmas break.

"You're in high school now, ladies," he said in response to

the groans after that announcement. "You don't want to leave your brains to idle thought—or worse—for two weeks."

"Worse . . . like what?" Kendra Hyde, who sits across the aisle, leaned over and whispered to Carley.

She shrugged. "Sex, drugs, rock and roll?"

"I know, right? It's like he thinks we're all wild, partying sluts or something. Speaking of which . . . want to come to my New Year's Eve party?" Kendra grinned.

Carley was surprised—and pleased—to be invited.

Kendra doesn't talk much, and she's not cliquish like the other girls. When she found herself invited to her party, Carley thought they might wind up good friends.

"I can't," she told Kendra reluctantly. "I already have plans for New Year's Eve." She didn't specify that they were the same plans her family always had: to ring in the holiday at her grandparents' house, surrounded by family and a couple of priests from the neighborhood parish. That suddenly seemed lame.

"No big deal. Some other time," Kendra said with a shrug.

But there would be no other time. After the others started ganging up on Carley, Kendra stopped talking to her, just like everyone else.

Now, whenever Carley is in math class, she keeps her head turned straight at the board, or bent to focus on her work. She doesn't dare look to the left, at Kendra, or to the right, at Melissa Kovacs, queen of the mean girls, or at any of the others. She knows they'll only glare, or smirk, or mouth nasty things.

"You have fifteen minutes left," Mr. Sterne announces, strolling up the aisle, his scuffed black shoes making squeaking noises on the tile floor. "If you've finished, use the remaining time to double-check your work."

Finished?

Carley has barely begun the test.

Miserably, she tries again to concentrate on the algebra problem before her.

$$13 + (b \times 12) - 18 = 271$$

While math has always been her most difficult subject, she's managed to stay on top of it by working extra hard. Ever since all the trouble began with the other girls, though, she's had a hard time focusing on schoolwork at all. She told her mother she has an 87 so far this term, but that was before she missed three homework assignments—all resulting in zeros—and failed a quiz last week.

She really needs to get a decent grade on today's test. It's the only reason she's here at all. Mom told her to stay home and not worry about algebra, but . . .

Mom doesn't understand that it's not just about that. She doesn't understand the seriousness of her situation, or that if Carley makes things easy on herself even just this once, she'll be tempted to do it every day.

That's what Angel said.

force urself to keep showing up evry day becuz if u dont then they winnnnnn

Angel was talking about the other girls, of course—the ones who have been tormenting her.

When Carley told her about Nicki, and about Mom wanting to let her skip school today to go to the wake, Angel didn't think that was a good idea, either.

u dont want to fall behind what if u flunk mathhhhhh

Angel was right, of course. Carley told her so last night.

im alwys rite listen to me and u will b fine lolololollllllll

"Ten minutes, ladies," Mr. Sterne announces.

Carley chews the eraser tip and stares miserably down at the problem.

$$13 + (b \times 12) - 18 = 271$$

A teardrop splashes onto the test paper. And then another. Again, she wipes her eyes.

Maybe, just this once, Angel was wrong. Maybe she should have stayed home.

Something hits her on her leg beneath the desk. She looks down to see a piece of paper folded into a triangular football.

Uncertain where it came from, she looks around. The other girls are studiously bent over their work. Mr. Sterne is at the board, writing out a series of problems for his seventh period juniors.

Glancing down again at the wad of paper, Carley sees that her name is written on it.

Certain it's some kind of trick, she reaches out her leg and is about to kick it away when Mr. Sterne suddenly turns around and looks right at her.

"Carley? Is there a problem?"

"No. I was just . . . trying to figure something out."

"You have nine minutes and thirty seconds to do it." He turns back to the board.

She thinks better of kicking the note away. Who knows what it says? The last thing she needs is for Mr. Sterne to come across it later and find a reason to dislike her even more.

Surreptitiously, she bends to pick it up instead. She's about to put it into the pocket of her skirt when curiosity gets the better of her. Instead, she quickly unfolds it on her lap.

It takes her a moment to realize that the rows of numbers and letters are the answers to the algebra test, complete with the equations that show how the problems were solved.

Why would anyone want to help her?

Maybe because you're sitting here crying, and someone in here heard what happened to Nicki and actually has a heart?

Could it be Kendra?

She no longer makes conversation with Carley, much less

invites her to anything, but she's not one of the mean girls.

But even if it came from Kendra—why would she assume Carley would want to cheat?

Maybe that's no big deal to someone like her. Maybe she's just trying to help.

So now what?

Would Carley cheat?

Absolutely not, she reminds herself firmly.

She glances up at the clock just in time to see the big black minute hand jump to the next notch.

She looks back down at her nearly blank test page, and then, reluctantly, at the unfolded paper in her lap.

The drafty corridors of Sacred Sisters look exactly the same as they did decades ago: beige and black speckled tile floors, yellow-painted interior concrete block walls, rows of tall, narrow, battleship gray lockers.

If Jen had walked in while classes were changing, those locker doors would be slamming amid the sound of female chatter. But sixth period is in full swing and her footsteps echo in the empty halls, past hushed classrooms where teachers' voices drone or students are bent over their desks, pencils in hand.

She passes the tree an artistic hippie nun painted on the wall back in the seventies, its bare branches always seasonally decorated by a couple of lucky students. Right now, the tree is covered in small green construction paper buds. Soon, Jen knows, they'll be swapped out for large green construction paper leaves.

It's momentarily comforting to know that in this little corner of the world, at least, even the things that are meant to symbolize change never change.

Comforting—until she remembers the bullies who have made Carley miserable here.

Jen passes the memorial plaques and photos on the wall

outside the principal's office. When she was in school, there were just a handful, and the only one she knew was Ruthie Bell, killed in that car accident during their sophomore year.

Ruth Ann Bell: 1969–1986.

Jen still can't bear to look at that plain, familiar face, frozen in grainy black and white; can't bear the memories even after all these years.

Now there are at least a dozen additional tributes to students who have since walked the halls of Sacred Sisters, but tragically died before graduation.

Is there a similar wall at Woodsbridge High, where Nicole Denise Olivera will be memorialized?

Stop.

Go.

She walks on, searching for other memories. Happier memories.

She allows herself to glance into the glass display case outside the coach's office, filled with trophies and plaques, many of which are inscribed with her sisters Bennie and Frankie's names. And the gym, echoing with the sounds of bouncing ball and rubber sneaker soles squeaking on the varnished maple floorboards. And the health office, where she overhears the school nurse on the telephone telling a parent that it's just a low-grade fever, and glimpses a girl lying on a vinyl cot, furtively messaging on her cell phone beneath the watchful painted gaze of the Blessed Virgin.

Jen remembers playing hooky on that same orange cot beneath that same framed print of serene, blue-mantled Mary; remembers reading an issue of *Seventeen* magazine hidden in the pages of an oversized textbook while waiting for her mother to come pick her up.

More than the familiar sights and sounds of the school, it's the smell that, for Jen, is the most powerful memory trigger.

From the moment she stepped through the big glass double doors, she was struck by the familiar scents of pine floor cleaner, incense from the chapel, and what she and her friends used to call Eau de Sloppy Joe. Chances are, the cafeteria lunch ladies aren't even serving Sloppy Joe today, but for some reason it smells as if they are. Always has, and probably always will.

As the scent infiltrates her nostrils, memories of her days here at Sacred Sisters begin working their way into her brain. By the time she reaches the warren of second-floor offices that house various staff members who fall under the guidance department umbrella, she half expects to see old Mrs. Esposito manning the reception desk.

But she died years ago, and Jen isn't here to discuss her own college applications or SAT scores. She's here to introduce herself to the new social worker and find out how Carley is doing.

"Do you have an appointment?" the department secretary asks when Jen inquires whether Sister Linda is in today.

"No, but I won't keep her for more than five minutes."

The woman purses her lips. "Have a seat. I'll go find out if she's available."

As she disappears, Jen finds herself wondering why the people who sit at reception desks—at schools, at medical offices—so often seem to have dour personalities. Are those the kinds of people drawn to these jobs, or does the pressure of dealing with people all day, every day, eventually wear on them?

Back in Jen's day, Mrs. Esposito was such a force to be reckoned with that even the guidance counselor seemed intimidated by her. Jen remembers sitting in this very spot— perhaps on this very chair—under Mrs. Esposito's watchful gaze, trying not to reveal that she had a forbidden wad of strawberry Bubble Yum in her mouth.

"Sister Linda will be out in a few minutes," the receptionist announces, reappearing and settling back at her desk.

Jen's thoughts return to the past as her gaze settles on a

nearby bulletin board, where a thumbtacked poster adver-
tises an upcoming school trip to Italy and the Vatican over
Easter break.

When she was at Sisters, she begged her parents to
allow her to go on a similar trip. They refused, saying they
couldn't afford it. But after Jen took an after-school job to
earn the money herself, they still wouldn't agree to let her
go. "It wouldn't be fair to your sisters" was Mom's excuse.
"They didn't get to go to Italy. Even Daddy and I have never
been to Italy, and Grandma and Pop-Pop haven't been back
there since they left on the boat."

At the time, Jen was devastated. Even more so when her
boyfriend, Mike Morino, got to go on the same trip with his
classmates at Cardinal Ruffini, the all-boys Catholic school
he attended. She was certain he was going to fall in love
with someone else while he was there, and spent a miserable
Easter break envisioning Mike strolling the streets of Rome
hand in hand with another girl, a beautiful Italian girl who
looked like a young Sophia Loren.

It didn't happen . . .

Or more likely it did, but she never knew about it.

Looking back now, remembering how much that mattered then, she wonders, not for the first time, how Mike is
doing.

Driven by nothing more than idle curiosity, she's searched
for him a few times on the Internet. But he has a huge extended family that, in Italian tradition, names their sons
after fathers and grandfathers. There are a number of Mike
Morinos in the area. If she searched harder, she could probably figure out which one he is, but why bother?

"Mrs. Archer?"

Jen looks up to see a black-habited woman coming
toward her.

"I'm Sister Linda. I wasn't expecting you—"

"I know, I'm sorry, but I'm here to pick up Carley and I

was running early, so I thought I could stop in and see you if you have time."

"I do. Come on into my office." The social worker turns to the secretary. "Hold my calls, please, Lenore."

Appearing as pleased by that request as she is by anything else, Lenore gives a hard-faced nod.

Sister Linda leads Jen down the hall and through a maze of file cabinets and cubicle partitions.

This isn't the first time she's ventured into the guidance counseling department since her own days at Sacred Sisters. She was here for an evening academic orientation meeting last fall when Carley enrolled.

But she's never had any reason to visit the social worker. For all she knows, there wasn't even one on staff when she was a student here.

Sister Linda came on board last September to replace the school's previous part-time social worker, Sister Helen, who had passed away during the previous school year.

Jen recalls hearing about it at the family Memorial Day picnic last year, courtesy of her mother's grand plan to have all her daughters living close to home again. That might actually happen with recently divorced Maddie, an attorney who's in the process of trying to sell her Cleveland townhouse and return to the area. Mom is always sending her job leads for local law practices.

Unlike Maddie, Jen's sister Frankie has no intention of moving back. She has an MSW and works for the state Department of Social Services in Albany, making decent money with good benefits. But that didn't stop Mom from showing her the listing for the opening at Sacred Sisters.

"Did you see the starting salary, Ma?" Frankie shook her head. "There's no way I can afford to do that. Catholic schools pay peanuts—especially Sisters. That's why only nuns are on staff there. They've taken a vow of poverty."

"But you can at least apply and see what happens.

Wouldn't it be nice to work at your old school?" Mom coaxed. "And the cost of living here is lower . . ."

"Not low enough. I'd have to live in a cardboard box if I took that job. It's only part-time."

"You could move back home with Daddy and me. We've got plenty of space even with Maddie coming back, and your roommate could visit whenever she wanted."

Jen's sister, looking sufficiently horrified, quickly changed the subject.

Though Frankie came out to their parents years ago, Mom persists in referring to Patty as Frankie's "roommate"—her way of reconciling her daughter's lifestyle with her own staunch Catholicism. And as thrilled as she is that her first-born is thinking of moving home again, Theresa can't even begin to discuss the topic of Maddie's divorce.

"This is my office." As Sister Linda steps across the threshold of a tiny windowed room, Jen sizes her up.

She has a full, almost homely face, thick torso, and bulky limbs beneath her habit, worn with lug-soled black shoes and outdated granny glasses. Formidably old school, but of course that doesn't mean she isn't kindhearted, or that the girls can't relate to her.

Jen can't help but remember Sister Patricia, one of the few nuns who did wear a habit back in the old days, but used to throw on a pair of Nikes with sparkly pink laces to lead the girls in after-school aerobics classes. She was only a couple of years older than they were at the time.

I wonder whatever happened to her?

Sister Patricia, Mrs. Esposito, Mike Morino . . .

All part of another era, permanently erased from her life like resolved equations on a chalkboard. Now there's just Sister Linda, closing the office door and moving a stack of papers off the lone chair opposite a cluttered desk. "Here, have a seat."

"Thank you."

Jen watches her look around for a surface where she can put the displaced papers. With a shrug, she plops them on the floor.

"Sorry," she says as she pushes aside a couple of books with the toe of her sensible shoe. "I'm still trying to dig my way to the bottom of this mess I inherited. Sister Helen was a wonderful person, I'm sure, but she really was disorganized. Did you know her?"

"Me? No. Carley is just a freshman," Jen reminds her.

"I realize that, but you were a student here, too, weren't you?"

"Oh, I didn't know that was what you—yes. I did go here, back in the eighties. Did Carley tell you?"

The woman nods.

"We didn't have social workers back then. Just guidance counselors."

"I see." Sister Linda settles into her desk chair, pressing her palms together and propping the steepled fingers under her double chin as if in prayer. "You said you're picking up Carley. Does she have an early appointment, or . . . ?"

So she doesn't know.

That makes sense. Nicki Olivera wasn't a student here. If she had been, the social worker would be busily consoling students. The administrators would probably bring in grief counselors, too. For all the talk of teaching the girls to be independent and handle problems on their own, there are certain situations in which any modern school would step in with a support system.

It wasn't like that back in the old days. When Ruthie Bell was killed in that car accident, Jen is pretty sure that life marched on as usual here at Sacred Sisters, aside from a special prayer for her soul at daily Mass and the plaque that went up on the wall over the summer.

Things would be different now. Or maybe things would

have been different back then if poor Ruthie herself had been different; if she'd been the kind of girl whose loss had had great impact on the student body . . .

Uncomfortable with the path her thoughts have taken, Jen pushes Ruthie from her mind yet again and addresses Sister Linda's question.

"I'm picking up Carley early because we're going to a wake."

A shadow crosses the woman's eyes. "Oh . . . I'm sorry. Was it a family member, or . . . ?"

Jen finds herself irrationally annoyed with Sister Linda's stilted conversational habit of trailing off with questions half unspoken.

"It was a friend." She shifts her weight on the hard wooden chair. "Carley's best friend, actually, from the time they were two or three. She's not a student here, she goes to Woodsbridge High—*went* to Woodsbridge High," she amends, and drops her gaze to her hands clasped in her lap, feeling the familiar lump start to work its way into her throat.

"Oh, I'm so sorry. What *happened*?"

"She—died. Suddenly. I . . . I'd rather not get into the details. But between this and all that's been going on here at school, I'm worried about Carley."

"Has she mentioned any more trouble to you?"

"No. But that doesn't mean there isn't any. She doesn't like to talk about it with me."

"Why not?"

The question catches her off guard. It's probably meant in a benign way—of course it is—but to Jen, it feels almost as though the woman is accusing her of being an inadequate mother.

Come on, that's ridiculous. It's just a question, and a logical one, really.

She just wishes she knew the damned answer.

"Carley's always been a quiet kid. She keeps things to herself."

"Most teenagers do, Mrs. Archer." The social worker offers a faint smile and shakes her head. "You're not the first mother who's sat in that chair and told me that her daughter doesn't confide in her. I'm sure you won't be the last."

The words are meant to reassure her, but somehow, Jen only feels worse. She doesn't want her relationship with Carley to be just like everyone else's.

Why not? Because you're special? Because you're the perfect mother and she's the perfect daughter?

Carley's not perfect any more than Jen is perfect. But she's always been the good kid, the easy one, the one who doesn't make waves. The one who comes up to pat Jen's arm when she's upset over a brash comment from Emma or an argument with Thad or—

A shrill blast jars her: the tone announcing the end of sixth period. Already, she can feel the tide of movement as the students head to their next destination. Chairs scrape on wooden classroom floors above and below; voices and footsteps fill the hallways and stairwells.

Jen has run out of time to pump the social worker for the details of what happened to her daughter. Today isn't the day to dwell on that, anyway.

Opting to focus on the more immediate hurdle—Nicki's wake—she stands abruptly. "I have to go find Carley."

"All right. Keep me posted and let me know how she is."

Jen assures Sister Linda that she will. But as she makes her way out of the office, past an unsmiling Lenore, she can't help but think it should be the other way around.

In the hallway, there are slamming lockers and chattering girls. Their faces are unfamiliar, as are those of the habit-clad nuns who linger in classroom doorways talking to students.

Jen's journey into the school might have been a pleasant trip down memory lane, but it's as though she took a wrong turn into unfamiliar territory on the way back. Now everyone—everything—seems foreign.

She quickens her pace, eager to find Carley and get out of here.

Entry from the marble notebook

Wednesday, December 25, 1985

Christmas Day is the same as any other day of the year in our house (in other words, miserable), aside from being a weekday that feels like a Sunday because we have to go to church and then come home and pretend to listen while Mother reads Scripture out loud to us, same as she does on Sunday mornings.

We don't get presents. Naturally, Mother doesn't believe in the commercialism of Christmas. I feel bad for Adrian because he wonders why Santa skips our house, just like I used to wonder when I was little. So last night I snuck into his room with one of my old red knee socks and I filled it with stuff and left it on his bed.

It wasn't anything much—just little things I've been collecting, like packages of oyster crackers they have in the school cafeteria sometimes, a candy bar and some Matchbox cars I got at the dollar store, a couple of books from the library sale that look brand-new, plus a charcoal sketch of the two of us that I drew in art class. It's not perfect, but it's pretty good and I got an A on it. I put it into a wooden frame I found in the Dumpster behind the crafts store. Sometimes they throw away perfectly good stuff.

Adrian came running into my room with the stock-

ing when he woke up, and I pretended I didn't know anything about it. I told him he must have been a really good boy because Santa had found him and filled a stocking for him. I told him not to tell Mother and Father, because they don't even believe in Santa anyway, and I made him promise to hide the stuff, especially the books. Mother only lets him read Bible tales.

I've already read the new stories to him over and over again and he's so smart he practically has them memorized. One is about dinosaurs and the other is about trucks. He loves them both.

It was a pretty good Christmas for a change. I don't know what I'd do without my baby brother.

Chapter 7

"Hello?" Emma calls cautiously as she steps into the front hall, even though Mom's car isn't in the driveway.

She listens for a minute, hearing nothing but the hum of the refrigerator in the kitchen.

"Mom?" she calls, just in case. "Carley? Dad?"

No reply.

Satisfied the house is empty, she turns to the others. "Okay"—she opens the door wider—"come on in."

They file past her: Bridget, also in eighth grade at Saint Paul's; Brian, who lives next door, and his girlfriend, Miranda, both of whom are sophomores at Woodsbridge High; plus Gabe, the new kid who just moved in down the street with his dad.

Emma's had a major crush on him since she spotted him at the high school bus stop a few weeks ago. She promptly made it her business to meet him.

"Hi," she said, marching right over to him. "I'm Emma."

He unplugged one earbud. "Huh?"

"I'm Emma." She could hear loud music blasting from the tiny dangling speaker. Guitars and drums—rock, as opposed to hip-hop.

"Gabe. What's up?"

"I just thought someone should welcome you to the neighborhood."

"Thanks."

"Where are you from?"

"New York."

"This *is* New York."

He just looked at her from beneath those thick, manly eyebrows.

"Oh. You mean New York City?"

His expression suggested that he thought she was hopelessly unsophisticated.

To show that she wasn't, Emma managed to work into that first awkward, brief conversation that she's almost sixteen and that she goes to private school. Naturally, she didn't mention that it's a parochial elementary school.

"Not to be mean or anything, but if he's a senior and he's from New York City and so hot and so cool, then how come he wants to hang out with you?" Bridget asked when she first told her about Gabe.

"Gee, thanks a lot," said Emma, secretly pretty sure that if he weren't the new kid, Gabe wouldn't give her the time of day, even if she really was sixteen.

"So what does he look like?" Bridget wanted to know. "What makes him so cool?"

"He's like . . . he's not a boy. He's a man."

"In what way?"

"He's really tall, and he's always dressed in flannel shirts and jeans and work boots."

Bridget made a face. "Ew."

"What? Why 'ew'?"

"I like it when guys dress up."

"I like it when guys look rugged, not prissy."

"I didn't say—"

Emma went on, talking over her, "And he has shaggy dark hair and a little bit of a beard and dangerous eyes . . ."

"What do you mean dangerous eyes?"

"You know . . . really dark and kind of . . . just *dangerous*." Sometimes Bridget can be super clueless.

Plus, Emma can't help but notice that she looks like such a baby today. The sprinkling of freckles across her nose and cheeks aren't usually so noticeable at this time of year, but she got sunburned when her family went to Florida a few weeks ago. Her gingery hair is pulled back in a ponytail with a dorky blue satin ribbon tied around it, and of course she's wearing her school uniform.

Emma is wearing her navy Saint Paul's jumper, too, but she went into the girls' room before they left school and safety-pinned the shoulder straps to make it shorter. She wanted to do the same to Bridget's, but Bridget refused, saying her thighs are too chubby.

She's right about that, in Emma's opinion. But once when she advised Bridget that she really needs to lay off the bread and butter, Bridget got all pissy.

As she ushers the others toward the kitchen, Emma kicks a pair of Carley's sneakers out of the way. The sole of one hits the white baseboard and leaves a faint smudge.

Not my fault, Emma thinks. It's Carley's, for leaving them there. And Mom's, for being so wrapped up in what happened to Nicki that the house has been taken over by clutter. There are stacks of newspapers, magazines, and mail on every surface; a basket of folded laundry sitting at the foot of the stairs; coats draped over the backs of chairs.

"How long do we have?" Brian asks Emma, his fingers intertwined with Miranda's.

"My mother said the wake goes till four, and then she and my sister have to drive back down here, which takes, like, a half hour. So . . ."

"Are you sure? I mean, we don't want to take any chances," Bridget points out. "Your parents would kill you if they found out you skipped school plus had all these people over."

Emma rolls her eyes, wondering why she even bothered to include her today in the first place.

Actually, she knows why. It was because she herself was feeling a little shy about hanging out alone with the older kids.

Plus, Bridget is usually game for pretty much anything, which is why she's at the top of Emma's BFF list. Like, it was Bridget's idea to lie about hanging out at each other's houses one Saturday night so that they could go to a high school party. And it was Bridget's idea to help themselves at the mall to expensive eye makeup they couldn't afford and their mothers would never let them buy.

Today was Emma's idea. She thought of it the moment her mother mentioned that Woodsbridge was excusing kids early today to go to Nicki's wake. She made a beeline down to the Woodsbridge bus stop while her mother was in the shower.

Brian and Gabe were there, both plugged into their iPods. When Emma suggested that they sign out under the pretext of going to the funeral home, they were wary, but interested. Brian only vaguely knew who Nicki was, and Gabe didn't know her at all.

"Can Miranda come, too?" asked Brian, who's been dating her since freshman year.

"Sure."

"And you're positive no one will be home?"

"Positive. My dad will be working and my mom and sister will be at the wake."

"Don't *you* have school?" Brian asked, and Emma shot him a warning look. She'd already begged him not to tell Gabe how old she really was, and he agreed on the condition that she owed him a big favor.

"I'm faking a note from my mom," she said, "saying I have to leave early for the wake."

"Seriously?" Gabe looked impressed.

"Yeah, I do it all the time. No big deal."

Maybe she doesn't do it all the time, but she's done it before.

Well, once. And she was amazed at how easy it was to fool Sister Agatha, the elderly principal at Saint Paul's.

Today, Emma again faked a note for herself and wrote one for Bridget, too.

"Didn't you feel guilty," Bridget whispered to Emma after they handed in the notes, "when Sister Agatha blessed us and said she'd pray for Nicki's soul?"

"Nope. I'm just glad she said she's not going to the wake herself until tonight." Emma had stupidly forgotten that everyone at Saint Paul's knew Nicki, who'd graduated eighth grade there last year. "Can you imagine if she ran into my mom at the funeral home this afternoon and asked where I was?"

But that didn't happen. Things had worked out for Emma, as they always seem to have a way of doing, and now she and her friends have the house to themselves for a couple of hours. Bridget is just nervous because she likes to be the one in control, and she's not used to being the youngest kid in the group. Plus, she keeps sneaking these sideways looks at Gabe, like she's interested in him. When she's around a guy she likes, she tends to get flustered. Definitely not cool.

I shouldn't have invited her, Emma thinks again.

What if Gabe is into girls who are cute and perky, like Bridget? It doesn't seem likely, but you never know. Sometimes opposites attract.

Look at Emma's parents. Mom is outgoing and likes to run around doing things, and Dad is quiet and antisocial.

That's what Mom called him once last summer when they had a fight because she wanted to go to some patio party Dad had forgotten about, and he wanted to make up an excuse and stay home.

"I deal with people all day every day at work, Jen," he said. "On weekends, I like to lay low."

They don't argue that often; Emma listened with interest.

"I lay low every day," Mom shot back. "On weekends, I like to get out of the house."

She won the argument, of course. Unlike Dad, she's super good at talking. She had way more to say about why they should go out than Dad did about why they shouldn't. In the end, they went to the party and came home laughing and acting all lovey-dovey.

Nicki was sleeping over that night. Emma heard her tell Carley wistfully, "Your parents seem like they really love each other."

"Well, they're married, *duh*, Nicks."

"Yeah, but still . . . it's nice that they laugh and kiss and stuff."

Personally, Emma cringes whenever her parents get affectionate. Who wants to think about *that*?

"Do you guys want something to eat?" she asks, leading her four afternoon visitors toward the kitchen.

"Like what?" Gabe tosses his down jacket over a stool at the breakfast bar, sees the glass cookie jar, and opens the top to peek in. "Are these, like, homemade?"

"Yeah."

"Who made them? You?"

"My mom. They're peanut butter."

"Your mom *bakes cookies*?" he asks, wide-eyed, as if she just claimed that her mom raises the dead.

"She makes the best cookies," Bridget bubbles. "Have one!"

Gabe makes a face and pushes the cookie jar away. "Got any beer?"

"Sure." Without missing a beat, Emma opens the fridge.

She moves the condiments and milk cartons around and finds four bottles of Bud. Hopefully her dad won't notice if a couple are missing. He's not a big beer drinker, just keeps it on hand for company. When Dad drinks, it's usually whiskey. Emma snuck a sip once and nearly puked.

"You want a beer?" she asks the others casually, as if she does this every day.

Miranda and Brian, wrapped around each other in a corner, don't even seem to hear her. Good. Dad would definitely notice if all the beer disappeared overnight, and it's not like he'd ever suspect Carley.

"I'll have one, Em," says Bridget, munching a peanut butter cookie.

"We can share." She plunks two bottles on the counter and twists off the caps.

"Why do we have to share?"

Ignoring Bridget's question, Emma hands an open bottle to Gabe.

Brian extracts his mouth from Miranda's and announces, "Um, we're going to go upstairs for a bit."

"Whatever. Just don't go into my parents' room."

"Which one's yours?"

"Second door on the right at the top of the stairs."

Bridget, well aware that it's actually Carley's room, starts to open her mouth to protest, but closes it when Emma shoots her a look.

After they all leave, before her mother and sister get home, Emma will sneak in there and make sure nothing is disturbed. She doesn't really want Brian and Miranda rolling around in her own sheets. Plus, this way, her bedroom is vacant, just in case Bridget gets a clue and goes home, leaving Emma alone with Gabe. She'd rather take him to her own room than Carley's, with all those stupid stuffed animals and juvenile books she won't get rid of, and the frilly pastel color scheme. Emma recently got her parents to re-paint her own room in shades of blue and brown.

"Brown?" Mom asked dubiously. "Isn't that a little bit—"

"It's super chic," Emma assured her, only she mispro-nounced it—"chick"—and her parents and sister acted as though that was the funniest thing they'd ever heard. Some-times, they bring it up even now—"Hey, Em," Dad will say, "how's your chick brown room?"

Hilarious.

Sometimes, she really can't stand her family.

Emma looks over at Gabe and finds him looking right back at her. He smiles and her heart beats a little faster as she takes a sip of beer.

Then he asks, "So how come your friend blew her brains out?"

She blinks. "You mean Nicki?"

"You got another friend who blew her brains out?"

Emma looks at Bridget, who raises an eyebrow at her.

Yeah, it is a little insensitive of Gabe to phrase it like that, but you can't really blame him. After all, he's new in town and didn't even know Nicki.

"She didn't blow her brains out."

"No? What'd she do?"

"Slit her wrists."

"Yeah? How come?"

"She was depressed," Emma tells him with a shrug.

"Yeah?"

She nods. Actually, she has no idea what happened with Nicki. But you'd have to be pretty depressed to do what she did, right?

A couple of kids at Saint Paul's have asked Emma about Nicki, assuming she has the inside scoop because Carley was close to her. It made her feel kind of important.

"Did she leave a note or anything?" Gabe asks.

That's a good question—and one Emma herself had asked her mother when she found out the news. Mom didn't know the answer. But Emma doesn't want to admit to Gabe that she's that far outside the loop, so she nods.

"Yeah? What did it say?" Gabe wants to know.

"It said, 'Farewell, cruel world.'"

"Seriously?" Bridget's blue eyes are big and round. "You didn't tell me that."

Emma rolls her eyes. "I'm just kidding, you idiot. Who writes a note like that?"

The approval in Gabe's expression makes it easy for Emma to ignore the wounded look on Bridget's face and her muttered "How was I supposed to know?"

Grinning at Gabe, Emma takes another gulp of beer. "Want a tour of the house?"

"Sure."

"You know what, guys?" Bridget reaches for her jacket. "I'm going home. I'm not feeling great."

"See ya," Emma tells her, eyes locked on Gabe's.

Yeah. Definitely dark and dangerous.

Really dangerous.

And that's just fine with Emma.

After Sandra Lutz died, Angel called the real estate office, offered brief condolences, and told one of her colleagues to hold off on the listing.

"I've decided to hang on to the house for at least a while longer, make some repairs, and wait for the market to turn around."

"Just give me a call," the colleague said hurriedly, as phones rang in the background, "when you're ready to sell it."

"I will," Angel promised.

That might very well happen, someday, when the house has served Angel's purposes.

But for now, I need to be here, where it all began. And I don't want them to know I've come back.

Still, even for someone who's never exactly been a "people person," it's not always easy spending so much time alone behind drawn shades, confined, after dark, to the two rooms that have lamps set on timers.

Thank you, Sandra Lutz, for that brilliant idea.

Ironically, instead of keeping passersby from realizing the house is empty, the goal is now to prevent the neighbors from seeing that it's occupied.

Angel never comes and goes through the front door. Luckily, an overgrown evergreen shrub border surrounds the lot, and the back door of the house is completely shielded from neighboring homes. Under cover of darkness, Angel cuts through a rarely used gravel parking area behind the dry cleaner around the corner on Redbud Street.

Inside the house, Angel has learned to make the most of those precious hours when the master bedroom and living room lamps click on, not daring to flip a light switch elsewhere in the house for fear someone out on the street might notice.

That isn't the only potential risk. Though it can be unbearably hot and stuffy in here during the summer months, the windows must remain closed and locked at all times. But at least there's heat when it's cold outside, and hot water. Using online bill pay, Angel keeps up with the utilities and home maintenance services, withdrawing the money directly from Mother's checking account.

There's even a working stove and refrigerator. Angel had instructed Sandra Lutz to leave the appliances intact—aside from the old chest freezer in the basement.

"I don't remember seeing that," Sandra had said, long distance. "Are you sure it's still here?"

"Where else would it be?"

"Maybe your mother sold it. Did you know that people use them for makeshift root cellars? They're airtight and watertight, perfect for keeping out insects and dampness, and I read about a farmer in the Midwest who—"

"This isn't the Midwest!" Angel snapped, to make it stop.

"Well, your mother must have gotten rid of it somehow, then, before she—"

"What, do you think she carried it up the steps on her back? I don't want it moved into storage, and I don't want it left in the house. Do you understand me? I want it disposed of. *Please*."

"I understand."

"Thank you."

Days later, Sandra sent an e-mail saying she'd checked the basement again and the freezer wasn't there.

I don't know what to tell you, she wrote, *except that it's gone. Your parents must have disposed of it. But I've taken care of everything else, and I left the kitchen appliances intact and running.*

And so that was that.

Angel was forced to put aside nagging thoughts of the basement freezer, not even certain why it mattered so much anyway. Somewhere back in the dim shadows of memory, there might have been something . . .

But Angel isn't interested in dredging up any more childhood unpleasantness than is absolutely necessary.

I have enough to deal with as it is. Every time I reread that marble notebook . . .

Angel knows it by heart now—page by page, line by line, word by word of blue ballpoint handwriting.

When this is over—when everything has been made right—I'll burn it. I'll burn it, and the house, and I'll walk away and never look back.

For now, though, for however long it takes, Angel is compelled to stay under this roof, a restless ghost doomed to walk in the shadows, endlessly reliving the tragedies of the past.

Yes, now the old place really is haunted.

And no one in the neighborhood is any the wiser. As far as they're concerned, it's deserted.

You could have always gotten your own place—a regular apartment even right here in the neighborhood. No one would ever be the wiser.

But it wouldn't feel right.

Angel needs to be here again. Here, under this roof, it's impossible to lose sight of what needs to be accomplished.

There was just one real risk reclaiming the house after Mother died, and that was having wifi installed.

It had to be done. Regular Internet access is crucial to the plan. While it would be easy enough to tap into a neighbor's unprotected wifi service, that's far too dangerous. If anyone stumbled across Angel's online activities . . .

But no one will. The house now has its own password-protected wireless network. Shortly after moving in, Angel ordered it online using Mother's existing telephone service account, and was taken aback when informed that someone would have to show up here to install the equipment.

The technician, who was in his early sixties, introduced himself as George Berry. He was perfectly pleasant and didn't give Angel a second glance, though he did comment on the empty house.

"Did you just move in?" he asked, as their footsteps echoed through the empty rooms.

"Yes."

"It's a great neighborhood. I've lived here for years."

With that single innocuous comment, the installer sealed his fate, much as the overly chatty Sandra Lutz had sealed hers.

"Really? Where do you live?" Angel asked casually.

"You know that stretch of Denton Road where there are a

bunch of ugly little ranch houses that were built in the fifties and sixties? Yeah, that's where I live. In one of those."

"Nice."

"Not really. Not all that nice, and not big enough even for my wife and me. My entire house is less than a thousand square feet, and that includes the attached two-car garage. What I wouldn't give for a big, beautiful old house like this. You're lucky, you know that?"

Angel wasn't so sure about that, but one thing was certain: the technician was most unlucky.

As George Berry worked in the cellar, whistling and setting up the new network, Angel paced the first floor. What if he mentioned to one of the neighbors that the big old house on Lilac Avenue has a new occupant?

I can't take that chance.

"Are you going to be here for a while?" Angel called down the stairs.

"At least an hour," he said, "while I get this panel installed and get the service up and running."

"I have to run a quick errand. I'll be back soon."

George had left his jacket hanging over a doorknob. In the front pocket was a set of keys.

Angel slipped them out and went directly to the hardware store. Not the small mom-and-pop operation just two blocks away, where the elderly owner provides cheerful, hands-on service and proudly declares that he never forgets a customer's name or face, but the huge superstore just off the thruway exit.

There, a disinterested high school kid duplicated the entire set of keys without once glancing up or uttering anything more than a mumbled "Here you go," when the job was done.

Less than twenty-four hours later, George Berry and his wife, Arlene, met an untimely death due to carbon monoxide poisoning.

According to the newspaper coverage, one of them had absentmindedly forgotten to turn off the car engine after pulling into the garage and closing the door. Accompanying the article was a sidebar about the domestic hazards of even minor memory loss in the aging population.

No one would ever suspect that someone had slipped into the Berry home in the wee hours with a copied house key. It was a chilly September night; the windows were closed and locked and so was the garage, where a pair of Chevrolets, one a silver Malibu and the other a black Impala, were parked.

The keys to both were conveniently hanging on a hook just inside the kitchen door. With gloved fingers, Angel removed a set, started the Malibu, closed the door, and disappeared out into the night.

At least it was an easy way to go. Much easier than burning alive, or bleeding out.

Much easier than the fate that lies in store for the others.

Angel grins.

Sandra Lutz.

George and Arlene Berry.

Nicki Olivera.

Four down.

Two to go.

As they make the painstaking mourners' crawl up the freshly shoveled sidewalk and through the funeral home's carpeted foyer and anteroom, Jen occasionally wipes away tears and sees Carley doing the same.

They're hardly alone in their sorrow. Everyone else, strangers and familiar faces alike, is doing the same thing, punctuating the hush with muffled sniffles and whispered conversation.

But when the line inches forward through the archway into the chapel room, and the shiny white casket comes into view—closed, as Jen had assumed it would be—there is a noticeable shift in the subdued mood immediately surrounding them.

The whispering becomes murmuring, with a few audible "Oh my Gods," and the trio of teenage girls directly in front of Carley breaks down in tears.

Jen instinctively reaches for her daughter's hand, only to find that Carley's fingers, clammy and trembling, are already groping for hers.

"Are you okay?"

Rather than bristling at the latest inane question to escape her mother's lips, or claiming to be "fine," a pale Carley gives a slight shake of her head.

"Do you want to go back outside?"

"No. I just . . . I need a second." She takes a deep breath as if to steel herself for the ordeal ahead.

Jen finds herself wishing that they had waited until tonight's viewing hours to attend the wake with Thad, who's planning on coming after work. He's always a calming presence in a storm, and Carley isn't the only one who can use his quiet strength right now.

Jen's father would be the next best thing. She turns to scan the crowd over her shoulder, hoping to see her parents' faces.

They aren't there. She notices the middle-aged couple directly behind them watching something and turns to see that they're staring at Carley as she leans briefly against the back of a wingback chair near the archway. Jen notices, for the first time, that she's wearing stockings and flat leather loafers instead of sneakers with her school uniform today.

She would have suggested it if she'd thought of it herself. She swallows hard, touched that Carley did it on her own.

"Is she a friend of Nicole's?" the woman behind Jen asks sympathetically.

"Yes."

"Poor thing. She looks upset."

Jen nods. No kidding.

"I used to work as a paralegal in her father's office, years ago," the woman goes on. "Terrible tragedy."

Used to work . . . her father . . . years ago . . .

It takes a moment for Jen's thoughts, swirling with concern for Carley, to process that. *Her father, her father . . .*

Oh. Nicki's father. Debbie's husband, Andrew.

Jen doesn't know him very well. Despite her friendship with Debbie, they don't socialize as couples. Andrew is a busy attorney, rarely home, and the marriage isn't the most stable one around. In all those years of playground conversations and carpools, chaperoning class trips and girls nights out, Debbie hasn't ever gone into much detail about her relationship with her husband, other than to say they live separate lives.

"He does his thing and I do mine," she's often said, with a slight shake of her dark head, her eyes betraying not a hint of emotion.

Feeling a touch on her sleeve, Jen turns to see Carley motioning that the line has moved forward again.

"Are you sure you want to do this?" Jen asks her.

Carley nods, and together, they make their way toward the coffin. A large framed photograph of a grinning Nicki sits on a flower-bedecked pedestal beside it.

The unmistakable sickly-sweet perfume of Stargazer lilies permeates the room, mingling with the stale cigarette smoke and cooking smells wafting from the folds of mourners' coats. Jen can smell the flowers though she can't see them, and the distinct scent triggers an unpleasant memory that plays at the edges of her mind.

She refuses to let it in. Not here, especially. Not now.

Not so soon after walking the empty halls of Sacred Sisters, trying to forget . . .

Here, there are flowers, other flowers, everywhere—

mostly in chalky shades of white and cream. Standing out among them, Jen spots the large spray of roses she ordered from the neighborhood flower shop.

"Are you sure you want to do hot pink?" the florist had asked over the phone. "We're mostly doing whites . . ."

"Hot pink," Jen said firmly. It was Nicki's favorite color.

She sent the flowers with a card that reads simply, *With Deepest Sympathy, The Archer Family.*

"Is there anything else you want to say?" the florist asked.

Yes. So many other things she wants to say . . .

But none seems appropriate or meaningful enough to write on a card sent with funeral flowers for a fifteen-year-old girl who killed herself.

Positioned by the casket, flanked by her husband and her mother, Debbie Olivera seems to have aged a decade in the couple of weeks since Jen saw her last. The skin around her eyes and mouth is sallow and sunken; her shoulder-length auburn hair is streaked with wiry silver strands.

Ordinarily, she's a flashy dresser, layering on the jewelry and favoring bright colors like turquoise, coral, and her daughter's favorite hot pink. Today, she's subdued and frail in a simple black crepe dress that envelops her slender figure and renders her neck, wrists, and ankles inordinately spindly.

Seeing Jen and Carley, Debbie steps toward them and falls onto them, weeping uncontrollably. Jen can't find her voice and quickly stops trying, sobbing along with her heartbroken friend and her daughter until Nicki's father steps in.

"Deb," he says quietly, "pull yourself together."

Jen immediately resents the words.

But when she looks up and sees the stark pain in Andrew Olivera's eyes, she reconsiders.

You don't judge a grieving parent. Ever.

"I'm so sorry," she says thickly to Andrew, and to Debbie and her mother, Rosemary, before the trio is enveloped by a fresh cluster of mourners.

Jen looks at Carley. Her daughter appears shaken.

"Let's say a prayer," she suggests, and together, they walk over to wait their turn at the kneeler beside the flower-covered casket.

All around them, people are gathered in small groups. Some are wiping tears or leaning morosely on each other. Others are reconnecting with old friends, introducing them to spouses or children, the atmosphere one of an oddly re-strained cocktail party.

It's always this way at a wake, Jen thinks. People talk about how they only see each other when something terrible happens, and promise to get together again soon under happier circumstances.

But do they ever?

Probably not. Life has a way of sweeping you along in day-to-day business, and old friends and extended family are too easily lost.

"You really need to start social networking on Peeps," Jen's sister Bennie said in a recent phone conversation from the opposite coast. "Then we could be in touch every day."

"You mean Peopleportal?"

"Peopleportal, Tumblr, Twitter . . . I keep up online with tons of people I never thought I'd see again, Jen."

"Really? I thought that was mostly something teenagers do."

"Well, that's why I started in the first place—I wanted to keep an eye on what my kids were up to."

Probably nothing good, Jen thought, knowing her niece and nephew. Bennie's two children have been a handful since they were born.

"Now I think the kids have me blocked," her sister went on, "but I'm on Peeps all the time anyway. It's addictive."

"How do the kids have you blocked?"

"Oh, it's easy. There are settings so that you can choose who sees what, even if they're on your connections list."

Jen has never been comfortable with the thought of broadcasting any kind of personal information on the Internet, let alone allowing her daughters to do it. She said no when Emma asked if she could get a Peeps page last fall. Carley has never even brought it up.

"Mom."

"Hmm?" She snaps out of her reverie to see Carley gesturing at the empty kneeler.

"It's our turn."

As she sinks down and makes the sign of the cross, Jen finds herself on eye level with the fragrant bouquet of Stargazer lilies, positioned on the floor directly in front of the coffin.

They must be from someone who also knew Nicki well enough to be aware that bright pink was her favorite color.

Jen finds herself looking down at the florist's card to see who that might be, and is surprised to see that the signature reads only, *A friend*.

Who, Jen wonders, sends funeral flowers without putting a name on the card?

Particularly an elaborate bouquet of distinct blooms as these.

Enveloped in the scent, she again balks at the powerful memory trying to work its way into her consciousness. She hasn't allowed herself to give that unpleasant incident more than a passing thought in years. And now, twice in one day . . .

No. Don't let it in.

Pushing it away once again, she bows her head and closes her eyes, losing herself in silent prayer.

Afterward, she and Carley make their way over to sign the guest book lying open on a nearby stand.

"You can sign for both of us, Mom." Carley plucks a fresh tissue from a strategically placed box and wipes her red, swollen eyes. "I'm going to go find a ladies' room."

"Do you want me to come with you?"

"No thanks."

She watches Carley, with her head bent, weave her way through the crowd, then turns glumly to the guest book. After signing their names on the page, she scans the signatures above to see if her parents have already come and gone.

Just a few lines up, a name jumps out at her.

Michael Morino.

Startled to see it, she glances around, wondering what he's doing here.

He knew Debbie, of course, back in the old days, and not just because he and Jen were dating. Mike played sports for Cardinal Ruffini, and Debbie was on the Sacred Sisters squad that provided cheerleaders for the teams at the boys' school.

Jen herself hasn't seen Mike in . . . what? Twenty years? Twenty-five?

Not since they broke up that final time, right before she met Thad.

Is he still here?

She furtively checks out every tall, broad-shouldered man in the room who might possibly be Mike, wondering whether she'd even recognize him—and vice versa. After all, they're older, and—

Whoa. There he is, standing off to one side talking to Glenn Cicero. The two of them were good friends back in the old days.

Glenn looks every bit the middle-aged man, jowly with a scant fringe of graying hair around his ears.

But Mike hasn't changed a bit—dammit. It would have been somehow satisfying to see him balding with a beer gut. Instead, he's lean and handsome as ever, with a full head of dark hair that's shorter than it used to be. There's just enough wave in it to remind her of the days when she'd playfully— or passionately—run her fingers through it.

About to turn away before he spots her, she hears a voice calling, "Genevieve? Genevieve Bonafacio, is that you?"

Everyone in the vicinity—including Mike Morino—turns to look at her.

No one ever calls her by her given name these days, unless she's at her parents' house, surrounded by family. Even then, her sisters usually call her Jen, just as she refers to them by their American nicknames.

Which mildly offends their mother, because, as she says, "It's not like we're right off the boat. You girls are third-generation Americans! I gave you beautiful Italian names to celebrate your roots, and you have nothing to be ashamed of."

Jen and her sisters have long given up trying to convince their mother that it's not a matter of shame; it's a matter of convenience. It's much simpler to go through life as Jen, Bennie, Frankie, Jessie, and Maddie than as Genevieve, Benedetta, Francesca, Giuseppia, and Madonna.

"I thought that was you! I'd know you anywhere!"

"Marie!" Forgetting Mike, Jen finds herself face to face with a woman she hasn't seen since she was, what? Fourteen? Fifteen?

Yes—Carley's age.

And Nicki's age.

It's as if a taut bungee cord has jerked Jen back to the sickening reality of the present.

This is a wake. Nicki's wake.

Caught up in nostalgia for childhood innocence unmarred by senseless tragedy, her own and Carley's, Jen is once again on the brink of dissolving into a puddle of emotion.

"It's so good to see you after all these years, honey, but not like this. Not like this." Marie Bush pulls her into a bear hug.

Years ago, she was a frequent substitute teacher at Sacred Sisters and gave piano lessons to all the kids in the neighborhood. Everyone adored her, parents and daughters alike—even Debbie, who didn't see eye-to-eye with many teachers.

But it was impossible not to get along with bighearted Marie, an attractive woman with stylishly short blond hair, big blue eyes, and a hearty laugh.

Pulling back to look at her, Jen says to Marie exactly what she'd just been thinking about Mike: "You haven't changed a bit!"

"Thank you, honey. I'm in the herbal nutrition business now. Keeps me looking young. Feeling young, too."

"You don't teach piano anymore?"

"A little bit on the side. In fact"—she lowers her voice, shaking her head sorrowfully—"I had just started with Nicki this past fall."

Nicki was taking piano lessons? Debbie never told her that—nor did Carley. Suddenly, the recent rift between the girls seems even wider.

She remembers Carley mentioning that the Oliveras had bought a baby grand piano right around the time school got out—an eighth-grade graduation gift for Nicki.

"Wow—that's some present."

Jen and Thad had gotten Carley a pair of birthstone earrings and a bookstore gift card that was ostensibly from Emma, who, when Jen showed it to her ahead of time, declared it a lousy gift. She wanted to know what Jen was going to get for Carley to give her in return when it was *her* turn to graduate from eighth grade, because—"just saying, Mom"—she didn't like to read and would much rather get cash.

Carley loved the bookstore gift card and the earrings, and she didn't seem to resent that Nicki's graduation gift was far more extravagant than her own. She was used to the fact that money never seemed to be an object in the Olivera household. Andrew and Debbie were always buying expensive cars, artwork, the latest electronic gadgets.

"You should hear this piano, Mom," Carley said last June. "Nicki played it for me."

"I didn't know she plays."

"Just the bottom part of 'Heart and Soul.' But it sounds so much better on their piano than on ours."

Not surprising. The Archers' old upright hasn't been tuned since they got it.

Marie Bush looks over at the coffin, takes a deep breath, exhales heavily. "I just can't believe this happened."

"Neither can I."

Marie pats her arm.

For a moment, they're both silent, but comfortably so, with Marie's graceful piano-playing fingers resting on Jen's arm.

"What are you up to now, Genevieve? You're not still living here in the neighborhood, are you?"

"No, we're down in Woodsbridge. I'm married and we have two girls. My oldest, Carley, is—*was* a close friend of Nicki's."

Past tense is appropriate in more than one way.

"She was a nice girl. So talented. I never in a million years imagined that she could possibly . . ." Marie trails off, the four earrings dangling from her double-pierced ears swaying rapidly as she shakes her head.

"You know, my daughter Carley took piano lessons for a while," Jen says spontaneously, needing to change the subject lest she find herself on the verge, again, of erupting in tears. "I always thought she had a natural talent for it. If you're still teaching, maybe I should look into lessons again."

"Give me a call," Marie says promptly, reaching into her bag. "Here's my card. No pressure if she's not interested."

"I think it might be good for her."

God knows Carley's self-confidence and her spirits could use a lift, and it would be so nice if she found something at which she could excel.

"I give lessons in Woodsbridge on Friday afternoons,"

Marie tells her. "I'm usually booked solid, but I might be able to—oh."

Seeing the realization in her eyes, Jen easily reads her mind: Now she'll have a vacant slot available. Nicki's slot.

"Hi, Marie."

They both turn to see that Mike Morino has come up beside them.

"Michael." As Jen watches Marie embrace him just as fervently as she had Jen, he shoots a sidelong glance in her direction.

She shifts her own gaze uncomfortably. Though it was great chatting with Marie again after all these years, she wishes she had beaten a hasty retreat before Mike spotted her. Now she's stuck, and she isn't in the mood to make small talk with him, of all people.

There was a brief time, years ago—after Mike dumped her but before Thad came along—when she would have given anything to run into him somewhere and reconnect. After all, if you've spent years of your life loving, and gradually losing, somebody, you tend to crave some kind of closure. But God knows she's long past needing it at this point.

So, no, she doesn't want to talk to Mike right now, or ever.

All she wants is to take Carley home.

She looks around to see if her daughter has returned, but there's no sign of her.

I'll say a quick hello, she promises herself, *and then I'll go find Carley and get out of here.*

"Is Taylor with you?" Marie is asking Mike, and Jen assumes she must be referring to Mike's wife. She heard through the grapevine that he married years ago, and he's wearing a thick gold wedding band.

Taylor: The name belongs to a head turner. Jen wouldn't suspect anything less from Mike. He always did appreciate beautiful girls.

He tells Marie, "Taylor's not here. She didn't know Nicki."

"Genevieve's daughter was a friend of hers." Marie gestures at Jen.

At last, Mike looks directly at her, and she's bombarded with memories. Mostly about how much she once cared about him—and what a jerk he turned out to be.

How on earth did it take her so long to figure that out? His character—or lack thereof—is so obvious now. She's spent less than a minute in his company and can't miss the hint of self-importance in the air. Any longer, any closer, and it would be as sickening as the scent of those Stargazers, which only serve as further reminder of his cruel streak—especially now that her own daughter has been victimized by mean-spirited teenage bullies.

"Jen," he says with an outstretched arm, "it's good to see you again."

"You too," she lies, and goes to shake his hand. Instead, he clasps hers and gives it a lingering squeeze.

"So you two know each other? I was about to introduce you."

"We're old friends," Mike tells Marie, still looking at Jen. "How have you been?"

"Fine. You?"

"Fine."

Right. That covers twenty years' worth of life: *fine*.

"You're in Woodsbridge now?"

Surprised he knows, she nods.

"Debbie mentioned that."

How in the world, Jen wonders, did Debbie have the presence of mind—much less the inclination—to discuss her with Mike today?

Unless . . .

What if it wasn't today? What if the two of them have been in touch all along?

Why would they be? They weren't connected back in the

old days other than having met through Jen, and of course when Debbie cheered at his games.

If they did stay in touch—or even run into each other, years later—then why wouldn't Debbie have mentioned it to Jen, even just in passing?

It's a strange thought, and one that doesn't sit well for some reason.

But it would explain why Mike is here at the wake—unless, of course, it's sheer ghoulish nosiness. Jen wouldn't put that past some people she's met in her lifetime, but Mike? He doesn't go out of his way for many reasons—and morbid curiosity doesn't strike her as a likely one.

But you don't know him now, she reminds herself. *You only knew him when. People change. He might be different now, in a lot of ways.*

Catching him furtively checking out a quietly weeping woman in a snug-fitting black dress, something tells her that he's not.

"Hi, Marie," someone—Bob Witkowski, the locksmith—calls, beckoning her over to where he's standing with a group of neighborhood pals.

"I'm going to go say a quick hello to Bob," she tells Jen and Mike. "His daughters are my pupils. I'll be right back."

Jen wants to grab on to her and make her stay, or slip away along with her, but instead she's left alone with Mike Morino.

"She great, isn't she?"

"Marie?" Jen nods vigorously. Of course Marie is great. Everyone knows that. Everyone has always known that. Everyone thinks Marie is great, so . . .

I have to go, she thinks, but somehow, she can't verbalize the sentence.

"She teaches piano to Taylor."

"Oh . . . that's nice." For someone who's always been an expert conversationalist, she's having a hell of a time today.

"She's been taking lessons with Marie for about five years now, since middle school."

Oh. So either he's a cradle robber in addition to being an arrogant jerk, or Taylor is his daughter, not his wife.

"That's nice," Jen says again.

"She's pretty good."

Don't you dare say that's nice, Jen warns herself and instead asks, "How old is she?"

"Probably late sixties, maybe early seventies, but she doesn't look a day over forty-five, does she?"

Jen blinks. "What?"

"Oh . . . I thought you meant Marie." He grins. "No, I didn't think that, actually. I was just trying to break the ice with a joke."

She forces her mouth to quirk in vague semblance of a smile. "Good one."

"Taylor is seventeen going on eighteen. And she doesn't look a day over twenty-five," he adds wryly. "It's not easy being the father of a teenage girl when you were once a teenage boy yourself and you remember exactly what they have on their mind at all times."

Well, it's not easy being the grown woman who was once the teenage girl on Mike Morino's mind, either.

I have to go. I have to go.

Just say it.

Mike reaches into his pocket and holds something out to her. His wallet?

Oh. There's a section of vinyl inserts; he's showing her a photo of his daughter.

"That's Taylor."

Jen nods at the headshot of a drop-dead gorgeous brunette who does appear considerably older than seventeen. "She looks like you."

"Everyone says that. She looks like me, but she acts like

her mother. In other words, she's high maintenance." He puts his wallet away. "At least she's at an all-girls high school."

"Which one?" She guesses Griffin.

"Sisters. Your alma mater. She's a senior."

Sisters?

It probably shouldn't surprise her. After all, Mike attended Cardinal Ruffini in the same little corner of the world—a world that suddenly feels *too* small.

Don't, Jen warns herself. *Don't mention Carley, that she goes there.*

But then he asks, "So you have a daughter, too?"

"Did Debbie tell you that?"

"Marie just did, remember?"

Jen thinks back over the conversation, her mind clouded by grief and exhaustion. Now is not the ideal time to be getting reacquainted with her ex-boyfriend.

"She said your daughter was a friend of Nicki's," Mike clarifies, "but actually, Debbie has mentioned it before, too."

"You and Debbie . . . so you're in touch these days? Is that . . . through Marie?"

It makes sense, now that she thinks about it. Maybe they've run into each other at their daughters' piano recitals.

"Actually, I've been in touch with Marie all along. I mentioned her to Debbie when she got the baby grand for her daughter—you know she got her a baby grand, right? Last year, for graduation?"

Of course I know that. But why do you?

At Jen's nod, Mike goes on, "Deb said she'd always wanted Nicki to take lessons . . ."

Deb. As if they're so close.

Are they?

" . . . but she thought it was too late for her to start. I told her it's never too late."

The words, given the circumstances, fall flat and hard

between them. Mike's dark eyes cloud over and flick in the direction of the casket, then back at Jen.

"This is bad," he says, puffing his cheeks and exhaling loudly. "Really, really bad."

Yeah. Understatement of the year.

"Poor Deb. With something like this, for anyone who's left behind, there's never going to be closure."

Closure. He's talking about closure. The irony doesn't escape Jen.

"I wonder," she says without thinking, "whether she left a note."

Mike jerks his gaze away from hers abruptly. "No."

"No . . . what?"

"I don't think she did."

"Leave a note? How do you know that?"

"I just . . . I heard." Before she can ask him to elaborate, he goes on, "How is your daughter taking it?"

"Not well." Worried anew about Carley, she adds, "I'd better go find her."

"It was good seeing you again."

"You too," she lies.

"You look great, Jen," he lies.

No, you look great, Mike.

Not a lie.

But she curbs the impulse to say it, or anything other than "Thanks," before hurrying away to find Carley.

Entry from the marble notebook

Tuesday, January 7, 1986

Today is Adrian's birthday.

I took the long way home from school to stop at Sgaglio's and get a package of Hostess cupcakes. This time they didn't have orange—Adrian likes the orange—so I got chocolate. The price has gone up since last year, and I didn't have the extra nickel, but Mr. Sgaglio told me not to worry about it. He's always nice to me, and it makes me wonder why his daughter turned out so nasty. Lynnette Sgaglio is the one who told me someone had spit in my lunch a few years ago after I had eaten it, and it made me throw up right there in the cafeteria, and they all laughed like it was the most hilarious thing they'd ever seen.

Adrian seemed a little disappointed when he saw that the cupcake wasn't orange, but he hugged me anyway. I had saved the birthday candle from last year, and I stuck it into the cupcake and lit it. I sang to him and he made a wish—the same wish as last year, he said. And then he told me that sometimes, he pretends I really am his mother, and he wanted to know if maybe that was really the truth.

I told him that Mother is really his mother. I told him all about when he was born—how no one ever told me she had a baby in her belly, and I just thought she was getting really fat. And then one day, I came home from school and I thought the house was empty and I found blood in the bathroom—not a lot, but it was smeared by the bathtub and I got really scared.

I didn't tell Adrian that part.

I just told him how I ran through the house looking for her, and I found her in her bed, with this tiny little baby. And how surprised and thrilled I was when she told me it was my new baby brother. And how I called him my little angel right from that moment on.

I didn't tell him how at the time, I didn't think anything of the fact that she delivered him right here at home, all alone in the house, while I was at school and Father was at work—but now I know that babies are supposed to be born in hospitals, and kids are supposed to be told that they're on the way so that they can prepare to be big sisters.

It doesn't really matter, does it?

All that matters is that Adrian was born. He's the only good thing in my life.

Chapter 8

On Thursday afternoon, chin resting morosely in her hand, Carley watches Mr. Sterne walk up and down the aisles handing back test papers.

The classroom windows are open for the first time since October, but at this time of year, that's more unsettling than pleasant. The weather is oddly warm for March; the sky has taken on the ugly yellowish-purple tint of an angry bruise, and there's a strong wind blowing from the southwest, gusting every so often to drown out the rhythmic dripping of melting snow.

Carley's thoughts are on Nicki.

That's all she's been able to think about the past few days: Nicki taking a knife and slicing open her veins.

Did she feel anything when it happened?

Was there excruciating pain?

A split second of regret?

How long did it take her to die?

Is her spirit still alive somewhere?

Carley hasn't slept well ever since she found out. She lies in bed at night with every muscle clenched, afraid that if she allows herself to drift off, she'll have nightmares about Nicki. Being awake is just as frightening, though, when she considers the prospect of being visited by Nicki's ghost.

Yeah, that seems like a preposterous thought in broad daylight in the middle of math class . . .

But in the dead of night, alone in her room—

"All right, ladies." Mr. Sterne is back at his desk. "Please put your tests away and open your textbooks to page 223."

With a rustling of papers and pages, the others do as they're told.

Carley, realizing he didn't return her test, starts to raise her hand—then quickly lowers it as Mr. Sterne's gaze locks on hers.

"Miss Archer. See me after class."

He knows.

Her stomach gives a sickening lurch.

Somehow, he knows that she cheated.

A couple of the girls dart glances at her, and then each other. Realizing they're smirking, Carley quickly grasps the reason: they know, too.

They know, because they're behind it.

They didn't see her struggling that afternoon, overcome with grief, and take pity on her. No, they totally set her up.

How could she have let herself believe that it might be a sympathetic friend who tossed the folded note containing the answers? Of course it was the enemy. The enemy is all around her now, wherever she goes. She doesn't dare trust a soul, ever again.

Panic and nausea sweep over Carley. She's certain she's going to throw up, or pass out, or cry . . . or . . . or *die.*

I wish I could, she thinks. *I wish I could just lie down right here, right now, and close my eyes and make it all go away forever.*

Yesterday morning, the day after the funeral, Jen called Debbie to see if she needed anything.

"I don't think so." Debbie's voice was small and faraway.

"Are you sure? I can go to the store for you if you're out

of milk or bread, or I can run errands if you need me to, or just come and sit with you . . ."

"I don't think so," she repeated. "Not today."

This morning, Jen called again. This time, she didn't ask whether she could come over, just told Debbie she'd be dropping by with a jar of homemade soup and a basket of biscuits.

"I won't stay," she said, "unless you want me to."

Debbie wanted her to.

Like the Archers, the Oliveras live in a two-story Colonial on a cul-de-sac in a private development. But there are differences here, some none too subtle, courtesy of the Oliveras' higher income bracket and extravagant spending habits.

Andrew and Debbie opted for all the builders' upgrades. Their home is Georgian-style with an extra thousand square feet, a three-car garage instead of two, and a circular driveway that sweeps past the white-pillared portico. The exterior is clad in brick rather than plain old white siding.

Inside, there are crown moldings and custom window treatments; granite countertops and rich cherrywood cabinets with glass doors that reveal backlit shelves displaying china and glassware. The modern art on the walls was bought at galleries, and the furniture is heavy and expensive, each roomful purchased as a matching set.

Today, Jen notices the latest addition: the gleaming black baby grand piano Nicki was learning to play. It reminds her that just this morning, she called Marie Bush, arranging for her to come by over the weekend to meet Carley. She isn't sure her daughter will be interested in resuming piano lessons but it definitely won't hurt, after this trying week, for Carley to meet warmhearted Marie.

In the past, Jen has sat here on the rich leather couch in the Oliveras' home admiring, and sometimes even envying, all that Debbie has.

Today, facing the same framed photograph of Nicki that was displayed beside the casket, she pities her friend for what she's lost.

A wan-looking Debbie is perched on an adjacent wing-back chair, wrapped in a bright pink hoodie that belonged to Nicki.

"It still smells like her," she tells Jen, idly coiling the knotted hood cord around her fingertip, unwrapping it, wrapping it again. "Like that lotion she's always buying at Bath & Body Works, you know?"

Jen does know. Carley has the same lotion.

Like that lotion she's always buying . . .

Debbie makes it sound as though Nicki is still here.

To say, "that lotion she always bought" would imply that she's accepted that her daughter is gone forever. What would it take for her—for any mother—to make that leap to past tense?

What would it take for me?

Jen's mind returns to the dark place where it's been wandering for days now.

She pictures herself in Debbie's shoes, huddled in Carley's sweatshirt, or Emma's, mourning her lost child.

It's unthinkable, yet she can't seem to stop going there. If she closes her eyes she can all too easily see herself curled up on Carley's bed, hugging her daughter's beloved stuffed animals, feeling the soft synthetic fur against her cheek . . .

Fragmented images of her grief-stricken self are so vivid that they frighten her, seeming more like memories of something that actually happened than nightmarish flights of imagination.

What if it were one of my girls?

But of course, it couldn't have been. Neither Carley nor Emma would ever in a million years take her own life.

"I still can't believe it," Debbie says dully.

That's the most disconcerting aspect for Jen: that Debbie never saw this coming. No one did.

"She never said anything," Jen asks, "that made you worry that she might—"

"No. Never."

"Did something happen that night that might have—"

This time, Debbie doesn't interrupt her; Jen cuts herself off, sensing by the way Debbie tenses in her chair that she's entered uncomfortable territory.

She hesitates before quietly telling Jen, "She was fine when I left for dinner that night. I stuck my head into her room to tell her I was leaving, and she was video-chatting with one of her friends, laughing, happy . . ."

Debbie trails off, staring into space, and Jen bites down on her lower lip to suppress all the other questions that spring to mind.

Had Nicki been depressed lately, even if she wasn't at that particular moment?

Was she taking some kind of medication that might list suicidal tendencies as a side effect?

Had she ever attempted to harm herself before?

Who was the friend on her video chat?

Did Debbie ask whoever it was whether anything happened to upset Nicki after she left?

"I wish I could remember her that way," Debbie says with a catch in her voice, "instead of what I saw when I came home and found her . . ."

Jen swallows hard, trying to hold back her own tears for her friend's sake. Debbie hasn't yet broken down today; she said earlier that she's all cried out.

"I keep wondering," she says after a moment, "what would have happened if I had stayed home that night."

"Don't do that to yourself."

"I can't help it. I keep thinking I could have saved her, and

I have to live with that for the rest of my life, wondering . . ."

"Wondering why she did it," Jen finishes the sentence for her. "And there was no note?"

Again, the slight hesitation before Debbie answers. "No. No note."

She stares down at the pink sweatshirt cord, coiling it around her finger again.

"You were a good mom, Debbie."

The words spill easily from Jen's mouth. Maybe too easily.

Jen didn't agree with all her choices, to be sure, but still . . .

"Don't blame yourself. Please."

Debbie says nothing.

"Have you thought about talking to someone about all this?"

"You mean a shrink?"

"A therapist, or . . . I don't know, Father Peter?"

Now Debbie looks up at her, eyes flashing. "Father Peter? Nicki committed suicide, Jen. You know how the Catholic church views that. Or didn't you pay attention in theology class back at Sisters?"

"The church has modified its stance since then."

"Really? Good for the church."

Me and my big mouth, Jen thinks glumly, wishing she had stuck to what she'd told herself on the drive over: that she was coming here to listen, not to talk or ask questions.

Guilt can be a dangerous burden; she can't bear to think of Debbie blaming herself for what happened. It isn't her fault. No matter what. She and Nicki have always been close, sometimes treating each other more like sisters or friends.

Back when she and Jen were teenagers, Debbie would swear that she'd never treat her future children the way her mother had treated her. Rosemary Quattrone could be stodgy and strict—even Jen's mother thought so.

"You're so lucky," Debbie would tell Jen, "that your mom isn't breathing down your neck every second of every day."

"That's because I'm the fifth kid. She's too exhausted to breathe down anyone's neck."

But Debbie was an only child. As a teenager, she rebelled against her mother's hypervigilance with reckless behavior and sneaking around. And now . . .

Had her own permissive parenting backfired on her?

Jen hasn't seen much of Debbie since their daughters went their separate ways. She has no idea what their mother-daughter relationship was like these days; no idea what Nicki was like, whether she'd gotten into drinking and drugs or something . . .

Something, anything at all, that might explain how she could kill herself out of the blue.

Something that might set her apart from Carley and Emma, thus reassuring Jen that the tragedy that struck the Oliveras could never in a million years strike the Archers.

Mr. Sterne waits until the other girls have left the classroom, most of them tossing backward glances at Carley as they go. Some, especially Melissa Kovacs, are still smirking, a few just wear inquisitive expressions, and one—Kendra Hyde—seems to trail behind.

Carley only glimpses the sympathy in her eyes—or imagines it—for a split second before Kendra disappears into the hall, leaving her alone with Mr. Sterne.

He closes the door, snuffing the chatter and locker doors slamming out in the hall. The room is suddenly frightfully still. Carley listens to his dress shoes tapping on the tile floor as he walks over to his desk, to her own shallow breathing, and to the distinct click of the minute hand on the big black and white wall clock jumping ahead to the next number.

Mr. Sterne seems to be taking his time ruffling through

papers. She's going to be late for social studies. Though that's the least of her worries right now.

Finally, after removing a set of stapled sheets from a folder, he walks over to her desk. Without a word, he places her math test in front of her.

An enormous zero is scrawled at the top in angry red ink. "What do you have to say for yourself?"

She tries to swallow past the aching lump in her throat, shaking her head mutely.

Not waiting for her to find her voice, he says, "Your answers were copied verbatim from one of the students sitting in the row ahead, Miss Archer. Unfortunately, she is not one of the better students in this class, which always makes it easy for me to spot a cheater."

No! she wants to protest. *That isn't how it happened! I didn't copy off Wanda!*

She knows that's whom he's talking about: Wanda Durphy, a lump of a girl who plods dismally through academics—and life itself.

Mr. Sterne goes on, not naming names, "Every mistake that student made was reflected on your own test. She failed miserably with a 58. You failed with a zero because you blatantly violated the academic honesty policy."

"But . . ."

It's true, of course. She doesn't dare tell him that she had no intention of cheating, that she didn't copy off anyone sitting in front of her, that the incorrect answers were fed to her as a malicious prank.

Does that somehow make what she did less wrong?

She deserves the zero.

Yet something spurs her to make a feeble attempt to defend herself. "How do you know I'm the one who copied the answers? How do you know it wasn't Wa— the other person?"

"Because that student sits in front of you, Miss Archer.

Do you think I wouldn't have noticed someone facing in the wrong direction long enough to copy the test of the person sitting behind her?"

She shakes her head numbly.

"Do you think I didn't notice your demeanor during the test? You weren't focused on your work. Every time I looked in your direction, you were sitting straight up, looking around."

Silence as he allows her to digest that.

Then he asks her again what she has to say for herself.

"Nothing," she whispers. "Just . . . I'm sorry."

In Debbie's kitchen—easily twice the size of Jen's large kitchen, with a restaurant-grade six-burner stove, two built-in custom wood-paneled refrigerators, and two dishwashers— Jen stirs a kettle filled with the chicken soup she brought over.

She insisted on heating up some for Debbie, who keeps shivering and probably hasn't eaten in a week.

Staring out the window at swaying bare tree branches against a dismal sky, she finds herself thinking, once again, of Mike Morino. He wasn't just at the wake on Monday afternoon; he was at the funeral the next day, too. He came alone, wearing a dark suit, and slipped into a pew a few rows ahead of the one where Jen was sitting with Thad and the girls.

Naturally Thad didn't give Mike a second glance—why would he? He wouldn't recognize him; they'd never met. For that, Jen was grateful. The day was trying enough without having to make awkward introductions, or reintroductions.

She wasn't going to spend the entire Mass thinking about Mike, about their past, about how badly things had ended between them—or worrying about running into him at Sisters now that she knows his daughter also attends the school.

Her main focus was the service, from the moment that

shiny white coffin came down the aisle, trailed by a shattered Debbie and Andrew barely able to hold each other up.

But Jen didn't miss the look Debbie threw over her shoulder when she rose shakily for the first prayer; a look that sought, and then settled on, Mike.

Jen could see only the back of his head, but she had a clear vantage of the expression in Debbie's mascara-smeared eyes when they connected. Mingling with the traumatic grief was a fleeting mixture of relief and longing—as though she had found a measure of comfort just knowing Mike was there.

It was in that disconcerting moment that Jen first suspected something might be going on between the two of them. The more she's thought about it over the last forty-eight hours, the more certain she's become.

Mike wears a wedding band, but he always was a cad—he'd proven that years ago. And Debbie's marriage is anything but rock-solid.

Does it honestly matter, in the grand scheme of things, if they're having an affair?

Debbie lost a child. Now isn't the time to judge her. She's bearing more than enough guilt over her daughter's death.

Jen supposes that's only natural, and yet . . .

There's something else.

Staring down at the pot of bubbling soup, she thinks back to Monday.

Mike mentioned, at the wake, that Nicki hadn't left a suicide note. When she pressed him for more information, he stammered and acted cagey.

Then, a short time ago in the living room, when Jen asked Debbie about a note, she, too, suddenly seemed evasive.

What—if anything—does that mean?

It means it's none of your business, she reminds herself, and turns down the flame on the burner. *It means that as usual, you're tempted to overstep your bounds. If there's more to the story, and Debbie wanted you to know, she would have told you.*

With a sigh, she opens a drawer to get a spoon and finds herself staring at an assortment of kitchen knives. This, she knows, is where Nicki found the blade she used to slit her wrists. She grabs a spoon, slams the drawer shut, and opens a cupboard door to get a bowl.

On one shelf is a bottle of ear infection drops prescribed to Nicole Olivera; on another, the familiar refillable bright pink water bottle Nicki carried back and forth to day camp every day a few summers ago. Carley went to the same camp; they carpooled together. Jen would sit behind the wheel and smile to herself as the girls talked about how they'd be counselors together when they got to high school.

"I'd want us to be assigned to the elementary school boys," Nicki would say, "because they'd want to play kickball all day long and we'd get a lot of exercise so we wouldn't get fat."

"No way, Nicks! I hate kickball! I'd rather have the kindergarten girls. We could sit on the picnic tables and teach them how to braid friendship bracelets the way we did when we were little."

So many plans will never come to fruition . . .

So many memories pop up at every turn . . .

Eyes brimming with tears, Jen takes a bowl from the cupboard and a ladle from a drawer.

"Debbie," she calls, "come on in here and have some soup."

No reply from the next room.

"Deb?"

After a few more moments of silence, Jen turns down the flame and goes to investigate.

The living room, where she left Debbie, is empty. There's no sign of her on the first floor. Jen goes to the stairs. "Debbie?"

Reassured by a muffled response from upstairs, she hesitates, staring at the framed gallery of Nicki's eight-by-ten school photos diagonally lining the wall above the steps. Should she go up? Or does Debbie want to be alone right now?

Maybe I should just leave.

But what if she wants me to stay?

"Deb, are you all right?"

Stupid question.

Shaking her head, Jen pushes aside her uncertainty and goes up the stairs.

In the upstairs hall, the door to the master suite is ajar. Peeking inside, she takes in the rumpled bed, drawn shades, strewn clothing. Carelessly draped over one of the bedposts is the black crepe dress Debbie wore to her daughter's funeral. The room is empty.

Down the hall Jen goes, remembering the sunny May Saturday when she was last upstairs in the Oliveras' house. She'd come to pick up Carley, who'd slept over and summoned her up to Nicki's bedroom to see her new furniture.

"Be quiet," she whispered in the upstairs hall as they passed the master bedroom door. "Mrs. Olivera is still sleeping."

Jen had to grin at that. Debbie was always claiming that she never got out of bed before noon on a Saturday. "I tell Nicki to get herself some cereal and turn on the cartoons," she told Jen when the girls were preschoolers. "I don't want to be disturbed for anything less than fire or blood."

Now, remembering what happened last Saturday morning, Jen shudders. That sunny May morning seems to have unfolded in a long-ago century, in a distant universe.

"Look, Mom, isn't it great?" Carley asked as she showed Jen around Nicki's spacious bedroom, completely redone in honor of Nicki's transition from parochial school to high school. Carley, Nicki, and Debbie had kept Jen apprised of every detail of the months-long makeover project. "Don't you love the colors?"

The bold hot pink and splashy lime green accents were straight out of Pottery Barn Teen catalog and so was the decor, complete with state-of-the-art electronics, a dorm fridge, boxy lounge seating, and a study nook.

"And look, this is my bed, right, Nicks?" Carley giddily pulled a trundle from beneath the queen-sized bed. "It's super comfortable. I wish I could sleep over again tonight."

"You can!" Nicki said.

"Can I, Mom?"

"Carley, you can't sleep here every night."

"I wish I could."

"So do I." Nicki looked wistful.

"Well, you guys can be roommates when you get to college."

"But Mom, that's not going to happen until, like, forever!"

Now, as she peeks into Nicki's beautiful bedroom, Carley's words come back to haunt Jen.

It's not going to happen, *ever.*

Debbie is sitting on the bed hugging a fuchsia throw pillow between her knees and her chest. She looks up, and the ravaged expression in her eyes triggers more tears in Jen's.

"I heated up the soup . . ."

Debbie just gives a little shake of her head as though she doesn't have the strength to speak. She sits silently stroking the fringe on the pillow, staring off into space again.

Jen lingers despite feeling as though she's violating a private moment, not wanting to leave her friend alone unless she requests it.

If I left and she—if anything happened, I would never forgive myself.

Does she really think Debbie, sitting here in her dead daughter's room, is going to do what Nicki did?

Her gaze drifts around the room, from the bed with the trundle—Carley's trundle—tucked out of sight to the desk cluttered with open texts, notebooks, and an open laptop as though Nicki might show up any second to finish her homework.

Following Jen's gaze, Debbie says dully, "She was supposed to be doing her homework. She was failing earth science and I made her promise she wouldn't wait until Sunday night to study for the test she had Monday morning."

Jen nods, knowing Debbie is talking again about Friday night, perhaps remembering the very last conversation she had with her daughter.

Spying a book lying on the hutch shelf above the desk, Jen can't help but recoil when she reads the title on the binding.

The Virgin Suicides.

Her old book club read the novel years ago, and she dimly recalls that it was about five teenage sisters who killed themselves.

Before she can digest the perhaps noncoincidental irony of its presence here, her cell phone rings in the back pocket of her jeans.

She apologizes to Debbie, pulling it out and checking the caller ID.

The area code is local, but she doesn't recognize the number.

"Deb, I'll be right back. I'll just . . ."

Her friend doesn't even glance in her direction as she slips out into the hallway with the phone, walking toward the stairs so that her conversation won't disturb Debbie's mournful reverie.

"Hello?"

"Mrs. Archer?"

"Yes?"

"This is Kirk Newcomb, the principal at Sacred Sisters. I'm afraid we need you to come right over here."

Her heart stops.

Carley.

Something's happened to Carley.

A grim realization takes hold: this is why Jen hasn't been able to stop envisioning herself in Debbie's shoes; why her imagined grief has seemed so real—not as if it were a memory after all, but some kind of premonition.

Dear God.

Her liquid legs give out and she sinks down onto the top step.

"Is Carley . . . ?"

"She's been suspended, Mrs. Archer."

Swept by intense relief that the message isn't the one she was dreading, Jen fails to grasp the one that's been delivered.

All she can think is that Carley is alive.

She crosses herself. *Thank you, God.*

"Mrs. Archer?"

"I'm sorry . . . I was just . . . you're sure she's all right?"

Kirk Newcomb clears his throat. "She most definitely is *not* all right. I think you've misunderstood. Your daughter has received a mandatory suspension for violating school policy."

Suspended . . .

Carley?

"There must be some mistake. Are you talking about Emma?"

There's a pause. "Emma?"

Wait—of course he isn't talking about Emma. Emma doesn't go to Sacred Sisters; she goes to Saint Paul's.

But . . .

"I'm sorry," she tells the principal. "Emma is her sister. I was just . . . I mean, Carley couldn't have been suspended. She's not—"

"Mrs. Archer." His voice is firm, cutting her off. "We

need you to come over here right away. Carley *has* been suspended. She's in serious trouble."

Serious trouble.

Suspended.

And yet, she's alive. Whatever has happened to her at school, whatever she's done—no, whatever they mistakenly *think* she's done—Jen is certain can be easily cleared up.

"What happened, exactly, Mr. Newcomb?"

"Carley breached the school's code of ethics. We take that very seriously here."

The idea of conscientious, rule-follower Carley breaching the code of ethics is so preposterous that she wonders if the principal has her mixed up with another student.

But before she can ask, she hears a phone line ringing in the background, and Kirk Newcomb abruptly informs her that he has to take another call.

"All right, I'll be there as soon as I can," she tells him, and hangs up, thoughts spinning.

There's no way, absolutely no way that—

"Is everything okay?"

Startled, she looks up to see Debbie in the hallway behind her. Struck anew by her haggard appearance and the anguish that radiates from her, Jen nods.

"Everything is okay."

Everything that matters, anyway, she thinks as she gets to her feet.

Entry from the marble notebook

Wednesday, January 22, 1986

Father saved my life tonight.

I hate him for it. Mostly, because it meant I had to endure him touching me. I don't want him touching me, ever, for any reason. Not even to save my life. Although maybe if he were going to TAKE my life instead of save it—like, by strangling me—then I'd want him to touch me, just that one last time, just to kill me. Because if he kills me, I don't go to hell. He does. Jail first, then hell.

What happened was, I almost choked to death because there was a storm a few days ago, and the cellar flooded again, and the power went out. Well, really, I almost choked to death because of Mother. For dinner tonight, she made meat from the cellar freezer. It had thawed, and it smelled bad. I didn't want to eat it. I told her it might be contaminated, that it might make us sick, especially Adrian, because he's so little. But she forced me to eat it, just grabbed me and forced my mouth open and started shoving big hunks of meat into it. She was screaming, "Chew! Swallow! Eat it! Eat it!" like a crazy woman.

She IS a crazy woman. He may be pure evil, but she's pure evil AND insane.

A piece of meat got lodged in my windpipe, and I

couldn't breathe, I couldn't make a sound. The weird thing is, you'd think your instinct would be to fight to stay alive, and mine was . . . well, when I looked at my baby brother, I did want to stay alive, but only for him. He was so scared, looking at me with those big eyes. But then Mother told Father to do something— "Give her the Heimlich!" she kept shouting—and he came toward me and in that split second, I didn't want to stay alive anymore. It flashed into my mind that it could be over—that it was almost over, I was almost there, and it wasn't going to be so bad. Dying, I mean. Being dead.

But he came up behind me and he wrapped his arms around me and I could smell his tobacco and sweat and I swear I would have given anything to die. I tried to get away, I really did, but he wouldn't let go and then he squeezed me and the meat came flying out of my throat and I could breathe again. I probably could have talked again, too, except—I didn't want to. So I pretended I couldn't when Mother said, "Don't you even thank your father for saving your life?" When I didn't say a word, he said, "Don't worry, you can thank me later."

I ran straight to the bathroom and threw up. If only I could find a way to—

I have to close now. I'm in my room, and I can hear him coming down the hall.

I truly wish they had let me die.

Chapter 9

A mid-life crisis car. That's what I need, Al Witkowski thinks as he turns the corner onto Redbud Street late Thursday night.

Yeah. Something fast and sporty, like a Mustang or a Jaguar.

If Al had a car like that, the woman upon whom he'd just spent two hundred bucks for a fancy dinner at Salvatore's Italian Gardens would be coming home with him for a nightcap, instead of heading in the opposite direction.

It was a blind date—sort of. They'd met through the online matchmaking service someone had suggested to him. He's made connections with quite a few women over the past couple of months, but no one he wanted to see more than once—or, if he did, it wasn't mutual.

When he got to the restaurant tonight, his date was waiting for him. Marianne was a businesswoman—a big plus since Al is looking for a classy woman this time around. Someone the complete opposite of his ex-wife, whose heavy eyeliner and bleached blond hair he found much more alluring two decades ago when he accidentally got her pregnant. That was before all the body ink she started adding when she turned thirty. Ugh.

There was no way in hell Marianne had a tattoo hidden

under her prim gray skirt suit. That was another plus. He found her to be attractive enough, though—here came the negative—she was at least forty pounds heavier than in the photos he'd seen, and those didn't exactly show a slender woman to begin with.

The extra weight seemed less unappealing, though, as the evening wore on and the wine flowed.

Marianne seemed interested in him throughout dinner, and agreed to come to his place for a nightcap. But when they got outside and she spotted his old pickup truck, still sporting a big dent in the fender from where the street plow sideswiped it on Tuesday morning, she changed her mind.

Probably just as well.

Even if Al had convinced her to follow him over here, Marianne probably wouldn't have ventured into his small apartment above Chimera's Dry Cleaning. A woman like her in a place like that? No way.

He never thought it would come to this: living in a hole-in-the-wall, driving a dented piece-of-crap truck he can't afford to fix, his business flailing in the lousy economy, never seeing his son, who's in the army and stationed in Germany, or his daughter, married young and living in a Florida trailer park . . .

"It could be worse," his brother Bobby invariably says when he complains.

"Yeah? How?" Al always asks, even though he knows the answer. Bobby got all his stale wisecracks from their father.

"You could be dead."

Dead is about as bad as things can get. But life—at least as Al knows it right now—is just barely a step above.

If I could just find someone to share it with . . .

"Get a dog" was his brother's advice. Al ignored it.

But for Christmas, Bobby went and got him a puppy.

"Now you'll have someone to talk to," he said as the little mutt licked Al's stubbly chin.

"But not someone who can talk back to me."

"Trust me—that's not a bad thing" was his brother's reply. Bobby is long-married with three daughters.

Al named the puppy Roscoe. Having a dog does help with the loneliness, but it's not enough. He needs more.

Female companionship wouldn't make the rest of Al's problems magically disappear, but it would sure put a smile on his face for a change.

So he keeps putting himself out there. Chatting with women on Internet dating sites, on bar stools at happy hour, in the produce department at Wegman's—wherever, whenever he gets a chance.

The problem is, he's not the handsome man he was in his youth, not even when he shaves and puts on a nice dress shirt and shiny shoes. The women who would bother to give him a second glance aren't his type. They're the type who wear bifocals and Buffalo Bills sweatshirts, their curly hair cut short and their bright blue denim jeans cut short as well, riding slightly too high above their white rubber gym shoes.

Where, Al wonders, do you go to meet someone with looks, style, personality, and a solid career who wouldn't stick her nose in the air at a blue-collar guy who's a little worse for wear? Preferably a nice Catholic girl who lives right here in Buffalo; someone whose attitude, when it comes to marriage and babies, is been-there, done-that; someone old enough not to have kids still at home and young enough not to be a doting grandma . . .

Someone like Sandra Lutz.

Oh, Sandra . . .

He'd had a crush on her since they were kids growing up in this neighborhood. She was known as Snobby Sandy back then, in part because her father worked not in the local factories but as a dentist, and in part because she gave off a hint of sophistication even then. Her aloofness didn't bother

Al, though. It set her apart from the usual gaggle of gossipy, giggly girls.

For years, Al tried to work up the courage to ask her out. By the time he finally did, after she'd graduated from Fordham and moved back home, it was too late. She smiled and showed him the engagement ring on her left hand, and that was that. A few months later, he became the groom at a shotgun wedding.

He and Sandra lost track of each other for years as they dealt with the serious business of being married and raising kids. But eventually the kids were grown and she got her real estate license and he started running into her around the neighborhood again. By then he was divorced, she was divorced . . . he could have sworn it was meant to be.

He was wrong.

Not a day goes by that Al doesn't think about what happened to her.

It was such a shame . . .

The last time he saw her, he was personally overseeing a job she'd hired his company to do: emptying out the big old mansion around the corner on Lilac Street, directly behind his rented apartment.

The Addams House, they always called it back in the old days.

"Did you ever take a dare and sneak inside?" Sandra asked when he met her there on a long-ago summer day to give her an estimate for the moving and storage.

"Sure—how about you?"

"No. I was always too chicken. I thought it was haunted."

"You believe in that stuff?"

"Don't you?"

"Nah."

Ironic—there he was, acting all macho, when really he was too chicken to even ask her out. Every time he saw her, he tried to work up the nerve, but it was just like when they were kids. He kept beating around the bush, and the next thing he knew it was too late . . .

But this time, not because she was married.

This time, for good.

Sandra's death was a damned shame.

Every time Al looks out the back window of his apartment and glimpses the mansard roofline looming above the treetops on the next block, he's zapped with a bolt of regret, thinking of her and what might have been.

Too bad I can't move out of this neighborhood, or at least off the block, so I could get away from all this shoulda coulda woulda.

But the rent here is all he can afford, thanks to the economic situation and his lousy ex-wife.

"Guess she really took you to the cleaners—literally," Bobby likes to crack. He can be an insensitive jerk sometimes.

Al sighs. Time to put his latest romantic mishap behind him. Right now all he wants is to take Roscoe out for a few minutes, then sit on the couch, catch the tail end of the Sabres game, and drink a beer.

About to pull into the curbside spot where he usually parks, he thinks better of it. He probably shouldn't leave the truck on the street anymore. That's just asking for trouble. It might get hit again, or someone might break into it or steal it.

Are you kidding? Who'd want this piece of crap?

But he shouldn't take chances. He doesn't have the time, patience, or money to deal with further misfortune.

He backs up and pulls into the driveway that runs alongside the dry cleaner to a small rear parking lot occupied by a couple of Dumpsters, potholes, and weeds. The landlord told him he can park back here anytime, but he never does— mainly because he'd have to walk all the way back out to the street to get to his door.

God knows he can use the exercise after all that pasta tonight.

If only he had the money, he'd join a gym, get back into shape . . .

Maybe he should start taking the puppy for real walks instead of letting him briefly nose around the weeds growing in sidewalk cracks in front of the building, encouraging him to do his business so they can get back to the couch.

Yeah, it's not a bad idea. He can start off slow, just a couple of blocks, maybe five, ten minutes, and work up to a brisk half hour or more. The extra pounds would probably melt away in no time if he did that every day.

As the high beams illuminate puddle-filled ruts, Al steers recklessly through them rather than going around. Maybe all that spattered mud will hide the dented truck body, he thinks darkly as he notices, through the trees, the familiar mansard roof of the big old house on Lilac Street.

Sandra.

If he had asked her out on that last day he saw her— which turned out to be the day before she died—would she have said yes? If she had said yes, would they have gone out that night? If they had gone out, would he have gone back to her place?

He could have died in that fire, too.

Or he could have saved her life.

Maybe they'd be married right now, and instead of renting this depressing apartment, he'd be living over on Wayside Avenue in Sandra's—

As the headlights arc across the overgrown patch of property beyond the parking lot, Al instinctively hits the brakes, startled to see something . . .

No. *Someone.*

Someone is back there.

He only has a quick glimpse before the figure disappears into the trees bordering the yard of the Addams House.

Last he knew, the place was still sitting empty, just as it had for years when Al was a kid. He's driven past it a few times and seen light glowing in the front windows, but he knows it's coming from the lamp timers Sandra set so long ago. You'd think the bulbs would have burned out by now.

Has someone changed them?

Is someone really sneaking around the yard there?

Maybe, thanks to all the cabernet he drank at Salvatore's, he's just imagining things.

Yeah—or maybe it's Sandra's ghost, back to haunt the old place—and you.

For a moment, Al sits thoughtfully rubbing the stubble on his chin, his foot still on the brake.

Come on. You don't really believe in ghosts, do you?

Nah.

Still . . .

With an abrupt shake of his head, Al pulls the truck around and leaves the parking lot, deciding to take his chances on the street after all.

Angel 770 is online.

Seeing the message bubble pop onto her laptop screen, Carley sits up straight and pushes her glasses up higher on her nose. It's about time. She was on the verge of drifting off to sleep.

That wouldn't necessarily have been a bad thing. She'd welcome any means of escaping the latest nightmare . . .

Well—almost any.

While waiting hours for Angel to show up online tonight, she had revisited the anti-bullying forum, paying particular attention this time to the many threads about suicide. She was trying to get some insight into Nicki's frame of mind before she died, but wound up relating to some of the posts herself.

Yet as miserable as Carley's life has become, she can't imagine taking that final step—crossing the line between thinking she might be better off dead, and actually doing something about it.

No, she'd never do that, because when she dies, she wants to go to heaven. Otherwise, what's the point?

QT-Pi: where have u been today?

Angel 770: y whts up?

QT-Pi: trouble

Angel 770: ???????

Carley hesitates.

Angel 770: ru ok?

QT-Pi: no suspended

Angel 770: srsly?

"Yeah. Seriously," Carley whispers glumly, suddenly wondering why she'd been so eager to discuss what had happened.

It's not as though Angel can magically make it all better. Maybe she could if she were a friend IRL—Internet shorthand for *in real life*.

If Angel were a friend IRL, she could watch Carley's back at school and eat lunch with her and choose her for her team in gym. And this Saturday night—while the rest of the world, the Sacred Sisters world, anyway, goes to Spring Fling in the Cardinal Ruffini gym—they could have a sleepover and eat junk food and watch scary movies.

But Angel is just some girl who lives a few thousand miles away, in California.

Sunny California, where Nicki used to want to live.

Yeah.

No matter how great a listener Angel is, no matter how effective her insight into Carley's problems, she's still going to vanish into cyberspace at the end of this chat and Carley's going to be left feeling more alone than ever.

Especially now that Nicki's gone.

Carley's been thinking a lot tonight about the falling out she had with her best friend. She has a feeling it wouldn't have happened if they had still been connecting daily in person, rather than just over the Internet.

It all started with a post Nicki put on Carley's Peeps page last fall, not long after school started.

OMG carls whats up with your hairrrrrrrrr, she wrote beneath a photo Carley had posted.

Stung, Carley immediately deleted the photo, along with the string of comments beneath it. There were only a couple of them above Nicki's, and they'd been posted by a couple of the Sacred Sisters girls she'd recently met.

One said, *2 cute*

Another, *luv ittttttttt*

And then there was the insult from Carley's so-called best friend.

Maybe Nicki was just jealous, she thought at first. After all, the photo showed her with Sarah Bielecki, a girl from her art class. The teacher had chosen the two of them, along with Kendra Hyde, to tape yellow and red construction paper leaves to the bare branches of the big painted tree in the hallway—a good excuse to get out of the stuffy classroom on an Indian summer afternoon.

Kendra snapped the picture with her phone and posted it on both Carley's and Sarah's Peeps pages. When Carley saw it, she was warmed by the feeling of inclusion. There she was, smiling in a photo posted by a friend instead of by Carley herself; a photo that announced to the world that she was having fun in high school, involved and fitting in.

It never occurred to her that her hair wasn't looking its best until Nicki mentioned it. Instantly humiliated, she deleted the photo before she allowed herself to take a closer look at it, then found herself wondering how bad her hair actually looked.

Maybe it was kind of limp that day—it's usually a little limp, though. And Nicki was always the one who tried to make her feel better about it.

Then again, Nicki did like to tease, and once in a while she'd say something that would hurt Carley's feelings. Never anything too harsh, though. Like, if Carley tripped over her own feet—which she does a lot, having inherited her clumsiness from Mom—Nicki would say, "Nice going, Grace."

Grace—as in graceful. As in *not*.

Carley was used to Nicki's gently kidding her about being a klutz, but not to this harsh criticism—in public, no less—of her appearance.

She promptly sent Nicki a private Peeps message: *thanks a lot*

The reply: *4 whattttttt?*

joking about my hair

o that was no joke u need to do something about it Carls its kind of hideous

Hideous?

Stung, Carley didn't reply.

Maybe that was her first mistake.

No. Maybe her first mistake was believing that her friendship with her best friend would stay the same even now that they were in high school, growing up, growing apart.

The hair comment was just the beginning.

The next one Nicki made was about her weight.

And then her skin.

it's constructive criticism carls, Nicki messaged her, after Carley deleted the latest cruel comment so that no one else would see it.

Nicki added, *this is stuff u can fix, if u rly care*

She did care. A lot. Too much.

But when she texted Nicki, asking to get together and talk about it, Nicki made excuses. Then she came right out and said it.

Well, she didn't actually *say* it.

She sent a text: *i rly dont think we have much in common nemore*

wht do u mean? Carley texted back with shaky fingers.
take the hint do you rly need me to spell it out for u?
No. Carley did not.

She got the hint.

That was sometime in early October, when she was still thinking she might eventually become friends with some of the girls at Sacred Sisters. It wasn't going to be easy, given her shyness. And she's not exactly experienced at befriending new people, having met Nicki when she was a mere toddler. They had a comfortable circle of friends throughout the parochial school years—friends who sat with them at lunch and worked folded paper fortune tellers with them at recess and invited them to playdates and birthday parties . . .

Them. Carley and Nicki were a pair, always. Where one went, the other went, and their classmates at Saint Paul's knew it.

Some of those girls moved on to Woodsbridge High with Nicki; others scattered to Catholic schools. Not Sacred Sisters, though. It's too out of the way for most South Towns kids.

Why didn't Mom realize that was going to be a problem?
Why didn't I?

How was Carley supposed to make new friends at a school where no one lived in—or even near—her neighborhood? It wasn't like she could walk home with the other girls after school or stop over on weekends, even if they were friendly—and, hard as it is to remember, some were, sort of, at the beginning of the school year.

Still, back in the fall—when Nicki dumped her—making new friends wasn't out of the question, either.

Not then. Not yet.

That was before the second phase of Carley's troubles began, with the bullying at school and online.

So what is this, then? Phase three? Getting suspended for cheating?

How much more, Carley wonders, *can I take before . . .*

Before what?

What are you going to do?

There's nothing to do, except force herself to get out of bed every morning and go through the motions of another day . . .

Right?

She swallows hard, trying not to think of Nicki, who obviously concluded there was another choice after all.

come on meet me just for 2 secs

Reading Gabe's latest text on her phone, Emma takes a screen shot of the text so that she can show it to Bridget at school tomorrow, then texts back wickedly, *sex?*

Of course she knows *secs* is short for *seconds*. But she can't resist flirting with him and holds her breath for the reply, which comes quickly.

sounds good!

Wow. He's interested in her, all right. Too bad she can't do anything about it right now.

told u i cant

y not?

Martha is still up

Martha would be Martha Stewart—otherwise known as Mom.

Gabe has been calling her Martha Stewart—in a derogatory way—ever since the other day, when he found out she bakes cookies from scratch.

Emma found herself wishing she had a normal mother—the kind who works full-time and buys Oreos—or maybe even no mother at all, like Gabe.

She's not sure if his mother left him and his dad or is dead, but either way, she's out of the picture. And Gabe's father is never home. Which means Gabe gets to come and go as he pleases.

Emma, on the other hand, is a prisoner in her room at the moment. On a normal night, Mom would have gone to bed hours ago. But it's long after midnight and she's still downstairs in the family room, watching television.

still up? is Gabe's reply. *what is she a vampire?*

Emma snickers at the idea of her mother in a black cloak and fangs instead of the ratty bathrobe and pajamas she was wearing when Emma snuck downstairs to check on her about an hour ago, the first time Gabe begged her to sneak out of the house and meet him.

She was hoping to find Mom dozing, in which case she might have actually risked slipping out for a few minutes.

But her mother was wide awake, and called from the couch, "Em? What are you doing up?"

"Getting a glass of water."

"There are Dixie cups by the sink upstairs."

Duh. As if she doesn't know that. She's lived in this house fourteen years, and there have always been Dixie cups by the bathroom sink.

"I want a real glass, and the downstairs faucet is colder."

"Well, hurry up and get to bed. It's a school night."

Emma got water and made the return trip up to her room to report to Gabe that she couldn't meet him. Instead, they video-chatted for about a half hour, mostly about music.

Gabe told her he plays guitar and asked if she plays any instrument.

"Piano," Emma told him—which was stretching it. She took lessons years ago because her mother made her.

But she really wants Gabe to like her.

It seems like he does, considering that he's back again, persistently texting her about meeting him.

She thumb-types a reply to his last text: *MS is not a vampire just a PITA who wont go to bed*

? is his response.

it means pain in the—

no, he cuts in, *i mean y wont she go to bed?*

Remembering how he teased her about her cookie-baking mother and, later, about having the perfect all-American family, she writes back, *she's pissed b/c my sister F'd up bigtime @ school and got suspended for a week*

There. That should show him that her family isn't all that perfect.

SRSLY??? WAT DID SHE DOO??

Translation: *Seriously? What did she do?*

Emma's thoughts whirl.

Rather than tell him the boring truth—cheating on a math test is super lame, in the grand scheme of things—she texts, *no clue something pretty bad tho*

as bad as sneaking out of the house to meet me for sex?

She grins and writes, *You mean secs*

nope

u dont give up do u?

nope

too bad its not going to happen. not tonight anyway. how bout 2morrow?

maybe, he texts back, and then, *gtg*

Got to go.

Disappointed, she signs off, wondering why he'd ended their conversation so abruptly. It's not like his father would care that he's still up at this hour. Even when he's home, he apparently doesn't care what Gabe does.

Must be nice, Emma thinks again, slipping beneath her brown and blue comforter and leaning back against the pillows.

Her mind wanders back to Monday afternoon, when she fooled around with Gabe right here in her room, in her bed, in this very spot.

Later, when Bridget asked how far they went, Emma said, "All the way."

In truth, they didn't go *that* far. She was planning to, but then chickened out. After he left, she worried that he'd decided she's just a tease and lost interest in her.

If anything, though, it's been exactly the opposite.

Next time, Emma promises herself, *I really will go all the way with him.*

She can just imagine what her parents would do if they ever found out about that. Look at how they'd reacted to what Carley did.

Emma has to admit, she was pretty impressed when she heard what her sister did. She didn't think Miss Goody-Goody had it in her. In fact, she still doesn't quite believe it. But she eavesdropped on her parents talking and found out that apparently, Carley had admitted to cheating on the test.

Emma knocked on her bedroom door earlier, wanting to—well, not congratulate her, exactly. More like offer her some support, now that she knows her sister isn't as strait-laced as she thought.

"Go away," Carley said through the door.

"It's me, Emma."

"I know. Go away."

Emma did, annoyed. You'd think Carley would want to talk to the one person who's on her side—sort of.

Mom is always saying that someday, she and Carley will be the best of friends again, the way they were when they were little.

Maybe she'll actually turn out to be right about something for a change.

Opening the creaky door just off the kitchen, Angel is greeted by a pungent wave of musty mildew.

Ah, the cellar.

That's what they always called it when they were living in the house, as opposed to the "basement."

Back in the late seventies and early eighties, the word

"basement," in Angel's opinion, evoked pleasant images of finished rec rooms with drop ceilings and wood paneling and indoor-outdoor carpet installed over concrete floors.

But this dank, rambling cavern beneath the house, with its clammy stone walls, dirt floor, low, cobweb-draped, rudimentary ceiling beams and exposed pipe work . . . this is a *cellar*.

Angel quite understandably never spent much time there back then and hasn't lately, either.

Unfortunately, at the moment, it's a necessity.

The eighteen inches of snow that fell earlier in the week melted rapidly, seeping into the already saturated ground around the house. This flood-prone cellar that was supposed to be somebody else's problem is Angel's problem now, and has been for almost two years.

Tonight, Angel put off dealing with it as long as possible.

Just like I put off dealing with Carley . . .

But for different reasons.

Knowing Carley was going to want to talk about what happened in school today, Angel took perverse pleasure in allowing her to cool her heels for most of the evening. But when they did finally connect, it was hardly satisfying. Carley seemed distant and ended the conversation rather abruptly.

That isn't good.

One problem at a time, though.

Flashlight in hand, Angel descends the rickety cellar stairs to assess the latest flood damage, shuddering at the memory unearthed by the familiar creaking sounds and echoing drip from somewhere below.

Water rising in the cellar . . .

Mother.

The old chest freezer.

Angel stops midway down the flight, trying to grasp a thought that swoops in like a twilight bat, only to fly away again.

What is it about the freezer?

Why is the thought of it so unsettling all these years later?

If the power went out—and it often did—Mother would don the rubber waders Father used to wear for creek fishing, and she'd clump down these steps to the freezer. Angel would hear her sloshing across the floor, heaving open the heavy lid, foraging amid the wrapped packets . . .

They'd have to eat whatever had started to thaw, and it never tasted good, but—"Eat it!" Mother's voice booms.

"But the freezer was sitting in all that muddy water . . . what if it's contaminated? What if I get sick?"

"Don't be ridiculous! How many times do I have to tell you the freezer is waterproof? Now eat it or I'll force it down your throat!"

And she would, and she didn't care if you gasped and vomited and choked. One time—

With a shudder, Angel blocks out the memory.

It's all right. That was a long time ago. Mother is dead. The freezer is gone. It's time to move on.

Angel continues the descent.

The bottom tread of the stairway has been swallowed by several inches of standing water.

With a grimace, Angel steps onto it, barefoot, and then the floor.

Even if those waders were still around, I wouldn't wear them. I wouldn't touch anything that reminded me of her.

But of course, the waders are long gone. The freezer. Mother.

All gone.

Angel sloshes across in the general direction of the clogged drain, bare feet scuffing along in the mud.

Last time, it took nearly half an hour of probing around until the flat edge of the submerged metal grate was located.

I really should put some sort of marker near the drain for next time. Just a yardstick poking up out of the ground would—

"Ouch!"

Big toe stubbing into something that protrudes from the mud, Angel flails and nearly goes down with a splash.

"Dammit!"

What the hell *was* that?

Not the drain, that's for sure.

Angel reaches down into the water and feels around for the offending object.

There. There it is.

It feels like some kind of metal bar, or . . .

No, it's a handle.

A handle sticking up from the ground?

Probing the mud surrounding it, Angel's fingers encounter a flat, hard, rectangular surface buried beneath a relatively shallow top layer of mud.

It appears to be some kind of trapdoor in the floor.

So.

The old house has revealed yet another secret.

Staring down at the murky water that obscures it—for now—Angel wonders whether the contents of this compartment will prove to be as interesting as the last.

Too bad I'm going to have to wait until the water's gone to find out.

If there was a pump, or a shop vac, the water could be gone in no time. But that would mean another trip to the hardware store, and . . .

No. That's all right.

Mother always said patience is a virtue.

Then again, Mother said a lot of things—not all of them true.

Bitter memories churning once again, Angel resumes looking for the drain in the mud.

Crawling into bed in the dark beside Thad, Jen looks at the digital clock on the nightstand.

It's almost three A.M., but she's wide awake. She figures she should at least try to get a few hours' sleep, unlikely as it is that she'll manage to drift off. Until now, she's been sitting downstairs in the family room for hours, staring absently at the Weather Channel—the most inane wee-hour programming she could find—and mulling over the bizarre events that unfolded this afternoon.

As the meteorologist droned on about the freakishly warm weather that's settled over the Northeast, Jen concluded that the world as she knew it had somehow spun off its axis—not just today, but in the past couple of weeks.

Yes, somewhere along the way, she woke up to find herself inhabiting this bizarre alternate reality where her reliable, respectable daughter is blatantly cheating on tests and has become a social outcast; where that daughter's squeamish best friend, who had everything to live for, had slit her own wrists open and bled to death, leaving a shattered mother . . .

A mother who's apparently been having a secret affair with none other than Jen's own first love.

You don't know that for sure, she reminds herself as she pushes the down comforter away. Even with the windows cracked open, it's warm enough tonight with just a sheet and blanket. Too warm.

An earthy scent wafts in the air. Ordinarily Jen would welcome it as the first hint of spring, but now it brings to mind the cemetery on Tuesday. Standing beside an ominous heap of snow-crusted mud at Nicki's open grave, watching the white coffin being lowered into the ground . . .

No. Don't think about that. Think about something else. Something pleasant.

Like what? Carley getting suspended?

After a few moments of restless tossing and turning, Jen realizes that her husband, whose rhythmic, gentle snoring usually lulls her to sleep, is lying awake beside her.

"Thad?"

"Yeah."

"You're not sleeping."

"No."

For a long time, they're both silent.

Then Jen asks, "What are you thinking about?"

"One guess."

"Me too."

"I'm still having a hard time wrapping my brain around it," Thad says. "She's such a stickler for rules. She knows the difference between right and wrong."

Of course she does. But Jen herself had tried to convince her that not every rule is set in stone.

Right and wrong . . .

Black and white . . .

Did Carley decide there was gray area somewhere in the school's code of ethics and that it was okay to cheat? Is that the message she took from Monday morning's conversation?

Thad sighs. "You know, I don't think I'd believe it at all if Carley hadn't admitted it—"

But she had.

When Jen arrived at the school this afternoon, she found a stricken-looking Carley waiting for her in the receptionist's area outside the principal's office.

Jen went straight to her as the receptionist picked up the phone to tell Mr. Newcomb she'd arrived.

Carley sat stiffly within the circle of Jen's arms until she pulled back to look at her daughter's angst-ridden face. "What happened? Tell me."

"I cheated on my math test on Monday" was the straightforward—and absurd—reply.

Before a stunned Jen could ask her to elaborate, they were ushered into Mr. Newcomb's office.

The principal, a stocky, no-nonsense man whom Jen had previously only seen from her auditorium seat during last fall's school orientation, got right down to business. As he explained that her daughter had copied algebra equations off another student's paper, Carley sat quietly crying beside Jen, who kept an arm tightly around her rigid shoulders.

She scarcely believed it. Not then, and not when they got into the car to drive home and she asked Carley, once again, what really happened.

Her daughter stuck to her story, miserably explaining that she'd been feeling desperate because the clock was running down and she didn't know the answers.

"But you studied."

"Not hard enough, I guess."

When they got home, Carley went straight to her room and Jen called Thad. He asked all the questions Jen had asked of the principal and of Carley herself, and he kept asking, "But are you *sure*?"

"All I can think," Jen tells him now, "is that she was so shell-shocked by Nicki's death that she wasn't in her right mind."

"Even so . . ."

"I know."

What Carley had done was so completely out of character—and so serious—that Jen can't help but wonder if there isn't more to the story.

Just like I wonder if there's more to Debbie's story about Nicki's suicide note . . .

Or lack thereof.

In the twelve hours or so since she left the Oliveras' house, she's given that situation little thought, too wrapped up in her own troubles with Carley.

Now, however, the misgivings come rushing back and she finds herself starting to tell Thad about it, but quickly thinks better of getting into too much detail. She doesn't want to mention Mike to him right now, if only because she's suddenly exhausted—emotionally and physically. She can save the rest of the story to tell him later—or not at all.

But now that she's brought it up, Thad is curious. "So you're saying you think there really was a note, and Debbie lied about it?"

It wasn't just Debbie. And it isn't just about the note. I think she was having an affair.

"I don't know—maybe it was just my imagination," she tells him. "I just thought she seemed a little evasive when I asked her about it."

And I thought Mike Morino did the same thing when I asked him about it.

"Maybe she didn't want to discuss it. Maybe it's too painful."

"I'm sure it is. Leave it to me to ask too many questions."

Thad reaches over and finds her hand, giving it a warm squeeze. "You were being a good friend."

"I was trying."

Just like she's been trying to be a good mom.

But Carley has completely withdrawn from her, and from Thad as well. She wouldn't tell them anything more about what had happened in math class and she wouldn't come out of her room, even to eat. Jen isn't sure whether to be furious with her or feel sorry for her.

I'll figure it out tomorrow, she decides, and yawns deeply, inhaling the earthy fresh air as she rolls onto her side.

She can feel herself drifting off and welcomes the promised reprieve from the latest round of troubles . . .

She's at the funeral home again. Nicki's wake. There are bouquets of bright pink Stargazer lilies everywhere, a whole wall of them obliterating her view of the casket.

Their overpowering fragrance clogs her nostrils, making it difficult to breathe, bringing back a dim memory she tries to push back.

No, don't think about that. It was a long time ago.

Think about what's happening right now. Think about the wake. About Nicki, lying there in the casket.

As she works her way closer, she turns to ask Carley if she's all right, but somehow Carley isn't there.

Where did she go?

She was with Jen just a moment ago. They came in here together, after she picked up Carley from school.

Panic starts to sweep through her as she looks around, scanning the room filled with black-clad mourners. There are flowers, so many flowers, lilies, again their sickening sweet perfume reminding her . . .

No!

No, don't think about it. It was so mean . . .

There's Debbie, wearing her Sacred Sisters uniform beneath Nicki's hot pink sweatshirt, standing by the casket, arm in arm with Andrew . . .

Then Jen realizes that it isn't Andrew at all.

It's Mike.

"What's going on between you two?" she asks, and they start to laugh heartily, Mike and Debbie, a terrible sound that echoes through the room.

Jen covers her ears to block it out and again walks toward the casket.

In horror, she sees that it's wide open.

"My son Connor is the best in the business," Glenn Cicero is saying. "Go ahead. Look at her. Didn't he do a beautiful job?"

"He's just a little boy. How could he—"

"Connor's the best in the business," Glenn repeats, and pushes her forward. "Go on. Look."

No . . . no, it's going to be gruesome. She turns to tell Carley to stay back; again, she realizes Carley isn't there.

Where is she?

"Carley?" Jen calls, but Debbie and Mike are still laughing and the sound drowns out her voice.

Glenn gives her a hard shove toward the open casket.

She sees that something is poking out from the satin lining.

Pink synthetic fur, clutched in a waxy-looking hand . . .

"That's Bubblegum," Debbie whispers into her ear, suddenly beside her. "She sleeps with him every night, so she wanted to be buried with him."

Yes, of course.

Wait—no! No, that doesn't make sense.

Bubblegum doesn't belong to Nicki; Nicki gave him to Carley, and Carley's the one who . . .

"Go on," Glenn croons. "Look at her. She's beautiful, isn't she?"

Taking one final step toward the open casket, Jen lets out a bloodcurdling scream as the corpse's mangled head, with a worm squirming out of the eye socket, comes into view.

It isn't Nicki.

It's Carley.

Entry from the marble notebook

Sunday, February 2, 1986

This morning, when we got into the car to go to church, it wouldn't start. It turned out the battery was dead. Father said he needed to get it jumped, and he wanted to ask our next-door neighbor who was out there snow-blowing his driveway, but Mother wouldn't let him do that. She never wants us to have anything to do with any of the neighbors, or anyone, really. She told Father to call the service station and have them send someone over to jump the battery.

They didn't come for a couple of hours, and we ended up not getting to church until eleven-thirty Mass. That was way more crowded than seven o'clock Mass. We had to sit way in the back, instead of in the front row, and Mother was not happy about that.

I was happy about it, though, because guess who was sitting in the pew right in front of us?

The boy from Cardinal Ruffini, the one who was in the backseat with me the day his friend drove me home without a license after Father had his heart attack.

I stared at the back of his head through the whole Mass and I didn't even listen to a word of the sermon. Mother would have been furious, but she couldn't tell, because I'm sure she thought I was looking at the priest.

I passed him in the line as I was going up to get Communion and he was coming back. He looked right at me, but I don't think he remembers me.

I wish I knew his name.

And I wish we could go to eleven-thirty Mass every week.

Chapter 10

On Friday afternoon, the ground is still muddy from Monday's snow when Jen pokes her trowel into it and sees a fat, pinkish-brown earthworm wriggling out of harm's way.

At least she didn't bisect this one with the sharp metal edge the way she did another a few minutes ago, while trying to dig out yet another dandelion taproot. She read somewhere once that only half of the worm will die when that happens, but that didn't make her any less squeamish.

Dirt . . . worms . . .

She can't stop thinking of the cemetery on Tuesday; the heap of mud beside the yawning grave; her own nightmare.

Frustrated, she sits back on her heels and tosses the trowel aside, closing her eyes and tilting her face to the warm sun that feels more suited to May than March. The last few dirt-speckled patches of slush have melted away. The oak and elm branches have yet to bud and there's still no sign of a crocus or robin, but soon . . .

Soon this dark season will draw to a close. Not soon enough, but at least a hint of hope floats on the earthy breeze today and Jen will take it. She'll take whatever she can get; anything to absorb some positive energy.

It's useless to waste precious daylight trying to get rid of

weeds this early in the season—a job that seems futile at any
time of year. No, she's ready to move on and start planting.

She picks up the trowel again. Time to transform this
bare—other than the weeds, anyway—patch bordering the
low front shrubbery into a collage of splashy purple and
yellow blooms. Flowers can't fix everything—oh hell, they
can't fix anything—but she can't allow herself to sit around
dwelling on the drama.

Carley shouldn't, either.

It's perfect gardening weather—or so she tried to convince her daughter earlier. But Carley refused to tag along
to the nursery to buy flowering plants; refused the offer of
lunch at the Cheesecake Factory; refused to even come out
of her room.

"I'm not sure you should be encouraging that anyway,"
Thad said when Jen talked to him at noon. "She's home from
school because she's been suspended. Shopping and lunch-
ing aren't exactly punishment."

Of course not. But Jen can't help but want to coax Carley
out anyway. What happened in math class was such a devia-
tion from her ordinary behavior that there must be a logical explanation—something other than the one she gave her
parents yesterday:

"I panicked, and I was afraid I was going to fail, so I took
the easy way out."

Maybe that's part of it. But it's not the whole story.

Jen e-mailed Sister Linda this morning, asking to set up a
meeting to discuss the situation. Then she went to the nursery herself, and stopped off at church on the way home to
pray a novena to Saint Anne, the patron saint of mothers.

Kneeling in the deserted sanctuary, praying for special
graces in the strength and wisdom to ease her daughter's
troubles, she felt a sense of peace she hasn't experienced in
weeks.

I can see her through this, she thought as she stepped

back out into the beautiful spring day, rejuvenated by her plan to repeat the devotion for nine consecutive days, as she was taught back at Sacred Sisters.

She stopped at a café to buy Carley's favorite chicken parm sandwich. Only when she noticed all the fish on the specials board did she remember it was a Lenten Friday, and got the eggplant parm instead.

Carley didn't turn down the food—she must have been famished by then—but insisted on eating it in her room, alone. Her laptop was open, and she was studying.

"I have to do all my assignments," she said, "or I'll be way behind when I go back."

How could Jen argue with that? But it bothers her, seeing Carley cooped up all day in front of a screen.

After throwing on an old Buffalo Bills T-shirt and tattered jeans, she knocked once again on her daughter's door. "It's a beautiful day. If you want to take a break and get outside, I'll be in the front yard planting pansies."

"Okay."

"So you'll come out?"

"Maybe later."

She didn't really expect Carley to join her, but she can't help but be disappointed that she hasn't. Fresh air would do her good.

Oh well. At least it's doing me good.

Feeling the sun on her shoulders and inhaling the pungent scent of wet soil, Jen works the first plant out of the plastic cell pack, careful not to damage the roots.

Her mind wanders back to when the girls were little.

Pigtails, bandaged knees, molded plastic watering cans and toy trowels . . .

In those days, they both wanted to "help" Mommy with the garden, and it was a challenge to get anything done. Once, she planted an entire bed of bulbs only to have toddler Emma dig them all up again. Another time, tiny Carley surprised her with a bouquet of handpicked roses and handed them to her crying, her hands stung and bloody from the thorns.

I cried, too, that day, Jen remembers as she carefully tucks the tender little pansy into the waiting hole. *I was so touched that she'd gone through all that agony just for me*.

Her tears land in the dirt as she pats it around the plant, remembering that sweet little girl, longing for simpler times. If only she could soothe away this new pain with kisses and drugstore balm.

She rubs her wet cheekbones against one shoulder and then the other, and her streaming nose, too. She can hear a car coming up the street and hopes it's not a neighbor who will want to stop and chat. It's been quiet out here all afternoon, but now the kids will be coming home from school and their moms will be shuttling them off to dance lessons and hockey leagues and countless other activities that encompass the lives of overscheduled offspring here in postmillennial suburbia.

The car is slowing as it passes the house, tires crunching the gravelly salt left behind by the road crews in the storm.

Busily digging a new hole, Jen doesn't turn around, hoping whoever it is will just drive on. She isn't in the mood for small talk—nor is she about to tell a casual acquaintance about anything that's gone on lately.

Behind her, she hears the car pull to a stop at the curb.

Dammit.

With a sigh, she turns to see who it is. Maybe from that distance, they won't be able to see her tearstained face and T-shirt. Or maybe they will see and take the hint to drive on.

She instantly recognizes the white compact car—and, through the open window, the driver. Relief courses through her and she tosses the trowel aside, on her feet in an instant. "Frankie!"

Her sister climbs out of the car and arches her lean body

in a backward stretch with her hands clasped behind her head. Her shoulder-length wavy dark hair is pulled back in a simple headband and she's dressed in her usual uniform: jeans, sneakers, and a sweater.

Jen hurries over, about to throw her arms around her sister, then remembers—"I'm covered in dirt."

Frankie hugs her anyway. "It's okay. I'm covered in orange Chee-tos dust. I ate an entire bag on the road."

Good old Frankie. Addicted to salty crunch since they were kids, she counterbalances the junk food habit with daily exercise—running, spinning, yoga . . .

"You should try yoga," she recently urged Jen, claiming there's more to it than stretching and chanting. "It would be good for you. It quiets the mind."

"You mean the mouth?"

"I don't know if anything could quiet *your* mouth," Frankie teased. "They don't call you the Yapster for nothing."

"News bulletin: They don't call me the Yapster at all. Not anymore, anyway. Not around here."

Well, Debbie sometimes does.

Debbie . . . Nicki . . . Carley.

Right and wrong.

Black and white . . .

Black and white. Dominoes tip over in Jen's brain, and she remembers why she summoned Frankie for this weekend visit.

Tears spring to her eyes.

"You okay?" Frankie doesn't miss a thing.

"I'm just so glad to see you. It's been kind of . . . hard lately. I've been feeling kind of alone in all this. I really need you."

"Aw." Frankie gives her another hug, and Jen sees tears on her cheeks, too.

Yeah. It's one of those messy Bonafacio attributes. Cry at the drop of a hat; laugh at the drop of a hat.

Jen rubs her wrist across her eyes, telling her sister, "You must have been doing a hundred and fifty miles an hour to get here so soon. Not that I'm not thrilled to see you—and believe me, you're about the only person in the world I'd be happy to see right now, other than Thad—but I wasn't expecting you until tonight."

"I canceled my afternoon appointments and snuck out of work at lunch. You didn't tell Ma I was coming a day early, did you? If she finds out, she'll have us both over there deboning fish for Sunday."

Sunday—that's right. The Saint Joseph's feast at their parents' house. They're supposed to spend all day tomorrow helping their mother prepare the food. Jen had forgotten all about it.

"I left you a message earlier reminding you not to mention it to Ma," Frankie goes on. "Didn't you get it?"

"No, I was out and I guess I forgot to check the voice mail when I got back. Carley was home all day, but—"

But apparently she couldn't be bothered to answer the phone when it rang.

"No school today?" Frankie asks. "Is it a holy day of obligation or something?"

"What do you think?"

"I think . . . there are no holy days of obligation in March that I can recall. What's going on?"

Jen fills her in on the situation as quickly as she can, watching her sister's brown eyes go from curious to concerned.

"Where is she now?"

"In her room."

Frankie opens the trunk, pulls out a duffel bag, and slings it over her shoulder. "I'm going to go throw my stuff in the guest room and have a talk with Miss Carley."

"She might not be willing."

Frankie shrugs. "I'm used to convincing tough kids to open up."

"Wow."

"What?"

"I just never thought of Carley as a tough kid."

"They all have their moments. I'll see if I can find out what's going on. You go back and play in the dirt for a while."

Jen flashes her a grateful smile. "Thanks, Frankie."

Backpack dangling from one hand and jacket tied around her waist, Emma walks quickly along the road leading to her development.

I should have just left everything at school.

It's much too warm for down, and there's nothing in the bag but a pack of gum and the eye makeup she snuck out of her mother's drawer this morning. But if her parents see her come home empty-handed, they'll start in on her about keeping better track of her belongings and about her grades and how she could do much better if she'd bring her books home and spend her weekends studying like Carley does.

Then again . . . maybe they won't be so quick to hold her sister up as an example now that Carley has fallen from grace.

In any case, Emma opted to transport everything back home again on this sunny Friday afternoon, and when she gets to the house, she'll put the backpack on her back and hunch over as if it's filled with heavy texts. Then maybe her mother will leave her alone.

But she won't be home for a while. First, she has another stop to make.

After passing the low brick wall that marks the entrance to the development, she makes a turn, walks past several large homes in various states of construction, and turns again. Here, the pavement ends abruptly at what will eventually be a paved cul-de-sac lined with houses that have yet to be built. Right now, it's a gravel road bordered by dozens of tree stumps and large, overgrown lots marked off in string and posts, with a dense thicket down at the end.

Emma can see Gabe waiting for her there, leaning against a tree, shrouded in long, late, afternoon shadows.

Hating that she's suddenly nervous, she does her best to put some swagger into her stride.

"Hey," she calls, swinging her bag like she doesn't have a care in the world, "what's up?"

"Not much." He watches her approach, and she realizes he's smoking a cigarette.

And that surprises you because . . . ?

She should have guessed he smokes. It goes with the whole dark, dangerous image he's got going on. And he looks sexy doing it.

But the nuns are always talking about how smoking is deadly. Plus, Bridget's uncle, who was even younger than Dad, was a heavy smoker and he just died of lung cancer.

I don't want Gabe to die. I'm in love with him.

Maybe she should tell him cigarettes cause lung cancer, just in case—

No, he probably knows that, right?

Yeah. Everyone knows. She shouldn't remind him.

"C'mere," Gabe says, and the hand that's not holding a cigarette reaches toward her.

Should she tell him, before this goes any further, that she's supposed to be home from school right about now?

She tried to walk twice as fast as usual to free up some extra time, but her mother's going to notice if she's not home in, like, fifteen minutes.

Not a lot can happen in fifteen minutes.

Can it?

"What's wrong?"

"Nothing!" She moves closer.

He snakes his arm around her neck and kisses her. He tastes like tobacco, but in a good way, and she no longer cares about anything but this.

Breaking off the kiss, he pulls back and looks at her.

She tries to think of something to say. Her heart is pounding.

"How was your day?" pops out of her mouth, and she wants to cringe. She's always blurting out stupid things, like her mother.

No. Don't think about her right now.

"It sucked," Gabe says. "How was yours?"

"It sucked." Not really, but . . .

"I bet your sister's day sucked even more."

"My sister?" Emma blinks.

"Yeah. I saw her Peeps page. She said she wishes she was dead."

"Why . . . How did you find her on Peeps?" The first question that came to mind also applies, though. *Why* did he find her on Peeps?

Why would he care about Carley?

"I plugged in her name and it popped up," he says in a *duh* tone.

"How do you even know her name?"

"Um, because it's the same as yours?"

"No, that's not what I meant. Not her last name." Frustrated that he's talking to her as though she's an idiot, she explains, "She just uses Carley Theresa—that's her middle name—on her Peeps page."

"Since when?"

"Since she was born."

"She's had a Peeps page since she was born?"

"No! I mean ever since she's had one—for, like a year or something—she's always used just Carley Theresa on it."

"Yeah? You sure about that?"

"I should know—she's my sister."

He shrugs. "Okay."

"What do you mean?"

"I mean okay. What else would I mean?"

"I have no idea."

She watches him look down at his cigarette and take a drag.

He's obviously losing interest fast. In the conversation. In being here. In her.

But then he stubs out the cigarette with the toe of his boot and looks directly at Emma again. "So you want to go into the woods, or what?"

Relieved, Emma tilts her head and flashes him what she hopes is a sexy smile. "Sure."

As he grabs her hand and leads her toward the shadows, she thinks about what he told her about her sister's Peeps account. There must be another Carley Archer on the Peopleportal site. It's not that uncommon a name, is it?

Unless . . .

What if Gabe's right? What if, after all her prissy warnings to Emma about using her real name online, she went and changed her own account to do the same?

Like it even matters. It's not like she ever posts anything interesting—mostly just lame quotes from supposedly famous people Emma never heard of and cheesy pictures of fuzzy kittens and daisies, stuff like that.

Then again, Carley seems to have changed lately. Maybe her Peeps page—if she's really behind the one Gabe found—has changed, too. Maybe now she'll back off whenever Emma does something the slightest bit wrong.

First thing I'm going to do when I get home is call her out on it, Emma decides—then thinks better of that.

No. Carley might just change her settings and block me the way I did her. Better to just check it out and not let her know I know.

QT-Pi: gotta go in a min my aunt just got here
    Angel 770: your mothers sister?
    QT-Pi: yeah she has 4 but the 1 whos here now is the best

Angel 770: family with 5 girlsssss? HAHA!! Ever read
The Virgin Suicides?
QT-Pi: ???????
Angel 770: book abt messed-up family w 5 sisters who all
want to kill themselves
QT-Pi: do they?
Angel 770: not telling read it AWESOME BOOK

Carley shifts her weight uncomfortably, not sure how to react to that overenthusiastic reply. Maybe Angel forgot that her best friend just committed suicide. Or maybe the book has a happy ending and she's thinking it'll cheer up Carley.

Whatever. She hears footsteps coming up the steps and down the hall now. A few minutes ago, when she heard a car door slam outside and saw her Aunt Frankie through the window, she had to fight the urge to run down there and give her a huge hug.

Any other day, she would have.

But today, she's not interested in seeing or talking to anyone.

Well, anyone other than Angel. She was so glad when her online friend popped up this morning to keep her company. Otherwise, it would have been weird and lonely, staying home from school when she's not sick and there's no blizzard outside—although, in the grand scheme of things, she's relieved that she wasn't forced to endure school today, of all days.

Spring Fling is tomorrow. The other girls would have been talking about what they're wearing, and who's going with whom. The decorating committee, during their free periods, would have been hauling the gigantic, glittery floral decorations from the storage locker in the basement through the halls to the gym for its annual transformation into a colorful enchanted garden.

When Carley was first elected freshman princess, she pored over photos other girls had posted online of Spring

Fling in years past, picturing herself posing this year among the oversized plywood daffodils and gigantic tissue paper butterflies suspended from the ceiling.

Yes, it was much better to be here at home, especially with Angel to keep her company. She was surprised Angel herself wasn't at school today, but she reminded Carley that they're on different schedules. She said she doesn't even have to be in homeroom until noon East Coast time. When noon rolled around, Carley expected her to sign off, but she said she'd decided not to go today.

wont ur mom make u? Carley asked, surprised.

The answer was simply: *no*

Angel doesn't like to talk about her mom, she noticed. Or her dad. Or even her sister. Back in the beginning, she said she has one sister, but hers is, like, ten years older.

There's a knock on Carley's bedroom door, and Aunt Frankie's voice calls, "Hey, guess who?"

Carley quickly types *gtg—got to go*—into her computer and closes the screen without waiting for Angel's reply.

As she gets off her bed, she sees herself reflected in the mirror on her closet door and cringes. She's still wearing the sweatshirt she put on when she came home yesterday afternoon and her hair is still matted from last night's restless sleep. She didn't even bother to brush her teeth or wash her face this morning.

Not much she can do about it right now. She crosses to the door, opens it, and is immediately enveloped in Aunt Frankie's arms.

"I've missed you, babe. Are you okay?"

Caught off guard by an unexpected wave of emotion, Carley opens her mouth but finds it impossible to push any sound past the lump in her throat.

Aunt Frankie pulls back to look at her, then reaches out to gently push a clump of hair back from Carley's forehead.

"Hey," she says. "I'm so sorry about everything. Your mom told me."

Carley swallows hard and manages to ask, "You mean that I cheated?"

Aunt Frankie nods. "And about Nicki. I can't imagine how you felt, losing your best friend to—"

"She wasn't."

"What?"

"She wasn't my best friend. I mean, she *was*—before—but not anymore. Not in a long time."

"Since . . . ?"

"Since last fall."

Since she went off to a different school and got a whole bunch of new friends and started criticizing me and making fun of me in public, and blowing me off in private.

"That sucks."

Aunt Frankie never minces words. It's one of the things Carley loves most about her.

"Want to see what I brought you?" she asks, reaching into her duffel bag. She pulls out a white gift bag with lavender tissue—Carley's favorite color—poking out of the top and hands it over.

Inside is a stuffed purple kitten with a long tail and big green eyes that look real.

"Thank you, Aunt Frankie." She tries to dredge up some enthusiasm. "She's so sweet."

"What are you going to name her?"

"I don't know."

"You always come up with the perfect names for your stuffed animals."

"I know. I will. I just . . . I'll have to think about it."

Carley walks across the room and sets the kitten on the window seat between Noodle the plush snake and Haberdasher the tuxedoed penguin.

Through the glass, she can see Mom below her, on her hands and knees, planting flowers.

It would be so nice, Carley thinks, to be her. She doesn't have to worry about any of this stuff—school, or friends, or what she looks like, or what people think of her.

But even when her mother was her age, she probably didn't worry. She was popular enough to be Spring Fling princess sophomore year, and she had a boyfriend—his name was Mike, Carley knows. Not because her mother told her, but because Nicki did.

"My mom is really good friends with your mother's old boyfriend," she said once.

"What do you mean?"

"This guy, Mike. We ran into him around last Christmas when we were shopping at the Galleria, and he invited my mom to lunch to catch up, and sometimes they still see each other."

"That's weird."

"That my mom hangs out with some guy? They're just friends!" Nicki said quickly—too quickly.

"No, I mean it's weird that my mom has some old boyfriend."

"Yeah. My mom said they had a super bad breakup, so, like, she didn't want me to bring him up to you or your mom. But, like, I always tell you everything, so—just don't mention it to your mom."

"I won't," Carley promised, and it was easy not to. She doesn't even like to think about her mother—even as a teenager—dating, or caring about, or breaking up with, some guy who isn't Dad.

Behind her, Aunt Frankie asks, "So you hadn't talked to her lately?"

"Mom?"

"Nicki."

"Oh. Um, no. She went to public school. I'm at Sisters.

The only place we'd ever run into each other would be Mass, and she didn't go that often."

"What about on the phone? You didn't talk on the phone?"

"We texted. But not after—I mean, we kind of had a fight."

"In person?"

"No . . ."

"On the phone?"

"Kind of." She quickly explains to her aunt that nearly all of her interaction with Nicki since school began had been written—the final drama unfolding in texts and online. Not that that's unusual.

"Hardly anyone I know uses the phone for anything other than texting," she says, and Aunt Frankie nods.

"It's a different world, that's for sure. Communications technology, social media—pretty ironic phrasing, I think. You guys have so many ways of getting in touch now, but it makes you antisocial, if anything."

"What do you mean?"

"Kids are much more isolated these days than we ever were. It must be kind of lonely, growing up that way."

Carley is about to agree, but then she thinks of Angel, quickly becoming her new best friend. "Not really. I'm not lonely. I have friends."

"At school?"

"At school," she lies, "and, like, all over the place."

"Online?"

"All over. So how have you been?"

"Fine. What about—"

"How's Aunt Patty?"

"She's good. You—"

"I wish she could've come with you."

"Yeah, well, she's working. Do you—"

"She works, like, all the time."

"Sometimes it seems that way. So—"

"How are Dorito and Funyun?" Those are Aunt Frankie's cats.

"They're fine. Okay, I get the hint."

"What hint?"

"You're not in the mood to spill your guts to your old aunt. Got it." She heads for the door.

"Wait—Aunt Frankie. I'm sorry. I didn't mean to keep interrupting. I just . . ."

"I know. Don't worry. I'm going to go take a shower and wash off the road dust—and Chee-tos dust—and then we'll go out to dinner. And you can tell me about all this stuff that's been going on . . . or not. Okay? I'll listen if you want to talk, and if you don't . . . I'll talk. You listen. Sound good?"

It does, actually. Really good.

Carley smiles. "Yeah. Deal."

Aunt Frankie leaves the room, and she starts to open her laptop again, then changes her mind and goes over to the bookshelves.

Maybe it's time to give the Internet a break for a while.

Getting to her feet at last, Jen straightens with a wince and brushes the garden soil off the knees of her jeans. Her back and shoulders are killing her after kneeling and digging for hours, but the bare patch has been transformed into a colorful flowerbed.

The hard physical work and fresh air were cathartic enough that she didn't even dwell on Carley's problems the whole time, or wonder how things are going between her and Frankie inside the house.

Now, though, she's ready to go find out. She needs to check her e-mail, too, to see whether Sister Linda got back to her. Maybe she can shed some light on the situation.

She peels off her gardening gloves, grabs the empty black plastic cell packs and her trowel, and starts toward the open garage door.

Behind her, she hears jingling dog tags and someone calling her name.

Amy Janicek is waving from the curb, where she's walking Thayer, her yellow Lab. Glad to see her, as opposed to one of the more talky, gossipy neighbors who will want to chat and linger, she waves back.

"How's it going?" she calls, and is surprised when Amy—who, though not standoffish, usually keeps a polite distance—beckons her closer.

Jen doesn't know her very well. Her kids are younger, twin seven-year-old boys and a nine-year-old daughter, all of whom go to Saint Paul's. Carley told Jen how well behaved they are; how they brush their teeth and fold their clothes without being told, put their games away neatly with all the pieces intact, and consider baby carrots and cut-up fruit a treat.

"Wow. They sound like perfect kids," Jen said mildly, trying to keep the edge from her voice. "Their mom must be a great mom—or at least, she must run a really tight ship."

"She's kind of proper—but she's really nice and normal," Carley added hastily, as though fearing Jen might equate proper with abnormal and not nice.

Of course she wouldn't.

Well, not really.

The truth is, she's always found Amy—albeit from a polite, neighborly distance—to be a bit too buttoned-up for her taste. It's not that she's ever proven herself to be a judgmental prude . . . but Jen senses that she's very . . .

"Different," is how she described it once to Thad. "She's just different."

"Different how?"

"Different from me."

In other words, Amy Janicek is not the kind of woman who would ever act on impulse, burst out laughing or crying, trip over her own feet or tongue, blurt out the wrong thing at the wrong time to the precisely wrong person . . .

Unlike Jen.

Thad found that amusing, and reminded her—with affection—that he's never met anyone quite like her. "You're unique, Jen."

"In a good way?" she asked, and he grinned and kissed her on the forehead.

"Of course in a good way."

"Only you think that."

"We all have our quirks."

Not Thad. Not really. Not potentially embarrassing ones.

And this woman—Amy Janicek—she doesn't seem like a quirky person, either. Or the type who would give someone a pass for a minor—or major—digression.

"Sorry—I don't want Thayer to tear up your lawn," she explains as Jen crosses the yard toward her, "and I don't want to shout it and be overheard."

Uh-oh. Shout what?

Did she find out, somehow, about the trouble at Sacred Sisters? If that's the case, she's probably wondering about Carley's integrity, questioning whether she should be allowed to continue babysitting the Janicek children.

What am I going to say if she asks about the suspension? Jen wonders as she reluctantly crosses the grass toward the tall, wiry woman whose straight, shoulder-length blond hair, pulled back in a navy visor, is just a shade dull enough to be courtesy of genetics and not a salon.

Amy wastes no time getting to the point. "I hate to even bring this up, because I'm a mom, too, and you might feel that it's none of my business, but when I saw you out here, I realized I can't just walk on by without mentioning it."

Immediately on the defensive, Jen wonders how she even found out about it in the first place.

"I mean, if it were my daughter, I'd want to know. I figure you would, too."

Jen decides to play dumb. "Want to know what?"

"I was just walking Thayer over by the entrance to the development—I wear a pedometer and it's exactly a mile from here down to the end of that new road where they're about to start building—and I saw your daughter going into the woods."

"What?" Startled, Jen immediately looks back at the house, at Carley's bedroom window. Did she sneak out somehow? Is that why she didn't answer the phone earlier, when Frankie called?

No, that can't be. Jen saw her after she got back from the nursery, and anyway, Frankie would have come down to tell her if she found the house empty. So what the heck is Amy talk—

Wait a minute . . .

"Which daughter?"

"Your younger one."

Jen's heart flutters a bit, as if deciding whether to sink or not. "Emma."

"Yes, Emma. She was going into the woods."

Terrific. Jen glances at her watch and sees that her youngest should have been home from school twenty minutes ago. She was so busy worrying about Carley—and all right, planting pansies—that she completely lost track of time. Caught in the act of running a loose ship while Emma was in the woods doing God only knows what.

Jen feels sick inside, pretty willing to bet she wasn't bird watching or foraging for morels.

"She wasn't alone," Amy informs her.

No. No, of course she wasn't.

"She was with Gabe."

"Gabe? Who—"

"The boy who moved in next door to us."

Oh. Right. The new neighbors.

In another lifetime, Jen made a sponge cake to welcome them, but brought it over to Debbie's instead . . .

Debbie . . .

Nicki . . .

Carley.

Dominoes falling again.

"What were they doing?" she asks Amy, who is distract-edly wrapping the dog's leash around her hand to keep him close as he tries to tug her away.

"In the woods?"

"Yes. In the woods. What were they *doing*?" Jen realizes, as she repeats the ridiculous question, that of course Amy doesn't know the answer to that, but she can probably take a wild guess . . .

And so can I.

Dammit.

Motherhood is starting to feel like Whac-A-Mole. No sooner does she manage to stamp out one problem than an-other pops up.

No . . . it's not like that at all. She hasn't stamped out any problems.

Okay, so maybe motherhood is more like pulling weeds. They're everywhere, all the time. Even when you think you've eliminated them, the taproot is there, just beneath the surface, waiting to sprout again.

My girls . . . my little girls . . . how is this happening?

"I really—I have no idea what they were doing." Amy shakes her head. "I'm sorry. Maybe I shouldn't have—"

"No, it's fine, thank you for telling me. I'll talk to Emma when she gets home."

"All right. I mean . . . I'd want to know, if it were my own daughter," Amy says again, but Jen can tell she's thinking that it never would be her own daughter.

No, because we never think that, do we?

We assume that our kids are the good ones, the perfect ones who aren't going to sneak around or get into trouble at school or . . .

Or worse.

Again, her mind goes to Debbie and Nicki, and the nightmare she had last night.

"Are you okay?"

Opening her eyes, she sees Amy Janicek peering at her, looking concerned.

"Thank you. Really. I appreciate the heads-up."

"No problem. The thing is—" Amy breaks off to scold the dog, still straining at the leash, "Thayer, stop that! Sit!"

Imperfect Thayer ignores her, nose to the ground, sniffing, pulling.

"The thing is, he's— Thayer!" After a brief tug of war, Amy shakes her head and allows the dog to jerk her onto the grass. "I'm sorry. He's just bad news."

For a moment, Jen thinks she's talking about the dog. Then she realizes—Gabe. Gabe is bad news.

"In what way?" she asks.

"No supervision whatsoever. The father is never home. I only met him once, in passing, when he was leaving and I was walking the dog, and I welcomed him to the neighborhood. He wasn't friendly at all. He didn't bother to thank me for the casserole I dropped off with the son on the day they moved in—didn't seem to know anything about it, didn't even know where my dish was, and it was one of my good Corningwares. I need it back."

"And the son . . . ?"

"Comes and goes at all hours. He dresses like a bum—I know kids dress down these days, but come on. You live here in this development, you can afford a decent wardrobe right?" Not waiting for an answer, she shakes her head, adding, "There's just something shady about him. They're

from New York City, did you know that? I told my kids to
steer clear of that side of the yard, because you just never
know what— Thayer, stop that! Sit!"

"What else do you know about Gabe?" Jen asks. "I mean,
is there anything specific . . . ?"

*Other than assumptions you've made based on things he
might not be able to help.*

She's feeling prickly, listening to Amy's rant.

Then again, that boy—Gabe—might have lured her innocent eighth-grader into the woods and, for all she knows—

"He's just bad news," Amy says with a shrug, unwinding
a length of leash to allow the dog to graze further onto the
lawn. "What does he want with a girl Emma's age?"

Jen shakes her head, mouth set grimly.

"I didn't mean to upset you, but—"

"You didn't upset me. I just—I'd better get inside. My
sister is here visiting, and Carley is . . . she's . . ."

She's a good girl. She is.

"Oh, tell Carley I may be calling her to babysit for a few
hours tomorrow night so that Pete can take me out to a nice
dinner. I really need a break. It's been a crazy week."

Yeah. Tell me about it.

For a moment, she considers informing Amy that this
isn't a good weekend for Carley—without mentioning, of
course, her best friend's suicide or the suspension from
school. She'll just say they'll be busy tomorrow helping her
mother with the Saint Joseph's Day cooking, an annual task
Carley has always looked forward to.

Then again, that might prolong the conversation, and Jen
is eager to get rid of Amy. She merely says, "I'll tell her,"
and is grateful when Amy turns away at last, pulling the dog
back out onto the pavement.

"Have a great weekend," she calls over her shoulder.

Jen doesn't bother to reply.

Entry from the marble notebook

Thursday, February 6, 1986

Father came into my room last night.

Before he left, he told me that he signed me up for my road test. When I told him I'm not ready to take it yet, he said you have to sign up way in advance and that it isn't scheduled until March. He said that leaves us plenty of time to practice driving, and the way he said it . . .

Whenever I drive, he sits so close to me that I can smell his breath and it makes me gag. I don't know how much longer I can stand it. Sometimes, when he's sitting on the passenger side, I'm so tempted to turn the wheel really, really hard and drive him right into a tree. There are so many huge old ones right next to the street in our neighborhood. It wouldn't be hard to do. I could pretend it was an accident.

But God would know. And He would punish me in hell.

Sometimes, I wonder how much worse that would be than anything else I've gone through.

Chapter 11

To her credit, Aunt Frankie waits until they've ordered dessert—peanut butter fudge ripple cheesecake for Carley and tiramisu cheesecake for her—to bring up what happened at school.

Carley was starting to think—hope—that the topic wouldn't come up at all, but she should have known better. That's the whole reason they're here, isn't it? It's why Aunt Frankie drove all this way on a Friday afternoon, and why Mom and Dad and Emma didn't tag along for dinner.

Even if they had intended to come, the plan probably would have been derailed by the latest trouble with Emma. Carley has no idea what her sister did this time, but she heard Mom downstairs yelling at her like crazy when she got home from school. Carley was curious—it sounded a lot worse than the usual battles between her mother and sister—but not curious enough to emerge from her room to investigate.

At last her mother was focused on something other than Carley, and she didn't want to risk drawing attention back to herself.

She stayed behind closed doors, reading, until Aunt Frankie knocked and said it was time to go. As they left, she could hear Emma slamming things around in her room. Dad was just pulling into the driveway, and Mom was sitting in the living room waiting for him, grim-faced.

If Aunt Frankie knew what was up with Emma, she didn't bring it up during the drive over, and Carley didn't ask. She has enough problems of her own.

Aunt Frankie had told her she doesn't have to discuss it if she doesn't want to. She probably wouldn't have wanted to, if the subject had come up at the beginning of the evening.

But she gradually relaxed as they talked about other topics. Movies, music, books, celebrities—Aunt Frankie can have an effortless conversation about absolutely anything. That's always been one of Carley's favorite things about her, but it's especially the case tonight.

What a relief to spend time with someone who isn't scolding her, or peering nervously at her—both of which her parents did in the past twenty-four hours, before Emma got into trouble again.

Even now, Aunt Frankie is totally casual as she leans back in the booth, takes a sip of her cappuccino, and asks, "So . . . your mother tells me you're suspended for cheating?"

Carley nods. What is there to say to that?

"What the heck happened? You're smarter than that, babe."

Too relaxed—or maybe just too weary—to be defensive, Carley can only agree with a shrug. "I know."

"Did you go in there planning to cheat, or was it something that—"

"No! I would never *plan* it. I would never cheat on purpose."

"So you cheated *by accident*?"

"Not exactly. It was . . ." She hesitates, wondering if she can trust her aunt with the truth. "I really don't want to get into this with my mother. She'd freak out."

"Why?"

"Because she's always worried about what goes on at

school, and—I don't want her to get involved. It was really my own fault. It's just . . ."

"What happened, Carley?"

"I was sitting there during the test and I couldn't focus and time was running out, and then out of the blue, someone threw me a note with the answers. Only it was a setup. They were mostly the wrong answers, copied off this girl who's failing math."

"Who threw the note?"

"I have no idea." Actually, that's not entirely the case. She has some idea. It had to be someone sitting close enough to not only toss her the note, but to copy the answers from Wanda Durphy's test paper. Kendra Hyde, maybe, or Melissa Kovacs . . .

Aunt Frankie shakes her head, looking disgusted. "So basically, someone baited you, and you took it?"

"Exactly. My guard was down, because . . ." Because she was upset about Nicki. But she doesn't say it. That's no excuse for what she did. She should have known better; she doesn't need to hear Aunt Frankie tell her that.

"Because Monday was your best friend's wake," Aunt Frankie says gently. "Right? Did the other girls know about that?"

"I don't know. Maybe. It doesn't matter. They wouldn't care anyway."

"Why not?"

"Because they hate me."

"Who hates you?"

"Everyone."

" 'Hate' is a strong word. I'm sure they don't—"

"You have to hate someone to do what they did to me."

The awful story spills out of her—about how they elected her Spring Fling princess, as a joke. Only Carley didn't know it was a joke for the first few days. She tells her aunt how happy she was, and how happy her mother was, too.

"We were going to go shopping that weekend to buy a dress for me to wear. Mom couldn't wait. And I don't even like to shop, but I . . . I couldn't wait, either. And then I was in the locker room, changing for gym, when I heard these two girls talking . . ."

Even the memory of it makes her queasy. She can still hear their voices. One of them was Melissa Kovacs. She was whining to the other girl, Renee, about how this thing had gone far enough, and she was missing out on all the fun that leads up to being Spring Fling princess . . .

At first, Carley thought she was just jealous that she hadn't been elected.

Then Melissa said, "It's time to tell Princess Carley that everyone wrote her name down as a joke."

"You'd think she'd have figured it out by now."

"You'd think she'd have figured it out the second they read her name over the intercom. I mean, come on! Since when is a fat, zit-faced klutz royal court material?"

Emotion jams Carley's throat as she repeats the cruel words to Aunt Frankie, whose brown eyes are shiny with tears. She reaches out and holds Carley's hands in her own, silently listening to the rest of it.

There isn't much left to tell.

Carley doesn't mention that when she fled the locker room in tears, she crashed right into Johnny, the janitor, right outside in the hall—so close he might very well have heard every word Melissa and Renee said.

"Hey, what's wrong?" he called after Carley, but she kept her head down, running . . . running . . .

"I just wanted to go home," she tells Aunt Frankie, "so I went to the nurse, but when I got there, she was with two other girls and I didn't want them to know something was wrong."

"So what did you do?"

"I went to Sister Linda, the social worker."

"That was a good move."

Carley shrugs. "That's what we're supposed to do if we have a problem, and . . ."

"And you've always tried to follow the rules, do the right thing." Aunt Frankie gets it, gets her. "What did Sister Linda say when you told her what happened?"

"She said she understood why I believed they had elected me princess. She said, 'There are none so blind as those who will not see.'"

Aunt Frankie frowns, but says nothing.

"She said not to worry, that she would handle it with the other girls," Carley said, "and she called Mom and now Melissa is Spring Fling princess like she should have been all along."

"Wait," Aunt Frankie says, "you lost me. How is she Spring Fling princess now?"

"I told Sister Linda that I obviously couldn't do it," she says, and continues talking over Aunt Frankie, who starts to interrupt, because she knows what her aunt is going to say: that she should have taken a stand and insisted on being Spring Fling princess.

But Carley was nowhere near strong enough to go through with something like that.

"Sister Linda said she'd talk to our class advisors for me and explain," she hurries on with her story, "and they ended up holding another election without saying why even though everyone knew why, and Melissa won."

At last, Carley stops talking. She takes off her glasses. Her eyes are hot and swimming with tears.

"That's disgusting."

"Melissa?" Carley nods. "I didn't vote for her. I didn't vote at all. I handed in a blank ballot."

"The whole thing is disgusting. The way it was handled . . ." Aunt Frankie shakes her head. "That girl should have been punished, not rewarded, and—"

"It wasn't just her, it was everyone, and it doesn't matter, it's—" Carley's voice breaks. She grabs her napkin off her lap, turns toward the wall, and surreptitiously wipes her eyes, hoping no one sees.

"Here." Aunt Frankie slides a little tissue packet across the table to her. "Want to go to the ladies' room?"

In other words, does she want to parade, sobbing, through the busy restaurant? Carley shakes her head furiously, clearing her throat. "I'm okay."

"No, you aren't. But you will be."

"No, I won't."

"You will," Aunt Frankie counters. "I promise. Trust me."

She looks up at her aunt. It's so easy for her to say, sitting there. She's pretty and athletic, with a job and a car and a house, and she has Aunt Patty and two cuddly cats and tons of friends.

What do I have?

Nothing.

Not even a friend.

Except for Angel, Carley reminds herself.

Thank God, thank God for my guardian angel.

When at last it was unearthed from beneath a shallow layer of mud in the basement floor, the trapdoor turned out to be long—much longer than Angel expected. It's a wooden door with recessed panels, one that, standing vertically, would fit any of the doorways upstairs.

That, Angel suspects, is probably exactly where it came from. Up on the no-frills third floor in what was once the servants' quarters, some of the shelved closets are open, with hinge marks indicating that they once had doors.

This one on the basement floor has a metal plate covering the place where the knob hole would have been drilled, and someone affixed a sturdy metal handle—which stubbed Angel's shuffling toes—precisely in the middle.

Simply tugging on that handle wasn't enough to get it open, though.

No, this has been one hell of a job. It's required not just patience, waiting for the floodwaters to subside, but also, once the task had commenced earlier this evening, a disruptive road trip to go purchase a heavy metal crowbar from the hardware superstore off the thruway.

Tonight, the clerk wasn't a disinterested high school kid but a silver-haired retiree who asked Angel about the weather: "How is it out there now that the sun's gone down? Still warm like it was all day? Feels like spring, don't it?"

Inwardly cringing at the grammatical error, Angel nodded politely and paid for the purchase in cash, wanting only to get out of there and back to the job at hand.

"You have a nice night now. Don't work too hard, whatever it is you're doing."

It's none of your damned business what I'm doing.

Jaw clenched, Angel left the store vowing to shop somewhere else next time. You can't have people talking to you, asking questions—even about the weather. Because then they recognize you, and they notice what you buy—*Oh, you're the one who got the crowbar that time, and a while back, you had the keys copied, and now you're getting rope and duct tape? What's this for?*

That's how it goes in small, friendly cities like this, where people don't ignore each other and keep their distance the way they do in, say, New York.

At least the crowbar does the trick. The door makes a splintering sound as Angel pries it open at last, letting it thud over onto the damp dirt floor.

Breathing hard from the exertion, Angel grabs a flashlight—also purchased in a hardware store, but at the mom-and-pop one two blocks away.

That was last year, in the beginning, before I knew any

better. Before I realized that I'd need to be able to come and go around here without attracting any attention.

Aiming the beam into the hole, Angel is startled to see that it's lined with concrete.

What on earth . . . ?

Tilting the flashlight's angle deeper into the hole, wondering whether it leads to an underground bunker of some sort, or perhaps a passageway leftover from the Underground Railroad era—*no matter what that twit Sandra Lutz said about it*—Angel expects to see a tunnel.

But that's not the case. The hole is fairly shallow, maybe three feet deep from the opening to the bottom . . .

Except, upon closer examination, what appears to be the bottom isn't the bottom.

Peering into the hole, Angel sees that it's actually the top—of Mother's old chest freezer.

But you knew it was here, didn't you?

No!

Of course I didn't know! I asked Sandra Lutz to get rid of it, and she said . . .

She said . . .

How many times do I have to tell you the freezer is waterproof?

It isn't Sandra's voice that seeps into Angel's brain; it's Mother's.

Mother, with her secrets and lies . . .

Mother who—with Father's help, of course; he did everything she asked—had buried the freezer in this strange, concrete-lined vault beneath the basement floor, the lid secured with a large padlock, protecting . . .

Protecting . . .

God only knows what's inside.

No.

Not just God. You know, too.

You do. In the back of your mind, you've always known, haven't you? Even before you read the marble notebook. You've known ever since . . .

Winter. Cold. Dark. Late. Flashlights.

The power has gone out again, or . . .

Or they don't want to turn on a light down here. They don't want anyone to see.

But I see. I'm crouched on the stairs, and I see what they're doing, and I smell the dirt, and I hear choking sobs . . .

Father. Father is crying.

"Hush!" Mother's voice, cold as the bitter January wind that rattled windowpanes and banged shutters upstairs, jarring Angel from a sound sleep.

Father: "I can't help it! I can't stop thinking of—"

Mother: "Don't think of her. Just dig! Dig!"

Shovels digging into the damp earthen floor, rasping, scraping . . .

Father's sobs . . .

Mother's voice . . .

Fingertips to temples, Angel can no longer block it out, any of it.

"You're ruining my life!" Emma screams at her parents, who are sitting calmly on the couch as she strides around the living room. "How can you do this to me?"

"*You* did this to you," Dad tells her. "You have to take responsibility for your own actions. If you want to go sneaking around in the woods with some kid who's too old for you, some kid we don't even know, then you'd better be prepared to—"

"*I* know him, and he's not too old for me! I'm fourteen!"

"Exactly. You're fourteen," Mom cuts in. "You—"

"I wasn't doing anything wrong!"

That's what Emma keeps reminding herself. When two people are in love, physical intimacy is natural and right.

Even if it's also scary and kind of embarrassing and painful, too.

Anyway, her parents aren't aware of what, exactly, went on between her and Gabe. They just accused her of being in the woods with him, nothing more.

Emma has no idea how they even found out about that part.

All she knows is that Mom was lying in wait for her when she got home. She grounded Emma until further notice, took away her phone and laptop, and had already changed the password on the household wifi to keep her from getting online using any of the other computers in the house.

"You can't just cut me off like this!" Emma protests, turning her back on them and pacing over to the window.

The lamplight allows her to see only her own scowling reflection, but she imagines that Gabe is out there in the night, gazing longingly at her silhouette in the glass. She turns her head so that he won't see her profile; she hates the way her nose protrudes from that angle.

He's got to be worried about her, wondering why he hasn't heard from her.

"I'll text you first thing when I get home," she promised him just before she scurried away this afternoon, having forgotten all about her earlier decision to go straight to her laptop to look up Carley's Peeps page.

Now she can't do either of those things. She can't do anything, thanks to her stupid parents.

"It will be good for you to get unplugged and away from screens for a while," her mother is saying. "It's not healthy for anyone to spend so much time on the phone and computer."

"You didn't unplug Carley!" Emma hurls, whirling away from the window. "Perfect Carley goes around cheating and breaking school rules and getting suspended and you let her keep her phone and her computer? And you don't even ground her? She's out to dinner with Aunt Frankie! How is that fair?"

Her parents look at each other.

I'm right, she realizes. *They know I'm right. It isn't fair.*

But they're not about to admit it. Of course not. They would never give her the upper hand in an argument.

"That's between us and your sister," Dad tells her. "And this is between us and you. We don't—"

"Does Carley have the new wifi password?"

"No."

"Are you going to give it to her?"

"That has nothing to do with—"

"I hate you!" Emma screams, and storms away.

"It's okay, Jen," she hears Dad say as she stomps up the stairs. "She doesn't mean it."

"I *do* mean it! I wish you were dead. And Carley, too! I wish she was dead!"

"Don't you *ever* say that!" Mom yells. "*Ever!* Do you hear me?"

Ignoring her, Emma slams her bedroom door and leans against it, breathing hard.

"I do mean it," she says again, this time in a whisper, hating her sister with all her might. "I wish she was dead."

And so, she remembers, does Carley herself, according to Gabe and the Peeps page Emma can't even look at now.

"How did this happen?" Jen asks Thad, watching him pour a generous amount of Jack Daniel's into a glass on the kitchen counter.

"You mean Emma?"

"Emma, Carley . . . I keep looking back, trying to figure out what we did wrong."

"Maybe we didn't do anything wrong."

She just looks at him.

He shrugs, tilts the glass, takes a long sip, and plunks it down. "Sure you don't want some?"

She shakes her head and tells him, just as she did the first time he offered, "I don't like whiskey."

"Have some wine, then. Do you want me to open some for you?"

"No, thanks." She slept so little last night and the day has been so challenging that all she wants is to go to bed as soon as Emma settles down up there—which isn't likely to be soon, given the way she's still stomping around her room. Anyway, one of them had better keep a clear head in case their daughter bounces back downstairs for another round.

Thad sits heavily on the stool beside hers, both hands clasped around his glass. "Maybe we were too permissive. Maybe we spoiled them."

"By we, you mean me."

"If I meant you, I'd have said you. We've both had our moments, especially with Emma, where it was easier to give in than deal with an overblown theatrical scene."

"I've had a lot more of them than you have."

"It's because you're the one who's here most of the time. I feel guilty that I'm not. I feel guilty that I have to work all day tomorrow instead of staying here to help you pick up the pieces. And you can't blame yourself. You've been a terrific mother."

His words echo, almost exactly, the ones she spoke to Debbie just yesterday. If she herself is suffering guilt over the difficulties with her girls, imagine what her friend feels? For her, there will be no chance to turn things around.

"Maybe," Thad muses, "in the grand scheme of things, it's not so bad."

"Oh, it's bad."

"Maybe it's just that it all happened at once, and that it was this week, with Nicki . . ." He trails off, lifts the glass to his lips to sip and swallow again. "It's that old saying, what is it . . . ?"

"All hell is breaking loose?"

"I meant 'It never rains, but it pours.'" He offers her a wry, faint smile that doesn't even approach his blue eyes. "But, yeah. Basically, all hell is breaking loose, too."

Jen can't pull off even a hint of a smile. She sits glumly thinking of her girls, her sweet babies, caught up in lying and sneaking and cheating and Lord only knows what else.

Is this what happens when they grow up?

Is it going to get worse before it gets better?

Is it even going to get better?

"The thing with Emma, by itself, wouldn't surprise me," Thad says after a long moment. "She's always been—"

"She's never done anything like this, Thad!"

"That we know of. If Amy Janicek hadn't come along and seen her, and then told you, we'd still be in the dark. Who knows? Maybe it's better that way."

"Are you serious?" She looks at him, seeing not dependable, sensible Thad but a man with a drink in his hand and whiskey on his breath.

Mike. Mike Morino used to drink, back when they were teenagers. He'd steal whiskey from his father's liquor cabinet and drink it straight from the bottle, passing it around at parties.

Sometimes Jen would imbibe a bit. She was no saint. But she wasn't the kind of girl who regularly got drunk, either. Mike used to tease her about that, saying she should loosen up, be more like . . .

Debbie.

He was always fond of Debbie. Out of all Jen's friends— and there were many—she was the only one Mike didn't complain about having around.

Were the two of them having a fling even then?

Are they now?

Jen's speculation is cut short by the sound of car doors slamming outside.

"Your sister and Carley are home," Thad observes, looking expectantly toward the hall.

Moments later, the front door opens, and Carley's voice reaches their ears.

"—straight up to bed," she's saying, "but thanks, Aunt Frankie, for dinner, and for . . . well, you know. Sorry I got all upset."

"You're allowed, kiddo. See you in the morning. We've got a lot of cooking to do over at Grandma's house. Oh, and remember what I told you."

What? Jen wonders. What did Frankie tell her? What did Carley tell Frankie?

Hearing her sister's footsteps approach the kitchen, she wants to start firing off questions, but manages—just barely—to hold her tongue.

"Hi, guys." Frankie sticks her head in. "I'm glad you're up. Midnight snack?"

Thad silently holds up his glass.

"Oh. That kind of snack. I was hoping for popcorn."

"Want some?"

"Popcorn? No thanks."

"I meant Jack." Thad indicates the bottle.

"No, thanks again. That stuff would knock me out until noon. But if you have any wine . . ."

"We do. How was dinner?" Thad gets up and busies himself opening a bottle of cabernet as Frankie fills the seat he vacated. Jen manages to merely listen as Frankie talks about what she ordered, what Carley ordered.

After taking two stemmed glasses from the cupboard, Thad pours wine into each and slides one across the breakfast bar to Frankie, the other to Jen.

She accepts it without protest and when Frankie pauses for a breath after describing her tiramisu cheesecake, she asks, "Did Carley talk to you about what happened?"

So much for holding your tongue.

Frankie swirls the wine in her glass. "She did. But she asked me not to talk to you guys about it."

Jen's knee-jerk instinct is resentment. But then Thad catches her eye and gives a little nod, as if to say it's okay.

He's right. Isn't this what she was hoping for? That Carley would open up to someone?

"I told her she should fill you in," Frankie goes on, "because she's had a lot to deal with and you can help her."

"So there's more to the story than she told us?" Thad reaches across the breakfast bar for his whiskey.

"There's always more to every story," Frankie returns simply.

"I'm glad she talked to you," Jen says. "Just tell me—should I be worried?"

"You mean more than you already are? Look, I don't—" Her sister breaks off, looking at the ceiling as footsteps pound overhead, then down the stairs.

Bracing herself for another bout with Emma, Jen is surprised to see Carley appear in the kitchen doorway, still fully dressed and looking disturbed.

"There's something wrong with the Internet," she announces. "I can't get online."

"There's nothing wrong with the Internet," Thad tells her. "Your mother changed the password."

"Why?" Carley's gaze, behind her glasses, darts to Jen, who sighs inwardly.

Suddenly, she's too exhausted to get into Emma's situation now. "I think everyone needs to take a break from the computer stuff for a while."

"What? But—you can't do that!"

Taken aback by the reaction, Jen manages to say evenly, "I can, and I did."

It would be so much easier in her exhausted state to just give Carley the new password. That's what she was planning to do all along, whenever she got around to asking for it.

But Emma's earlier accusations of favoritism aren't sitting well with Jen tonight. If losing online access is fair punishment for one daughter, why isn't it fair punishment for the other?

Because there's more to every story, and this isn't like Carley . . .

It's what Jen's been telling herself all along, but—

Maybe she really was too lenient with the girls—both of them. Maybe it's time to toughen up.

"No Internet," she tells Carley firmly.

"For how long?"

"Until I decide it's time to change the password back."

"Noooooo!"

Thad plunks his glass down on the counter. "Do *not* shout at your mother."

"But it's not fair!"

That's what Emma said earlier. It's what she says often.

But not Carley.

"Give me your cell phone." Jen stretches out a hand. She took Emma's phone; she should take Carley's as well.

"Mom, you can't do this!"

"Give me your phone."

"But I need it!"

"Now? It's almost midnight."

"So?"

Jen cringes. Nothing presses her buttons like a belligerent *So?*

Carley, well aware of that, takes it down a notch. "I need it to get online for school stuff."

"It's a Friday, and anyway, you weren't even *in* school today, remember?"

"I still have to keep up with my work, *remember*?" Carley snaps back, completely out of character.

Why is she making such a big deal about something Jen hadn't even expected to impact her much? Carley isn't one of those kids who spends a lot of time online . . .

Or is she?

Hasn't she spent most of her time alone in her room for months now?

And hasn't Jen spent the last twenty-four hours realizing that she doesn't know her daughter as well as she thought? Hasn't she spent the last week, in the wake of Nicki's suicide, realizing that maybe no parent ever does?

She glances over at her sister and sees that Frankie is watching Carley intently, chin propped on her fist.

She knows more than we do. I need to find out what it is.

"Hand over your phone, Carley," Thad says firmly.

"But—"

"Carley."

She whirls to face Jen. "Mom, please, you have to let me go online. I—"

"No means no." Jen folds her arms, pressing her shaking hands against the sides of her ribs, feeling her heart pounding hard.

With a frustrated groan, Carley thrusts her cell phone into her father's outstretched hand.

"Good. Now go to bed."

Sobbing, Carley runs from the room and up the stairs, slamming her bedroom door for the first time in her life.

Frustrated, Angel paces across the hardwoods of the small third-floor bedroom at the back of the house, the best place to ensure that the glow of the laptop screen, however faint, won't be seen from outside.

It's past three A.M., so chances are most everyone in the neighborhood is asleep, but you never know.

Really, the basement would be the safest place of all for Angel to hide with a lit-up screen. But the thought of descending those stairs again is hardly appealing. Not with the gaping hole in the earth floor, and the padlock that stubbornly protects Mother's sickening secret after all these years.

Angel tried hard to break it open, but it proved impossible without the proper tools on hand.

Tomorrow, I'll make yet another trip to yet another hardware store for a pair of bolt cutters.

For now, I'll just have to wait to see what's inside.

As if I don't already know. But I need to see for myself.

Meanwhile . . .

Where the hell is Carley?

She's been absent from the Internet all night. It isn't like her.

Angel stops pacing and crouches before the open laptop on the floor to check, yet again, for her sign-on alert.

Still nothing.

But . . . look at that, the lovely Taylor Morino—who tomorrow evening will reign as senior class queen at the Spring Fling dance—has just posted something on her Peopleportal page.

With the disregard for discretion and dramatic flair so typical of girls her age, Taylor has announced to the world—at least, the Peeps world: *worst night EVERRRRRRR cant sleep @ all so i guess i shouldnt have had a dble espresso at the mallllllllll*

Ordinarily, her posts are greeted with a flurry of comments from her lengthy list of Peeps connections, but the vast majority of her admirers must be asleep because there's just a smattering of response.

dude i have something u can take for that, writes a

wholesome-looking kid whose profile states that he's a sophomore at Saint Francis.

*awwww poor baby maybe u shd ask J to come sing you
a lullaby*, writes a girl whose portrait shows a pretty blonde
Angel recognizes as a senior at Sacred Sisters and part of
Taylor Morino's wide circle of friends. No telling who J is,
and it doesn't matter.

Wheels turning, Angel logs into the pseudonymous Peeps
page created months ago to gain access to Taylor Morino.
The official connection isn't necessary to interact publicly
on Taylor's page—which would be too risky anyway—
but it's the only means of interacting privately through the
Peeps mailbox system.

Angel correctly assumed that a girl who already had over
two thousand connections wouldn't bother to double-check
whether she actually knew a "Rachel Riley," Angel's fictional alter ego.

Taylor had accepted the connection request without
question, but if she had asked how they knew each other,
"Rachel" would have responded they'd met at a party last
summer. Taylor had attended plenty of those, according
to Angel's research—and chances were, Miss Popularity
wouldn't remember every detail of her social adventures the
morning after, let alone months later.

Angel had cleverly given Rachel a background that placed
her in Taylor's periphery but not in her direct circles. Supposedly, she's a junior at a public high school in the Buffalo
suburbs. Angel downloaded Rachel's official Peeps portrait
from a stranger's collection of candids posted on a foreign
travel Web site. She's a fresh-faced teen with brown hair and
brown eyes; pretty, but not too pretty; the kind of girl who'd
be fairly inconspicuous in any group.

For the past few weeks, "Rachel" has been telling Taylor
about her "cousin," Rick Riley, a handsome tight end for the
Buffalo Bills. The real Rick Riley is ostensibly spending the

off-season dating women his own age, but Angel came up with an ingenious plan. Rachel told Taylor that her cousin Rick had spotted Taylor's photo on her own Peeps page. Taylor has gobbled up Rachel's private messages about how Rick has been asking to meet her.

Now, Angel types a quick note: *me & rick r hanging out @ his house w/ a bunch of ppl & we just noticed ur still up so wanna come over? i can pick u up, just tell me ur address*

That last line is added for a note of authenticity. Of course Angel is familiar with the small house a few blocks from Sacred Sisters where Taylor lives with her mother, Susan, an ER nurse. That's where the flower arrangement—signed *From a secret admirer*—was delivered just the other day, courtesy of the same online florist that delivered the anonymously sent Stargazer lilies to Nicki Olivera's wake.

Angel would have preferred to have Taylor's flowers sent to her father's suburban town house, but she hasn't visited him in a while. Besides, he might not even grasp the significance; Debbie Olivera might not have, either.

They were sent more for Angel's own benefit; sent to symbolize the penance for that long-ago sin.

If only Taylor were spending the night at her father's home this weekend. If only he could be the one to find her lifeless body.

But I can't wait any longer. I need . . .

I need to do something. Something . . .

I need to do this. It's time. It's her turn.

Angel checks again to see if Carley has signed on yet—no—then goes back to pacing, waiting for her to materialize online, waiting for Taylor to write back, waiting, waiting, frustration building . . .

Taylor . . .

Carley . . .

They're just like Nicki. Foolish, self-absorbed, oblivious little twits.

They deserve what Nicki got. They deserve worse.

So do their parents.

Taylor Morino might not live with her father, but she's a daddy's girl through and through. And Carley Archer's doting mother was so convinced her little sweetheart could do no wrong.

They're in for a rude awakening, both of them. They're going to know what it's like to—

An electronic tone shatters the silence, indicating a response to Angel's message.

hi Rachel i would luv thattttttt

Grinning with relief, Angel types a quick note back: *GREATTTTTTTT be there in 10 mins and whatevr u do dont tell anyone b/c rick is super private*

It's tempting to wait for Taylor's reply, but that probably isn't a good idea. She might change her mind, and then what?

Now that everything is in motion, Angel has no interest in prolonging it any longer.

It's been almost three decades since the heinous deed that set all this in motion; three decades since the three of them—Debbie, Mike, and Jen—destroyed their innocent victim as surely as if they had taken a razor-sharp knife with a fancy brand name etched into the wooden handle, and severed her veins . . .

The way Nicki Olivera supposedly did.

Guilt-tainted grief must be eating her mother alive. Good. Now Debbie Quattrone Olivera knows exactly what it's like to be left behind, bereft, filled with regret and questions that can never be answered. Now she can pay that penance for the rest of her days on this earth.

It's time for Michael Morino to suffer the same sacrifice, and on the eve of the Spring Fling dance where his darling daughter would have worn the coveted tiara.

Then it will be Genevieve Bonafacio Archer's turn.

Only then will Angel be at peace.

Then I'll be able to decide where to go from here.

Or whether to go on from here at all. After so many months in this house, consumed by vengeance, haunted by memories. . . .

And now, faced with whatever has lain buried beneath the basement floor for nearly thirty years . . .

You know what it is. You know!

Eyes stinging, Angel abruptly closes the laptop and leaves the room, dogged by Mother's voice.

Are you crying?

What's wrong with you?

"Shut up, Mother! Shut up!"

You're a sissy, that's what you are.

"Shut up!"

Boys don't cry!

"But I'm not—"

Angel stops short, halfway down the stairs, remembering something.

Go back and get it, you big crybaby. Without it, the whole plan is worthless.

Focus. Focus!

Angel strides back to the laptop and removes the memory stick, pocketing it before opening a closet door and reaching high up on the shelf. Two copies remain of the three that were originally purchased at a local bookstore—for a book club, Angel told the nosy clerk who asked.

But I only need one tonight.

Angel takes the book and scurries back to the stairs, smiling at last in anticipation of what is to come.

Taylor Morino leans into the bathroom mirror, checking to make sure her hastily applied lip gloss went on evenly.

Yup—her mouth looks perfectly kissable, and with any

luck, that's just what she'll be doing soon: kissing Rick Riley.

She's dying to post that on her Peeps page, but Rachel asked her not to tell anyone. Bummer.

Back in her room, she glances at the huge bouquet of pink Stargazer lilies on the nightstand.

She has a pretty good idea who the secret admirer is. When she sees Rick tonight, should she come right out and thank him, or make him wonder if they even arrived? The latter option might make him sign the card next time. Then she'd have something to show her friends.

She slips her phone into the back pocket of her jeans, then switches it to the front pocket, where she can reach it more easily. At least she'll be able to sneak a picture of her and Rick to share later, regardless of how things go between them. If it turns out to be just a one-night thing, she'll still have photo evidence, and if it turns into more than that . . .

It would be pretty cool to have a picture of the night they met, to show their kids someday, just like Taylor's parents did.

Of course, Mom and Dad aren't even married anymore, but whatever. Taylor still likes to look at the old snapshot, a group picture taken at Mom's five-year high school class reunion. She'd gone to Immaculata, and one of her former classmates brought Dad as her date. In the picture, Mom and Dad are looking at each other while everyone else looks at the camera.

When Mom first showed it to Taylor years ago, she said that Dad flirted with her all night, and his date got mad and left early.

"I just knew that first night," she used to say, "that he was the one. From the second we saw each other, we both knew, didn't we, Mike?"

Dad would agree, of course, but Taylor always got the feeling that he was just going along with Mom's romantic version of their story. Long before they split up, she could tell that her father wasn't as content being married as her mother was. She secretly wondered why he'd ever proposed in the first place—until she got old enough to do the math and realized Mom was three months pregnant with her at their wedding.

That explained it. Her parents both came from old-fashioned, religious Catholic families; neither of them believed in abortion or having children out of wedlock. For that, Taylor is grateful—otherwise she wouldn't exist.

She can barely remember what it was like to live with both her parents under the same roof in a much nicer neighborhood than where she lives now.

After the divorce, Mom and Taylor rented this small ranch house on Dogwood Street because it was affordable and close to the hospital where she works, and to good Catholic schools as well. Dad, who didn't have custody of Taylor, didn't have to worry about those things and moved to an "adult townhouse community" in a wealthy suburb.

Mom works the overnight shift every weekend, and Taylor used to stay at her father's, but not anymore. She's old enough to spend the night alone. Plus, she and Sharon, her latest stepmother—this is Dad's third marriage—don't always see eye-to-eye.

Dad and Sharon don't see eye-to-eye, either, lately, Taylor's noticed. She has a feeling Dad's lost interest in her after two years of marriage, and that Sharon is trying hard to recapture his attention.

Bev, Taylor's last stepmother, did the same thing. So did Mom.

Taylor has done it, too, for that matter.

Notice me, Dad. Come on, stop looking at your watch and fidgeting with your keys. Notice me.

He hardly ever seems to, not even when they're spending "quality time" together.

But I don't really care. Not anymore.

Soon enough, she'll be off to college—Catholic college, of course, because it's what her parents want, and having spent her formative years in their stormy household, she learned not to make waves.

She has only a few more weeks to make up her mind where she's going to school—or rather, a few more weeks for her parents to decide where she's going. If Dad gets his way, it'll be Saint Bonaventure, his alma mater; Canisius or Niagara if Mom gets hers. She herself went to Xavier in Cincinnati for her nursing degree, but she wants Taylor to stay closer to home.

"You're all I have," Mom tells her often. "My whole world."

Yeah. No pressure there.

Taylor is kind of hoping that since Dad is the one who's paying tuition, he'll get his way and she'll be off to Saint Bonnie in August. Some distance would be good for everyone. But then again, Dad paid for high school, too, and Mom won that battle. Dad wanted her to go to Griffin Academy and live there; Mom wanted Sisters because it's in the neighborhood.

"If she goes to Griffin, Mike," Mom said, "she's going to commute as a day student, and you'll have to come up here and drive her to and from every morning and afternoon because that's when I sleep."

Apparently, Dad wasn't interested in doing that—"It would cramp his style," Mom told her, which hurt Taylor's feelings at the time.

But it was all for the best. She's had a decent four years at Sisters, graduation is right around the corner, and she was voted queen of Spring Fling tomorrow night. She's going to the dance with Josh Keller, the best-looking guy in the Cardinal Ruffini senior class, but who cares about him right now?

She has a hot date with a handsome, famous, rich NFL player.

Taylor slips her feet into a pair of heeled black boots. Rick Riley is six-four, and his cousin Rachel mentioned once that he likes tall girls. Taylor is five-eight barefoot, but it won't hurt to add a couple of inches.

She checks her reflection one last time in the full-length mirror on the back of her closet door. Ordinarily, she's more than pleased with what she sees, but right now, her eye is extra critical. She's going out with Rick Riley.

Going out? More like staying in, she thinks, grinning at herself in the mirror.

With any luck, they'll soon be able to ditch his cousin and whoever else is hanging around his house.

Hearing a car coming down the street, Taylor turns away from the mirror and grabs the suede jacket that makes her look at least twenty-one. Of course, Rachel must have told Rick how old she really is, but obviously, it doesn't matter to him. He wants to meet her anyway.

Taylor takes a deep breath of air sweetly perfumed by the Stargazer lilies and turns off her bedroom light.

As she walks down the hall, she can see a silhouette in the glass front door, and her heart beats a little faster.

The pace quickens when she opens the door and sees the person standing on the threshold.

It isn't Rick Riley.

And it isn't his cousin Rachel.

Of all people, it's—

"What are you doing here?" Taylor asks incredulously. "Is this some kind of—"

She breaks off, seeing the gun, and she looks into those familiar eyes for a hint of humor.

But one glance into those lethal depths tells her this is no joke.

Entry from the marble notebook

Friday, February 7, 1986

It's no accident that I was practicing parallel parking on the street near Cardinal Ruffini this afternoon. I remembered that it was a Friday when Father had his heart attack, right around five o'clock. I figured the basketball team must leave practice around that time every Friday, because I noticed on the sign out front that there's bingo in the school gym every Friday night at six-thirty, so the team would have to leave early that day so that all the tables can be set up.

Pretty smart, right?

Right! Because sure enough, at a few minutes after five, the doors opened and out came a bunch of guys in basketball jackets.

I spotted the cute one right away. I haven't been able to stop thinking about him since I sat behind him at church on Sunday. He was even better-looking than I thought, which was based on the first time I saw him under traumatic circumstances and the second time when it was mostly just the back of his head.

I pretended not to see him and his friends, but they obviously saw us. My car window was open because Father kept making me stick my head out to see how close I was to the curb.

I heard one of the guys—it turned out to be Eric,

the one who drove—shouting to us. He was asking how Father was feeling.

I let Father do all the talking when the boys came over to the car, but I couldn't stop looking at the cute one. He didn't say anything, just stood there dribbling his basketball.

Father was pretty nice to the guys—he actually managed to make himself seem like a normal person, which I've seen him do before, whenever he's out in public. No one would ever guess what a monster he really is.

While the other guys were talking to Father and I was staring at the cute one, I noticed him noticing me. He kind of smiled at me.

And this crazy thought popped into my head right then: What if he likes me, too?

I can't stop thinking about it.

I can't wait until next Friday.

Chapter 12

When the doorbell rings on Saturday morning, Jen breaks off in mid-conversation with Thad—about the girls' latest traumas, of course—to glance at the clock on the microwave.

"It's only five to nine. Who can that be?"

"Your parents. Who else?"

"They don't come over without calling anymore."

"Sometimes they do," Thad points out with a forced grin, followed by a wince as if it hurts just to move his facial muscles, courtesy of his fierce hangover.

"Not in a long time."

"Maybe they heard Frankie snuck into town yesterday without telling them and they want to scold her."

"But they never come to the front door and they don't ring the bell."

"Yeah, no kidding."

"I don't want to go to the door looking like this." Jen gestures at the flannel shirt and sweatpants she threw on when she rolled out of bed, and at the hair she hasn't brushed in almost twenty-four hours.

"I'm not looking so hot myself," Thad points out unnecessarily, "and I'm not feeling so hot, either."

"Really? I had no idea!"

Managing another grin, he forces himself to his feet. "Okay, okay . . . I'll go see who it is if you'll pour me a refill. I need more coffee if I'm going to get to the office."

"Maybe you can work at home today. We'll all be over at my mother's so the house will be quiet."

"Can't. I have clients coming in." He slides his empty coffee mug across the breakfast bar toward her and heads for the hall.

With a sigh, Jen puts her own empty coffee cup into the sink and dumps what's left in the carafe into Thad's, then sets about making a fresh pot. Frankie is still upstairs asleep, as are the girls, but judging by the amount of red wine she consumed last night, she'll be looking for strong black coffee when she wakes up, just as Thad was.

As her husband and sister overindulged into the wee hours and got into a string of lively, good-natured debates— about religion, politics, sports—Jen sat brooding about her daughters. Finally, she left the two of them in the kitchen and went to bed. Somehow, she managed to fall into a deep, blessedly dreamless sleep, only to be jarred awake when Thad crawled in beside her at three-thirty.

He was snoring within seconds, but her mind kicked right back into gear and she lay sleepless until dawn. Finally, she got up and checked her e-mail, which she hadn't had a chance to do yesterday.

There was a message from Sister Linda suggesting a meeting on Monday afternoon. Jen confirmed that she'd be there.

Then she shut down the computer and started doing all the laundry that's been piling up for a week. Between loads, she cleared clutter from surfaces, went through stacks of neglected mail, sorted the contents of kitchen drawers that didn't really need sorting.

Anything to keep busy. Anything to keep her mind away from persistent dark thoughts. She was looking forward to going to church later to pray her novena to Saint Anne.

When Thad came downstairs half an hour ago looking decidedly green, Jen wanted to feel sorry for him, but instead found herself resentful. She can count on one hand the number of times he's overindulged, and he's certainly paying for it today. Yet it stills seems somehow unfair that he got to enjoy a few hours of lighthearted reprieve from parental concern while her every waking moment has been consumed by worry.

Now, standing at the sink running water into the coffeepot and staring at the overcast morning beyond the window, Jen remembers, yet again, how Carley lashed out at her last night. It was one thing for Emma to act as though Jen had severed her lifeline when she took away the Internet, but *Carley*?

The coffeepot overflows and Jen turns off the tap in time to hear Thad coming back to the kitchen talking to someone—a female voice, but it isn't Frankie's.

Startled, then dismayed, to see the impeccably dressed Marie Bush in the doorway beside rumpled, stubbly, bleary-eyed Thad, Jen belatedly remembers: She'd invited Marie to come by on Saturday morning to discuss piano lessons for Carley, telling her to come early, before they had to leave for her parents' house to do the cooking.

"Genevieve—it's so good to see you again." Marie sweeps in to hug her, smelling of lavender and mint and fresh air, leaving Jen feeling all the more stale and disheveled.

"Marie, I—I'm so sorry—I completely forgot. Carley is—she's not—she's—"

"I'll go get her out of bed," Thad offers, and quickly disappears.

"Wait a minute, don't wake her up. If you weren't expecting me then I can come back another—"

"No, it's okay," he calls, already on his way up the stairs, "she'll be down in a few minutes."

Marie looks at Jen, who musters a smile. "Um, that was Thad. My husband. I should have introduced you."

"We met," Marie tells her with a little laugh. "He seems like a nice man."

"He is. He's . . ." *He's got a raging hangover from drinking too much whiskey, but . . .* "He's a nice man. Have a seat, Marie. I was just about to make another pot of coffee."

"Is everything all right?"

Jen nods.

"Are you sure? I'm intuitive, you know."

Jen smiles.

"I'm serious. I spend my summers down at Lily Dale. Ever hear of it?"

Jen raises an eyebrow. "Of course."

Everyone in western New York is familiar with Lily Dale, a summer colony about an hour south of Buffalo, populated by psychics and spiritualists. Her parents always dismissed it as "a hocus-pocus circus" and said that believing in that stuff went against the teachings of their own faith.

"So you're psychic?" she asks Marie.

"Psychic, intuitive. . . . whatever you choose to call it. But it doesn't take much to know everything is not all right with you today. What's going on, sweetie?"

"It's just been a rough week, between Nicki and . . . you know."

Marie squeezes her arm gently. "I know."

But she doesn't know. And no matter how intuitive she is, she couldn't possibly guess.

Tempted to pour out her troubles, Jen thinks better of it. Marie, who's raised three kids of her own, would undoubtedly lend a sympathetic ear. But Jen finds herself wanting to protect Carley, lest Marie get the wrong idea about her before she even meets her.

She's a good girl who made one bad decision . . .

As far as Jen knows, anyway.

Frankie said there's more to the story. Jen wanted to steer her sister back to that topic of conversation last night, shamelessly hoping her guard would be down once she'd had some wine. But it didn't happen.

I wish I were psychic.

"Genevieve—" Marie is watching her closely. "Are you sure it wouldn't be better if I—"

"No, please, sit down," she says quickly, "and call me Jen. Here, let me take your coat and I'll make some fresh coffee."

They make small talk as she hangs Marie's tan trench over a hook by the door and gets the coffee going. Footsteps creak into the hall bathroom overhead and water gushes into the pipes.

"That must be Carley in the shower. I'm sure she'll be down soon."

"How has she been coping?"

For a moment, Jen assumes Marie is referring to the school suspension. Then she realizes—Nicki.

"It's not easy."

"No, it isn't." Marie pauses. "Nicki's piano lessons were scheduled for Friday afternoons at four. Yesterday would have been the day, but—well . . . Anyway, I was in the neighborhood, so I stopped over there at four to see Debbie."

"How was she?" Jen asks.

"As well as you'd expect. She was alone. She said her husband went back to work on Thursday morning. I have to admit, that surprised me. She said it was his way of coping."

Debbie had told Jen the same thing when she visited.

At the time Jen found herself trying to fathom Thad leaving her and going back to work under those circumstances, then hated herself for entertaining the heinous scenario yet again.

"To each his own, I suppose," Marie says now.

Jen nods, sitting beside her at the breakfast bar. "I suppose."

Suddenly remembering that *The Virgin Suicides* was sitting on Nicki's bedroom shelf, she wonders if Debbie even noticed it there. If she'd seen the book before her daughter's death, was she beating herself up because it was a red flag she should have noticed? And if she hadn't spotted it until afterward, when it was too late, was she blaming herself for not having paid more attention to the little things, to *everything*?

Was that the source of her guilt, or was there something more to it?

"The loss of a child has destroyed even the strongest of marriages."

Jen wonders whether Marie deliberately meant to imply weakness in Debbie and Andrew's. Catching a hint of a gleam in her eye, she decides that she might have.

Don't ask her about it, she warns herself.

But when she opens her mouth, words—the wrong words—fall out of it. "I was surprised to see Mike Morino at the funeral."

"Oh?"

Marie knows something. Or at the very least, she's been suspicious, too.

"I didn't realize they were in touch again," Jen says. "Debbie and Mike, I mean. I'm surprised she didn't mention it to me."

"Why is that?"

"Because Mike and I dated all through high school, and it seems . . . it just seems like something you would mention. You know, that after all these years, you've been in touch with someone's ex. Doesn't it?"

"It does," Marie agrees, studying the pattern on the granite breakfast bar, and Jen abruptly decides it's time to stop sidestepping the elephant in the room.

"Do you think they were seeing each other, Marie?"

"Who?"

She knows darn well, but Jen obliges with a patient, "Debbie and Mike Morino."

"I don't like to gossip."

"I don't, either. I just picked up on something between them."

"So you're psychic, too."

Marie is teasing, Jen knows. But when she thinks about the nightmare that felt like a premonition, a strange apprehension oozes into her gut.

"Not psychic at all," she tells Marie, "but . . . I wondered about it, that's all. I've been so worried about Debbie, and Mike is . . . well, he's not . . . he's . . ."

He's a bastard; that's what he is. He's the last thing Debbie needs in her fragile state.

"Look, I've known Mike for years," Marie tells her. "Not well, but he's always been pleasant to me, so who am I to speculate about his personal life?"

"You're right. I'm sorry. I was just concerned about Debbie, and . . ."

No. Something more about the possible connection, something beyond worry for Debbie's welfare, is bothering her.

What about the suicide note?

If there in fact was a note, Mike and Debbie chose to cover it up. Why? To protect themselves, or to protect Nicki?

Who am I to drag it out into the open?

"Forget it, Marie. I shouldn't have brought it up. I don't want to spread rumors. In the grand scheme of things, I guess it really doesn't matter whether Mike and Debbie are involved, does it?"

"No, it doesn't matter, but . . ." Marie tilts her chic blond head, as if she's deciding whether to confide something. Then, mind apparently made up, she says, "Just so you know you're not the only one with suspicions . . . It wouldn't have even crossed my mind until yesterday . . ."

Jen's pulse quickens. "Why? What happened yesterday?"

"While I was visiting Debbie, Mike stopped over. Obviously he didn't expect to find anyone there with her. It was such a nice day that I had left my car parked around the corner, where I had my three o'clock lesson, and walked over to the Oliveras' . . ."

"So Mike just showed up there?"

"Yes. And it was awkward."

"How?"

"She went to answer the door and the way he started talking to her—then I guess she must have shushed him and he realized I was in the next room, and he changed his tone completely."

"I wish I could talk to her about it."

"And tell her what?"

"I don't know . . . warn her, maybe, that he's a jerk?" Even as she says it, Jen realizes it sounds ludicrous.

Her warning would be based on the teenage Mike she once knew. But Debbie knew him, too. Knew how he'd treated Jen; knew about the cheating and the lies; knew he wasn't the nicest guy in town, by any stretch. It follows that Debbie also knew—should have known—better than to get involved with him.

Anyway, maybe he's changed. Maybe—

Come on, who are you kidding?

Mike hasn't changed one bit. He's married, having an affair . . .

And what he does now is none of your business, Jen reminds herself.

"I'm sorry," she tells Marie as the coffeemaker beeps to indicate that it's finished brewing. "I didn't mean to even bring this up. But sometimes my tongue ignores my brain."

Marie smiles. "That's because you care about people—not because you don't."

"That might be one of the nicest things anyone has ever said to me. Thank you." Jen stands and goes over to the counter to pour Marie a cup of coffee. As she lifts the pot, a loud rapping startles her and she nearly spills it.

Turning, she sees that someone is standing on the deck, knocking on the sliding glass door. Two *someones*.

"That just about gave me a heart attack." Marie presses a hand to her breastbone.

"I'm sorry. It's my parents." Jen carefully sets down the coffeepot and hurries over to the door, shaking her head.

Her mother is wearing pantyhose, makeup, and a dark coat; her father, a blazer and dress shoes. They've just been to Mass at Our Lady, Jen knows, and they've undoubtedly brought over a box of doughnuts. Her mother probably wants to go over the menu for Sunday and talk about the cooking they'll be doing today.

Unlocking the door and sliding it open, she's about to remind them that they're supposed to call first when she realizes that they haven't brought doughnuts after all—and that her mother looks upset.

Uh-oh. Did she find out Frankie snuck into town early?

"Hi, Ma, hi, Dad. What's going on?" Jen steps back to let them in, along with a blast of damp chill.

"I wanted to call first," her father says as they quickly take turns hugging and kissing Jen, "but your mother didn't want to stop back home first, and we didn't have our cell phone with us."

"Is that Frankie's car out front?" Theresa Bonafacio asks.

"It is. She's—"

"When did she get here?"

"She—"

"Is that . . . Marie?" Theresa interrupts, catching sight of her beyond Jen's shoulder. "Marie Bush?"

"Hi, Theresa, Aldo. It's been years, hasn't it!" Marie greets Jen's parents with warm hugs.

"Years," Jen's father agrees.

"Years," echoes Jen's mother. "What are you doing here?"

"We're talking about piano lessons for Carley. What are *you* doing here?" Jen asks her parents in return, closing the door behind them.

They exchange a glance, and the troubled expression her mother was wearing at the door settles over her features once again.

"We didn't mean to barge in," her father says.

"We thought you'd want to know, though."

"Know what?" So this isn't about Frankie being in town after all, or about the feast preparation.

"We were on our way to church earlier when we saw a commotion over on Dogwood Street. Police cars, flashing lights. Then after Mass, we went to Tim Horton's for coffee—we do that every morning," her mother breaks off to explain for Marie's benefit. "A big group of us. Now that we're all retired, we can do that."

Marie nods politely.

"So what happened?" Jen prods, trying to recall whether she knows anyone who still lives on Dogwood in the old neighborhood, not far from Sacred Sisters. "Was it a fire?"

"No, not a fire. Joe Dinella—do you remember Mr. Dinella, Genevieve? He was in the Knights of Columbus with Dad years ago."

"Something happened to Mr. Dinella?" she asks, feeling a twinge of guilt over her immediate sense of relief. Based on her mother's expression, she'd been expecting to hear news of a tragedy.

Nothing against Joe Dinella, but he must be in his late eighties, early nineties, even. Maybe he had a fall and had to be taken to the hospital, or maybe he even died in his sleep. That would be sad, but hardly tragic.

"No, no, Joe is fine. But he lives on Dogwood, next door to the house where we saw all that commotion, and he told us what happened."

"What *happened*?" Jen asks yet again, jaw clenching.

"The woman who lives there—her name is Susan Morino."

Morino.

Okay.

There are a lot of Morinos in Buffalo . . .

"I know her," Marie speaks up. "She's Michael Morino's ex-wife."

His *ex*-wife? Jen had assumed, based on the wedding ring he'd been wearing, that he was married.

See? Maybe you were being too hard on him after all.

No—because Debbie is married. Is it any less sinful to fool around with another man's wife than it is to cheat on your own?

"Genevieve went with Mike for years when they were in school," her mother is telling Marie. "That's why I thought she'd want to know . . ."

"Know what? Did something happen to his wife, Mom?"

Ex-wife. *Ex.*

Theresa shakes her head. "No, not to her. They have a daughter . . ."

Yes. Taylor.

A chill creeps over Jen as she remembers her conversation with Mike that day at the funeral home, remembers the photo he pulled from his wallet, remembers the smell of Stargazer lilies filling her lungs every time she took a breath, filling her head with memories she's tried to bury for almost three decades . . .

"Taylor. Her name is Taylor." Marie touches, clutches, Mom's arm. "Did something happen to her?"

"I'm so sorry. You knew her?"

Past tense. Oh, God.

"What happened?" Marie's question is taut with dread.

"She . . . died."

Her mother's shocking words slam into Jen, taking her breath away.

Died—"died" is the wrong word.

Seventeen-year-old girls don't just *die*.

Not like little old men who might close their eyes one night and never wake up.

High school girls don't die without warning, without being sick . . .

How do you know she wasn't sick?

Because Mike didn't mention it?

Why would he share something like that with you?

Maybe that's why he's been there for Debbie. Maybe he knew he would soon be facing a terrible loss himself.

Awash in self-loathing, Jen remembers all the terrible things she's been thinking, and yes, now even saying, about Mike.

You don't judge a grieving parent.

You don't—

"Her mother came home from working the night shift and found her," Theresa Bonafacio reports gravely. "It's a terrible coincidence. She killed herself, just like Nicki Olivera."

Stunned, Jen presses her hands against her mouth.

Humming a made-up tune, Angel cracks a second egg into the cast-iron skillet on the stove and tilts the pan to spread the white a little. A pair of fried eggs, sunny side up, will hit the spot after all the strenuous activity of the early morning hours.

It was unearthing the buried freezer that took up most of the energy—not what happened afterward, with Taylor.

She didn't even put up much of a fight. One look at the gun pointed at her, and that was it. She'd have done anything. Anything at all.

She didn't have to do much, though.

Just walk calmly and quietly to her bedroom with the gun poking into the small of her back. It was gratifying to see the bouquet of vibrant pink lilies displayed on her bedside table.

"I see you got my flowers."

She made a small whimpering sound.

"What's that? You didn't know they were from me? Who'd you think they were from? Your dear old dad? Well, I guess I don't blame you. It wouldn't be the first time he sent someone a bouquet of Stargazers. Oh, that's right—you don't know about that."

Taylor sat on a chair as directed, her back to Angel. It was easy, from there, to slip the noose around her neck and tighten it in one swift motion.

It took a long time for Taylor Morino to die, though.

She strangled slowly, her polished fingernails clutching at the noose and her heeled boots kicking until they toppled a lamp, shattering the light bulb on the hardwoods.

"Now look what you've done," Angel chided, still holding on tightly to the noose. "I'm going to have to clean that up when this is over. I should make you do it. Oh, wait—you can't, because you'll be dead."

Angel found that hilarious for some reason, and almost lost hold of the rope thanks to a slaphappy burst of laughter. Almost, but not quite, thanks to a thick pair of work gloves meant to prevent rope burns—and fingerprints.

At last, Taylor's body went still. Only when a full minute, maybe two, passed without writhing or kicking or even twitching, did Angel finally let go of the noose.

Then it was time to remove Taylor's clothing from the closet. It had sturdy double bars, the top one too high to reach without standing on something. That would serve the purpose nicely. Angel heaped piles of dresses, shirts, and jackets, all on their hangers and some wrapped in plastic, on the bed and floor. Some items were familiar, from pictures Taylor had posted on her Peeps page: the slinky black dress she'd worn at her homecoming dance, the red velvet sheath she'd had on when she posed in front of a Christmas tree, and a sequined gown with price tags still on it, presumably purchased for the Spring Fling dance.

Then there were the school uniforms she'd worn every weekday, unaware that her friend "Rachel" was right there, watching her, waiting . . .

Now the waiting had finally come to an end. It was over.

Angel dragged Taylor's lifeless body over to the closet, threw the rope over the top bar, and strung her up until her corpse swayed gently, black heeled boots dangling a foot above the floor. Then came the chair, set into position beneath the girl, then toppled with a hard kick.

Trading the work gloves for thin latex gloves, Angel turned to Taylor's laptop, still open on the desk. She was still logged into her Peopleportal page, which made it a breeze to delete every trace of Rachel Riley, including the private messages exchanged less than an hour ago.

Then, in Taylor's status box, Angel swiftly typed a quote memorized solely for this occasion: *Numbing the pain for a while will make it worse when you finally feel it.*

The words had been spoken by the character Albus Dumbledore in J. K. Rowling's *Harry Potter and the Goblet of Fire.*

The entire hardcover series was neatly lined up in the bookcase beside Taylor's bed, right where Angel had seen it on an early visit to the house when no one was home.

With gloved fingers, Angel plucked the fourth dog-eared volume from the shelf, found the page with the quote, and folded the corner down. The book went back into the row with the others, but pulled slightly forward, as though someone—Taylor—had recently been rereading it.

Then it was time for the other book—the one Angel had bought, kept on the closet shelf, and brought to the house.

It took a few moments to figure out the best place to leave it: somewhere unobtrusive, where it would appear as though Taylor herself had been reading it and set it down.

The bedside table was too obvious, under the pillow too stagey, the desk too similar to where it had been left in Nicki's room.

Angel finally looked at the bookshelf again, finding it too full to fit another hardcover vertically among the others. But the volume fit sideways, right on top of the row of Harry Potter books.

The final step was to insert the memory stick and upload the letter that had been painstakingly written and rewritten, just like the one Angel planted in Nicki's laptop.

Nicki's suicide note had blamed her mother for what she was about to do.

Taylor's note blames her father.

But both make reference to the sinful affair between Mike Morino and Debbie Quattrone Olivera. Both were created with one explicit purpose: to fill the surviving parents with shame and guilt for the rest of their days.

After ejecting and pocketing the memory stick, Angel left the laptop open to the document and looked in the utility closet for a broom, an empty plastic shopping bag, and a new light bulb. The lamp was righted with the bulb screwed into place; the broken shards were swept into the bag. On the way home, Angel tossed the bag into a Dumpster in the parking lot behind the dry cleaner on Redbud Street, the same place where the other household garbage has been deposited—not that there's ever been much.

And that was it.

So simple.

All told, it had been a satisfying night.

Rather, morning.

And now it's time for a good hot breakfast, eaten in civilized fashion, not squatting on the kitchen linoleum, but rather, perched on the built-in seat beneath drawn shades that cover the dining room's bay windows.

In a house cleared of furniture, one learns to improvise.

Still humming, Angel opens a drawer to find a couple of paper packets of salt and a plastic fork among the seasonings and utensils collected and hoarded over many months of consuming fast food. It would be nice to cook in a well-equipped kitchen for a change, rather than making do with odds and ends here or dining yet again on McDonald's, Chinese, or prepackaged crap from 7-Eleven.

After plucking a couple of salt packets from the litter of takeout ketchup and soy sauce, Angel rummages through the spoons and knives looking for a fork. There's one wedged in the back of the drawer, but it snaps in half when Angel tries to pull it out, and—

A memory barges in.

On that last day, when they did the walk-through, Sandra Lutz didn't hand over just the marble notebook wrapped in rosary beads. There was a plastic bag, too, filled with odds and ends. One was a tarnished, bent fork that had been left behind in a kitchen drawer.

Another was a key, forgotten on a high nail by the cellar door.

Forgotten . . . or hidden?

Angel takes the stairs two at a time and hurries down the wide second-floor hallway to the back bedroom where the bag is stashed, along with the journal.

Yes. There it is.

Key in hand, Angel bolts back down the stairs, races through the first floor, opens the basement door, and flips the wall switch without thinking.

Halfway down the creaky flight, the realization hits: *You turned on the light!*

A serious violation of Angel's foremost rule, and yet, it's broad daylight outside, and this is merely a basement light.

There are only a few windows there anyway, narrow, low to the ground, recessed in little alcoves built into the foundation. In the front of the house, they're completely shrouded by dense shrubbery. In the back, they're more visible, but the backyard is private, and you'd have to be standing right there, on ground level, to even see the basement windows in the first place.

Still, Angel doesn't like to take chances. The smart thing to do would be to turn off the light, go back upstairs, and find a flashlight, and yet . . .

I've been patient long enough.

The gaping hole awaits, and the key to the lock—the key to the past—might be in hand at long last. Besides, this won't take long at all. Either the key won't fit the lock, or it will.

If it does, Angel decides, *I'll go back for a flashlight before I do anything else. But I just need to know. Now.*

Fingering the key, Angel crosses the dirt floor and kneels, reaching down, down, down to the padlock holding the old freezer chest closed.

It might not fit.

It probably won't fit.

But . . .

It does.

The bolt springs free and the lock falls away, dropping into the depths of the hole. Angel's intention to go back for a flashlight vanishes in an instant.

I have to see inside the freezer. Now.

Are you sure you want to know what's there?

I already know. I just have to see for myself. For . . . for her sake.

Angel leans forward and takes hold of the edge of the freezer lid, tugging it upward . . .

All at once, a deafening, high-pitched sound blasts from the first floor.

What the—?

It's the smoke alarm.

The eggs—the eggs are on the stove burner, undoubtedly scorched by now.

Sandra Lutz's voice rises above the screeching alarm, filling Angel's head

. . . airtight and watertight, perfect for keeping out insects and dampness . . .

Angel glances toward the stairway. Someone is going to hear that piercing sound, even with all the windows closed.

Hurry! Get upstairs and turn it off!

I will, but first—

This can wait a few more minutes! It's been buried down here for almost thirty years.

Buried down here in the murky basement. . . . buried in the darkest corner of Angel's brain. Buried long enough.

Angel gives the lid a mighty, final tug, and this time, it opens.

Putrid air spills forth.

The light from the overhead bulb fails to permeate the freezer's depths, making it impossible for Angel to see her. But she's there.

Been there all these years, all along.

"Oh, Ruthie . . . Ruthie . . ."

Leash in hand, Al Witkowski frowns, looking down at his puppy.

One moment they were walking briskly along Redbud Street, and the next, Roscoe stopped in his tracks and started whimpering.

"What's the matter, boy? Did you step on something? Here, let me take a look."

Al crouches beside the dog and begins lifting his paws, looking for embedded broken glass or sharp bits of metal, finding nothing.

But something is clearly bothering Roscoe. He only whines like this when he's in pain.

Stumped, Al tugs on the leash. "Come on, boy. Even I'm not hurting yet, and I'm in worse shape than you are. It's only been two blocks and we're almost home."

Roscoe digs in his paws, head tilted, looking toward the dry cleaner a few doors down.

"We're almost there, Roscoe. Let's get home. I have a job to get to."

Still the dog refuses to budge. Frustrated, Al bends over and picks him up. "Fine. If you can't walk, I'll carry you."

He strides on down the block with the dog squirming in his arms. He might have to take his morning walks without the puppy from now on, if this is how it's going to—

Al stops short a few steps away from the building.

There's a faint, high-pitched tone coming from some-where.

"Is that what it is, boy? Is that sound hurting you?"

It must be. Dogs' ears are much more sensitive than humans'. Poor guy.

What the hell *is* that sound? A shrill electronic hum, it seems to be coming from out back somewhere.

He quickly puts the dog back inside, then heads out to investigate, walking up the rutted drive alongside the building. The rutted parking lot looks the same as always: empty, except for a couple of Dumpsters.

The high-pitched buzz seems to be coming from the field

behind the parking lot . . . or maybe, Al realizes, from the block beyond. He begins picking his way through the weeds, then remembers the figure he thought he glimpsed in this very spot a few nights ago.

A ghost? he wondered at the time. Sandra's ghost?

In broad daylight, the idea is almost laughable. Almost.

The sound does seem to be coming from the gloomy, abandoned Victorian he can see through the trees. And now that he's closer to it, he recognizes it as the distinctive peal of a smoke alarm.

His thoughts immediately go to Sandra, who might have lived if only the smoke detectors in her house had been in working order.

If only . . .

Al pushes thoughts of Sandra aside.

Is the old place on fire?

It seems pretty damned unlikely that an empty house would spontaneously combust, which means that either the resident ghosts set a fire or someone is—

The sound is abruptly curtailed, as if the button was pushed to turn off the alarm.

Knitting his bushy gray-blond eyebrows, Al moves closer to the house, sidestepping a rusted tire rim and gingerly skirting a clump of pricker bushes. An overgrown evergreen border separates the lot from the backyard of the Addams House, thinner in some spots than in others.

Al works his way toward what looks almost like an opening and realizes that he's reached a path of sorts, following a trail where the weeds have been bent and broken, as though someone has walked here. Sure enough, in a muddy patch close to the opening in the border, he spots a couple of indentations that look like footprints.

Maybe he really did see a person heading back here the other night.

Maybe whoever it was just wanted to cut through to the

next block—although there's a far easier path from Redbud to Lilac behind a long-shuttered warehouse a couple of doors down. All the neighborhood kids use it.

So why would anyone come this way?

Reaching the evergreens, Al parts a couple of boughs to get a better look at the big old house. It looks foreboding as always, rising against a backdrop of bare branches and a gloomy morning sky. But as he peers at it, he spots something.

A faint light glows in the basement windows.

For a long time, Al stands there, looking at it.

He's seen light in the front windows, where the lamps on timers are located, but . . .

Who puts a timer lamp in a basement?

Is someone renting the place now? Probably.

Wait . . .

Would a legitimate renter sneak through an empty lot at night?

No.

It must be kids, Al decides. After all, the house, when it was abandoned back in the seventies, was a magnet for him and his cronies. It stands to reason that a new generation of neighborhood children has discovered the Addams House.

He turns away, satisfied with the explanation.

But as he makes his way back home, he thinks about the smoke alarm going off. And about Sandra.

He remembers how her eyes had lit up when she showed him around the old house on that long-ago day. "I've always wondered what this place was like inside. Isn't this woodwork magnificent, Al?"

She used fancy words like that. *Magnificent.*

Oh, Sandra. You *were magnificent.*

It's wrong for a bunch of careless kids to be trespassing, running loose through the old house, probably vandalizing it, smoking cigarettes . . .

What if they burn the place down?

No. No way. I won't let that happen.

Maybe Sandra didn't live there, but it was the last place Al saw her alive. He still thinks of her whenever he sees the house, thinks of what might have been . . .

Al makes up his mind to go over there and take a look around. Not now, because he has a moving job to oversee. And not later, because he's meeting his brother Bobby and Glenn Cicero at Louie's, a neighborhood bar, to watch the Sabres game over beer and wings.

But I will, he vows, *just as soon as I have a chance.*

Entry from the marble notebook

Thursday, February 13, 1986

Wouldn't you know it? All week, I've been looking forward to practicing my parallel parking over in
front of Cardinal Ruffini after school tomorrow, but
Father mentioned he has to stay late for a meeting at
the bank so we won't be able to go driving.

"You look disappointed," he said, like he thought
it was because I wouldn't get to spend two hours in
the car alone with him.

All I could think was that now I won't get to see my
cute guy for another whole week.

On days Mother works, I walk home the long way
so that I can detour past Cardinal Ruffini in case he's
hanging around outside, but he never is.

I've been trying to find out his name so that I can
figure out where he lives because maybe I can walk
past his house. I check all the sports articles in the
newspaper, and they print the roster so I know all the
possible names he could have.

I wish I knew which one is his. It would make me
feel like I know him a little better. Still, I honestly
think I'm falling in love with him. How am I going to
wait a whole week to see him again?

Chapter 13

Stepping out of the shower, Carley grabs a towel and swipes a jagged window into the steamed-over mirror. Her own bloodshot eyes, still swollen from tears and rimmed by dark circles, stare morosely back at her.

Thanks to her mother changing the wifi password, she just spent a largely sleepless night mourning her dead friend instead of chatting online with Angel, her new friend. Her *only* friend.

Until now, she hasn't truly allowed herself to wallow in what happened to Nicki—no, in what Nicki *did*. For a week now, she's been doing her best to distract herself with schoolwork, with a book, or—mostly—with the Internet.

Not last night. Last night—this morning, really—she finally let the brutal truth hit her full force, maybe to punish herself for her own stupid lapse in judgment. Yes, she deserves pain, deserves to suffer.

With the inevitable tears came anger—fresh anger, not over the way Nicki destroyed their friendship, but that Nicki took her own life.

How could you do that to yourself? To your parents? To me?

It just doesn't make sense.

Nicki just wasn't capable of hurting herself, let alone destroying her parents' lives and damaging everyone who ever knew and loved her.

Obviously, she changed, Carley reminded herself. *She was a different person when she did what she did.*

But somehow, in all those hours tossing her head on a sodden pillow as black shadows faded to blue, and finally to filmy gray, Carley couldn't seem to accept that fact as the simple answer. People don't change that drastically.

Hearing a knock on the bathroom door, she turns abruptly away from the mirror.

It's probably Aunt Frankie. It can't be Emma, because she would never get up this early on a Saturday—and even if she did, she would bang on the door and holler, not rap gently.

"I'm in here," Carley calls.

"I know."

Surprised to hear her sister's voice, and not Aunt Frankie's, she frowns. "Go use the one in Mom and Dad's room."

"For one thing, Dad is in the shower and for another thing, I don't have to go to the bathroom. I just need to come in."

"But I'm in here!"

"I know! Duh! I have to tell you something."

Exasperated, Carley wraps herself in the towel and opens the door a crack.

"What?"

"Let me in."

"Why?"

"Because I don't want to shout it so the whole world can hear, okay?"

As irked as she is intrigued, Carley steps backward into the steamy bathroom. Her sister pushes in after her, clad in the snug-fitting yoga pants and a T-shirt she wears as pajamas.

Carley envies her trim figure, as always.

It wouldn't be so frustrating if Emma at least worked at being in shape, but she's one of those people who can eat whatever she wants, lie around all day, and wear a size two.

"Don't worry, it'll catch up with her sooner or later," Nicki used to say. She, too, was in good shape, but unlike Emma, she sweated and starved to squeeze into teeny sizes.

And for what?

Now her slim, toned body is lying in a coffin, buried in the ground.

"Something crazy just happened," Emma announces, closing the bathroom door.

"Crazy good?"

"Crazy bad. Really bad. Do you know some girl named Taylor Morino?"

Carley nods.

Taylor Morino is yet another annoyingly perfect-looking girl, one who has a ton of friends, gets good grades, and dates the best-looking athletes at Cardinal Ruffini. The seniors voted her Spring Fling queen—and not, by any means, as a joke.

"I know who she is. She goes to Sisters. Why?"

"She killed herself last night."

"*What?*"

"Yes." A quirky hint of an odd smirk plays at the edges of Emma's mouth, as if she's secretly delighted at this terrible news, or maybe just delighted by her own importance in delivering it.

"But . . . why?"

Why would a girl like Taylor Morino kill herself?

Why would Nicki?

Why would anyone?

"I have no idea, but I swear, it's like an epidemic or something," Emma says. "You know?"

Carley thinks of that novel, the one Angel told her to

read: *The Virgin Suicides*. Last night, when she and Aunt
Frankie were talking about books, she asked Aunt Frankie
if she'd ever read that one.

"Yep. It's about an old-fashioned Catholic family with
five sisters," Aunt Frankie said wryly. "How's that for coincidence?"

"Is that why you read it?"

"*Everyone* read it. It was one of those books, fifteen years
ago, maybe twenty."

"Did my mom read it?"

"Probably. Ask her."

But Carley didn't want to do that. Not with a title like
The Virgin Suicides. It would open the door to yet another
conversation she doesn't feel like having.

"So what happens in the book?" she asked Aunt Frankie,
feigning complete cluelessness even though Angel had given
her a hint of the plot. "Does one of the sisters kill herself or
something?"

"They all kill themselves."

Carley's eyes widened. "Why?"

"It wasn't really clear. It was . . . look, it's a dark book,
Carley. Why are you asking about it?"

She shrugged. "No reason."

"Were you thinking of reading it? Because I don't know
if that's such a good idea for you, especially now."

But Angel thought it was. Carley fully intended to ask
her more about it, but of course she couldn't even get online
when she got home last night.

Remembering the scene she'd caused in the kitchen, she
feels a familiar pang of guilt.

But she couldn't seem to help flying into a rage. Angel is
her only friend in the world lately, and the Internet is Carley's only means of reaching her.

*And now . . . especially now, right now . . . I really need
to connect with her.*

"Epidemic" might be an overly dramatic word, but still . . . another suicide, so close to home, and just a week after Nicki's?

"How did you find out about it?" she asks her sister.

"I was downstairs in the family room a few minutes ago, and, like, no one knew I was there . . ."

Carley raises an eyebrow at her.

"Okay. I actually snuck in there," Emma amends, "because I figured Mom must have written down the new wifi password someplace. I really need to get online."

Ordinarily, Carley would, in proper big sister mode, chide Emma for snooping. But today, she only nods. Yes. She gets it. She really needs to get online, too.

"So anyway, some lady is here with Mom in the kitchen—"

"The piano teacher." Carley nods. That's why Dad woke her up, not long after she finally managed to drift off to sleep.

At first she thought she was dreaming when he said there's a piano teacher here to see her, because she hasn't taken piano lessons in ages. But then Dad explained that Mom had forgotten to tell her about it, and that she thought it would be good for Carley.

Which made no sense at all, and she told her father that.

"I don't know, Mom thinks it will help you . . . you know, feel better about . . . everything."

That was funny, because Nicki took piano lessons and it obviously didn't help her feel better about anything.

But Dad wasn't in his usual patient mood—he'd mentioned that he had to get ready for work and he wasn't feeling very good today—and he added, in his I-mean-business tone, "Listen, just hurry up and get down there."

Carley did what she was told.

I always do what I'm told.

Right. The good girl, never in trouble, and now—

"What piano teacher?" Emma is asking. "Is she making us take lessons again?"

"Just me, I think."

"Oh, right. I forgot you're getting punished, too." Her sister regards her with an expression Carley has never seen before—not directed at her, anyway: a combination of approval and respect.

Suddenly, Carley feels something akin to just that as she looks at her kid sister.

Being in trouble at school and at home is the story of Emma's life, yet she always manages to act as though it doesn't bother her. But how can it not?

This sucks, losing privileges and feeling like no one understands you and the world is against you . . .

Carley isn't used to it. She's used to being the good sister.

And I don't think I can let the bad stuff just roll off me the way Emma does.

"So then *anyway*," Emma goes on again with her story, "Grandma and Grandpa show up, and they don't even call first, and they tell Mom and the piano lady that this girl Taylor killed herself, and she goes to your school. Do you know who she is?"

"Yeah. Everyone knows who she is."

"That's not what I meant. Do you know who her dad is?"

"Her dad? Why would I—"

"He's Mom's old boyfriend!"

"Seriously?"

"That's what Grandma said. Isn't that crazy?"

Carley stares at her sister, remembering something Nicki told her a long time ago.

"Is his name Mike? The old boyfriend?"

Emma's eyebrows shoot up. "Yeah. Why?"

"No reason, I just . . ."

"You knew about him?"

"No. I mean, just that Mom had an old boyfriend named Mike. But I had no idea that he was Taylor's dad."

"How did you even know about him and Mom? Did she tell you?"

Emma is jealous, she realizes, imagining some cozy mother-daughter conversation that she wasn't privy to. To be fair, there have been plenty of those, but . . . not this time.

"Nicki told me that her mom was friends with him, and that he was Mom's old boyfriend. That's it."

"Well now Nicki's dead, and his daughter's dead, and you—" Emma breaks off, looking troubled.

"And I what?"

"You *wish* you were dead. You're not going to do anything stupid, are you?"

"What are you talking about?"

"You know . . . like kill yourself or something."

"*Kill myself?* No! Why would you even . . . God, no!"

"But you said you wanted to."

"I did not!" Leave it to Emma to put such dramatic words into someone else's mouth.

"Okay, maybe you didn't *say* it, but you *wrote* it."

Carley stares at her. "I did not write it. What are you talking about?"

"On Peeps."

"Emma, trust me—I did *not* write on Peeps that I wanted to kill myself."

"Gabe said he saw it on your page."

"Who the heck is Gabe?"

"My boyfriend. He's super hot."

Her *boyfriend*? Dumbfounded, Carley can only shake her head.

"Gabe said he checked out your page. Which means you lied, because you told me you had it set to private, and obviously you don't, because he could see it. And you obviously have me blocked, because I *can't* see it."

"First of all, I do have my page set to private. No one can

see anything I write unless I accept a connection request. And trust me, I never got one from some little kid I don't even know."

"Gabe's not a little kid. He's older than you, and he's super cool."

"Cool? Really? I thought you just said he was hot."

"He *is* hot. And cool."

"Okay. *Whatever* . . . I never got a request from your hot, cool *boyfriend*."

"You don't have to say it like that."

Yeah. I do.

Carley can't help it.

She's never even been out on a date, and Emma has a boyfriend. An older boyfriend, besides.

Come on . . . is it any surprise? Look at Emma.

Look at me.

She catches sight of herself in the fog-free spot in the bathroom mirror. The image is blurry—her glasses are on her bedside table—but not blurry enough to obscure the fleshy face, neck, and upper arms above the towel, acne on her cheeks and shoulders, hair wet and matted . . .

Yuck.

She turns back to her sister. "Em, second of all, I don't have you blocked. I don't have anyone blocked."

"Then why—"

"Look, if someone is lying about this, it's—"

Don't say "your boyfriend" again in that snotty tone, Carley warns herself. *Just don't. Why put her on the defensive?*

"It's not *me*," she says instead. "I'm not the one who's lying."

"So what does that mean? You think he is?"

"Obviously, since I haven't even written anything in a while. I've been a little busy lately with upsetting stuff, in case you haven't noticed."

"I *have* noticed. That's why I was worried! That's why I thought I should ask. I was just trying to—but, hey, you know what? Forget it. Die if you want to. I really could care less."

Emma jerks open the door and storms off down the hall.

Shaken, Carley closes the door after her.

People are always warning that the Internet is a dangerous place; that nothing you do online is ever truly private. She's spent a lot of time on those bullying message boards, perusing the suicide threads, but not because she actually . . .

Die if you want to!

But I don't *want to.*

Nicki did.

And Taylor did.

Was it a coincidence?

Or some kind of copycat thing?

Maybe, but not . . . not an epidemic. Leave it to Emma to blow it up into something it's not. You don't have an epidemic with just two occurrences of something. An epidemic means, what? Dozens? Hundreds? A lot more than two.

And there won't be any more, Carley tells herself firmly, if uneasily. *There can't be any more.*

Yet as she turns back to the mirror, reaching for a hairbrush, her sister's bizarre claim rings in her ears. What kind of guy is Emma mixed up with? Why would he make up something so horrible about Carley?

I should talk to Mom about this, she thinks—before remembering that she doesn't really want to talk to Mom about anything. Not right now, while she's suspended and being punished and trapped in the house—without Internet, without Angel, even—for another whole week.

Anyway, chances are her mother knows all about Emma's older boyfriend. That's probably why they were fighting yesterday, much more heatedly than usual.

I'm staying out of it, Carley decides, plugging in the hair dryer, wondering why she's even bothering to make herself presentable. No one downstairs is going to want to discuss piano lessons after this bombshell—Carley included.

And that's really too bad, because while she was in the shower, she found herself thinking that it might actually be kind of nice to get back into music. Unlike Emma, she used to enjoy practicing and would often sit at the keyboard long after she'd finished her scales and assigned sheet music, playing songs from the old 1970s songbooks she found inside the bench or picking out by ear the melodies of favorite tunes from her iPod playlists.

Yeah. Maybe Mom is right. Maybe she will want to take piano lessons again, after all of this blows over and things get back to normal.

Normal . . . what is normal like? She can barely remember.

Brows knit, she thinks again of the argument she just had with her sister. Of all the things Emma's jerk of an older boyfriend could possibly say about her, that was just mean. Sick and twisted, too, since he obviously must know what happened to her best friend.

Ex–best friend, she starts to correct herself, then stops.

Best friend, period.

All those years together . . .

Feelings don't just vanish overnight when someone hurts you, drops you. You can pretend you don't care, and you can try not to care, but . . .

You still care. You always will.

No. Don't cry. Aren't you tired of crying?

Carley wipes her eyes and furiously begins brushing the knots out of her wet hair, yanking the bristles hard through the tangles so that the hair pulls and her scalp hurts.

She stares into the mirror, brushing, aching, thinking of Nicki, thinking of Taylor . . . and of Taylor's dad.

My mom said they had a super bad breakup, Nicki had

told Carley, and made her swear she wouldn't tell her mother that Mrs. Olivera was still friends with him. Good friends, Nicki had said.

Did Nicki and Taylor know each other as well? Were they friends, too? Did they . . .

What if they made some kind of suicide pact or something?

Carley is so startled by the idea that she fumbles the hairbrush, dropping it into the sink.

As she reaches for it, there's another knock at the door.

"Go away, Emma! I don't want to—"

"Carley? It's me. I wasn't sure if anyone was in here."

"Oh . . . sorry." She opens the door to see Aunt Frankie standing there, barefoot in the same clothes she had on last night, toothbrush in hand and looking kind of ashen. Maybe she's sick, too, like Dad.

Maybe there's a bug going around, Carley thinks hopefully, out of habit, *and I can catch it and I won't have to go to school on Monday.*

Then she remembers—she doesn't have to go to school on Monday.

Which is worse: having to go to school and being ostracized by everyone in every class, or having to stay home because you're not allowed at school?

"I'll come back," Aunt Frankie tells her.

"It's okay. I was just going to dry my hair, but I can do that in my room." Carley grabs the brush and blow dryer. "By the way, Grandma and Grandpa are here."

"Oh no, really? Not that I don't love them, but I'm just a little under the weather, so . . ."

"They came over to tell Mom something about her old boyfriend—do you know him? His name was Mike."

An expression of distaste crosses Aunt Frankie's face. "I did know him, a long time ago, when he went out with your mom."

"And you didn't like him?"

"Not really."

"Why not?"

"Want the short list?" Aunt Frankie begins ticking off on her fingers. "He was bossy, he was sneaky, he thought he was God's gift to the world, and he was not a nice person. And I probably shouldn't be talking about him like this after all these years, but it's early, and—wait, *is* it early?" She looks at her watch, which she appears to have slept in, along with her clothes. "It's not *that* early, but I haven't had my coffee yet so I can't be blamed for anything, right?"

"Um—"

"Never mind, sweetie. So Mom and Dad—Grandma and Grandpa—came over here to talk about Mike Morino? Why? What's going on with him?"

"His daughter killed herself. She went to my school, and—" She breaks off, mortified to feel a lump rising in her throat. Why? She didn't even *know* Taylor.

"Come here." Aunt Frankie's arms wrap around her, good and tight.

She can't help it. She finds herself crying again.

"Oh, Carley . . . I'm so sorry."

"No, I'm okay. It's not like . . ." Carley reaches for a Kleenex from the box on top of the toilet tank. "I mean, she wasn't my *friend*, or anything. I knew who she was, but I didn't . . . it's not like Nicki. Not like that. I'm just . . . I'm just kind of shocked."

"Of course you are. This is just . . . unbelievably tragic." Aunt Frankie pulls back and shakes her head, looking at Carley, brushing her damp hair away from her wet cheeks.

"I'm a mess," Carley comments dully, not sure whether she's referring to her physical state, or her emotional one. Both, really.

"Anyone would have a difficult time with this. You've

been through a lot. Just take a deep breath . . . There, good. Better?"

Carley shrugs, feeling faint, swaddled in moist, over-heated air.

"Keep breathing. Where's your mom?"

"Downstairs. She doesn't know I know. Emma told me."

"Is Emma upset, too?"

"Emma never gets upset."

"Some people are better at not showing it."

Carley shrugs, not wanting to tell her aunt that it isn't like that. With Emma . . . it's almost as if she *likes* this kind of thing, in some weird way. Likes the drama of it. She probably can't wait to talk about it with her ghoulish boyfriend, the way she must have talked about Nicki. Why else would he have made up that stuff about Carley talking about suicide on her Peeps page?

She shudders.

"Are you cold?" Aunt Frankie asks.

Not in the least, but she nods anyway, deciding to go with it. That's better than trying to explain what her sister told her just now. It would just be one more stressful thing she'd ultimately end up having to discuss with her parents. If they hear that some idiot creep is spreading rumors about her Peeps page, she'll never be allowed to get back online. She'll lose Angel forever.

"Go dry your hair and get dressed, Carley, and I'll see you downstairs, okay? Just remember to breathe. Deep breaths. You okay?"

Okay? She's never been farther from okay in her life.

But she nods again and slips gratefully away, into the cool, welcoming air of the hallway.

Sitting down on the dining room window seat at last with a plate of freshly made eggs—the burned batch having been scraped into the trash—Angel sighs. It isn't a contented sigh, exactly; rather, an exhausted one. The long night that turned into a long early morning has now given way to what now promises to be a long, sleepless day ahead.

"No rest for the weary, right?" Angel asks around a spoonful of eggs—as opposed to a forkful, because a fork never did turn up in the kitchen drawer. But it doesn't matter now.

Nothing matters now but having found Ruthie.

The last time Angel ever saw her alive was in this very room. They were seated across from each other at the long dining room table, the one that could seat twelve with the extra leaves inserted. Of course they were never inserted; there were never more than four people at that table . . .

Until there were only three.

But on that last night with Ruthie, there were still four.

A harsh March wind howled off the lakes, rattling the dining room window panes. Sleet had been falling when they left for Sunday morning services, and it changed over to snow when the temperature dropped sharply. The pastor warned exiting churchgoers to be careful on the drive home.

"The roads are covered in a sheet of ice," he cautioned, "and this storm is only going to get worse."

The warning would come back to haunt Angel in the wee hours of the morning following the accident, and forever afterward. Surely they haunted Mother and Father as well. But at the time the words were spoken, they went in one ear and out the other, just like the pastor's fiery sermons.

Dinner that night was boiled beef with carrots and potatoes, same as it was every Sunday evening.

Ruthie pushed hers around on her plate, the tines of her fork chinking the china amid the wet sounds of their father eating. He could never breathe through his nose—allergies, he said—so he always chewed with his mouth open. That disgusted Ruthie—everything about him disgusted Ruthie, though Angel wouldn't grasp the deep-seated reasons for her distaste until the marble notebook surfaced.

But on that final night, she didn't even seem to notice the sounds. She stared off into space, not even catching Angel's eye across the table as Father chewed and china chinked and Mother gave occasional terse directions—*Put your napkin on your lap* and *Please pass the salt*—and the large mantel clock ticked toward seven o'clock.

After dinner, Ruthie silently helped Mother clear the dishes, and Angel bundled up in a warm coat, gloves, and hat to help Father carry wood from the woodpile.

After Father's heart attack a few months earlier, Mother had decided Angel should start helping with that particular chore.

"He's not old enough or strong enough to be hauling logs around," Father said the first time.

That was true. But Mother insisted; she blamed it on his bad heart but she probably didn't want Father to continue to disappear outside for a good half hour every evening after dinner to smoke his forbidden pipe and, Angel and Ruthie suspected, stay as far away from Mother as he could, for as long as possible.

Their distaste for each other was palpable. Angular with high cheekbones and slate blue eyes, Mother could conceivably have been a handsome woman if she'd ever smiled in her life—but Angel was convinced she had not. Father, with his bushy red sideburns, ruddy pock-marked skin, and overbite, was known to grin on occasion, revealing an uneven row of yellow teeth, but it was usually brought on by some kind of perverse pleasure, like purposely stepping on the tail of the stray cat who used to prowl the yard.

Angel knew why they were married to each other: because no one else would have either of them. But why, Angel wondered for many years, bother to get married at all?

The likely answer turned up in a highlighted passage in the dog-eared Bible Mother had used as a young literalist, and later used for theology lessons when homeschooling Angel: "But because of the temptation to immorality, each man should have his own wife and each woman her own husband."

Mother had found a husband because the Bible instructed her to.

What, then, had been Father's motivation?

Did he believe marriage would allow him to obscure his pedophilia? Was he counting on a wife to eventually give him daughters?

Oh, Ruthie . . .

Angel caught a final glimpse of her on that last night before slipping out the back door into the hush of swirling white darkness. Ruthie stood alone in the dining room, head bent, lost in thought while clearing the table.

Was her mind already made up, or was she still wrestling with her decision? Had she already written the final entry in the marble notebook, the one Angel would read years later in the turret room? Or was she composing it in her head even then, choosing the words that would become her last while scraping watery, greasy sludge and scraps of gristle from one plate onto another?

Outside, the branches were glazed in ice and fringed with snow. Every so often, there would be a distant cracking sound and somewhere, a limb would fall to the ground. Father leaned against the woodpile, puffing gray tobacco smoke into the night as Angel threw snowballs against fat tree trunks to make faces.

Eyes—*wham, wham*—nose—*wham* . . .

The mouths were the tricky part. You had to line up several snowballs in an upward curve in order to get a smile. Angel's aim left something to be desired. When it was time to take the wood and go inside, the yard was filled with sad, scowling trees that years later seemed an eerie harbinger of what the night would bring.

The kitchen was clean and deserted now, lit only by the dim bulb in the stove hood. The rest of the first floor was still: Ruthie was already upstairs in her bedroom; Mother in hers. The air still smelled of boiled meat and onions, but there was another faint, lingering fragrance.

The large bouquet of pink lilies had arrived a few days earlier, addressed to Ruthie. Angel didn't know who sent them—not when they arrived, anyway. Ruthie had brushed away her little brother's initial questions about the floral delivery wearing a happy, mysterious smile for the first and only time Angel could remember.

That night, as always, the house felt warm for the first few minutes after the bitter cold outdoors, but of course, that was mere perception. Even during the harsh winter months, the thermostat was always set just high enough to keep the pipes from freezing. The only relatively warm spot was on the sofa directly in front of the living room fireplace. That was where Angel settled with a book of Bible pictures and Father with the Sunday papers, just out of sightline to the stairs and the hall.

When someone creaked down the flight a little while later, they both looked up.

"Ruth?" Father called, recognizing her tread.

She didn't answer.

There was a jangling sound: car keys being removed from the pocket of Father's Sunday overcoat, hanging on a coat tree in the foyer. Then the front door opened and closed, and she was gone.

With a curse, Father stood and strode to the hall. He opened the door, and Angel heard the sound of the family car driving off down the street.

That was shocking for many reasons.

Meek Ruthie was newly licensed and had never even

driven alone yet. She certainly wasn't allowed to take the car without permission, let alone at night, in a snowstorm.

Angel wasn't particularly worried, though—just impressed at Ruthie's bold move.

Father, it seemed, was neither worried nor impressed; he was furious. He muttered something, slammed the door, and strode up the stairs. Angel heard him up there talking to Mother.

Angel tried to eavesdrop, but it was too hard to hear. Eventually, the boring book and all that snowball tossing and log carrying and the warmth of the crackling fire took effect and drowsiness set in . . .

The next thing Angel knew, Mother was screaming that Ruthie was dead.

"But I didn't know why," Angel ponders aloud. "Not then. I thought it was an accident. I didn't know whose fault it really was. I didn't know what really happened to you. If you hadn't written it down in the notebook, I never would have known."

Of course Ruthie doesn't answer. Not out loud. But Angel hears her voice, clear as day.

Thank you, Angel.

That was the nickname Ruthie had bestowed from the moment she became a big sister.

"You're my little Angel," she used to say. "I'll always take care of you."

But she didn't. She left Angel all alone in that awful house with their parents. All those years, Angel believed that she hadn't meant to leave. She never would have abandoned her little Angel.

And now that you know the truth . . .

"I'm still your Angel, Ruthie. Your guardian angel. I promise I'll make them pay for what they did to you. Two of them already have, and the third will be soon."

Now, Angel. Don't wait any longer. Please. It's been long enough.

Angel sets aside the breakfast plate, now empty, and turns to Ruthie, propped on the window seat.

"Tonight." Patting the rotted, blackened flesh clinging to her skeletal hand, Angel assures her, "I promise I'll do it tonight."

Under any other circumstances, Jen knows, Carley and Marie Bush would have hit it off very well. But today, when at last her daughter shows up in the kitchen, she walks into a somber conversation about Taylor Morino's shocking death.

"Carley!" Jen's mother is the first to spot her standing there in a bulky sweatshirt and jeans that look too snug. Her hair appears to be blown dry but not styled, pulled back in a barrette that's parked crookedly at the nape of her neck. Her eyes, behind her glasses, betray too little sleep; too many tears.

"Hi, Grandma. Hi, Grandpa." Carley dutifully hugs one, then the other, and turns to Jen. "Dad said I needed to come downstairs."

Yes. That was before the world tilted even more crazily. Longing for ordinary Saturday mornings of not so long ago—when the worst imaginable disruption was her parents popping in with doughnuts—Jen introduces her daughter to a subdued Marie.

"Ms. Bush is here to talk to you about piano lessons, but we just got some news that's—"

"I already know," Carley cuts her off. "About Taylor Morino, right?"

"How did you hear? Were your friends talking about it online already?" Jen asks, before remembering she'd changed the wifi password.

"I'm not allowed to be online anymore," her daughter says pointedly, "and I don't have any friends."

"Don't be silly." Jen's mother brushes strands of hair back from her granddaughter's face, out of her eyes. "Of course you have friends. Why aren't you allowed to be online?"

Carley glances uncertainly at Jen, who gives a slight shake of her head to indicate that her grandmother doesn't know about the trouble at school.

There's no need to tell her, either—not now anyway, with Marie here and everything else that's going on.

"The Internet is a dangerous place for kids," Jen's father declares. "On *60 Minutes*, they said—"

"Aldo," Jen's mother interrupts him. "We're not talking about *60 Minutes* right now."

"We were talking about the Internet, Theresa, and I said—"

"What's going on?" Thad asks from the doorway, dressed for work in khakis and a trench coat and carrying a satchel.

Silence falls over the kitchen.

Carley is the one who breaks it, telling her father, "A girl from my school killed herself last night."

Thad's blue eyes widen. He looks at Jen, then back at Carley. "Did you know her?"

"Not really. I just know who she is."

"Who is she?"

"Her name," Jen tells Thad, "is Taylor Morino. Her father is Mike Morino."

"Mike Morino—he's the one you—"

"Yes."

Thad nods. "I didn't know he had a daughter who went to Sisters."

"Neither did I, until—"

"I didn't know Taylor Morino's father was your old boy-friend," Carley cuts in—accusingly, as though Jen deliberately denied her something of great significance.

Her head is suddenly throbbing.

"That was a long time ago, before your mom met your

dad and fell in love with him," Jen's mother needlessly informs Carley.

"For what it's worth, I never liked him," Jen's father says. "Wouldn't trust him as far as I could throw him."

"Aldo! His daughter just—"

"That doesn't change—"

As her parents begin to argue, then find the self-awareness to shush themselves and each other, Jen presses her fingertips to her temples.

She looks at Carley, wishing they could have this conversation alone. "How did you find out about Taylor?"

"Emma told me. She heard you talking about it. About how you used to go out with Mr. Morino and how Taylor had killed herself."

Jen didn't even realize Emma was awake yet today. She must have snuck downstairs, probably searching the house for her cell phone or the wifi password. Well aware that their younger daughter has a tendency to snoop, Thad locked both her phone and Carley's into the trunk of his car, and they probably should have done the same with the password.

A long moment of silence is broken by Thad pulling his keys out of his coat pocket. "I have to go," he tells Jen apologetically. "I have a client coming in. I'll call you from the office."

He quickly says his good-byes and heads out the door, casting one last, helpless-looking glance over his shoulder at Jen, as if to apologize for leaving her to deal with the fallout.

She shrugs at him. What else is new?

Her father jangles his own keys. "We should get going, too, Theresa, if you want to stop at the supermarket."

"I can't even remember what I needed to get. You're still coming to help me with the cooking, Genevieve, aren't you?" her mother asks. "You and Frankie and the girls?"

"Oh . . . I . . . yes. We'll be there as soon as we can."

What else is there to say? In the end, Taylor Morino's

death isn't going to impact the day's plans, and yet it's left Jen chilled to the bone.

Leaving Marie and Carley alone together in the kitchen, she walks her parents to the door. Her father kisses her on the cheek and heads outside, but her mother, flustered, lingers.

"I needed something from Wegman's, but for the life of me, I can't remember what it is. I'm getting old."

"It's okay, Mom. I'll go and pick up whatever you need before I come over. Just call when you remember what it is."

"You're a good daughter, Genevieve."

"And you're a good mom."

Her mother smiles. "So are you. A good daughter *and* a good mom."

The words catch Jen off guard. If her mother only knew that both her girls have been in serious trouble and are barely speaking to her.

Maybe she should tell her. Mom raised five daughters and made it look so easy.

Maybe it was easy back then. The world was less complicated. Kids weren't faced with distraction and temptation to the extent that they are now . . .

Or were they?

"Mom," Jen begins—only to be interrupted by the sound of a car honking outside.

Her mother sighs. "Your father is losing his patience. I'll see you in a little while."

Jen swallows against the ache in her throat as she closes the door and rests her forehead against it for a moment, feeling utterly abandoned. Reminding herself that she isn't, not really, she offers a silent, familiar prayer for strength.

Then she returns to the kitchen, where Marie and Carley are having what sounds like a painstaking conversation about piano. The ordinarily effervescent Marie is clearly preoccupied by the news of Taylor's death, and Carley— Carley isn't herself this morning, by any means.

She hasn't been herself in so long that maybe, Jen finds herself speculating, this is who she really is now. Maybe she's always going to be this brooding, dejected soul capable of volatile behavior like last night's explosion; capable of God only knows what else.

No!

Not my daughter. Not my daughter.

"Sweetie . . ." Jen reaches out to rest a hand on her shoulder, feeling the tension emanating from her body. "Do you want to take piano lessons again? Wouldn't that be fun?"

"Maybe. I . . . maybe." Carley attempts to shrug away her mother's touch along with the question.

"You don't have to decide right this minute." Marie checks her watch and reaches for her coat. "Think it over."

"I will. Thank you. It was nice meeting you," Carley says politely, and turns abruptly to face her mother, succeeding in shaking the hand from her shoulder. "Can I go back upstairs?"

"Don't you want breakfast?"

"I'm not hungry," Carley tosses over her shoulder, already on her way to her room.

Marie pulls on her coat and wraps a filmy floral lavender scarf around her neck. "She seems like a sweet girl."

"She is. She's . . ." Jen finds herself swallowing hard. "She's very sweet."

And she's hurting and I can't reach her and I can't help her.

"Why don't you give me a call later this week? We'll talk about lessons then. Right now, I really have to get going."

Jen walks her to the door and touches her arm as she reaches for the knob. "Marie . . . wait. What we were talking about before my parents showed up . . . I can't stop thinking about it."

"Debbie and Mike."

Jen nods. "If they really were—really are—connected in some way, then what happened to Taylor is either a tragic coincidence or . . ."

"Or it isn't," Marie says simply. "You're thinking she might have been influenced by what Nicki did?"

"I'm not sure what I'm thinking." Jen rakes a frustrated, confused hand through her hair. "I think I'm going to talk to Debbie about it. Maybe if we both went over there right now and—"

"Even if I thought that was a good idea," Marie cuts her off, "I can't. I have back-to-back lessons for the rest of the day, and I'm late already. I'm sorry to run out on you like this, but . . ."

"No, it's okay. I understand. Thank you for coming to talk to Carley. And Marie . . . I'm sorry to hear about Taylor. When you see Mike . . . please give him my sympathy."

"You won't come to the wake?"

Jen hesitates, then shakes her head. "I don't really know him anymore. That was all so . . ."

"Long ago and far away?"

"Exactly." And that's exactly how Jen had expected it to stay. "I just—I feel bad about assuming he was still married."

"He *is* married. Again. Wife number three," Marie adds with an ironic little smile and nod. "Good-bye, Genevieve. Take care of yourself—and take care of your daughter."

Marie's parting words seem to linger ominously after Jen closes the door after her.

"Was that Mom and Dad?"

She looks up to see Frankie at the top of the stairs behind her, pulling a sweatshirt over her head.

"They left a few minutes ago. That was Marie Bush."

"I would have loved to have seen her after all these years."

"I'm sure she would have, too, but this probably isn't the best time."

Frankie nods, descending the flight. "I heard what happened."

"Did Emma tell you, too? I didn't even know she was down here listening."

"No, Carley told me." Frankie puts her arm around Jen. "Are you okay?"

"I'm . . . I'm just so glad you're here. Come on. I'll get you some breakfast."

Frankie winces. "Maybe just some strong black coffee."

In the kitchen, Jen pours her a cup, then quickly loads the other ones into the dishwasher, starts it, and sinks wearily onto a stool beside her sister.

"I didn't realize you'd even seen Mike Morino in years," Frankie tells her.

"I hadn't, until Nicki's wake. He was there," she says simply, opting not to get into her suspicions about him and Debbie, "and that's when I found out his daughter is at Sisters with Carley. What are the odds that two girls who are connected to her—two girls with everything going for them—would do something like this in the space of a week?"

"Higher than you might think."

Frankie's response catches her by surprise. "What do you mean?"

"Kids who kill themselves sometimes trigger other kids who have been thinking about it to take action. There have been quite a few high-profile teen suicide rashes—I went to a seminar a few years ago where we studied the case in Minnesota where nine kids in the same school district killed themselves. Most of them had been bullied in one way or another."

The word sets off shrill warning sirens in Jen's brain.

"Carley was tortured by what happened with the Spring Fling princess election, Frankie, and ever since . . ."

"I know. She told me about it last night. I didn't let on to her that I already knew about it. It broke my heart, hearing her trying to articulate the pain . . . but I thought it was good for her to talk it out."

"I'm glad you were there for her. I keep praying she'll let me be there for her, too, but she's shut me out."

"It's because she feels like she's let you down."

"Why? I've let her know every chance I've had that I'm with her and I'm proud of her. I've tried to do everything right, but . . ." Jen trails off helplessly, flailing in a tidal wave of emotion.

"She's disappointed in herself, I think. She feels weak. And it's not just that, Jen." Frankie glances at the doorway, as if to make sure no one is there, and lowers her voice. "She told me what happened in math class. She didn't take it upon herself to cheat on that test. Those girls set her up. It was more bullying."

Jen's stomach turns over. "What happened?"

As Frankie relays what Carley told her last night, fury sweeps in to push back the sorrow.

"She told me in confidence, and I wasn't going to tell you, but . . . I thought you should know after I heard about this second suicide. And there's one more thing."

"What?"

"She was asking me about a book—*The Virgin Suicides*. Do you remember it?"

The title is a fist in Jen's gut. "I read it years ago for book club, but . . . Nicki was reading it. I saw a copy in her room, after . . ."

Frankie nods. "She must have told Carley about it."

"I don't think—I mean, they weren't even really friends anymore."

"Maybe it was a while ago. I think you need to get some professional help for Carley, Jen."

"A shrink?"

"One who specializes in kids."

"Where do I find one?"

"The school social worker should be able to give you a couple of names."

"I'm meeting with her on Monday."

"That's good. And in the meantime, we'll keep an eye

on Carley all weekend and keep the lines of communication open."

"She doesn't talk to me as it is. And I'm not sure she has any friends to talk to, but if she does, I just brilliantly cut her off from them when I took away the Internet."

"You were doing what you thought was best for her."

Jen shakes her head glumly.

"Don't worry, Jen. She's going to get through this and be okay. Where are you going?" Frankie asks, as she pushes back her stool abruptly.

"Upstairs to talk to Carley. I just want to make sure . . ."

"You probably shouldn't mention that I told you about what happened in math class. She told me in confidence."

"Don't worry. I won't," Jen assures her.

The last thing she wants to do is cut off yet another line of communication.

"Where *is* she?" Angel asks Ruthie, after checking the laptop yet again to see if QT-Pi has signed on and seeing that she hasn't. "This isn't like her at all."

Still propped in the dining room window seat, Ruthie sits silently by, but her empty sockets seem expectantly trained on Angel.

"Don't worry. I'm sure she'll turn up any second now."

Angel even impulsively text-messaged Carley's phone, hoping she wouldn't remember that she'd never provided her cell number. If she asked about it, Angel would say she'd given it a while back and must have forgotten because of everything that's gone on.

The text read simply: *where ru? im worried and i have a great surprise for u*

When this is over, it'll be just as easy to delete the message from Carley's phone as it will be to wipe away traces of their correspondence on her laptop. Angel just has to remember to find the phone from her pocket or bag—wherever she keeps it. One thing is certain: There's no danger of a teenage girl leaving her house without it.

For now, it's back to pacing, from the dining room through the archway into the living room, past the worn spot on the oak floor where Mother's favorite chair once sat, gradually wearing away the finish, the wooden rockers tilting back and forth, back and forth, year after year after year until . . .

"I did it, you know," Angel tells Ruthie. "But that time, it wasn't for you. It was for me. For what she did to me."

Turning to note that Ruthie's teeth are bared in a silent grin, Angel knows she approves.

"I know it might not seem so terrible, compared to what Father did to you, but . . . You know, Ruthie, that's the irony. I didn't know about that—about how he was abusing you—until I found the notebook. If I had—well, maybe I would have understood why Mother did what she did to me. Maybe I would have seen that she was trying to protect me from him, in her own bizarre way. But by the time I figured that out, it was too late."

Angel turns again to look at the spot where Mother was sitting on that spring night two years ago.

"It was my shrink's idea. Dr. Ellis is his name. He thought I should make the trip back here to confront Mother, maybe give her a chance to apologize. He thought it was important for me to make peace with her, because she was getting old, and I had spent so many years in therapy, trying to reconcile it all on my own, and it wasn't working . . ."

Angel can see Mother there, rocking, working her rosary beads in her hands. They were the heavy wooden rosary beads she'd had for many years, not the pink glass ones found wrapped around the marble notebook. Those had belonged to Ruthie. They used to sit in a shallow glass dish on her bedside table, a lost memory that was rekindled after Sandra Lutz handed over the notebook.

"I didn't call to tell Mother I was coming. I thought she

might tell me not to. I wasn't even sure she was going to let me in that night when I knocked on the door, but she did. She saw me standing there, and she didn't say a word, just opened the door and motioned for me to come in. I was only going to talk to her—well, really, what I wanted was for her to talk to me. But she refused. I talked, and then I cried and I begged—I begged her, Ruthie, for something. For an explanation, an apology, some words of regret, something. I got nothing. She just rocked and worked those rosary beads in her hands and I don't even think she was listening."

Ruthie is, though. Angel senses her rapt attention.

"Finally, I couldn't stand it another second. I picked up one of the pillows from the sofa and I walked over to her, and I pressed it against her face. I smothered her, Ruthie. And when she stopped moving, I put the pillow back on the sofa and I walked out of that house—no, not out the front door, or the back door, because she had those new locks with the keys in them . . ."

Angel smiles faintly, remembering the long-ago day Sandra Lutz had pointed out the new locks, never imagining that Angel already knew all about them.

"Mother and Father had never repaired the lock on the window in your room. Maybe they never even knew that it was broken. I knew, because I used to spend a lot of time in there, after you were gone. It made me feel closer to you. Anyway, that night—the night that I—the night that Mother died, I still had no idea why that window lock was broken. I just remembered that it was, and so I went upstairs and opened that window, and I climbed out onto the mudroom roof, and I pushed the window back down from the other side. I drove away—I drove nine straight hours back to Long Island. And then I waited. The more time that went by, the more certain I was that by the time they found her, she would be too far gone for anyone to guess that she'd died of anything other than natural causes. And even if they had guessed . . . no one would ever suspect me. As far as they knew, I hadn't visited that poor old woman in years."

Remembering the disapproval etched on Sandra Lutz's face, Angel sighs.

Really, Sandra got what she deserved.

As did Mother.

And now . . .

Striding back over to the laptop, Angel leans into the screen, hoping to see that QT-Pi has resurfaced.

She hasn't.

What if she's suspicious? What if . . .

No. Don't get all worked up.

If you can't make her come to you one way, you'll get to her another. You'll just have to bide your time.

Rushing things could be dangerous. That's when mistakes happen. There's no reason to take chances.

But you promised me it would be tonight, Ruthie's voice explodes inside Angel's brain. *You said you'd take care of it!*

"I will! I'll do it!"

Hands clenched into fists, Angel glares at the computer screen, willing Carley Archer to cooperate one final, fatal time.

Carley is lying on her bed, arms folded across her chest, staring at the ceiling, when someone knocks on her door.

"What?"

"Carley, it's me. Can I come in?"

She wonders what her mother would do if she said no. Probably just turn the knob and walk right in.

How stupid for a house not to have locks on bedroom doors. How cruel of her parents to deny Carley's request last fall that they add one to hers in order to put a stop to Emma's snooping. If she had a lock, her mother could stand out there in the hall and talk to her all she wants, and Carley wouldn't have to let her in.

"Carley?"

She sighs. "Yeah."

The door opens. "What are you doing?"

"Resting."

Her mother's footsteps cross the floor as she continues to stare at the ceiling, tracing a faint crease in the paint that runs from the ceiling fan light fixture to the slightly cob-webby corner above the window.

"You didn't eat any breakfast. I was thinking of making some pancakes."

"No, thanks."

"Would you rather have eggs?"

"No, thanks."

"Carley." Her mother sits on her bed, all but forcing Carley to shift her gaze in her direction.

"What?"

Her mother hesitates. She doesn't look like her usual cheerful—or forced-cheerful—self today, that's for sure.

"I'm worried about you."

"Don't be."

"I was thinking . . . maybe it would be a good idea for you to talk to someone."

"About what?"

"About whatever's on your mind."

"The only thing that's on my mind," Carley tells her, "is that I'm in solitary confinement and it's not fair. I'm not al-lowed to go to school, and I'm not allowed to get online . . ."

"I've been rethinking that."

Carley blinks. "You have?"

Her mother nods. "Maybe that wasn't fair to do to you. You've never abused that privilege."

"No."

"I'll tell you what. I'll give you the wifi password so that you can spend some time catching up online. I have to run a couple of errands on the way over to Grandma's, and you can meet me over there later with Aunt Frankie and Emma."

Carley is so relieved at the promise of getting back online that she doesn't bother to mention that she'd forgotten all about going to her grandmother's to help prepare the holiday feast today.

In years past, she's always looked forward to that tradition: three generations of females gathered in that cozy, familiar kitchen, chatting and preparing Sicilian recipes that had been handed down by her grandmother's grandmother.

Today, she's not in the mood.

There's only one thing she wants to do: get in touch with Angel.

And now she can, thanks to her mother.

"What about my phone?" she asks.

"That'll have to be up to Daddy. He put it away someplace and he's at the office for the day. You can talk to him about it tonight. Okay?"

"Okay. Thanks, Mom," she says softly, and smiles at her for the first time in days.

To her horror, her mother's eyes fill with tears. "You're welcome. I just . . . I love you so much, Carley. I hope you know that."

I love you, too, she wants to say as her mother wraps her arms around her, but somehow, the words are lodged in her throat.

"Well, it's about time. Look . . ." Angel grins, holding the open laptop in front of Ruthie's skull with its blackened, withered skin. "You see that?"

At long last . . .

QT-Pi is online.

Entry from the marble notebook

Friday, February 14, 1986

The most unbelievable thing just happened!!!!!!!!!

The doorbell rang not long after I got home from school, and I answered it! This man was standing on the porch with a big package wrapped in green tissue paper, and I saw the florist truck parked at the curb.

He asked me my name, and when I told him, he smiled and said, "These are for you, then."

I thought it was a mistake, and I told him that, but then he pointed to my name on the little white envelope attached to the package.

It turned out to be a HUGE bouquet of beautiful bright pink flowers that smell better than roses or lilacs, even.

The card inside the envelope was pink. All it said was Happy Valentine's Day *(printed on the card) and then it was signed,* From your Secret Admirer!

Mother and Father are still at work, so I brought the bouquet up to my room, and I can't stop shaking and I can't stop staring at them.

I wonder who sent them?

I'm so afraid to even guess, in case I'm wrong.

LATER

I thought I could hide the flowers from Mother, and I probably could have if they didn't smell so good.

The minute she came home, she came charging up to my room like some rabid bloodhound. I tried to stash them in my closet but she found them.

She didn't believe me when I told her I have no idea who sent them, and she called me all kinds of terrible names.

Then she handed me a pair of shears and she made me cut them up and throw them into the garbage.

Of all the cruel punishments she's ever given me, I think that was the worst of all. The whole time I was doing it, I was crying so hard I could barely see.

Before I threw the garbage bag into the shed out back, I saved a couple of petals. I'm going to press them in this page and I'm hoping the scent won't ever fade away, but it probably will. Everything does.

Chapter 14

Seeing Debbie's silver Lexus parked beside the portico when she pulls up in front of the Oliveras' brick Colonial just before one o'clock, Jen knows immediately that her friend has left the house at least once today. Debbie always keeps her car in the garage overnight, then leaves it on the circular driveway during the day as she's coming and going.

But she never stirs on a Saturday morning unless it's absolutely necessary.

I don't want to be disturbed for anything less than fire or blood.

Blood . . .

Nicki died on a Saturday morning.

And now Taylor Morino.

Did Debbie go to Mike when she heard the news?

What if she *hasn't* heard the news?

Maybe I should have called her first.

Too late now. Jen is already out of the car and putting up the hood on her raincoat as she walks toward the door, carrying a bouquet of pink tulips that caught her eye at Wegman's. She'd stopped there after her mother called to say she needed dry lentils for the soup she always served as a first course at the Saint Joseph's table.

The ordinariness of that interlude—walking the brightly

lit, bustling aisles of the supermarket—should have brought a measure of comfort. Instead, it left her even more troubled. Everywhere she looked, there were mothers and daughters: mothers with pink-clad babies in slings; mothers pushing pigtailed toddlers riding in cart seats; mothers chaperoning Girl Scouts at the cookie table set up outside the door; mothers clashing with chubby daughters in the junk food aisle. Serene-as-the-Madonna mothers and harried mothers; prettily pouting daughters and daughters clutching American Girl dolls in outfits that matched their own. . . .

Mothers with no clue, it seemed, of how fragile it all is; how you can wake up one morning to find that your little girl has become a stranger—or that she's no longer alive.

When she left the house, both Carley and Emma were still in their respective bedrooms.

Emma—presumably unaware that her sister has the new password and is back online—was unwilling to come along to her grandmother's this afternoon, even when Jen reminded her that she's still being punished and not allowed to leave the house otherwise.

"I don't care" was the response, spoken through the closed door.

"Don't push it," Frankie advised. "I'll see what I can do. With or without her, Carley and I will meet you over at Mom and Dad's at around two. Go ahead and run your errands, and try not to worry for a little while."

Jen promised to try. She didn't tell her sister that one of her errands entailed dropping by the Oliveras' house.

She isn't sure why she's here, exactly. She just felt compelled to reach out to Debbie when she heard about Taylor's death, and . . .

And maybe you want to figure out the connection between Taylor and Nicki . . .

Between Debbie and Mike . . .

Maybe you want to make sure that what happened to them doesn't happen to you.

Jen rings the doorbell. Listening to the steady rain splashing into puddles, dripping from the eaves, and pinging into the downspout, she wonders what she's going to say.

I'm sure you'll think of something. You always do.

Too bad it's usually not the right thing.

She's still second-guessing her impulsive decision to lift the Internet ban for Carley, violating one of her and Thad's cardinal rules of parenting: Never reverse a punishment. If Thad had been home, she'd have talked it over with him. But she was so spooked by what her sister said about the suicide epidemics that she didn't bother to think it through.

The last thing she wants to do is isolate Carley even further.

When she thinks about what those wretched girls in her math class did . . .

The thought is curtailed as Debbie opens the door.

This time, she's wearing not her dead daughter's sweatshirt, but a simple white blouse, black blazer, jeans, and boots. Her face is fully made up, but there's no mistaking the raw traces of tears. It's been only a couple of days since Jen last saw her, but she looks as though she hasn't slept since, and has dropped another five pounds she couldn't afford to lose.

"Jen! What's going on?"

"I wanted to stop by to talk to you for a minute. Is Andrew home?"

"Andrew," Debbie says grimly, "is never home. Why?"

"I just heard what happened." No need to waste time getting to the point; no need, either, for Debbie to pretend she doesn't know what Jen is talking about.

"You mean Taylor Morino."

"Yes. I'm so . . ." Jen pauses, not sure what to say. She's

sorry, yes, but this loss is not Debbie's. She's disturbed by it, of course, but the girl was a stranger. She's upset, concerned, so many things, but she's not sure what, exactly, to say until she knows for sure about Debbie's connection to Mike.

Then go ahead and ask. Just get it over with.

"Debbie, did you see Mike this morning?"

Obviously taken aback by the question, Debbie bites down on her lower lip. Then, with a hint of resignation, she opens the door wider. "Come on in."

Jen steps over the threshold, almost expecting to find disorder in the house given the emotional chaos endured by its occupants, but she should have known better. The Oliveras have a housekeeper. Everything is perfect as always. A stack of sympathy cards on the hall table beside a framed photo of smiling Nicki is the only hint that something is amiss.

Jen hands over her wet jacket, wipes her feet on the doormat, and asks Debbie if she should take off her sneakers. This has always been a leave-your-shoes-at-the-door kind of house.

"Don't worry about it," Debbie says in a desolate tone. "I really could care less about the floors today."

She leads the way into the living room, turns on a lamp to dispel the gloom falling through the tall windows, and they sit.

For a long time, the only sound is the patter of falling rain and the rhythmic swaying of the pendulum wall clock. Jen fights not to start blurting questions. The ball is out of her court.

"He called me when he heard," Debbie finally tells her, not looking at her. "Mike."

Jen waits.

"I went to meet him. He's a mess, and . . . look, I don't know what to say."

"About Taylor?"

"About . . . any of it. How did you find out?"

"About Taylor?" Jen asks again, then reinterprets Debbie's question when Debbie allows eye contact at last. "Oh. You mean how did I find out about you and Mike?"

Debbie nods.

So it's true.

Jen chooses her words carefully. "If you're worried that I heard about it somehow, you know, around Woodsbridge, or—I didn't. I guess I just picked up on some kind of vibe between the two of you."

"When did you even see us together?"

"I haven't, other than . . . It was at the funeral," she admits uncomfortably.

Debbie seems to need to digest that before moving on. Her fingers clench and unclench, her sparkling diamond wedding band catching the lamplight.

Jen battles her own instinct to fill the silence, only to be caught off guard by Debbie's next question.

"So Carley didn't say anything to you?"

"Carley? No! Why? Does she know about it?" She can't stomach the thought of her daughter, with everything else she's gone through, wrestling with the secret of a sordid extramarital affair.

"I don't know. I wondered if maybe Nicki mentioned it to her before . . ."

Before the two girls drifted apart? Or before Nicki died?

Jen shakes her head, silently waiting for elaboration, trying hard not to judge her friend, wishing it weren't so easy to do so.

It isn't that Debbie was having—is still having?—an affair . . .

Come on, Jen. Who are you kidding? Yes, it is. Partly, anyway.

But Jen can't help it. She's old-fashioned enough, or moral enough, to have a problem with adultery.

And beyond that: Why Mike?

Who are you to wonder about that? You went out with him for years, even after you knew he wasn't the nicest guy in the world.

Only now, though, does she see him for what he really is—a bully, no better than the girls who tormented her own daughter.

Back then, though, Jen was just a kid: secretly insecure, like most teenagers, and charmed by Mike's good looks and his line and the fact that every girl at Sacred Sisters would have killed to date him.

But Debbie was a grown woman when she got involved; a wife and mother with a lot more to lose than her self-respect and her virginity. She should have known better.

And you've done plenty of things in your adult life that you shouldn't have done, haven't you? Everyone has. So get off your moral high horse.

"Jen . . . Look, I need to talk to you. I can't carry this around with me anymore; I feel like it's going to suffocate me."

Recognizing the guilt in her friend's eyes, she shakes her head. "You've got to stop blaming yourself. It's not your—"

"No, Jen, I don't. I don't have to stop. It's not just me blaming myself. It's Nicki."

"What are you talking about?"

"I wasn't going to tell you—I wasn't going to tell anyone, except . . . look, I trust you. You've always been good with secrets. Promise you won't tell anyone."

"I promise." As soon as the words leave her mouth, she wants to take them back.

No. This isn't like it was back then.

"Promise you won't tell, Jen," Debbie said on that long ago night. It was March, just as it is now, and raining then, too. But it changed over to snow the next morning, and the world went from sodden to brittle in an instant.

"Don't worry," Mike said. "She won't tell. She's good with secrets."

She is. But that was different; it was . . .

Long ago and far away.

Debbie's voice cuts into her memories: "Nicki blamed me."

"For what?"

"For not wanting to live. For what she did. You asked about a note, and I lied. She did leave one."

"What did it say?"

"It was horrible. I found it on her laptop, and I . . . I deleted it. I couldn't let anyone see. It was about me—me and Mike. How she knew what was going on, and how ashamed she was, and she couldn't live with me, couldn't stand the sight of me. She called me terrible things, Jen. My own daughter . . ."

Jen rests an arm on her shoulders. "I'm so sorry."

"How can I go on without her, knowing . . . How can I live with myself? How can I live with the guilt?"

"Don't do this, Debbie. You were a good mom."

A good mom . . .

She said the same thing the other day, even though she had her share of doubts.

And her own mother just told her the exact same thing about herself, oblivious to the fact that one granddaughter was sneaking around in the woods with an older boy and the other was suspended from school for cheating.

Yeah. I'm a terrific mom.

"My daughter didn't think I was a good mom." Debbie fumbles in the pocket of her blazer, finding a crumpled tissue to wipe her eyes.

"That's not true. She was always talking about all the things you did for her, Deb. Her beautiful bedroom, and the piano, and all the times you took her shopping, everything, all the mother-daughter spa days and getaway weekends . . . I never heard her complain about you."

"That doesn't mean much, apparently . . . because I didn't, either. Not once."

"So she never confronted you about anything she wrote in the note?"

"No! That's the thing I can't get over. If she had just told me, I would have explained that her father and I . . . look, we're together, but it hasn't been a true marriage in years. Andrew and I understand each other and we give each other space."

"He knows about you and Mike, then?"

"No. Let's put it this way, though: It wouldn't break his heart if he found out. But if he realized that it was the reason Nicki did what she did . . ." She shakes her head. "He would never forgive me for that. And I wouldn't expect him to."

"So Andrew doesn't know about the note?"

"No. I told you, no one knows—except you."

"And Mike. He knows, too, doesn't he?"

Debbie opens her mouth as if she's going to deny it.

"Don't, Deb. It's okay."

She takes a deep, shaky breath. "I told him. I knew he wouldn't think—I knew . . . Mike and I understand each other."

Just like you and Andrew understand each other? Jen wants to ask, but she refrains. Let Debbie cling to her rationalizations. Let Debbie do whatever she needs to do in order to keep getting out of bed in the morning and facing another day without the daughter she loved more than anything in the world.

That, Jen knows, is the undisputed truth. No one who ever saw Debbie and Nicki together would deny that Debbie's world revolved around Nicki, making it all the more horrific that her own actions inadvertently led to her daughter's death.

I still can't believe it, Jen thinks, and yet . . .

There was a damning suicide note.

"How long," she asks her friend, "have you and Mike been . . . ?"

"A year or so."

"What about back when we were in school?"

Seeing the flicker of culpability in her friend's eyes, Jen knows the answer even before Debbie offers an evasive one. "Back in school he was your boyfriend, Jen."

"Right."

And I thought you had my back. All those times when you rode the team bus with him and came back to tell me how the other cheerleaders were flirting with him and how lucky I was to have you there to keep an eye on him for me. . .

But it's ancient history now. She has a solid marriage to a loyal, loving husband, and Debbie has . . .

Nothing worth having.

"You know, I hadn't seen Mike since—well, really, since you guys broke up and we all drifted apart," Debbie tells her. "But then out of the blue, in the craziest coincidence, we ran into each other at—"

She breaks off, interrupted by Jen's ringing cell phone.

Maybe it's her mother, remembering something else she needed, or Frankie, calling to say that the girls are coming after all.

Jen apologizes and pulls her phone out of her pocket. This time, she instantly recognizes the number on caller ID: It's Sacred Sisters. With an apprehensive sense of déjà vu, she answers the phone.

This time, it isn't the principal. It's an automated voice system, the same one that calls before dawn on stormy mornings to inform parents of school closings.

Jen listens to the message and then hangs up, aware of Debbie's questioning gaze on her.

"Who was that?"

"The school," Jen tells her, noticing that her battery is almost worn down and glad she has a charger in the car. "They said that due to the tragic death of one of the students, they're canceling Spring Fling tonight and will have counselors and the social worker on hand tomorrow at the school to talk to kids who need it."

"They did that at Woodsbridge, too, when Nicki . . ." Debbie shakes her head. "I mean the counselors for the other kids. Not Spring Fling . . . oh, Lord, I had forgotten all about Spring Fling. It was one of the few good things about going to that school. I can't believe they're still doing it after all these years. Was Carley going to go?"

Jen doesn't have the heart to get into the topic of her daughter and Spring Fling right now. She shakes her head.

"Did that phone call give any details?"

"None at all. Not even her name."

"I would imagine most of the kids have heard by now."

"Probably. You know how—" She breaks off. Of course Debbie knows how quickly bad news circulates. Last Saturday, it was her own daughter.

Has it truly only been a week?

"How did you find out about Taylor?" Debbie asks.

"My parents heard from one of the neighbors. But there wasn't anything specific. I mean, I don't know how it happened, or why it happened," she says, assuming Debbie does know.

"She hung herself, Jen."

Jen presses a hand to her heart and shakes her head mutely, stunned at the violence of it, just as she'd been stunned about Nicki and the knife.

"So that's the *how* of it. As for the *why* of it . . . who knows? She had everything going for her, the last kid you'd ever think would—well, she and Nicki were the last kids you'd ever think . . ."

She falls to bleak silence again, leaving Jen to try to wrap her head around the catastrophic coincidence that feels like anything but.

That two lovely girls from good homes—perhaps not with happily married parents, but decent homes just the same—could so violently take their own lives within days of each other simply defies reason.

"Did the girls know each other?" Jen asks Debbie.

"No. They never met. Sometimes Mike and I would fantasize about getting them together—we thought they would like each other—but of course, we assumed that wasn't going to ever happen."

"Did Taylor . . ." Jen clears her throat. "Did she leave a note, do you know?"

Debbie nods slowly. "I didn't see it. Mike didn't, either. His ex-wife told him about it. It was on the computer and it sounds like . . . it sounds exactly like Nicki's note. Blaming Mike."

"And the affair?"

"Yes."

"What about *The Virgin Suicides*?"

"What do you mean?"

"The book—I saw it in Nicki's room, the other day. She must have been reading it."

Debbie just looks at her. Then, wordlessly, she stands and heads for the stairway, motioning for Jen to follow her.

Together, they climb to the second floor. Nicki's pink and green bedroom is exactly as it was the other day, still with the fuchsia throw pillow askew and a distinct indentation on the quilt where Debbie sat grieving.

"Where is it?" she asks Jen, who walks over to the desk, pulls the book off the hutch shelf, and silently passes it to her, noticing that there's a bookmark stuck between the pages.

Debbie looks at the novel, turns it over, opens it, reads the inside flap.

"I didn't know she was reading this. And that's strange, because . . ." She shakes her head and looks up at Jen. "In November, we joined a mother-daughter book club at Woodsbridge with a bunch of her new friends from school. Her English teacher suggested it and I was so glad Nicki wanted to join, because she was never very big on reading, remember?"

Jen remembers, distinctly. From the time they were little girls, bookworm Carley was always trying to get Nicki to take some novel she'd loved, hoping she'd read it so that they could discuss it. It became a joke between them.

"You read the book," Nicki would say, "and I'll watch the movie with you."

And that was what they did for *The Sisterhood of the Traveling Pants*, *The Hunger Games*, *Twilight* . . .

But Nicki was even reluctant about some of the movies. Jen remembers driving the two of them to the cineplex to see the final Harry Potter installment, and Nicki nervously asking Carley's reassurance that it wouldn't be violent.

"Scary is one thing," said the girl who would carve her own wrists with a butcher knife, "but you know I can't deal with blood and gore, Carls."

"Don't worry, Nicks. If there's a gory scene, I'll hold your hand and you can close your eyes and I'll tell you when it's over."

Pushing past another wave of sorrow, and wondering how Debbie manages to function at all beneath the weight of grief and guilt, Jen suggests, "Maybe her English teacher assigned *The Virgin Suicides*."

Debbie shakes her head, passing the book back to Jen. "It was all classics. They were reading *Of Mice and Men*, and they had just finished *Romeo and Juliet*—you know, in February, for Valentine's Day. They read it aloud in class and Nicki got to be Juliet. She liked that because—" Her voice breaks.

Jen hugs her. "It's okay, Deb. I didn't mean to . . . I'm sorry."

A cell phone rings, breaking the silence. This time, it's Debbie's. She looks at it. "Mike. He was going over to the house, and he must be . . ."

"Go ahead, take it. I can go. I—"

"No, wait. I won't be long." Debbie quickly leaves the room, answering the phone with a gentle "Hey."

Left alone, Jen turns the book over and over as Debbie had done, as if it might reveal some insight into Nicki's last days. There's a price sticker on the back, indicating that it was bought at Talking Leaves, Carley's favorite bookstore.

Noticing that Nicki apparently didn't get very far in her reading, she opens the novel to the spot Nicki left marked and sees that it's page one, with its description of the youngest of the five sisters slitting her wrists.

The book flies from her grasp as if snatched away by the icy gust of revulsion that blasts through her.

"What?" Debbie asks, behind her, and she turns to see her standing there, phone poised in her hand as if to indicate Mike is still on the line. "Why did you throw that?" Without waiting for a reply, she goes on, "Mike said Taylor was reading it, too. It was in her room. He has her copy in his hand. He said she got it at Talking Leaves, too. But she hadn't just started reading it, like Nicki. She was almost finished reading it."

"There's a bookmark? Do you know what page?"

Debbie rephrases the question into the phone, listens, then relays the answer: "It was stuck between pages 214 and 215."

Hand trembling, Jen picks up Nicki's copy and flips through it until she finds the spot.

"What? What is it?" Debbie asks, watching her.

Jen can only stare numbly at the pages depicting the scene where fifteen-year-old Bonnie hangs herself, and she knows Mike has just seen the same thing, because she can hear his voice telling Debbie.

"Maybe they did know each other after all," Jen murmurs, mostly to herself. "Nicki and Taylor."

And maybe—

The ominous thought barges into her brain:

Maybe one of them suggested that Carley read the book, too. Maybe they even suggested that she—

No. They wouldn't have done that.

And even if they did—

Carley wouldn't do it. She wouldn't.

Yes, Jen had been terrified about the possibility before she talked to Carley in her bedroom this morning; before she saw the tremulous smile when she reinstated her Internet privileges; before her daughter not only allowed herself to be hugged, but also hugged her back.

She left the house feeling better about everything.

Carley is in good hands with Frankie, and Jen will be with her the rest of today and all day tomorrow, and then on Monday they'll talk to Sister Linda and find some professional help.

It's going to be all right. It really is.

Carley waits to put on her sneakers until she hears Aunt Frankie go into the bathroom down the hall and close the door. Moments later, the pipes groan, indicating she's stepped into the shower.

With a pang of guilt that's fleeting enough not to stop her in her tracks, Carley grabs the backpack containing her laptop and tiptoes over to open her bedroom door as quietly as she can, willing it not to creak. She pokes her head out into the hall just in time to see Emma doing the same thing from her room.

"What are you doing?" they ask each other in unison.

"Nothing!" they answer each other in unison.

Then, wearing a defiant expression along with her jacket and too much eye makeup, Emma steps all the way out into the hall.

"Where are you going?" Carley calls after her—but in a

whisper, lest Aunt Frankie hear. This is her one chance to sneak away, and Emma had better not blow it for her.

"Jailbreak," is Emma's terse reply as she heads for the stairs with a shrug.

A moment later, the front door opens and closes.

Now what?

Aunt Frankie is going to come out of the shower and find both of them missing?

She's going to be super worried. Darn that Emma anyway. Unless . . .

Carley hurries over to her desk, finds a sheet of paper, and scrawls a quick note.

Aunt Frankie—

Emma took off so I'm going after her. Be back soon.

XOXO
Carley

Again, she suffers a pang of guilt.

Again, it fails to deter her.

This is important. Angel flew all the way here on the red-eye just to meet her.

i was worried abt u, she wrote as soon as Carley signed onto the Internet. *where have u been?????*

Warmed by her friend's concern, Carley typed a brief explanation about her mother taking away the Internet as punishment.

That sux was the reply.

Then: *ru grounded?*

When Carley told her she isn't, Angel wrote, *great cuz I have a surprise 4 u wat is it?*

promise u wont tell ur prnts

tell them what??? Carley asked, growing anxious and impatient.

Angel explained that she'd jumped on a plane last night, using allowance and birthday money she'd been saving up.

so can u hang out 2day?

Carley thought about her mom, and Aunt Frankie, and her grandma.

i have to do this family thing so how bout 2nite

cant i have to fly back 2nite

Carley hesitated.

Then came another message: *pleaseeeeeeee?!?!!?!?!?!?*

my prnts wd kill me if i snuck out

ur already in trouble how much worse can it be

Angel had a good point.

cmon this is our 1 chance to meet and i came all this wayyyy

Another good point.

That was when Aunt Frankie knocked on Carley's door to say she was going to jump into the shower.

And now . . .

I'm really doing it.

Carley's sneakers carry her down the stairs into the kitchen, where she leaves the note on the counter for Aunt Frankie to find—just not right away. She needs a head start to get out of the development, and she's crossing her fingers that the metro bus will come pretty quickly. She doesn't know the Saturday schedule.

Outside, she's just in time to see Emma disappear down the driveway of the house next door to the Janiceks', where a new family moved in last month.

It dawns on her: Emma's new cool-hot boyfriend must be the teenage son of the single dad who bought the house.

I just hope she knows what she's doing, she thinks as she scurries down the street. For that matter . . .

I hope I do, too.

After dashing down the street in the rain, Emma lowers the hood of her jacket, shakes out her hair, and knocks on the back door of Gabe's house. She'd decided against ringing the front bell, not wanting Aunt Frankie to spot her if she happens to look out the bathroom window, which faces this end of the cul-de-sac.

It takes a long time for Gabe to answer the door, and when he does, he's wearing his coat.

"Oh, hey," he says. "What are you doing here?"

"Don't sound so thrilled."

"Sorry, I was . . . just on my way out."

"Where are you going?"

"To meet a friend."

She wants to ask if it's a girl, but decides she'd better not. She doesn't want him to think she's jealous.

Even though I am.

"Where's your dad?"

"Out."

"He's always out, isn't he?"

"Pretty much."

"So . . . is it a girl?" Emma hears herself ask.

"Is what a girl?"

"The friend you're going to meet."

"No. Why?"

He's lying, she decides. She can tell by the way he keeps shifting his weight from one foot to the other, refusing to make eye contact with her.

"Just wondering. I mean, I haven't seen you in, like, twenty-four hours and—"

"It hasn't been that long. It was after school yesterday."

"—*and*," she talks over him, "I feel like you aren't even glad to see me."

"Well, I didn't know you were coming over. You should have texted me first."

"I couldn't. I . . . lost my phone." No way is she going to tell him her parents took it away from her. "But I figured you were probably texting me and wondering why I wasn't answering."

"What? Oh. Yeah."

"You were texting me?"

"Yeah. So . . . maybe we can hang out tomorrow or some-thing. I've really got to—"

"Can you wait a couple of minutes? I need to see some-thing."

"What?"

Wow. He's not being romantic at all today.

It was obviously a mistake for her to have come over. But Emma couldn't stand not seeing him after everything they shared.

Anyway, she has a legitimate purpose for being here. She made sure of that.

"Remember when you said you saw something on my sis-ter's Peeps page?" she asks him briskly, as if that's the only reason she came. "Can you show it to me?"

"Now?" Gabe glances over his shoulder and she follows his gaze.

The kitchen behind him is a mess. Not just a pots-and-pans-in-the-sink, cereal-boxes-on-the-counter kind of mess, but truly cluttered and dirty. Even from here, Emma can smell an unpleasant aroma of sour milk and garbage. Every inch of counter space is covered in stuff, cabinets are open, dry food spills out of a pet bowl on the floor.

Hoping it doesn't belong to a cat, Emma looks again at Gabe. "Please? The Internet's down at our house and . . .

something terrible happened this morning and I'm, like, super scared."

"What happened?"

"Another one of my sister's friends committed suicide," she tells him—a bit of an exaggeration, since Carley said she didn't actually *know* Taylor Morino. But the situation is a lot more compelling this way.

Gabe smirks a little. "Dude, what is your sister, the Terminator?"

"Gabe, I'm seriously terrified that she's going to be next."

Okay, she's not exactly *terrified*. Not really even particularly worried. More like . . . curious.

Either Carley's lying about what she wrote on her Peeps page, or Gabe is. If it's him, he won't want her to see it.

And if it's Carley . . . why would she write that? To get attention?

The ironic thing about that: Carley isn't the one who usually likes attention.

I am.

And right now, she definitely has Gabe's.

"Come on in," he says, sounding resigned, but opening the door wider.

"Thanks," Emma says, and sneezes as she steps over the threshold. Definitely a cat.

"But you can't stay long. I've got to go."

She nods, wondering, suddenly, if he's lying about that, too. Maybe he saw her coming through the window and put on his jacket so that he could pretend he was leaving.

Maybe he doesn't love her after all. Maybe he doesn't even like her. He sure isn't acting as if he does.

"Come on," Gabe says brusquely. "The computer's in my room."

Entry from the marble notebook

Friday, February 28, 1986

My hand is shaking so badly I can barely write
this.

Today after school, I was practicing parallel parking over by Cardinal Ruffini again. My guy—I think
of him as my guy, I can't help it—came outside with
his friends.

This time, there was a girl with them, though. I
know her—Debbie Quattrone, one of the cheerleaders. She's stuck up and when I saw her with the guys, I
got a sinking feeling because I bet she's going out with
one of them. I was hoping it's not with my guy.

Just like before, they all came over to the car to say
hi. Even Debbie was nice, smiling and calling me by
name as if we're friends at school, which we're not.

I saw Father checking her out and it made me sick.

Then something UNBELIEVABLE happened!

The cute guy—my guy—slipped me a folded up
piece of paper, and he winked at me. No one saw. I
shoved the paper into my pocket until we got back
home.

Here it is.

Separate sheet of paper taped
into the marble notebook

Dear Ruthie,

I hope you got the flowers I sent you for Valentine's Day and that they were a nice surprise. I was wondering if you want to go to Spring Fling with me? If the answer is yes, then be wearing a pink ribbon in your hair when I see you next Friday.

Love,
Mike

Chapter 15

Driving over to her mother's house, Jen belatedly wishes she'd taken the long way around. This route takes her right past Cicero and Son.

As she passes the funeral home, she spots Mike Morino walking up the front steps wearing a long dark overcoat and carrying an umbrella. He walks slowly, head bent, a large shopping bag in his hand.

His daughter's clothing, Jen guesses, and her heart goes out to him.

For a moment, she contemplates pulling over to the curb and calling out to him. But this isn't the time or place to offer condolences.

Maybe she should go to the wake after all.

The fact that she doesn't think much of him as a person doesn't change the fact that he's a grief-stricken man who needs all the support he can get right now. A flawed man whose daughter blamed him for her suicide.

She drives on, thinking of Mike and of Debbie, wondering how they're going to get through another day of torturous guilt, let alone the rest of their lives.

I couldn't bear it, she thinks. *I'm strong, but not that strong, and—*

Oh no.

She just remembered that she was planning to stop at church before she left Woodsbridge, to offer the second day's devotion in her novena to Saint Ann. If she waits until later, she might not have a chance. They're already getting a late start on the cooking.

She might as well make a detour over to Our Lady, the neighborhood parish where her parents attend daily Mass.

She turns the corner, crosses the tracks, and turns again onto Wayside Avenue. Sacred Sisters is right up ahead. Jen can see a male figure wearing a hooded raincoat standing beside the signboard, and the glass-fronted cover is standing open on its hinges. He's arranging new letter blocks immediately following today's date and "42ND ANNUAL SPRING FLING."

So far, they spell out C-A-N-C-E.

Jen drives on past as he pulls an L from his alphabet box and reaches toward the sign. She wonders whether the dance will be rescheduled later this spring.

Selfishly, she hopes not. It was difficult enough for Carley to endure a month's worth of buildup to the dance. Stretching it out even longer will make it harder for her to close this chapter and move on.

Remembering what Frankie told her about how the other girls coerced Carley into cheating in math class, Jen allows her fury—diluted earlier by a wave of shock and worry—to fully sink in. Most of it is directed at the other girls, though a good deal of it is aimed at herself, and she can't deny a bit of anger toward her own daughter as well.

From the time Carley was a tiny girl, Jen had tried to teach her to be a good person and get along with others when clearly, she should have spent more time teaching her to stand up for herself, and not let others push her around . . . not to mention never to cheat in school.

I'm the one who drummed into her how important it is to do well and get good grades . . .

When it comes to academics, though, Carley is much harder on herself than Jen ever has been.

I told her to stay home that day and take the math test later. She didn't want to do that. She was worried about breaking the rules . . .

Ironic, since she then went and broke one of the biggest rules of all.

But everyone has a breaking point, Jen reminds herself. Especially when her emotions have been endlessly beaten down, manipulated, and abused.

Besides, Carley insisted on sticking it out at Sacred Sisters when she could have switched schools. That took strength.

I should point that out to her, Jen decides. *She's stronger than I thought. Stronger than she herself even realizes.*

She parallel parks on the street and leaves her phone in the car, plugged into the charger. After feeding the parking meter, she heads toward the old stone church with its stained glass windows and towering steeple. Memories bombard her as she picks her way around puddles in the cracked sidewalk, just as she used to do when she was a little girl trying to keep her shiny white Sunday shoes from getting muddy.

So many milestones unfolded here at Our Lady. She and all four of her sisters and countless cousins were christened in the church, and every spring for many years, it seemed, someone was making a First Communion or Confirmation here.

As she climbs the wide stone steps, she remembers lining up with her classmates for pictures, shivering in her thin white Communion dress as May flurries fell. Years later, she and Thad were showered with birdseed as they held hands and ran down those same steps toward a "Just Married" car. And they posed here with infant Carley in her christening gown, not long before they moved to the suburbs and joined Saint Paul's.

That picture sits framed on Jen's dresser back at home.

Frankie was godmother, flanked by Jen and Thad, proudly cradling the white-bonneted bundle in her arms.

"I'll always be there for her," she tearfully promised Jen that day. "I'll never let anything happen to her, ever. I'll love her as if she were my own child."

Remembering that peaceful, joyous morning, Jen is comforted.

Maybe it's no accident that I forgot to stop at church in Woodsbridge, she thinks as she tugs open one of the massive arched double doors. *Maybe this is where I was supposed to be.*

She crosses herself at the holy water fount and slips into the incense-scented sanctuary. The altar is draped in Lenten purple, and the pews are deserted.

She sinks into one, pulls her prayer booklet from her coat pocket, and finds the devotion for the second day of the novena, to be followed by the Our Father, Hail Mary, and Glory Be to the Father.

Today, the ancient verses seem to have new and urgent meaning.

Lead us not into temptation; but deliver us from evil . . .

When she's finished, Jen adds a final, silent prayer for the souls of Taylor Morino and Nicki Olivera.

Emma's eyes tear up as she stares at the laptop screen, open to a Peopleportal profile page for her sister, the big fat liar.

"Do you have a tissue?" she asks Gabe, doubting it. Never in her life has she seen such a pigsty. His room is worse than the kitchen, with crap piled everywhere and a layer of cat fur over it all.

Sounding put out, he says, "Hang on," and leaves the room.

Fighting the urge to rub her itchy eyes, not wanting to smear the carefully applied mascara, Emma thinks about Carley, endlessly lecturing about the dangers of putting too much information out there on the Internet, and how she should just put her first name on her Peeps profile, and blah, blah, blah . . .

Meanwhile, that Carley Theresa page was obviously just a dummy page set up in case their parents looked at it.

"Here," Gabe says, back with a handful of . . . toilet paper. Nice.

The visit isn't going the way she'd imagined, by any stretch.

Emma blots her eyes, sniffles, and looks at the Peeps page again.

This one has her sister's full name, and a bunch of pictures, and it shows a side of Carley that Emma has never seen. It's not that there are particularly provocative pictures on there, or that her sister is up to anything particularly scandalous. No, it's more that . . .

"Your sister's a real bitch," Gabe observes, reading over Emma's shoulder, and he's right.

Here on Peeps, Carley has nothing nice to say about anyone—especially the girls at Sacred Sisters. Scrolling up the page, Emma can see that she's been making rude comments about them for months now. She accuses them of slutty behavior, and spreads rumors about them, and when it comes to their looks, she's merciless. In the comments section on one slightly overweight girl's picture, she wrote simply, "Moo."

She's always whining to Mom about how everyone hates her. Is it any wonder?

For that matter, she has nothing nice to say about Mom here, either. She complains about her constantly, calling her names and mocking her. If Mom ever saw this, she would be devastated.

In the profile questionnaire for this page, Carley lists her literary heroes and heroines not as E. B. White or Laura

Ingalls Wilder, as she does on her Carley Theresa page, but as "Sylvia Plath and Ernest Hemingway, because they were smart enough to check themselves out of the B.S. Hotel." Meanwhile, her daily posts have grown increasingly dark, sprinkled with quotes and stanzas of poetry.

The most recent posts went up a few days ago:

My ex-BFF killed herself. Good riddance. I just wish I had the guts to do the same thing . . . and *Suspended from school. I'd rather be dead than spend days on end stuck at home with my mother. God, I hate her almost as much as I hate myself. I wish I really were dead.*

"See? I told you," Gabe says, pointing at that post.

"I . . ." Emma hesitates, sneezes, "I never saw any of this."

Neglecting to bless her, Gabe asks, "How come? I mean, I noticed you're not connected to her on here, but neither am I, and I can see it, so it must be set to public visibility."

"Yeah, but you can still block people." Emma sneezes again and wipes her nose on the toilet tissue before reaching for the mouse, which is sticky and spattered with something that looks like coffee or Pepsi. "She obviously has me blocked in her settings. Here, look . . ."

Emma clicks out of Gabe's screen name and signs into her own. Then she types the name "Carley Archer" into the Peoplefinder search window.

There are no results, other than a Carla Archer—an older woman from Michigan—and some Mexican guy named Carlos Archevarios.

When she types in "Carley Theresa," though, the dummy page pops up.

"See?"

"Pretty smart of her," Gabe says admiringly.

"I'm sure she has my parents blocked, too. They'd be super pissed-off if they knew."

Not to mention super worried.

Maybe Emma should tell them.

I will, she decides, feeling Gabe's hands suddenly resting on her shoulders, *just . . . later.*

Now that she's here she plans to put aside thoughts of her sister—not to mention her cat allergy and the household squalor—and make the most of her time alone with Gabe, who seems to have forgotten all about having someone to meet.

Walking back to her car after leaving the church, Jen sees the telltale paper rectangle stuck beneath the windshield wiper and realizes that she was in the church much longer than she'd intended.

Oh well. A measure of inner peace is well worth the cost of a parking ticket. She shoves it into the back pocket of her jeans and climbs into the car.

It takes only a few minutes to cover the distance to her parents' house on a block lined with foursquare, vinyl-sided houses set so close together that when the windows are open in summertime, you can carry on conversations with the neighbors without setting foot out the door or picking up the phone. Jen knows, having done so plenty of times when she was growing up here.

Not seeing Frankie's car behind her parents' white Buick on their half of the shared driveway, she wonders if Emma decided, at the last minute, to join them after all. That would explain why they're running late. Her younger daughter tends to take forever to get ready to walk out the door, regardless of whether she's going to a party or just out to the mailbox.

Jen grabs the plastic bag from the supermarket, closes the car door, and starts for the house—only to see her parents throwing open the front door.

"Genevieve!" her mother calls. "Where are they?"

"Frankie and the girls? They must be—"

She stops short, seeing the look of concern on her father's face. "What do you mean? Where are who?"

"Where are the girls? Frankie has been calling. She was trying to reach you because she thought maybe they were with you but you didn't pick—"

"No, they're with her!" Even as she says the words, Jen realizes they aren't true. She registers the panic in her mother's eyes, and she hears her father say they'd better call the police, and she knows that despite her fears and her promises and her precautions and yes, even her prayers . . .

Something has happened to her daughters.

On weekday mornings, it takes about half an hour to get to Sacred Sisters on the metro bus. But today, Carley waited at least that long before a bus even pulled up, and this one is making local stops.

Slumped in a window seat with her knees pressed against the seat back in front of her, she stares at the rain and wishes the kid a few rows ahead would turn down the music on his iPod. He's wearing earphones, yet every lyric, guitar solo, and percussion blast is loud and clear.

If Carley had her cell phone, at least, she could get in touch with Angel to let her know she's running late.

She could also call her mother to say she'll meet her over at Grandma's house later. That seems like the logical plan, since she'll be right in the neighborhood.

By now, Aunt Frankie must have found the note. Carley plans on telling her—and Mom, too—that she'd hopped the bus because she thought Emma might be heading into the city.

She hasn't yet figured out why she'd have possibly come to that conclusion, but she can probably make the story work.

Or not.

Guiltily, she reminds herself that covering one lie with another is never a good idea.

But Mom would never understand how desperate she is to meet Angel in person—or how touched she is that she's flown all this way from California just to make sure Carley is okay.

She's my only friend in the entire world, Carley thinks as the bus turns, at long last, onto Wayside Avenue. *I'm going to see her, and then they can punish me all they want after she leaves tonight.*

She sits up straighter and picks up the backpack resting on the seat beside her.

When Carley asked Angel why she needed to bring her laptop along, she wrote, *cuz i dont have mine here and i want to show u something online so whatevr u do dont 4get*

Carley was about to point out that just a phone with Internet access would be sufficient when she remembered that her own phone is still hidden wherever Dad stashed it. She didn't want to get into explaining that to Angel, so she wrote back, *don't worry i wont 4get*

Her heart beats a little faster as she spots Sacred Sisters up ahead.

Angel was the one who suggested meeting at the school.

i wasnt sure where u live, qp, she wrote, *and you weren't online this morning so i came here to see if i could figure out a way to trace u. 2 bad the place is deserted 2day*

well duh, Carley typed back. *its saturdayyyyy*

yeah but doors r unlocked so get ur butt over here-eeeeeeee

She promised to meet Angel there as soon as possible.

Now, Carley pulls the cord to request the bus stop, which is up past the school, on the far corner. As the bus slows, she notices that the sign in front of Sacred Sisters has been altered.

"42ND ANNUAL SPRING FLING—CANCELED."

Beneath that is a new line: "GRIEF COUNSELORS ON HAND SUNDAY 2–4 P.M."

It's Johnny's job to change the sign. Maybe he's here today. Suddenly, she wishes she had taken some extra time to brush her hair.

But then she reminds herself that this isn't about Johnny.

It's about Angel.

Smiling with anticipation, Carley stands and makes her way to the front of the bus.

Decked out as an enchanted garden, the school gym has gone from festive to forlorn, giving off an air of abandonment— like a girl who got all dressed up for the big dance, only to be stood up by her date.

Ruthie.

That night, the night before she died, Angel watched in her bedroom as she fixed her hair and put on a shiny pink dress.

"Ruthie! That's a fairy princess dress! Where did you get it?"

"At Goodwill. It had a tear in the seam, so it was practically free, and I fixed it. You can't see it, can you? It doesn't smell like mothballs, does it?"

"What do mothballs smell like?"

The dress did smell funny, but Angel didn't want to hurt her feelings. People were always hurting her feelings. She talked about that a lot. Sometimes she came home from school and cried because of the way the other girls treated her.

It was so nice to see Ruthie happy for a change that night, with pink cheeks and sparkly eyes. Her orangey-red hair was pulled back from her face with a pink ribbon.

She was going to a dance. With a boy.

"Who is he, Ruthie?"

"Do you remember when the florist rang the doorbell and gave me that beautiful bouquet of pink flowers a few weeks ago?"

"The ones that smelled nice?"

"Yes. He's the one who sent them."

"Where are the flowers? Did they die?"

"No." Ruthie's glow faded. "They . . . they're gone. But I saved a few of the petals."

"Are you in love with the boy, Ruthie? Are you going to marry him so that he can be my dad and you can be my mom?"

"You're silly!" Ruthie laughed, and she picked up Angel and they spun around and around so that the skirt of her dress swished and swirled.

"Ruthie! What are you doing?"

"Dancing!" It was so good to hear her laughing that Angel didn't even care that much about being dizzy.

"Listen, you can't tell Mother and Father you saw me dressed up like this, okay? I'm going to sneak out of the house for a little while."

"How will you get out?"

"Through the window."

"How will you get back in?"

Ruthie smiled and walked over to the window that overlooked the roof of the mudroom. "The latch is broken, and it goes up and down really easily from the outside. Want to see?"

She climbed out the window, closed it, and then opened it again a moment later.

Before climbing back inside, she held up a clear plastic box that was stashed outside on the roof.

"What is that?" Angel asked.

"It's my corsage for the dance. The florist delivered it right after school yesterday, and I hid it out here so that Mother won't smell it. Please don't tell, okay?"

"I won't tell."

"You're my little angel . . ."

Eyes flying open at the distinct sound of a distant door opening and closing, Angel is back to reality, standing in the middle of a shadowy school gym decorated as an enchanted garden. *This is what it must have looked like that night* . . .

Somewhere in the school, closer to the gym, another door opens and closes. Footsteps echo in the deserted hallway; not the purposeful stride of a teacher or counselor paying a weekend visit to the workplace, but the uncertain steps of a teenage girl who ventured far from home, all alone, to meet a friend.

Just like Ruthie did that night.

And—like Ruthie—Carley Archer won't be finding a fairy-tale ending when she gets here.

Having found that Angel was right about the school doors being unlocked, Carley walks slowly down the halls with her computer bag over her shoulder. Angel had said she'd be in the gym; she was going to shoot some baskets while she waited.

Unnerved by the shadowy, deserted corridors, Carley listens for the sound of a basketball thumping.

She hears nothing but her own footsteps and steady breathing.

"Angel?" she calls.

No reply.

She stops walking, wondering what to do.

Maybe Angel got kicked out while Carley was on the bus trying to get here.

Maybe she's been trying to message about where to meet instead.

Carley doesn't have her phone, but she does have the laptop. If she can use it to get online, she can get in touch with Angel that way.

Carley turns and starts back down the hall.

Then a voice, a female voice, echoes from the direction of the gym, stopping her in her tracks. "Carley?"

"Yes!" Relieved, she calls back, "Angel?"

"Yes."

Carley hurries in that direction, grinning.

When she reaches the gym, though, she hesitates. The doors are propped open, but the interior is dark.

"Angel?" she calls again.

"In here."

Carley takes a few steps over the threshold and immediately comprehends why Angel wasn't playing basketball in here.

The gym is decorated for Spring Fling. Oversized, glitter-painted flowers, trees, and picket fences line the perimeter. Papier-mâché butterflies and bumblebees are suspended from the ceiling, motionless amid tissue paper clouds.

"Angel?"

"Hi, Carley."

The voice is behind her, so close to her ear that she gasps and whirls around.

But it isn't Angel standing there.

For a split second, she's terrified to see a figure looming behind her.

Then her eyes adjust and she recognizes the face.

Her first thought is that she's going to get into trouble for sneaking into the school on a Saturday.

Her next is that for some reason, Sister Linda isn't wearing her habit, dressed instead in an old-fashioned, full-skirted pink taffeta dress covered in brownish stains, and a pink ribbon tied around straggly ginger-colored hair.

Entry from the marble notebook

Friday, March 7, 1986

All day, I was so worried something would go wrong and I wouldn't get to go driving, or he wouldn't be there if I did.

As soon as the bell rang, I ran straight home from school and I tied a pink ribbon into my hair. It wasn't ribbon, really. It was seam binding from Mother's sewing box, but it was all I could find.

I never wear pink. I've always thought the color clashed with my hair, but when Adrian saw the ribbon in it, he told me I looked pretty. He asked where I was going and I said out driving with Father. Father heard and got this pleased smile on his face, as if I'd tried to look special for him. It made me sick.

Then Adrian tripped over his shoelace and fell down and started crying, and Mother freaked out the way she always does when he gets hurt, and Father yelled at him and said boys don't cry.

"I wish I were a girl," Adrian said, while I was bandaging his scraped knee, "because then I could cry all I wanted to."

I told him I'm glad he's not a girl. He asked why, and I just said, "Because then you wouldn't be you."

The truth is that it's because I don't have to worry, ever, that Father might do to him what he does to me.

He never gives Adrian the time of day because he only likes girls. Even tiny girls. I've seen him staring at the little four-year-old who lives a few doors down, and I shudder at what he's probably thinking.

So we went out driving and I was such a nervous wreck that while I was parallel parking, I hit the bumper of the car in back of me. Luckily, there was no damage.

Finally Mike and his friends came out of the school. When he saw me, he got this huge smile on his face and they all came walking toward the car. Father made some comment to me about what a friendly group of kids they are.

Mike must have been pretty sure I was going to say yes about the dance, because he already had a note written and folded up with my name on it. He threw it onto my lap when Father wasn't looking. Here it is.

Separate sheet of paper taped into the marble notebook

Dear Ruthie:

I'm so happy you want to go to Spring Fling with me!

I can tell your dad is kind of strict, and I've heard your mom is, too, so how about if I just meet you at the dance? Wear a pink dress for me, please, and the special gift that will be delivered on Friday afternoon after school. I'll be waiting for you by the punch bowl in the gym.

Love,
Mike

Chapter 16

Jen paces the length of the living room again, past her parents and Frankie, all of them grim-faced and perched on the very edges of their chair cushions, as if to ensure they'll be able to jump up at the slightest bit of good news . . .

Or bad.

She can hear Thad on the phone in the front hall, talking to the police. They've been in contact for the past few hours, but there's absolutely nothing to go on—and no reason, according to the authorities, to assume the worst.

Frankie isn't certain how long the girls had been gone before she came out of the bathroom after showering and blow-drying her hair. She assumed they were still in their rooms. When Amy Janicek called to ask Carley about babysitting tonight, Frankie answered the phone, went through the house hollering for Carley, and found the note she'd left on the counter.

Hearing Thad hang up the phone, Jen goes out into the hall. "Anything new?"

He shakes his head and opens his arms. She steps into them and rests her head against his chest.

"I can't believe I took away the girls' phones," she tells him. "I keep thinking that if they had their phones, they'd call. Or at least we could trace them with the built-in GPS systems."

"Emma's probably had hers disabled for months now anyway. Plus, I'm the one who stashed the phones in the car trunk, Jen. If I'd left them in the house, they would have found them."

"That was the point of *not* hiding them in the house. Emma snoops."

"I know, but . . ."

"Don't beat yourself up, Thad."

"You either."

They've been doing their best all afternoon to assuage each other's guilt . . .

Just as Jen had tried to do with Debbie.

Debbie . . .

The train of thought starts careening, and once again, Jen's recent nightmare pops into her head—the one about the casket at the funeral home. It's been coming back to her all afternoon, ever since she found out her girls were missing. Try as she might to banish it, the image of Carley in a coffin flits around in the back of her mind like a vengeful ghost.

Thad sighs. "I keep wondering why Carley, at least, hasn't found a phone somewhere and called us anyway."

"Me too."

It isn't like their responsible firstborn to let them worry like this.

"Maybe she's doing it on purpose," Thad suggests. "Letting us worry, to punish us for punishing her."

"I think she was over that."

"I don't know. She was pretty furious last night."

"I know, but when I saw her in her room earlier . . . I got the feeling that all was forgiven."

Seeing the look on Thad's face, Jen knows he thinks she misread Carley.

Or maybe it was an act, all of it; the subdued attitude, the gratitude for the wifi password, even the hug. Maybe Carley was still, deep down inside, steeped in resentment toward her mother.

Just like Nicki was.

Jen hasn't allowed herself much time to process what Debbie told her about the suicide note. But whenever her thoughts settle on it, she finds it hard to believe Nicki could harbor such deep-seated anger without ever betraying to her mother the slightest inkling of disapproval.

Maybe Debbie just couldn't admit the truth to Jen, or even to herself.

Now Mike Morino is in the same boat. Was he aware that his daughter, too, was distraught over his extramarital affair?

But Taylor's parents were already divorced—had been for years, according to Marie. Would she be so upset about his cheating on his third wife that she'd end her life over it?

Nothing makes sense—but right now, Jen is mainly concerned with her own daughters.

Thad stiffens suddenly and she looks up to see him staring over her shoulder, at the door. She turns her head just in time to see it open.

Emma is standing on the threshold.

"They're back!" she screams, grabbing Emma and holding her tight, releasing a sob of relief into her daughter's hair. "Where have you been?"

Emma's hair smells of stale cigarette smoke.

Jen lifts her head, turns to look around for Carley, certain she'll see her here, quietly pleased at having managed to deliver her sister safely home from whatever decadence . . .

But Carley isn't here.

"Where's your sister?" Thad is asking Emma. "Where's Carley?"

"How should I know?"

"What do you mean? She went out looking for you!"

"Well, she didn't find me, did she?" Emma asks with a bratty little shrug, and Jen clenches her hand against her side to keep from reaching out to shake her daughter.

"When was the last time you saw Carley?" she asks, fighting to keep her tone even. "*When?*"

Emma's gaze flicks from Jen to Thad to her grandparents and aunt standing expectantly in the living room doorway. Her smug expression fades.

"I haven't seen her since before I left," she says in a small voice. "Why?"

"Because she went after you," Thad tells her, "and she hasn't come back."

Jen spots a new, rarely seen emotion in her daughter's blue eyes: fear.

"Emma—"

"I swear I don't know where she is."

"But you know something, Emma. What do you know?"

"Mom, I don't—"

"You know something!"

Emma swallows audibly. "I'll show you. But I can't do it on my own laptop, and it probably won't show up on yours, either. Where's Carley's phone?"

"I'll get it," Thad says grimly, taking his car keys out of his pocket.

Louie's Bar is pleasantly crowded on this blustery late afternoon. There are several flat-screen televisions, all tuned to the same channel and positioned so that every table and every seat at the bar has a clear view of the Sabres game in progress.

Al Witkowski has been coming here ever since his fake ID and five bucks could get him a couple of Genny Cream

Ales, a dozen wings in a paper-lined plastic basket, and a decent tip for Phil, the bartender. Now that'll cost him fifteen. Still not bad, all things considered.

Phil—whose real name is Phyllis—was a skinny blond college dropout when Al first met her. Now she's a hefty, gray-haired, divorced grandma in a black T-shirt and jeans, world-weary but with the same quick wit that made her a favorite among the neighborhood "boys" as she still calls Al, Bobby, and Glenn Cicero, who graduated from Cardinal Ruffini in the class between the two brothers.

"What'll it be, boys?" she asks as they settle onto stools at the end of the bar, wearing Sabres jerseys like most of the other patrons.

Until recently, Phil would have added, "You want the usual?"

The usual would have been a round of Genny drafts and a bucket of wings, the hottest ones on the menu. Suicide wings, they call them here at Louie's.

But lately, they've been changing things up a bit. Al's trying to cut calories and drop a few pounds, so he sometimes orders a grilled chicken sandwich. So does Bobby, when his gall bladder is flaring up. And Glenn occasionally has a bottled import instead of whatever's on tap lately, which inevitably causes Phil to grin and ask him if business is booming over at the funeral home.

Today, Glenn orders a round of bourbon for the three of them, straight up. Business is booming, all right—but no one's smiling about it. And no one's ordering suicide wings.

Mike Morino—an old pal from the neighborhood—lost his daughter this morning.

"Last week, it was Debbie Quattrone's daughter. What the hell is going on with these kids," Bobby mutters, keeping one eye on the Sabres game on the flat-screen television behind the bar, "that makes them think killing themselves is going to solve anything?"

He's undoubtedly thinking about his own three teenage girls at home. Al's nieces are all bubbly, well-adjusted kids. But then so, he hears, was Morino's daughter. Al is grateful that his own kids are past high school and seem to be thriving young adults—although you just never know.

"You know, I've always thought Mikey had it all," Glenn says, "but right now I wouldn't trade places with that guy for all the tea in China."

"Tea?" Phil shakes her head as she slides three glasses of bourbon across the bar toward them. "Forget tea. And forget your damned wallet. This round's on the house. You want wings, boys?"

Al shakes his head and takes a sip of the bourbon, relishing the burn. "On a diet, Phil. Been trying to eat right and exercise."

"Good for you. Check out the salads. We've got a new one with chicken tenders in it."

"That doesn't sound very healthy."

"There's spinach in it, too." She hands over a couple of laminated menus and a printed sheet of paper headed "TONIGHT'S SPECIALS," then heads into the kitchen.

"What kind of exercise you doing, Al?" his brother wants to know.

"Walking, so far . . . starting off slow, you know. I just walked over here, and—"

"This is only two blocks from your apartment."

"I walked this morning, too."

"What, from the door to your truck?"

"No, I walked the dog around the neighborhood." Sensing that Bobby's warming up to bust his chops, Al heads him off. "Hey, remember the old Addams House?"

"What about it?"

"I thought it was empty, right?"

"It is empty." Glenn sets down his half-full glass, then picks it up again. "Why?"

"While I was out walking this morning, I thought I saw someone in there. And the same thing happened the other night. And today, I heard the smoke alarm going off."

"Yeah? Maybe it was a ghost."

"Yeah, sure it was," Al tells Bobby, rolling his eyes as if that's the most ridiculous thing he ever heard.

"I'm serious. If anyone was ever going to come back to haunt a place, it would be Old Lady Bell. She was one scary lady. Although that whole family was a freak show. Remember what Ma used to say about them?"

Al nods, remembering the day he told Sandra about that, when she was getting ready to list the Bell house. "Yeah, Ma was all upset after the daughter was killed because they weren't having a wake or funeral Mass."

"You think your mother was upset?" Glenn speaks up. "My pop embalms her, gets her all set to be laid out, and then he finds out that there's no wake, no funeral, and they haggle with him over the bill. I remember I rode over there with him the day he delivered the casket. They said they were going to bury her out West, where they came from, and—"

"Wait—you guys just deliver a dead body like . . . like a pizza?"

"Well not *exactly* like that, but yeah. If it was being released to the family and they'd made arrangements for transport, we'd drop it off, along with personal effects. That day, I had to carry the package that had the dress she was wearing when she died. It was pink, and it was . . . messed up," he says, wrinkling his nose in distaste.

"So that's it?" Bobby asks. "You and your father just show up at the door—'Here's your dead daughter, here's her bloody dress, see ya later'?"

"Well, there was paperwork, and God knows these days there are more hoops to jump through, but . . . What are you going to do? In the end, the family gets to bury their loved one wherever they want." Glenn sets down his glass again. This time, it's empty.

"Poor Ruthie Bell." Al shakes his head sadly. "She never had a chance. Her mother was a crazy freak, her father was a dirty old man—remember how he used to leer at all the little girls on the playground? And Ruthie's kid brother . . ."

"Don't even get me started on that little sissy." Bobby rolls his eyes.

"He might have been a sissy, but he was no mama's boy, that's for sure. He had his dearly departed mother cremated—probably not something a conservative person like her would have wanted—and he left her ashes sitting on a shelf in my funeral home."

"You're kidding."

"Nope." Glenn signals Phil to bring them another round of drinks. "I tried getting in touch with him a few times—he lives on Long Island now—well, he *did*. But the phone was disconnected and the e-mails bounced back. I guess he fell off the face of the earth after she died. Just walked away and abandoned her remains, and the house—"

"And everything that was in it," Al puts in. "The stuff is sitting in one of my storage units. The rent automatically gets paid every month, though. Maybe you should have charged him up front for shelf space for his mother, Glenn."

"Yeah, well, maybe I'll just drop her off at the house as long as it's empty, especially if she's haunting it anyway."

"It might be Ruthie Bell's ghost, though," Al points out, mostly kidding around—*mostly*. "Or maybe it's the old man's, or . . ."

Sandra's. Is it Sandra's? She died in a fire. Would her ghost make its presence known by setting off a smoke alarm?

"Or it might just be kids in there," Glenn says, "doing

what kids always do: drinking and writing graffiti on the walls and smoking pot."

"You talking about the Addams House?" Phil asks, standing in front of them and pouring three more bourbons.

"How'd you guess?"

"I heard you say Ruthie Bell. I remember her. She died in a car wreck in a snowstorm. Had her license only a couple of days and slammed into a tree. I was spooked to drive if even a few flakes were falling for a long time after that." Shaking her head, she hustles away as the three of them drink from their refilled glasses.

"So which one of the Bells do you think is haunting the house?" Al muses.

"Why don't you go find out?"

"Why don't *you*?"

"I love it when you two get into it. Just like the old days." Glenn grins and shakes his head. "I don't remember either of you ever going through with that dare."

"And *you* did?" Bobby asks.

"Hey, I spent most of my time in a funeral home. No one ever questioned whether I had guts."

"I was thinking," Al says, glass poised in front of his mouth, "that I should go over to the Addams House and check things out. If kids are vandalizing the place, it's a real shame and it should be reported before they burn the damned place down. I think I'll go over in the morning."

"Why wait?" Bobby asks with a gleam in his eye. "Why not go tonight?"

"Want to come with me?"

"Nah, the game is on."

Al gestures at the TV. "Who cares? They're losing. And you're the locksmith, remember?"

"Yeah, but that doesn't mean—"

"Come on, boys," Glenn says. "Drink up and let's go take a walk."

* * *

Seated at her desk in the cluttered office tucked away in the back of the second floor, Angel takes one last look at Carley's laptop screen.

Nice. Very nice.

The suicide note had been composed months ago, along with Nicki's and Taylor's. Angel uploaded it onto Carley's computer just now, after painstakingly deleting every trace of correspondence she'd ever shared with Angel 770.

This note, like the others, contains just the right mixture of contempt and despair. When Jen Archer reads it—in the very, *very* near future—there will be no doubt in her mind that her daughter hated her.

But this note was trickier to write than the others.

Debbie Olivera and Mike Morino had made themselves easy targets.

Those two were puppets in my hands, just like the Sacred Sisters girls.

Angel had instigated the bullying of Carley Archer, to be sure. But left to their own devices, the girls did the rest, and the bullying took on a life of its own.

Evil has a way of doing that. You just have to use it to your advantage, and Angel learned to do just that.

It all began a few months ago with the creation of dummy Peeps profile pages for both Carley and Nicki. Angel blocked the girls themselves, along with everyone in their immediate circles, from viewing them.

Then she had "Carley Archer" send a note to the real Nicki Olivera, as well as to the handful of Sacred Sisters girls with whom she'd connected on the social networking site. The note said that she'd created a new page so that her parents wouldn't see what she was up to online. No one questioned it. A lot of the girls did stuff like that.

Then it was just a matter of having "Carley" alienate

every tentative new relationship she'd established, slamming the girls online, criticizing their photos, bragging about herself and claiming she'd cleverly cheated her way to her good grades . . .

She alienated Nicki in the same manner—and vice versa.

From Nicki's new dummy Peeps page, Angel sent the insults "Nicki" supposedly wrote about Carley's hair and appearance.

As for the coldhearted texts the girls exchanged . . .

These days, kids never dial actual phone numbers when they want to call or text a friend. They simply pull up the friend's name—or in some cases, just a photo—from the list of contacts on their smart phone, press a button, and the phone connects to the preprogrammed number.

All Angel had to do was get her hands on both girls' cell phones long enough to alter their contact information for each other. It was easy enough to do with Carley: she dutifully left her phone in the locker room during gym. Nicki's phone was harder to obtain, but not impossible. She was careless enough to walk around the Galleria one day with her shoulder bag unzipped. Trailing her, Angel plucked the phone out, changed the contact information for Carley, and then turned in the phone to mall security, saying someone must have dropped it. It found its way back into Nicki's hands, and the trap was set.

From that point on, text messages Carley and Nicki thought they were sending to each other were actually now going to Angel; their voice mails to an in-box with an automated greeting. It was Angel who answered their texts to each other; Angel who listened to the voice mail messages; Angel who deleted them and didn't return the calls. By the time Carley and Nicki ran into each other again face to face, the cold war was on.

Human nature, Angel has decided, is a wonderful thing.

Social networking as "Rachel Riley," Angel connected with several of the Sisters freshmen and planted the seed for the Spring Fling prank as well as the math test debacle. She never mentioned Carley by name, just talked about how satisfying it would be to have a laugh at an enemy's expense.

By then, Carley was everyone's enemy. Even Nicki's.

What a shame that in the end, Carley and Nicki never even realized that they were victims of their own behavior. If either of them had simply reached out to each other in person, all of Angel's efforts could have been undone with a simple conversation.

But Angel was counting on the fact that they wouldn't do that, well aware that modern teenagers are, for all their "connections," isolated in an unprecedented way, tending to their relationships on screens and keyboards.

Some adults are just as guilty.

After getting to know both Mike and Debbie from afar, Angel could see that the two of them had a lot in common. Far more than Mike seemed to have in common with his ex-girlfriend Jen.

It took some fancy manipulation to get him and Debbie into a room together, but once that happened, human nature—or in this case, their own fatal flaws—took over.

Engaged in a full-blown affair, they became careless enough that they wouldn't question whether either—or even both—of their daughters had stumbled upon their secret. And teenage girls are such emotionally volatile creatures that it's entirely conceivable that a parent's adultery might be sufficient motive for suicide.

But Jen Archer is different.

She was never going to have an affair, or make any other glaring misstep.

It's been obvious from the start that she loves her husband, that she's a fine, upstanding, moral citizen and, above all, a good mom. It wasn't easy coming up with a legitimate reason for her own daughter to hate her.

But I did.

Rather, Carley did, when she poured her heart out to strangers online, describing how she felt as though she'd let her mother down when the whole Spring Fling princess debacle unfolded.

i feel like she wishes i could be more like her, she wrote on one of the bullying forums.

And, *sometimes i think shes ashamed of me even when she claims shes not . . .*

And, *no matter what she says abt loving me the way i am, i bet if she could snap her fingers and make me beautiful & popular she wd do it in a heartbeattttttt . . .*

Naturally, Angel fueled the fire at every opportunity and ran with that theme for the suicide note, embellishing until it became the heartbreaking masterpiece it is now.

With gloved fingertips, Angel pops the memory stick out of the laptop and starts to pocket it before remembering that she doesn't have pockets; she's not wearing the nun's habit she usually has on when she sits at this desk.

She did wear it into the building earlier, and it was a good thing, because Johnny the janitor was here.

He didn't seem surprised to see her. He told her the principal had instructed the head custodian to have him change the sign out front to indicate that the dance had been canceled and that grief counseling would be offered at school tomorrow afternoon.

"You heard what happened, right?" he asked. "That girl who killed herself?"

"That's why I'm here," Angel told him. "I'm going to be counseling the girls and I have some things I need to do to get ready."

Johnny nodded, disinterested, obviously in a hurry to get going.

"Big plans today, Johnny?"

"Yeah—going home to watch the Sabres game. Have a great day, Sister Linda," he tossed over his shoulder as he headed for the door. "I mean . . . well, maybe not so great. I'm sorry about what happened."

Angel nodded. "Many people are."

I am not one of them.

The first thing Jen sees when she looks at Carley's phone is a new text message on the home screen:

where ru? im worried and i have a great surprise for u

"Who the heck is that from?" Thad asks, looking over her shoulder at it.

"I can't tell . . ."

"Here, give it to me." Emma reaches impatiently for the phone, then seems to think better of her attitude and softens her tone. "You guys aren't very good at tech stuff. No offense."

Jen hands the phone to her. Obviously, someone out there noticed Carley's communications blackout. No wonder she was so upset last night.

It's nice to know that she has at least one friend. And whoever it is just might know where she is.

Emma looks at the phone and gasps.

"What? What's wrong?"

Wordlessly, Emma points at the name at the top of the screen, indicating the sender of the text.

Nicki.

Carley opens her eyes to blackness.

For the first couple of moments, she thinks she's at home, in her bed.

Then she feels the throbbing in her head and hard concrete beneath her and it comes back to her.

She's at school, and Sister Linda . . .

Something is terribly wrong with Sister Linda.

"Where's . . . where's Angel?" Carley had asked her, bewildered, when she first saw her standing there in the gym.

"There's no Angel, Carley. Not the way you think. There's just me. I'm your angel . . . your Angel of Death," Sister Linda added with a grin.

Carley still didn't understand what was going on.

Then she saw the gun.

"Come on, Carley," Sister Linda said, aiming it at her. "Let's go."

She forced Carley to walk down the stairs to the basement of the school. She tied Carley's hands and feet and put a gag in her mouth, then shoved her, hard, into a storage closet.

Carley must have hit her head and blacked out.

Now Carley's lying on the floor, alone in the dark. She goes over what happened, trying to piece together the bizarre series of events. But it's like trying to work a jigsaw puzzle without the picture from the box . . .

No, like trying to work a puzzle using a bunch of scattered pieces from different boxes, and none of them fit together.

What about Angel?

Was Angel . . .

Carley faces the harsh truth: *She doesn't even exist.*

There is no kind, empathetic friend from California who knows just how it feels to be bullied; who spent her allowance and birthday money to pay a surprise visit, just for today, because she knew what Carley had been through and she wanted to cheer her up.

There's no Angel.

Jolted by the loss, Carley allows despair to overtake her at last.

First Nicki, and now Angel . . .

It's too much to bear.

Carley rolls onto her side, staring into the blackness, tears rolling down her cheeks.

Angel stashes the memory stick in a desk drawer and stands up. She smooths the full pink skirt, enjoying the feel of the taffeta fabric against her legs.

The dress is one of only two things she took with her from her parents' house when she left home on her eighteenth birthday.

She'd found it years earlier, not long after Ruthie's death. It was still tagged from the coroner's office, wrapped in plastic and tucked away in the bottom drawer of Ruthie's dresser; still stained in Ruthie's blood.

The moment Angel saw it, she understood that her sister had died in this dress. But as she walked over to the mirror and pulled it over her head, Ruthie seemed to come alive again.

Or maybe it was Angel coming alive.

Was it in that moment, staring at her reflection, wearing the pink dress, that Angel first saw the glimmer of truth?

Or was it later, much later, when she was old enough to truly understand what her mother had done to her?

No—not to me. For me. She did it for me.

That was what she claimed on Angel's eighteenth birthday, confronted at last with questions Angel had never dared to ask.

"I did it for you," Mother said, "because I knew that your life would be much easier this way."

That made no sense then. Angel didn't understand until the marble notebook came to light, and it became clear what Father had done to Ruthie. Clear that he had built that secret compartment where either he or Mother eventually stashed the notebook and God knows what else over the years.

Angel had wondered why they didn't just burn it. But there is no logic when it comes to Mother.

Mother, who said, when Angel was eighteen, "I did it for you."

"But I'm not . . . I don't feel like . . ."

"It doesn't matter," Mother said firmly. "It doesn't matter what you feel like. You are what you are."

No, Mother. I am what you made me. You, with your twisted logic.

Years earlier, Mother had begun giving Angel special medicine every day. She brought pills home from the pharmacy in orange prescription bottles that didn't have labels.

"You're sick," she told Angel, "and you have to take this medicine."

Sick? Angel had never even been to a doctor, not ever. Mother was so paranoid about germ exposure that Angel later assumed OCD was part of her undiagnosed mental illness. But it wasn't just germs. She worried, too, that something would happen to Angel.

"Don't climb on that," she'd say, or, "Walk slowly, don't slip," or "Careful, careful!"

She was always warning me to be careful.

Once, Angel was trying to cut an apple and the knife slipped.

"Mother . . . my hand is bleeding!"

Mother wrapped the deep cut in gauze. It didn't stop the blood. When Father came home, he took one look at it and said, "That needs stitches."

Mother argued against an emergency room visit. She sterilized a needle and thread, and she stitched the cut herself.

She was so desperate to keep me hidden away, to keep her secret safe.

Angel was allowed out of the house only once a week,

to go to Sunday Mass. But never alone. Only with Mother and Father.

At church, Angel would sit between them and think about Ruthie, missing Ruthie desperately.

It was at Mass, too, Angel would watch the others, kids who were the same age, noticing details about them . . .

I didn't know what they looked like under their clothes, and I didn't know what I should look like under mine. But still . . .

I knew something wasn't right. Mother had made sure, though, that I'd been sheltered enough not to figure out what it was.

Cut off from the outside world, Angel's thoughts were molded by Mother, who taught daily lessons in theology, and arithmetic, and history . . .

But never biology. Sciences were conspicuously absent from the curriculum—and not merely because she was a creationist.

She didn't want me armed with the intellectual capability to figure it out. She thought that if she controlled what I knew, what I saw, what I did every minute of every day, she could keep the truth from me forever . . .

She tried, she really did. And she nearly succeeded.

Every day, Angel dutifully swallowed the pills Mother counted out.

"When can I stop taking this medicine, Mother? I don't feel sick."

"That's because it's helping you. You need it."

Angel took the pills month after month, year after year . . .

"You're turning into a man now, Adrian," Father said when Mother made him teach Angel to shave the hair that had begun growing on his lip and chin. There was fuzz on his legs, too, and under his arms, and his voice had deepened.

Father added in his scoffing way, "But you have a long, long way to go."

Years later, relaying that comment to Dr. Ellis, Angel almost found it comical.

Almost.

" 'Oh, Father . . . you have no idea how far I have to go'—that's what I should have said to him," Angel told Dr. Ellis.

A Manhattan psychiatrist who specialized in transgender identity conflict, the doctor examined the pills Mother had been doling out—Angel had kept samples—and identified them as masculine hormone therapies, undoubtedly stolen from the pharmacy where she worked.

"As you approached adolescence," Dr. Ellis said, "she realized that you were going to begin developing as a female. She made sure that didn't happen. In her own twisted way—"

"Don't tell me that she was doing it *for* me, Doctor."

Dr. Ellis was silent, then suggested that it might be a good idea to try to make peace with Mother after all these years.

"What about your father?"

"He's dead. He died of a heart attack a few years after I left."

"Did you ever try to talk to him about your suspicions?"

"Are you kidding? He was never interested in talking to me about anything. After my sister was killed, he shut down. He lived in the house with us, but he wasn't really there."

"I just have a hard time believing he never guessed the truth."

"About me?" Angel shrugged. "You didn't live in that house with us. You didn't see how we were. How we kept our distance from each other, how detached he was from my mother and me, especially after my sister was gone. We weren't the kind of family that left bathroom doors unlocked or walked around half dressed . . ."

"Many families don't do that. But still—"

"No, I'm sure of it. To his dying day, he thought I was his

son. That was what my mother told him from the moment I was born. It was what she'd told everybody, including Ruthie. Why would anyone doubt it? She delivered me at home, alone. She never filed any paperwork; I never went to school. I'm sure she was the only one who ever changed my diapers or bathed me. As far as most of the world was concerned, I didn't exist. And the few who knew I did exist believed I was a boy. Even I believed it. I thought I was Adrian."

"You *were* Adrian," Dr. Ellis said. "And now . . ."

Now I'm Angel.

At eighteen, it was too late to reverse some of the changes the hormonal drugs had caused—the hair growth, the deepened voice. Angel was never going to be the most feminine girl in town, but she made an effort to embrace her feminine side; to act like a woman, dress like a woman, speak like a woman . . .

She made a fresh start in New York, waitressing and working retail. She couldn't afford to live in Manhattan but she found a nice little apartment way out on Long Island, near the beach. She kept to herself mostly.

For a long time—a decade, maybe more—she managed to keep the past at bay. But some things aren't meant to stay buried forever.

Oh, Ruthie . . .

Memories seeped to the surface when Angel least expected it; fury exploded out of nowhere like lava from a dormant volcano. She found herself doing crazy things—lashing out at strangers, hurling glassware against the wall, tailgating the car in front of her on the Long Island Expressway, muttering to herself . . .

Finally, she found her way to Dr. Ellis.

She thought he might be able to help, and he did, to a certain extent. He helped her to sort out the truth and understand what had happened.

"You have to grieve and accept loss. You were robbed of your childhood, and robbed of your self-identity, Angel."

Dr. Ellis helped her grasp that she had been a victim, and that it was all right to feel anger.

The great irony: Dr. Ellis thought confronting her past would help Angel find closure and peace at last.

Maybe it would have, once Mother and Father were both dead, if they had been the only ones to blame for losing Ruthie.

Angel made the first trip back to Buffalo on a whim. She got into the car and started driving one day, and the next thing she knew, she was parked in front of the house on Lilac Street.

After all those years of trying to suppress grief, Angel was overwhelmed by it the moment she set foot in the house. Memories of Ruthie were everywhere.

That was when she realized that her pain wasn't just about losing her childhood and her self-identity. It was about losing the one person who ever cared: Ruthie.

Punishing Mother for her role in it was cathartic.

Now the healing can begin, Angel thought, leaving the old woman dead in her chair and driving back to New York. She told Dr. Ellis that Mother had died of natural causes, and that she would soon be returning to her hometown to settle the estate.

Dr. Ellis wanted her to work through her emotions first.

"You can't just walk into that house unprepared to be bombarded with difficult emotions," Dr. Ellis said, unaware that Angel had already done exactly that.

That summer Angel felt prepared to venture up to Buffalo to take one last look at the house before listing it.

"But I'm not going there as me. The Realtor is expecting my parents' son, Adrian," Angel told the doctor, "and that's who I'm going to be. Anything else would be too complicated."

Dr. Ellis didn't approve and so, Angel decided, to hell with Dr. Ellis.

For the first time in years, Angel became Adrian again, with short hair, a man's clothing, a masculine stride.

The ghosts of the past were waiting to greet him in the house even before Sandra Lutz handed over the notebook, thus opening the door to a truth far more complicated than Angel had ever imagined.

Now vengeance could begin in earnest.

Now she could live in that house and let the memories come at her, even the traumatic and ghoulish ones.

The freezer. The cellar . . .

Oh, Ruthie.

Now she was a woman again:

Sister Linda.

It could have gone any number of ways, though, in the beginning. She only knew she had to become a part of their world again one way or another; had to get close to Debbie Quattrone and Mike Morino and Genevieve Bonafacio. Close to their children.

No one ever suspected that old Sister Helen, the part-time social worker at Sacred Sisters, hadn't fallen down that flight of stairs, but had been pushed. No one ever bothered to double-check the impressive credentials for "Sister Linda" when she applied for the abruptly vacated job. No one had been suspicious that she'd provided just a mail-drop address.

But if they had checked, and hadn't hired me, I'd have found another way in. I'd have found another way to live right under their noses, watching their children, pulling strings and watching my puppets dance . . .

Now it's almost over.

Now, at last, there can be closure.

Angel reaches into a bottom file drawer, back, back, back behind the papers and folders. Her fingers close around the other precious keepsake she brought with her when she left her parents' house on her eighteenth birthday.

She pulls out the wooden frame that holds a charcoal drawing depicting a mother and son.

That's what Angel always saw, anyway, looking at it.

There are none so blind as those who will not see.

The signature in the corner reads *Ruth Ann Bell*, but she'd written a different message on the back of the paper.

For my little Christmas Angel with love from your big sister Ruthie, 12/25/85

Angel looks at the picture for a long time before carefully tucking it back into the drawer for safekeeping until this is all over.

"That has to be an old text," Jen tells her husband and daughter, her heart pounding wildly in her chest. "Nicki is . . . Nicki isn't sending texts."

"But it's from today!" Emma points to the date and time stamp. "See? It was sent this morning!"

"Someone must have Nicki's phone," Frankie says logically, hovering nearby with Jen's parents.

"I'm calling the number." Thad holds out his hand. "Give me the phone."

"No, Dad, don't use Carley's phone to call," Emma tells him. "Use yours."

"Why?"

"Because I have to show you guys something on her Peeps page, remember? And this is the only way I can log in, if she's saved her password on her phone. Here, can I . . ." She holds out her hand for the phone.

"Wait—what's Nicki's number?" Thad asks, his own phone in hand and finger poised to dial.

Jen shrugs helplessly. "I don't even know how to find it. All it shows is Nicki's name."

"You have to go into the contacts file. Here . . ." Emma takes the phone from her and presses a few buttons.

Then she begins reading off a number, with Thad dialing it as she goes.

"Six-three-one . . ."

"Wait, he needs the area code, doesn't he?"

"That is the area code, Mom."

"No, it isn't."

"Yes, it is. See?" Emma shows them the ten-digit number, which does, indeed begin with a parenthetical 631.

"That doesn't sound right," Jen says. "It should be 716, or maybe 585. Thad, can you do a Web search from your phone for the 631 area code?"

He does. "It's Long Island."

"Long Island!" Jen's father shakes his head. "That can't be right. Nicki lived here in Buffalo."

"We know that, Aldo!" Jen's mother swats his arm. "Shh!"

Alarmed, and not even sure why, exactly, Jen clutches Thad's arm. "Call that number," she says. "I don't like this at all."

I'm going to die. Oh God, I'm going to die.

Crying makes it even harder for Carley to swallow and breathe around the gag in her mouth, but she can't help it. She wants desperately to cry, to scream for help; she wants . . .

I want my mommy.

Oh God. I'm going to die without telling her that I love her. I should have said it this morning when I had the chance, but I didn't. I thought I could always say it later, but . . .

Time is running out.

She's going to come back and kill me.

Any second now, that door is going to open and she's going to shoot me.

Why didn't she do it right away?

She'd been muttering to herself as she tied Carley's arms. Something about having to set the stage.

For what?

Someone will find me. Someone will figure out where I am and save me . . .

When Mom and Dad realize she's gone, they'll go snooping into her computer files, and they'll see—

No, they won't.

The computer is here.

No wonder "Angel"—Sister Linda—had her bring it to the school.

Still, someone else might come along. Johnny—he must have changed the signboard today. Maybe he'll open the storage closet door and—

Yes. That would be a welcome miracle. Johnny coming along and saving her.

Remembering all those scary movies she used to watch with Nicki at sleepovers, she thinks about how Nicki used to cover her fear by scoffing at the helpless female characters.

"Come on," she'd say, "no one would ever just wait around for someone to save her, or for the bad guy to come back and kill her. She'd at least try to get away."

But in those movies, no one ever got away. The bad guy would pounce, and there would be blood, and Nicki would run out of the room shrieking, and . . .

And Carley would shout after her that it wasn't real, and call her a wimp.

Now who's the wimp, Carls?

Now who's waiting around, helpless, not even trying to get away?

Who's counting on a miracle to save her?

Carley struggles against the bonds, struggling to wrench them from her wrists and ankles. The ropes burn her flesh, and her body aches, but if she can just pull hard enough . . .

You can do it, Carls, Nicki's voice seems to say. *Come on. You have to try.*

Managing to get to her feet, she feels around the tiny closet with her bound hands, wiggling her fingers against the shelves, trying to find an edge that might be sharp enough to saw through ropes.

No. They're too tight and there's nothing in the closet but smooth surfaces: buckets and broom handles, paint cans and bottles of cleaning supplies.

Carley closes her eyes again and does the only thing, besides crying and exhausting herself in a futile effort to escape, that she can possibly do.

She prays.

Entry from the marble notebook

Sunday, March 16, 1986

Dear Mother and Father:

After all these months of keeping this journal hidden underneath my mattress, I'm leaving it out in the open for you to find after I'm gone.

I snuck out of my room last night to go to a dance at school. I did it because I had been invited by the boy I thought I loved, the boy who sent me flowers.

He told me to meet him there, and I did. I walked into that crowded gym wearing the pink dress he wanted me to wear and the corsage he sent me, and I didn't see him anywhere. The room was full of couples, and everyone was staring at me and whispering about me and I didn't know what to do. I really thought he was going to walk in any minute and everything would be okay.

But he didn't.

Only one person talked to me. It was Debbie Quattrone, the cheerleader.

"Waiting for someone, Ruthie?" she asked.

And so I told her I was. It felt so good to be like the rest of them for once, and I wanted her to know I had a date. When I told her who it was, she made sure *everyone around us heard, too. She kept repeating it. "You're waiting for Mike Morino? Are you sure?"*

That was when the staring and whispering turned into laughing. People were laughing right at me, right in my face.

I just held my head high. I kept thinking about how ridiculous they'd all feel when they saw me in Mike's arms. I knew he was going to show up.

And he did.

When I spotted him in that crowd, he was smiling at me. That's what I thought. That's what I saw.

But . . .

I guess you were right about one thing, Mother. You always said there are none so blind as those who will not see.

I walked toward Mike, and I realized that he wasn't smiling at me after all. He was smiling at his date, Jen Bonafacio.

I couldn't believe it. But it was true.

All day, I've been thinking about what happened last night. All day, I've been wondering how I can ever set foot in that school again tomorrow and face them, any of them, especially Mike and Debbie and Jen.

The answer is that I can't.

I won't.

I have two final requests. Granting them is the least you can do for me, under the circumstances.

1. I know you won't be able to give me a funeral Mass or a Catholic burial, and I'm not even sure God hears your prayers, because He doesn't hear mine, but just in case, will you please pray for mercy for my soul, that He might forgive my sin?

2. Please don't ever tell Adrian what I've done. When it's over and I'm gone, just tell him that it was an accident. Tell him to always remember how much I loved him, and that he was my little angel.

You know how, whenever someone dies, people say they're in a better place? Well, I know that I'm going to go to hell for what I'm going to do. But if Adrian asks where I am, you can say I'm in a better place.

All things considered, it won't be a lie.

Ruthie

Chapter 17

"See that? I told you!" Holding the flashlight he grabbed from his apartment before he and Bobby and Glenn cut through the yard, Al aims the beam at the footprints in the mud beside the back door of the Addams House. "Someone's been here."

"Well, they're not here now," his brother says, "unless they're hanging around in the dark."

He's right about that. Dusk has fallen, but no light spills from any of the windows in the Addams House.

They walk around the perimeter, just to be sure. The timers have yet to turn on the lamps in the front rooms. The place is dark, and feels deserted . . . for now.

"We need to go in there and see how much damage these kids have done," Al decides. "It makes me sick to think of them running wild, vandalizing the place."

"Why? It's not like it's your house," Bobby points out.

"No, but . . ." Al just shakes his head.

Bobby would never understand about Sandra and her respect for old houses. He would never understand Al's lingering feelings for her.

No, Bobby always called her Snobby Sandy, just like the others did.

He thinks of her in silence broken only by droplets plunking softly to the grass from the eaves and towering tree branches high overhead. The rain stopped a little while ago, giving way to damp mist.

"We need to go in," he says again, decisively.

"But—"

"He's right, Bobby. No one wants to see this old place burn down." Glenn slurs his words a little. "It's a neighborhood landmark."

"Exactly." Al looks at his brother. "Go ahead and do your thing, locksmith."

Carley says a silent Hail Mary, trembling violently when she gets to the last few words of the prayer. She'd never really paid close attention to them before.

Now and at the hour of our death . . .

Did Nicki pray before she slit her wrists?

Was she, too, chilled by the final line of the Hail Mary?

Maybe not, because she actually *chose* the hour of her death.

How could she have done it? Even now, Carley can't make sense of Nicki's suicide. Maybe she'll soon find out the answer, though. Maybe Nicki will be waiting on the other side to greet her, and—

Then she remembers: Nicki might not be in heaven, because Nicki took her own life.

Mom doesn't believe in that, though. She said that a merciful God would never punish a troubled soul.

Carley hopes she's right.

Oh, Mommy . . . I love you so much. You and Daddy and even Emma, and Grandma and Grandpa and Aunt Frankie . . .

Carley is crying again.

They're going to be so sad. Especially Mom. She cries over sappy television commercials; how is she ever going to get through something like this?

She prays that her family, especially her mother, will be all right without her, and that they'll somehow know how much she really did love them.

I should have told them. And it's too late now.

Now is the hour . . .

She begs God to make her death quick and painless, and to let Nicki be waiting for her . . .

If she is, she'll probably be pretty upset with Carley. She'll want to know how Carley got herself into this situation.

You're too gullible and naïve, she'll tell Carley, not for the first time.

And yeah, no kidding. If she weren't gullible and naïve, she wouldn't be here.

If she hadn't listened to Sister Linda on that long-ago day . . .

What are you going to do, Carley? Leave school? Let them win? Wouldn't you rather hold your head high and show them that they can't get the better of you?

But . . . I can't. I just . . . I can't . . .

You can't hold your head high? Sure you can, if you grow a spine . . .

I was a fool for listening to her . . .

A fool for believing that the girls had voted me Spring Fling princess in the first place.

That was her last happy day on earth, she knows now.

She remembers how thrilled she was, floating giddily around the school . . .

No. Don't waste precious time you have left thinking about that.

Now is the hour . . .

Seeking comfort, she thinks again of Nicki. Heaven wouldn't be so bad with her there.

Heaven isn't supposed to be so bad no matter what. It's supposed to be paradise, remember?

But Carley can't imagine being happy anyplace all alone, without her family.

So yes, Nicki has to be in heaven, too, waiting for her. She *has to* be. Nicki will be her old self, hugging Carley and talking a mile a minute . . .

Why the heck didn't you try harder to escape, Carls? she'll ask.

Maybe I could have, if my hands and legs were free, but there was no way. What was I supposed to do? Snap my fingers and pluck a magical pair of scissors out of the air so that I could saw through the . . .

Carley goes absolutely still.

Once again, that day comes back to her—the day she found out she'd been voted Spring Fling princess. But this time, she lets the memory in. She needs to remember every single detail as if her life depends on it . . .

Because it does.

Angel is on her way out of her office when she hears the muffled sound of a ringing cell phone.

Her own phone.

She left it in her desk drawer, along with the memory stick and a couple of other items she'll be back to retrieve as soon as . . .

Why is the phone ringing, though?

The only people she's ever contacted from this number are Nicki and . . .

Carley.

But only posing as each other . . . until this morning.

This morning, Angel remembers, in a tizzy over not being able to reach Carley, she'd sent a text to Carley's phone—forgetting that she herself had programmed in the number to coincide with Nicki Olivera's contact information.

See what happens when you get impatient? You make sloppy mistakes.

Yes, and in her eagerness to finish this job, Angel had confiscated the girl's laptop, but had sloppily forgotten to take her phone, too. It must be in her pocket.

But how can she possibly be dialing it?

She can't be, Angel assures herself, hurrying back to her office to check her ringing phone. *It must be a wrong number.*

Yes. When she pulls the phone out of her drawer, she sees that the call is, indeed, coming from an unfamiliar number with a 716 area code.

Deciding she'd better answer it, Angel presses a button and barks a gruff "Hello?"

There's a pause on the other end of the line.

Then a male voice asks, "Who is this?"

"Who is *this*?" Angel returns, irritated.

"I'm looking for—"

The line goes dead.

Angel stands for a long time, looking at the phone in her hand. Then, with a shrug, she turns it off and tucks it back into the drawer.

She'll deal with it later.

Carrying Carley's backpack—which contains her laptop and a hardcover copy of *The Virgin Suicides*—Angel leaves her office again.

First, she'll take these things down to the gym and get everything ready. That, of course, is where the suicidal would-be Spring Fling princess would go to kill herself. Right there, amid the garish decorations for the dance, Carley Archer is going to slit her wrists just as her best friend did.

Just like Ruthie . . .

No. Ruthie didn't slit her wrists, and she didn't die in the school gym at Spring Fling. Not officially, anyway.

But Angel knows the truth.

Ruthie's life was over the moment she walked alone into

the gym that night, looking for Mike Morino—and found him with Jen Archer in his arms.

"Why did you do that?" Thad asks Frankie, who all but shoved Jen and Emma aside to grab his cell phone out of his hand and disconnect his call in mid-sentence.

"Because you were going to say you were looking for Carley, and . . . I don't think that was a good idea."

"Why not?" Jen asks her sister.

"I think something strange is going on."

"It was a man who answered. We need to call Debbie," Thad says abruptly, "and find out where Nicki's cell phone is."

"I don't think that's Nicki's cell phone. Not with a Long Island area code. I think someone was playing a trick on Carley and programmed that number into her phone to make her think it was Nicki. Someone was posing as Nicki, saying terrible things Carley thought Nicki had said. That's how their friendship ended."

"What do you mean?" Jen asks her sister.

Frankie quickly explains about the girls' final interactions with each other—how everything unfolded via text and social networking sites.

"You mean they never even talked it out?" Thad asks incredulously. "After all those years of friendship?"

"I can't believe that." Jen shakes her head. "They were so close. They wouldn't just—"

"Mom, they used to see each other every day," Emma cuts in, "but not anymore. They were in different schools. How do you think they got in touch with each other? Online and by text."

"But that's—"

"That's all anyone does. Trust me."

"She's right," Frankie says. "These kids aren't doing a whole lot of talking or face-to-face problem resolution."

"So you're saying . . ." Thad frowns, shaking his head.

"You're saying one of these other girls—these bullies—was posing as Nicki, making Carley think Nicki—"

"I think there's a strong possibility," Frankie cuts in. "And I think you need to call the police right away and tell them about this."

"Why?" Jen's parents ask in unison, not following.

But Jen understands exactly what her sister is thinking, and she feels faint as the dreadful possibility hits her.

"Because someone might have been doing the same exact thing to Nicki," she says, "and now Nicki is dead."

The moment he walks into the Addams House, Al inhales a distinctly charred stench in the air.

So it wasn't Sandy's ghost signaling its presence by setting off the smoke alarm after all. Yeah, he didn't really think that anyway.

Not really.

"I told you someone burned something in here this morning," he tells his brother and Glenn.

"Why are you whispering?" Bobby asks.

"I have no idea." Al clears his throat and walks across the kitchen, bouncing the flashlight's beam around the room.

There's no mistaking the evidence that someone has been staying here. A frying pan and a plate sit soaking in the sink. There's a box of crackers on the counter. Al opens the refrigerator and finds a few basics: eggs, butter, milk. He checks the expiration dates. Next week, next month . . .

"I don't think it's kids," Glenn says, looking over his shoulder. "I think someone's squatting here. Some homeless person, probably."

"That's not good, either." Al closes the fridge and moves toward the doorway leading toward the front of the house.

"Wait, where are you going?" Bobby asks.

"To walk through the place and see what's what."

"Why?"

Because it reminds me of Sandra, that's why. The last time I saw her . . .

"Let's call the cops, go back to Louie's, have another drink . . . Maybe not in that order," Bobby adds.

Behind them, Glenn has opened the fridge again and taken out a bottle of beer. "You think this is any good?"

Bobby groans. "You're kidding, right?"

"No, I thought that if the milk is good, then this might be, but you're right. It might be skunky."

Leaving the two of them in the kitchen, Al crosses the threshold into the butler's pantry, lined with empty shelves behind glass doors, then into the dining room.

His footsteps echo on the bare hardwoods, and he shines the flashlight around the empty room, thinking of all that furniture sitting in his storage unit. What will become of it? How long will it be before some new family moves in here and makes the place their own?

The beam dances across the walls, across the floor . . .

Startled, Al realizes there's a laptop computer lying on the hardwoods across the room. And a book, or . . . no, it's a notebook, he realizes, walking toward it, keeping the light trained on the spot, right beneath the built-in window seat—

What the hell?

Shreds of rotted flesh clinging to skeletal human legs and feet . . .

Al lets out a bloodcurdling scream.

Finding the Peeps icon on her sister's cell phone, Emma hopes Carley saved her log-in information. If she didn't . . .

But she did.

Seeing the screen name and row of asterisks symbolizing a saved password, Emma quickly hits enter, and the page loads.

"Mom . . ." She reaches out to stop her mother, who keeps walking back and forth with her hands clasped against her chest. Emma isn't sure if she's praying, or just clenching. "Look at this."

"What is it?"

"Carley's Peeps page. She—"

Wait a minute. No, she didn't.

Emma frowns, staring at the profile that just popped up on the small screen.

Carley Theresa.

She quickly scrolls through.

Favorite authors: E. B. White and Laura Ingalls Wilder.

Cheesy pictures of kittens.

"What? What is it?" Her mother is looking over her shoulder.

Emma shakes her head, trying to figure out how to explain. She'd already admitted, earlier, that she'd snuck away to see Gabe today. Her parents opted not to add to her punishment for the moment—though she's sure they will when this is over and Carley is home.

If Carley comes home, Emma thinks, wondering what's going on with her.

"The reason I went over to Gabe's," she says, to boost her case for not being further punished, "was because he said Carley had a Peeps page where she was talking about killing herself."

"*What?*" Her mother grabs her upper arms, hard.

"Mom, wait—I did see the page, on Gabe's computer, and it did say all this stuff, but . . . it didn't sound like Carley at all. It was just really dark, and—"

"Emma! Why didn't you tell me?"

"I'm telling you now. I thought it was Carley's real page, and that she just had this fake page to hide what she was really doing, but . . . it looks like this is the page she's been using all along."

"I don't understand. What are you saying?"

"Maybe somebody set her up, Mom. Like . . . you know, a

joke. Kids do stuff like that all the time, especially to people like Carley."

"People like Carley . . ." Her mother's voice is all choked up. "She's a good kid. She never hurt anyone. Why would anyone want to hurt her?"

Emma shrugs. "It's just the way things are" is all she can possibly say to that.

At last, everything is ready.

The laptop, the book, and the knife are waiting in the gym. In a matter of minutes, this will all be over.

Angel descends the stairway toward the custodial area where she locked Carley into a closet, bound and gagged.

She couldn't just leave her there in the gym. What if someone came along?

No one but the custodial staff could possibly stumble across her down here, and the only person working today—Johnny—is long gone.

Still, Angel has to make this quick.

All is silent behind the door as she approaches.

The key to this closet was laughably easy to find and duplicate, days ago, just lying around the custodian's office.

Angel inserts it into the lock and turns the knob.

"It's time, Carley."

She expects to hear her captive whimper or moan as she opens the door, but the girl doesn't make a sound. Angel reaches up, feels around on the wall for the light switch, and flips it on.

The closet is empty.

The shrill ringing of a telephone shatters the silence.

Jen gasps and stops pacing.

"It's your cell." Thad, who was also pacing, is already beside her. "Who is it?"

Jen's hand shakes as she reaches into her pocket, fumbling for the phone.

Carley . . . please let it be Carley . . .

Her heart sinks when she sees the number on caller ID.

"It's just the school again," she says. "Sacred Sisters. Probably another automated announcement about the dance, or . . ."

It rings again.

"Maybe you should answer it, Mom."

She glances at Emma, sitting between her grandparents on the couch, looking like a small, frightened little girl. Then she looks at Thad.

"Should I pick it up? I'm afraid to tie up the line even for a second, in case Carley tries to call."

"I know, but . . ."

It rings a third time. Fraught with indecision, Jen makes up her mind. She presses the talk button.

"Too late," she tells Thad, shaking her head and going back to pacing. "It already went into voice mail."

"Hi! This is Jen! Please leave a message and I'll get right back to you!"

With a strangled cry of frustration, Carley disconnects the call.

Crouched on the floor of the principal's office with the desk phone in her hand, she can hear footsteps out in the hall.

Sister Linda is on the hunt.

It's only a matter of time before she finds Carley.

She can make one more phone call and pray that she can get her whispered message across in time to be rescued.

One more call . . .

Her mind races, running through her options.

Should she try the home number?

What if no one is there?

Her father's cell?

What if he doesn't hear it ring? He hardly ever does.

Emma always answers her phone immediately, but they took it away from her . . .

And Carley doesn't know Aunt Frankie's number by heart. It's programmed into her own phone.

She knows her grandparents' number, but they're hard of hearing, and she has to whisper.

She should just call 911. It's what she should have done in the first place, but her instinct was to dial her mother.

Frustrated, Carley holds her breath and swiftly dials again.

Please please please please—

"Nine-one-one. What is your emergency?"

"My name is—"

"Hang up the phone."

Sister Linda is standing over her with the gun.

Trembling, Carley obeys the command, cutting off her lifeline.

The Addams House is crawling with cops, its stately foyer bathed in fluid red light from the spinning domes of the police cars parked out front. Sitting on the grand stairway with Bobby and Glenn, Al listens to the footsteps overhead and below and to the methodical voices and the squawk of police radios coming from the dining room. It's impossible to make out what they're saying, but he's pretty sure they're trying to ID the hideous corpse in the dining room.

Bobby shakes his head. "It's got to be her. Who else would it be? It has red hair and everything."

He's talking, of course, about Al's macabre discovery; speculating about whether the dead body belongs to Ruthie Bell.

Al shudders, thinking of long strands of hair he glimpsed

projecting from the black skull before he bolted from the room.

"It sure as hell looked like her," Glenn agrees. He and Bobby got only a quick look as Al dialed 911.

"Why 911?" Bobby asked when he hung up. "Don't you think she's a little too far gone to be rescued?"

Leave it to Bobby to be a wise-ass at a time like that.

"I'd think the hair would have fallen out by now," his brother comments now. "You know, if it were Ruthie Bell. She's been dead twenty-five, thirty years. Wouldn't she have been a skeleton by now? Or dust?"

Glenn shrugs. "She was embalmed, and . . . it would just depend on where she's been for all these years, and under what conditions. Bodies can hold up pretty well in an airtight, watertight compartment, so . . ." He shrugs again.

"Do you think someone dug her up from the cemetery in California," Bobby asks, "and brought her here?"

"If she was ever even buried in California." Al shakes his head. "I wonder . . ."

"Why? Where do you think she's been?"

"I have no—" He breaks off, hearing footsteps pounding up the cellar steps into the kitchen.

"Hey, Sarge," a cop's voice calls, "I think I know where she came from. Come take a look at what we found down there."

"Please don't—"

"Shut up!" With a gloved hand, Angel jerks Carley by the arm, forcing her into the gym. "Come on. Let's get this over with."

"Get what—"

"Shut up!"

She drags Carley over to the raised platform covered in green indoor-outdoor carpeting meant to evoke grass. Backed by a latticework white arch entwined with plastic ivy, the platform holds a pair of matching thrones left over from the set of an ancient drama department production of *The King and I.*

It's where the royal court would have been crowned at the dance.

It's where Carley Archer will die.

"I can't stop thinking about what they did to her," Jen tells Frankie.

They're in the kitchen now, under the pretext of making coffee. When Jen asked if anyone wanted some, her father said yes. Her mother immediately scolded him, then said she would make it. But Jen welcomed the distraction.

Frankie, who trailed her in here saying she'd help, leans morosely against the counter. "You can't stop thinking about what who did to her?"

"Those girls. The ones who voted her Spring Fling princess, and—God only knows what else. She was so happy that day—" Jen's voice breaks. "How could they have been so cruel?"

Frankie shakes her head. "The school should have handled it differently. When I think about what that social worker said to her . . ."

"Sister Linda?"

"Yes. Carley told me about it last night. It's been bothering me ever since."

"Why? What did she say?"

"She said, 'There are none so blind as those who will not see,' almost like it was Carley's fault for believing the girls really wanted her to be their princess."

Jen drops the coffee scoop back into the can of grounds. "None so blind . . ."

"It's an old saying. It means—"

"No," Jen cuts her sister off, "I know it is. I just . . . I've heard it before."

"Right. So have I. Like I said, it's an old . . ."

Jen closes her eyes, remembering, and her sister's voice fades away, and the pungent aroma of coffee grounds gives way to the stomach-turning fragrance of Stargazer lilies.

Angel gestures at the knife lying at Carley's feet.

"Pick that up."

"No . . ." Trembling, Carley shakes her head.

"Pick it up!"

Still, Carley doesn't move. "Please, just . . . Why?"

Angel wants nothing more than to pick up that knife herself and drive it into the girl's heart.

But that would be a waste. This has to be done right. Her fingerprints need to be on it.

"Why?" she asks. "Because you have to pay. Your mother has to pay for what she did to my sister."

"Your sister . . . ?"

"She killed herself. She left me all alone. And now you're going to do the same thing to your mother."

Carley's legs wobble. "I don't—"

"Shut up!" Angel snarls. "Shut up and do what I told you to do. Pick up that knife!"

Yes, all she needs to do is pick it up, and then Angel can take it from her and use it to slice open her veins.

Carley still isn't budging.

Panicky, Angel tries a new tactic.

"If you don't do what I say"—her voice is deadly calm—"I will go to your house, and I will use this knife on your mother and your father and your sister. Do you understand?"

She sees the stricken look on Carley's face.

Sees the resignation in her eyes.

Sees her bend over, at last, to pick up the knife.

Jen is back at Sacred Sisters, exhilarated about the Spring Fling dance.

She's been voted sophomore princess. Her date, Mike Morino, was voted sophomore prince at Cardinal Ruffini. When the time comes, their names will be announced and they'll climb the steps to the platform and pose for pictures.

Jen is wearing a beautiful dress the soft shade of cotton candy. Mike loves her in pink. There's a pink corsage pinned to her dress—much too close to her nose.

When the florist truck pulled up in front of the Bonafacio house this afternoon, Jen was excited until she saw what was in the clear plastic box.

The blossom was gigantic and waxy and a gaudy shade of pink.

"It's a Stargazer lily," her mother told her. "I love the way it smells, don't you?" Jen didn't. She thought it stunk to high heaven.

But when Mike came to pick her up—late as usual, long after her older sisters had left, one by one, with their own dates—she politely told him she loved it. She let him pin it to her spaghetti strap as her mother took pictures.

"Your friend Debbie helped me pick it out," he told Jen. "She said you were wearing a pink dress just for me."

Jen made a mental note to tell Debbie to go with a nice, muted pastel next time she helped Mike choose a corsage.

Finally, they've made it to the dance. The gym is crowded. A couple of Mike's friends pull him aside to whisper in his ear, and they all snicker.

"What's going on?" Jen asks him, but he just grins and shakes his head.

They're walking toward the dance floor when Jen spots Ruthie Bell. She's wearing an enormous pink dress that can best be described as a "frock," the kind of dress the brides-maids wore at Jen's parents wedding back in the fifties. Her gingery hair is pulled back in a ribbon that matches the flush poking through the freckles on her cheeks, and she's walk-ing right toward them.

Jen smells mothballs as Ruthie approaches, a scent strong enough to permeate the perfume of the lily pinned inches from her nose. Then she sees that Ruthie, too, is wearing a Stargazer corsage.

Debbie comes up beside them. "Mike, there you are! Ruthie's been looking for you! I really hope you didn't stand her up!"

Ruthie steps closer . . .

Closer . . .

Close enough to see that Mike has his arm around Jen.

Ruthie stands there, taking it in, and then she shakes her head, with tears in her eyes, and murmurs something.

Somehow, Jen hears it above the laughter and the music.

"None so blind," Ruthie Bell says to herself, and she flees the gym.

Jen turns to Mike. He's laughing.

"What's so funny?"

"Did you see that?"

"What?"

"Are you kidding, Jen? Ruthie!" Debbie is laughing, too. "She thought Mike invited her to be his Spring Fling date! Can you imagine?"

"Why did she think that?" Jen looks from Debbie to Mike.

"Who knows? She's crazy."

Before Jen can ask any more questions, the loudspeaker clicks on. "We'll now present the royal court . . ."

The whole time she's there on the platform, clasping Mike's arm as flashbulbs flash, she smiles. Smiles so hard her jaw and her cheekbones hurt.

The minute it's over, when Debbie comes up to gush, Jen pulls her to the door.

"What? Where are we going?"

"Outside. I need some air."

"But it's raining."

"I don't care. Just tell me. Tell me why Ruthie thought Mike invited her to the dance."

Debbie burst out laughing. "Did you see the look on her face?"

"Are we talking about Ruthie?" Mike is there, too. He's followed them. He's grinning.

"Who else?" Debbie indicates Jen. "She wants to know what happened."

"Did you tell her?"

"I was about to. Should I?"

Mike shrugs.

"Promise you won't tell, Jen," Debbie says.

"Don't worry. She won't tell. She's good with secrets. Right, Jen?"

She can't answer. She's shivering. The night is turning colder. The rain is supposed to change over to snow in the morning.

Mike puts his arm around her.

And then they tell her.

They tell her what they did to poor Ruthie Bell.

"Jen?"

She blinks.

Frankie is waving a hand in front of her face.

"Are you okay?"

Jen nods, reaching again for the coffee scoop, numbly thinking about that night. About how she broke up with Mike—for the first time, anyway—the following morning.

And about Ruthie Bell, who was killed in a car accident in a snowstorm, a scant twenty-four hours after she'd fled the Spring Fling dance.

When Jen heard about the accident, she wondered . . .

She still wonders. All these years later. Wonders if Ruthie was so distraught that she drove her car into that tree on purpose.

There was no funeral Mass or Catholic burial. Why not?

Because Ruthie killed herself, that's why.

She didn't slash her wrists like Nicki did, or hang herself like Taylor did, but . . .

The roads were bad that night, a sheet of ice. It wouldn't have been very hard, under those conditions, to make a death wish come true.

Someone—Ruthie's parents?—might have guessed it, or maybe they even knew for sure. Maybe they covered it up somehow.

Jen never told a soul what she suspected.

Like Mike said a long time ago—she was good with secrets.

Most teenagers are.

"Frankie," she says, "you don't think that Peeps page Emma saw really belonged to Carley, do you? You don't think she really does want to kill herself?"

Her sister puts an arm around her in an effort to be reassuring, but Jen can tell she's choosing her words carefully. "Even if the thought has crossed her mind . . . look, I think she has a lot of problems, and I think she's been depressed, but . . . she's got one hell of a support system in you and Thad, and she's a strong kid. She'll come through this."

"Whatever 'this' is . . . and if it's even up to her."

"What do you mean?"

"If someone is manipulating her—if those other girls are trying to hurt her . . . I keep wondering how far they'll try to push her."

"I hate to say it, but . . . kids can be really cruel."

"I know they can." Jen swallows hard and closes her eyes, again seeing Ruthie Bell's face.

Carley's trembling fingers close around the knife handle.

"Good girl," Sister Linda says. "Now hand it to me."

Carley thinks about what's going to happen.

She thinks about the other knife—Johnny's pocket knife.

The day she'd talked to him near the closet—the day she'd been voted Spring Fling princess, her last happy day— she'd seen him use a pocket knife to peel an apple. She remembered that he'd stashed it on the shelf behind the bottles of cleaning supplies.

It was still there. She'd managed to work open the blade; managed to saw through the rope that bound her hands until it frayed enough to break.

She tried the door to make sure it wasn't locked from the inside. Luck was with her. She untied her feet, pulled the gag from her mouth, and slipped out of the closet mere seconds before she heard footsteps approaching.

She went up the back staircase as Sister Linda was coming down the front . . .

All for nothing.

She managed to escape, and she tried to call for help, but it wasn't meant to be. She just wasn't quick enough, or strong enough, or smart enough, or brave enough . . .

Now no one will ever know that she really did try, though. That she almost made it.

Almost . . .

No.

No!

Almost isn't good enough.

It's her mother's voice, now, that's in her head. That's what Mom always says.

Almost isn't good enough, Carley. Don't settle for it. Try harder.

I will, Mom. I will . . .

Adrenaline and resolve surge through her.

Now will *not* be the hour of her death.

Seeing the white-draped stretcher roll into the foyer, Al reaches for the banister to pull himself to his feet. Beside him, in silence, Bobby and Glenn do the same.

They watch as a female police officer accompanies two attendants to the front door and opens it. The men roll it onto the porch, then carry it down the steps and along the wet, shiny pavement toward the waiting van from the medical examiner's office.

Closing the door, the police officer looks up at them.

"Was that Ruthie Bell?" Al asks, a bit hoarsely.

"We think it probably was, based on the evidence we found in there, but—"

"You mean the computer and the notebook?" Bobby asks.

The officer shrugs, shaking her head as if to indicate that she can't say anything more. Then she tells them that someone will be back shortly to take additional statements from them, and returns to the dining room.

"Poor Ruthie." Glenn shakes his bald head. "Her life was hell, her death was hell, and if that was her lying under that sheet, then she wasn't even able to rest in peace."

"Now she will." Al settles onto the steps again and crosses himself, offering a silent prayer for Ruthie.

"Yeah, but . . ." Bobby sits beside him. "I just wonder what kind of sick, twisted person has been living in this house with her."

"It has to be the brother." Glenn plops himself down on the step below. "He must have come back."

Al nods grimly, remembering Adrian Bell, whose only real crime was to be an oddball born into a crazy, creepy family.

Back then, anyway.

God only knows what he's done since.

"I feel sorry for him," Sandra Lutz said when Al told her about Adrian. "When I see him in person, I'm going to be extra nice. Sometimes a single act of kindness can make all the difference."

On her last day alive, Al remembers, Sandra was meeting Adrian Bell here at the house for the final walk-through. He wonders if that ever happened, and—

He sits up straight. What if—

"What's wrong?" Bobby asks him.

"Nothing, I . . . I just thought of something."

"What?"

Al shakes his head slowly. "It's probably nothing."

Sandra's death had been ruled an accident. She was careless with a candle. That's all.

Still . . .

When Al talks to the cops again, he's going to mention her connection to this house, and to Adrian Bell.

The knife handle is clenched in Carley's hand.

Sister Linda is reaching for it.

Before she can touch it, Carley thrusts blindly until the blade makes contact.

For a split second, she's too stunned—as stunned as the woman she just stabbed—to make another move.

Then Sister Linda lets out an unearthly howl. She reaches for the bleeding gash in her upper arm, feeling for the knife with her opposite hand.

She's quick, but Carley is quicker.

Quick and stronger and smarter and braver . . .

She pulls the knife out of Sister Linda's wound and takes aim again, this time for her gut.

When the phone rings, Jen is standing alone in the kitchen, glumly watching the coffee drip steadily into the glass carafe.

A moment ago, Frankie went back into the next room to see how many cups they need to fill as Jen tried to imagine herself sitting in there with the others, sipping coffee while her daughter—

But now the phone is ringing.

It might mean nothing at all, or it might mean . . .

Good news.

Or bad.

Jen lurches to grab the receiver.

"Mom?"

Every bit of air goes out of Jen's lungs. She braces herself against the counter with one hand, clutching the phone hard to her ear with the other.

"Carley! Carley, where are you?"

There's a pause.

Then Jen hears a quaking sob that stops her heart.

"Are you all right, Carley? Please, just . . . please answer me. Please tell me—"

"I'm all right! Not really. But—I am. I just want to come home."

She's crying, hard, and so is Jen—too hard to speak. But Thad is beside her now, gently taking the phone out of her hand, asking the questions Jen can't ask, and her parents and Frankie and Emma are crowding into the kitchen, too . . .

"Where is she, Genevieve?"

"What's going on?"

"Is Carley okay, Mom?"

Jen's heart is racing and her eyes remain glued to Thad. He's nodding and grabbing a pen to write something down.

"Okay, just stay calm," he says into the phone, pen poised. "Listen, you need to call—what? You already did?"

He smiles, a teary-eyed smile.

"Good job, sweetheart," he says into the phone, with a catch in his voice. "That was the right thing to do. They'll be there any second now. I'm going to call them to make sure. Just sit tight."

"Who, Dad? Who will be there?" Emma asks, tugging his sleeve.

Police, he mouths.

Police.

Carley had to call the police?

"You're not hurt, are you?" Thad is asking. He listens for

a minute and then, seeing Jen's expression, nods and flashes a thumbs-up.

Jen breathes.

"Good," Thad says, "That's really good. Mommy and I are going to get right into the car and—what's that? Sure, sweetheart. Sure. Hang on a second." Thad looks at Jen. "She wants to talk to you."

"Is she all right?"

He nods, closing his eyes and tilting his face toward the ceiling as he holds out the phone to her.

"Carley?"

"I'm sorry I didn't say it before. I should have, and I—I love you, Mom. I love you so much."

Jen smiles through her tears. She opens her mouth to speak, but nothing comes out.

"Mommy? Are you there?"

She nods—but of course, Carley can't see her nodding.

Say something. Hurry, before she hangs up. Say anything at all.

She swallows hard, clears her throat, and manages just four words: "I love you, too."

And for once, she's certain she's said exactly the right thing.

Epilogue

The auditorium is packed on this second Sunday afternoon in May. Onstage, a blond teenage girl—Bob Witkowski's youngest daughter—is seated at the piano, her fingers expertly flying over the keys as she delivers the rousing final notes of Rachmaninoff's Prelude in G minor.

Jen and Thad, with Emma between them, are in the third row; Jen's parents, Frankie, and Patty are scattered in seats someplace behind them. Her sister Maddie is just ahead in the second row with the Witkowski family. She's been dating Bob's brother Al ever since she moved back home from Cleveland last summer, and recently confided in Jen that they've been talking about getting married this fall.

A wedding in the family . . .

Jen feels giddy just thinking about it. God knows they can all use a joyful celebration; something to look forward to after all these difficult months spent trying to overcome the past.

Though last spring's nightmare is more than a year behind them now, the repercussions have yet to completely subside. Fourteen months after her best friend's murder, Carley continues to shed tears over the loss. And though her days as a bullying victim are long over, she can't quite shake the heartache—not to mention the post-traumatic stress of having been held captive on that awful March day.

That she managed to fight back—stabbing her tormentor, which allowed her to escape and call for help—has gone a long way toward healing her residual emotional pain.

So has her weekly volunteer work at an animal shelter, where she cuddles baby kittens to her heart's content.

Most cathartic of all, perhaps, is the fact that she hasn't ever set foot back in Sacred Sisters.

There was never any question in Jen's mind that Carley was going to change schools after what happened, and this time, her daughter didn't argue.

Letting go of the school—of tradition—was easier than Jen expected. She'll always carry her own happy memories of Sacred Sisters, but she's since come to realize that her affection isn't necessarily for the place itself. It's for the people who were there when she was: supportive staff and loving friends who have long since moved on.

Now the school is just a familiar building populated by unfamiliar faces. Even aside from the violence of that final day, Sisters holds too many unpleasant memories for Carley. It doesn't matter that the bullying hadn't been instigated by her schoolmates themselves. They went along with it, taking it to new levels; that alone was reason enough for Carley to seek a fresh start.

Carley was initially hesitant to transfer to Woodsbridge High because it had been Nicki's school. But she longed to be closer to home, and the therapist she's been seeing since the trauma urged her to give it a try.

From the moment she started there last spring, she felt comfortable. Nicki had made a close circle of friends in her six months at Woodsbridge, and they welcomed Carley with open arms.

Now, a year later, she goes to school smiling and comes

home smiling. Her weekends are filled with extracurricular activities, and she even has a couple of dates under her belt.

She managed to survive not making the honor roll as she finished her freshman year—though she's made it every quarter this year—and got past an unrequited crush on her biology lab partner. All things considered, she's making great progress.

Still, every so often, she wakes up screaming in the middle of the night. When that happens, Jen races down the hall to Carley's room and holds her close, drying her tears and staying with her until she finally falls asleep again. Even on nights when Carley is peaceful, Jen often doesn't sleep soundly, battling nightmares of her own.

They'd been fewer and farther between until lately.

That, she knows, is because of another looming status hearing. Late last year, after finally recovering from her physical wounds, Adrian Bell began the lengthy process of mental health treatment and evaluation. This coming week, the judge will decide whether she's fit to stand trial for multiple murders.

It's troubling enough for Jen to imagine facing her in a courtroom. But when she thinks about putting Carley on the stand . . .

"If she goes to trial, I need to do that, Mom," her daughter tells her, whenever the topic comes up. "For Nicki's sake. I need to make sure that she stays in prison for the rest of her life for what she did to her and to Taylor . . ."

And to Sandra Lutz, whose accidental death in a house fire has since been ruled a murder to which Bell initially confessed.

Carley is so much stronger and braver than Jen ever imagined; than she herself ever imagined. Jen reminds her of that every chance she gets.

"You're going to be just fine," she says when nightmares keep her daughter from sleeping.

"When? I just want to be able to close my eyes some night and not see her—him—*it*."

So do I, Jen thinks. But she doesn't say it. She doesn't say a lot of things that have been on her mind—not to anyone but Thad, anyway, and usually only in the wee hours.

Whenever she allows herself to think about "Sister Linda's" diabolical charade, she's incredulous that she didn't pick up on the fact that something was seriously off about the so-called woman. Incredulous—and infuriated.

"But no one else figured it out, either, Jen," Thad reminds her whenever she goes down that road. "The people at Sisters saw her all day, every day, and no one ever suspected a thing."

It's true. But when Jen thinks about how close she came to losing her daughter to that monster . . .

Thunderous applause erupts in the auditorium as the pianist stands to take a bow. Seeing Emma offer a few perfunctory handclaps before pulling out her cell phone, Jen elbows her.

"I'm just checking my texts," she whispers.

"Put it away."

With a scowl, Emma returns the phone to her pocket. Now a freshman at Woodsbridge, she's still a handful—though Jen keeps a closer rein on her than ever.

As the applause subsides and an expectant lull falls over the audience, Jen and Thad exchange a glance. She can tell he's thinking the same thing she is: *That performance is going to be a tough act to follow.*

Mic in hand, Marie Bush steps back onstage. "Thank you, Brittany. Wasn't that wonderful? And now I'm pleased to introduce our next young lady, who has been studying with me for less than a year, although you'd never guess, hearing her play. Ladies and gentlemen . . . Carley Archer."

Jen's breath catches in her throat as her daughter walks from the wings into the spotlight. She doesn't quite carry herself with the poise of Brittany Witkowski, but she doesn't teeter on her heels or fumble her way forward, either, the way Jen would have imagined her doing a year ago.

A year ago? Just days ago, Carley was thinking about backing out of the recital, a nervous wreck at the thought of being onstage in front of a roomful of people.

"You can do it," Jen told her. "You're going to be just fine."

"How do you know? You've barely heard me play lately."

That's true. Last winter, when the keys on their own piano started sticking and Jen was searching around for someone to repair it, Carley started practicing on the baby grand piano over at the Oliveras' house. That was Debbie's idea.

"Won't it be hard for you?" Jen asked her friend, well aware that the news that Nicki hadn't killed herself had served more as a second blow than as a measure of relief for Debbie.

"No—it would be nice to have someone play that piano," Debbie insisted. "Nicki would have wanted her to."

Now, though their own piano has long since been repaired, Carley goes over there almost every day to practice.

"It sounds so much better on a baby grand," she tells her mother, and Jen doesn't doubt that. But it's not the only reason she lets her go.

"What does Mrs. Olivera do while you're there?" Jen asked Carley not long ago.

"She just sits in the next room and listens. I think she's glad I'm there."

Jen knows she is. She prays for Debbie every day, and was gratified when her friend told her last summer that she'd broken things off with Mike and had decided to go into marriage counseling with Andrew.

"Maybe there's still hope for us," Debbie said, though her tremulous tone revealed that she didn't quite believe it.

Jen doesn't know whether she does, either—but at least it's a step in the right direction.

She sees Carley's chin lift a notch as she accepts the microphone from Marie. She's steeling her nerves, Jen knows, for what she considers the hardest part of the performance: introducing the audience to the piece she's about to play.

Even to Jen, she looks almost like a stranger standing up there: all dressed up in a pale lavender sheath, her hair back in a sleek ponytail, and her glasses relegated to a nightstand drawer after she got contact lenses just a few weeks ago.

She's been working out regularly ever since Frankie convinced her that physical activity would help speed her emotional recovery.

Carley hasn't quite made it past the physically awkward stage—she's not quite as slender as she'd like to be, and her skin flares up whenever she's stressed—but she's finally growing out of it, growing up.

"Thank you," she says shyly into the mic, and winces at a faint screech of feedback. Moving it a little farther back from her mouth, she goes on, her voice wavering just a little, "The classical piece I'm going to play was originally known as Johannes Brahms's *Wiegenlied*, Opus 49, Number 4. But you might recognize it by its popular name, Brahms's Lullaby. Because it's Mother's Day, and because my mom used to sing it to me when she rocked me to sleep when I was little, and because . . . well, because of a lot of other reasons, I'd like to dedicate this performance to her."

Jen's breath catches in her throat, and tears spring to her eyes. She feels Thad's hand coming past Emma to rest gently on her shoulder. He knows that Jen's days of rocking Carley to sleep aren't over yet. Sometimes, even now, as she strokes the worried creases from her daughter's forehead, she hums the lilting melody.

She presses her palms into her eyes and wipes away the blur in time to see Carley arrive at the piano bench.

Her daughter remembers to smooth the skirt of her dress behind her before sitting down and opening her sheet music.

Seeing her fingertips tremble as she positions them over the piano keys, Jen says a silent prayer for her.

Then Carley begins to play.

The lilting fluidity of the music—and a few fresh tears, happy tears—wash away every bit of apprehension.

She's good. Really good. Gifted.

The final note of the piece seems to hang over the hushed auditorium like a delicate glass orb suspended from a gossamer thread. Then it falls away, shattered by thunderous applause.

Onstage, Carley breaks into a relieved smile and rises from the bench. She bends her head in a little bow, then straightens, squinting a bit, still not entirely used to her contacts as her eyes search the vast room.

Jen fights the urge to jump to her feet and wave her arms in a wild burst of pride. Instead, she stops clapping and lifts her right hand slightly overhead, until Emma grabs it with a mortified "Mom! Stop!"

"She's looking for us!"

"No, she isn't!"

Yes, she is.

And now she's found them.

As her daughter's eyes meet hers, Jen smiles broadly and she gives a little nod—a nod that says not just *Great job*, and *I love you*, but also *See? I told you so*.

Carley really is going to be just fine.

Stay tuned for a sneak peek of

Wendy Corsi Staub's thrilling new book

THE PERFECT STRANGER

Coming 2014 from Harper

When the doctor's receptionist called this morning to say that they had the results, it never dawned on her that it might be bad news. Janine casually requested that she come by in person this afternoon; she even used just that phrasing, and it was a question, as opposed to a command: "Can you come by the office in person this afternoon?"

Come by.

So breezy. So inconsequential. So . . . so everything this situation is not.

What if she'd told Janine, over the phone, that she was busy this afternoon? Would the receptionist then have at least hinted that her presence at the office was urgent; that it was, in fact, a command rather than a request?

But she wasn't busy and so here she is, blindsided, numbly staring at the doctor pointing the tip of a ballpoint pen at the left breast on the anatomical diagram.

The doctor keeps talking, talking, talking; tapping, tapping, tapping the paper with the pen point to indicate exactly where the cancerous tissue is growing, leaving ominous black ink pockmarks.

She nods as though she's listening intently, not betraying

that every word after "malignancy" has been drowned out
by the warning bells clanging in her brain.

I'm going to die, she thinks with the absolute certainty
of someone trapped on a railroad track, staring helplessly
into the glaring roar of an oncoming freight train. *I'm going
to be one of those ravaged bald women lying dwarfed in a
hospital bed, terrified and exhausted and dying an awful,
solitary death . . .*

She's seen that person before, too many times—in the
movies, and in real life . . . but she never thought she'd ever
actually *become* that person. Or did she?

Well, yes—you worry, whenever a horrific fate befalls
someone else, that it could happen to you. But then you reassure yourself that it won't, and you push the thought from
your head, and you move on.

This time, there is no reassurance, no pushing, no moving.
The image won't budge.

Me . . . sick . . . bald . . . dying.

Dead.

Me. Dead.

The tinny taste of fear fills her mouth, joined by bile as
her stomach pitches and rolls, attempting to eject the tuna
sandwich she devoured in the carefree life she was still
living at lunchtime.

Carefree? Really?

No. Just last night, she lost sleep over the usual conflicts
involving money and work and household mishaps. When
she woke this morning, her first thought was that there would
be too few hours in the day ahead to resolve everything that
needed to be dealt with. She actually welcomed the call from
Janine the receptionist, thinking a detour to the doctor's office
would be a distraction from her other problems.

How could I have thought those problems were problems?

Stomach churning, she manages to excuse herself, lurches

to her feet, and rushes for the door, out into the hall, toward the small restroom.

Kneeling and retching, she finds herself wondering if this is what it will be like when she goes through chemotherapy. You hear that it makes patients sick to their stomachs.

Me . . . sick . . .

Dead.

How can she possibly wrap her head around that idea? If only she could magically escape to her bed right now, where she'd be alone to cry or scream or sleep . . .

But she can't. She has to pull herself together somehow, make herself presentable and coherent enough to walk back down the hall to the doctor's office . . . and then, dear God, the nurses and Janine and a waiting room full of patients still lie between her and solitude.

I can't do this. I can't.

I need to be alone . . .

Five minutes later, shaken, she emerges from the bathroom, returns to the still-ajar door marked with the physician's name.

As she crosses the threshold again, the doctor looks up, wearing a nonplussed expression that makes it clear this isn't the first time that a patient on the receiving end of a malignant diagnosis has behaved in such a manner. "Feeling better now? Come on in."

"I—I'm sorry," she stammers, making her way back to the seat opposite the desk, where the anatomical diagram still sits like a signed, sealed, and delivered execution notice awaiting final action.

"It's all right. Here . . . drink some water."

She takes the paper cup the doctor offers. Sips.

As the lukewarm water slides along her throat left raw from retching, she nearly gags again.

"I'm sorry," she repeats, and sets aside the cup.

"No need. Would you like to call someone?"

Call someone . . .

Would you like to call someone . . .

Unable to process the question, she stares at the doctor.

"A friend, or a family member . . . someone who can come over here and—"

"Oh. No. No, thank you." *I just want to be alone. Can't you see that?*

"Are you sure?"

"Yes. I'm . . . I'll be fine. I just needed a few minutes to . . ."

To throw up my lunch and splash water on my face and look into the mirror and try to absorb the news that I have cancer and I'm going to die.

Me . . .

Dead.

It's unfathomable that her worst fear is actually going to come to fruition after all these years, but then . . .

Isn't it everyone's worst fear?

We're all mortal, aren't we?

I'm not the only person in the world who's ever lain awake at night, tossing and turning, terrified that I'm going to die, only to have it actually happen.

No. But it becomes second nature to reassure yourself that it's not going to happen—not really, or at least, not anytime soon. You almost believe you're safe, that you've escaped the inevitable, and then suddenly . . .

"I know it's difficult to hear news like this," the doctor is saying, "but the important thing is that we caught it early. We're going to discuss your treatment options, and there are many, new ones being developed every day. The bottom line is that the survival rates for a stage one malignancy are . . ."

Treatment options . . .

Survival rates . . .

Stage one . . .

And here she is, right back to *malignancy.*

Jaw set grimly, she wills herself not to cry, but the tears come anyway.

About to climb into her side of the bed she shares with her husband—when he's not up in Cleveland, in the process of moving his elderly mother from condo to nursing home—Meredith Heywood winces and reaches back to rest a hand against her spine.

The ache is even worse now than it was before she took a hot bath, hoping in vain that it would relax her muscles. An entire Saturday spent working in the yard—followed by a few hours hunched over her laptop, writing about the garden she just planted—had been inarguably good for the soul. But for her middle-aged, cancer-tainted bones . . . eh, not so much.

"Why don't you wait until I get home to do the planting?" Hank had asked on the phone this morning when she told him of her plans.

"It's getting too late in the season."

"It's not even summer yet, Mer."

"I know, but we usually get the vegetables in on Memorial Day—that was a week ago." They'd been planning to do it then, but Hank's mother took a bad fall just as the holiday weekend got under way, and he had to jump into his truck and head to his hometown. He's been there ever since, trying to convince the stubborn woman that at ninety-three, she's too old to live alone.

Mission finally accomplished.

"I can handle the planting," Meredith assured him when he called this morning to tell her that it will be at least a few more days before he gets his mother settled. "It's going to rain for the next couple of days, so this is the perfect time to get the seedlings in."

"Why don't you call the kids to help you?"

"Maybe I will," she lied. Their daughter and sons, all

married and scattered within an hour or so drive of Cincinnati, have their hands full with jobs, young children, household obligations of their own. Meredith wasn't about to bother any of them to come help her.

Especially since . . .

Well, they don't know yet that her cancer has returned a third time, and spread. And she doesn't want them to suspect anything until she's ready to tell them. No need for anyone to worry until it's absolutely necessary.

Only Hank is aware of the truth. He's having a rough time with it.

"There are so many things we've been waiting to do until I retire," he said one night, head in hands.

"We'll do them now."

"Now, when I have no job and we're broke?"

"We're not broke yet. Don't worry. You'll find another job."

"Where? Not here. And we can't move, not with—" He cleared his throat. "I mean, you need to be near your doctors now."

"You'll find something else," she assured him. "Here. Some other kind of work."

"With decent pay? And benefits? If I don't find something before our medical insurance runs out . . . I can't believe this is happening."

"Not just to us. Teddy's in the same boat, and with a baby on the way." Their firstborn lost his job and healthcare last year and has been struggling to keep a roof over his family's heads and food on the table. Hank and Meredith have been giving him whatever they can spare—but now that's gone from very little to nothing at all.

"Then there's my mother . . ." Hank was on a roll. "She doesn't have long-term care insurance and she can't keep living alone. And I'm responsible for her since my brother fell off the face of the earth." They'd had a family falling out years ago, and Hank's only sibling had stopped speaking to both him and his mother.

It would have been easier if Hank's mother hadn't fallen last weekend, accelerating the need to get her out of her condo and into the only available—though not necessarily affordable—facility.

Easier, too, if the old woman wasn't so adamant about not leaving Cleveland. They could have moved her to Cincinnati years ago to make things easier on Hank—though certainly not under their own roof. Even if Meredith were healthy enough to be a caregiver—as opposed to facing the eventual need for one herself—her mother-in-law is downright impossible.

"She's never living with us, no matter what happens," Hank said flatly many years ago, when his mother was widowed shortly after their engagement. At the time, Meredith found the statement unduly harsh and started having second thoughts, wondering what kind of man would say such a thing.

That was before she got to know his mother—in small doses and from a distance, thank goodness.

"She's probably going to live to be a hundred," Hank says frequently—and dismally.

He's probably right. But whenever he brings it up, Meredith duly points out that he's lucky to have her, having lost her own mother when her kids were young—and having faced her own mortality at this age.

"I know. I just . . . I'm worried about having to deal with her while I'm trying to help you, and find a job, and healthcare . . . in the end, it always comes down to money we don't have. Story of our lives, right?"

Money? In the end it comes down to money? He didn't realize what he was saying. That's what she told herself. She knew he was just stressed, knew he loved her, knew that deep down, his priorities are straight. He's only human.

But—being only human herself—she couldn't help saying, "Hey, you can always push me off a cliff and collect on my term life insurance policy now instead of later. I mean, it's going to happen anyway, right? So why not put us both out of our misery—the sooner, the better."

His jaw dropped. "What kind of thing is that to say?"

"I'm sorry. I was kidding. Come on, Hank. Look at the bright side."

To his credit, he didn't say, "What bright side?"

If he had, she might have broken down and cried.

Instead, he'd hugged her and apologized. "I just want to make sure that we do everything we ever said we were going to do. No more putting things off—not because I don't think you're going to be around, but because . . . well, I don't like to waste time. That's all."

Right. And because she doesn't have time to waste.

Why dwell on the past when you can focus on the future?

That was the title of an optimistic blog post she wrote back when she was in treatment and assuming she was going to beat this disease. It was met with a mixed reaction from her followers, depending on their stage of the disease. Those who were in remission shared her mindset. Those who were not—those with very little future left—didn't want to think about what might lie ahead. They found comfort in reflecting upon happier times.

Now I get it. Now I'm sorry. I wish I could have told some of them . . .

But it's too late.

Too late . . . too late . . .

Meredith arches her back, stretching, trying to work out the kinks as a warm breeze flutters the peach and yellow paisley curtains at the window.

Through the screen, she can hear only crickets, a distant dog barking, and the occasional sound of traffic out on the main road. The houses in this neighborhood may be of the no frills, cookie-cutter architectural style, but they're set far apart on relatively large lots.

It was the quiet, private setting that drew Meredith and Hank here well over three decades ago, when they were living downtown in a one-bedroom apartment with two toddlers and an oops baby on the way. This seventeen-hundred square-foot house—with an eat-in kitchen, three bedrooms and one and a half baths—seemed palatial by comparison.

They felt like they'd be living in the lap of luxury and promised each other they were going to grow old here.

The place was showing wear and tear and they'd outgrown it by the time the kids were teenagers with friends coming and going at all hours. But who could afford to add on or buy anything bigger on Hank's salary and what Meredith made working at a local daycare? Not with three college tuitions looming in the near future.

Somehow, they survived the old plumbing and wiring and constant repairs; the crowds of kids, the lack of privacy and closet space. Eventually, their sons and daughter moved on and although their finances aren't terrific, thanks to the economy and a series of bad investments, at least Meredith and Hank grew back into their house.

It may be shabby, but it's home.

Now, the mere idea of growing old anywhere at all . . . that in itself is a luxury.

"Ouch," she says aloud, wincing again as she rolls her shoulders.

It's going to take a hell of a lot more than stretching, a hot bath, or even lying down on the memory foam mattress they splurged on last September when Macy's had a sale. That was when she was assuming their old, saggy mattress was causing the dull ache in her back. The pricey new one was their early Christmas present to each other, along with the bright, cheerful paisley bedding and curtains that at least made it look like springtime in here all winter long . . . even after she found out the memory wasn't going to cure her hurting bones. Nothing was.

She wishes now that she'd allowed her doctor to prescribe something for the pain during her last visit, but she was afraid she'd become dependent.

"That's crazy," Hank said when she told him. "Why would you think that?"

"You hear stories—all those celebrities addicted to prescription pain medication . . . and some of my blogger friends have had issues, too."

Hank shook his head. "Next time you go, let them give you something. Why suffer?"

"Suffer"—such a strong word. Especially since she isn't truly suffering. Not yet, anyway.

There will be plenty of time down the road for Percocet or morphine or whatever it is the doctors prescribe in the final stages . . .

Plenty of time—please, God, let there be plenty of time.

She's not against pain medication, but even now, while they still have insurance, their prescription plan isn't the best. Her medications have already cost them a fortune out of pocket—and a lot of good they did.

Plain old ibuprofen might help, but Hank must have packed the Advil they keep in the master bathroom medicine cabinet. She just looked for it, and it wasn't there. She's too tired to go hunt for another bottle.

What she really needs right now, as much as, if not more than, medication, is a good, stiff shot of Kentucky bourbon. There's plenty of that downstairs, courtesy of living a stone's throw from some of the world's finest distilleries.

In the old days—well, in the few years' window after the kids were grown but before Meredith got sick—she and Hank spent some deliciously decadent weekend afternoons with fellow empty-nester friends, sipping their way along the bourbon trail that lies in the bluegrass hills south of Cincinnati.

She was never a big drinker; just a social one. But that came to a complete halt after her breast cancer diagnosis, when she became hyper-vigilant about everything she put into her body. She lightened up a bit after five years in remission, but last year, a routine test betrayed a resurgence of microscopic cancer cells in her remaining breast tissue, and she went right back on the wagon. Not a drop of liquor, no soy products, only organic fruits and vegetables . . .

"I don't know about that," one of the other bloggers commented on a post where Meredith outlined her stringent habits. *"What good is being alive if you sacrifice all the fun stuff?"*

"I'm just trying to improve my odds. To each his own," Meredith wrote back.

And then—that's right, now she remembers, the blogger was Elena—Elena wrote back, *"My mother was a health nut who did everything right, and she was hit by a train before her thirtieth birthday. I did everything right, and I was diagnosed with cancer right after mine. I have to admit: I'm sick of being good."*

Meredith understood how Elena felt—and she hoped Elena understood why she herself wasn't—*isn't*—taking any chances.

Certainly not now the cancer has metastasized to her bones. But of course, Elena doesn't know about that.

"How long do I have?" Meredith asked the oncologist matter-of-factly when she first got the news.

"Don't jump the gun, there," said the doctor, a straight shooter. "It's a relatively small spot, and we're going to treat it. Radiation, chemotherapy . . ."

Yes. She knows the drill.

They treat it until everything stops working, and it continues to spread.

That, she suspects, is where they're headed now. A few weeks ago, the morning after an idyllic Mother's Day spent with Hank and the kids and grandkids, the doctor gave her some discouraging test results, then told her they're going to try this current treatment—which she knows is basically her last hope—a little longer and take some more tests to see whether it's working.

She has a feeling it isn't.

She's been doing her best to prepare herself for what lies ahead—if not in the immediate future, then at some point down the road.

Sooner or later, she'll be told to call hospice and get her affairs in order.

Even then, she knows, many doctors aren't able—or perhaps, aren't willing--to provide a time frame.

She's seen it happen to her online friends time and again, and now it's going to happen to her. Maybe not this year, maybe not even next, but eventually this damned disease is going to get the best of her.

She's privately told a few of her online friends of her situation, but not everyone. Eventually, she'll have to write an official blog post about it. The moment it goes live, she'll become *that* person—the doomed friend everyone rallies around.

I'm not ready. I don't want to be her. *Not yet. I want to be* me *for as long as I can.*

There's only one way to do that: pretend this isn't really happening.

The lyrics to an old Styx song—one she and Hank used to listen to on vinyl back in their dating days—keep running through her head.

You're fooling yourself . . . you don't believe it . . .

She'll get through her days staying busy so that she won't have to dwell on the future—and get through her nights the best she can.

Right now, she'll have to settle for over-the-counter pain relievers without courtesy of bourbon to numb the pain in

her back—or the disquieting, morbid thoughts that sometimes strike at night, especially when she's here alone.

With a sigh, she leaves the lamplit bedroom and flicks on
the hallway light. As she makes her way to the stairs, she
hears a whisper of movement below.

"Hank?" she calls.

No answer.

Of course not. He's in Cleveland. She spoke to him a half
hour ago on the phone, although . . .

He could very well have just *said* he was in Cleveland.
Maybe he was really on the road, headed home early to surprise her.

"Hank! Is that you?"

Absolutely still, poised midflight with her hand on the
banister, Meredith is enveloped in complete silence.

"Is someone there?"

No.

And yet—she did hear something before. Or perhaps it's
more just a sensation of not being alone in the house . . .

Or did you just imagine it altogether?

For a long time, she stands there, listening—one moment,
certain she can feel someone there, the next, certain she's
losing it.

Just last week, she blogged about this very scenario. Not
about things that go bump in the night, per se, but about getting older and potentially senile.

That entry stemmed from Hank's report that his
mother suspected her neighbor—a distinguished widowed
professor—of sneaking into her condo in the wee hours,
trying on her clothes and taking perfumed bubble baths in
her tub.

Meredith's blog entry was written entirely tongue in
cheek, as so many of them are. Even during the darkest days
of her cancer treatment, she's always managed to find a hu-
morous angle.

She'd started the blog at the suggestion of her therapist, who knew she'd dreamed of going to college and becoming a journalist before marriage and motherhood set her on a different path. Even the title of the blog page—Pink Stinks—is meant to be an irreverent poke at the breast cancer awareness movement.

Determined to keep her latest diagnosis to herself, she wrote last week about the inevitability of aging and the many signs, now that she's past her sixtieth birthday, that the process is well underway: *I can't recognize a single musician on the cover of Rolling Stone, I can't remember my user names and passwords if they're not saved in my laptop or phone, I can't see a blessed thing without my bifocals and if they're not on my head chances are I have no idea where I left them . . .*

She ended the post on an upbeat, if bittersweet, note: *Faced with the prospects of old age and senility—or not sticking around long enough to grow old and senile—I'll take the prior.*

That post was greeted by a barrage of positive, amusing comments from her regular followers and a couple of newcomers who have since stuck around. Someone—who was it?—wrote that she was wise and had a tough outer shell, like a turtle, and turtles are known for their longevity—"So I'm sure you're going to live a good long time!"

From your lips to God's ears, Meredith wanted to respond to whoever it was, but of course, she didn't.

Standing on the stairway, listening for movement below and wondering if she should go back to the bedroom for the baseball bat Hank keeps under his side of the bed, she mentally composes the opening of a new blog post she'll write tomorrow.

So there I was, armed and dangerous in my granny nightgown . . .

Oh, geez. She really is losing it, isn't she?

And her taut posture as she stands clenched from head to toe, clutching the railing, isn't helping her back pain.

Either turn around and go to bed, or go downstairs, get what you need, and then go to bed.

Meredith opts for the latter. She flips a wall switch at the foot of the stairs, then another in the living room, and the one in the dining room, reassured as she makes her way through familiar rooms bathed in light. As always, she notices not just the threadbare area rug, the worn spots on the furniture, the chipped paint on the baseboards, but also the clay bowl Beck had made in Girl Scouts, the bookshelf lined with Hardy Boys books Hank had handed down to his sons, the faint pencil marks on the doorjamb where they marked their growing kids' height over the years . . .

It's a good house. It's been a good life here.

In the kitchen cabinet where she keeps her daily vitamins and the medications prescribed to keep cancer at bay for as long as possible, she finds a bottle of drugstore-brand painkillers.

Having left her glasses upstairs on the nightstand, she can't quite make out the label. It looks to her like they expired last year, but they're probably fine. Fine, as in safe to swallow, if not as effective as they might have been.

She takes three, just in case they're less potent. Washing them down with tap water, she wonders how long it will take before the pills ease the tension in her muscles.

It really is too bad she can't take something stronger.

Not medicine. Just a nip of something that will warm her from the inside out, and let her sleep.

She glances longingly at the high cupboard above the fridge where they've kept the booze since their firstborn, Teddy, reached high school—as if keeping the stash out of arm's reach would deter him and his friends from getting into it. It didn't work, they discovered belatedly, when Hank realized that one of the kids—by then, all three were in college—had replaced the contents of a bottle of Woodford Reserve with iced tea.

Still, they were good kids, Meredith remembers as she sets the empty water glass into the sink. Spirited, but good. She's blessed to have watched them grow up and give her grandchildren—three grandsons so far between Teddy and Neal and their wives, with another little stinkerdoodle on the way this fall.

That's what Meredith calls her grandchildren, just as she always called her own children: the stinkerdoodles.

Everyone is hoping for a girl this time. Everyone but Meredith. Secretly, she worries about passing the cancer gene to a new generation.

"Men get breast cancer, too," one of her blogger friends pointed out when she wrote about that.

True. But it's not nearly as common.

She can't help but worry about the health of her daughter and future granddaughters. She's been warning Rebecca that she needs to do self-exams, and start her yearly mammogram screening in another couple of years.

Beck, of course, waves her mother off. She's too young and full of life to worry about illness.

So was I at her age. I never thought something like this could happen. No family history . . .

You just never know. Oh, well . . .

It's been over a year now since Beck married Keith. They'll probably be starting a family too, soon.

Meredith has so much to live for. If only . . .

Shaking her head, she turns off the light and leaves the kitchen, never noticing the cut screen on the window facing the newly planted garden out back, or the shadow of a human figure lurking in the far corner.